"As Christ walked on the waters
so in my vision I walked.
But I descended from the cross
for I am afraid of heights
and do not preach the resurrection."

– Mahmoud Darwish

TRANSLATOR'S NOTE

The protagonists of this novel are Christians who belong to the Syriac (or Syrian) Orthodox Church, who speak (or are descendants of those who spoke) a language that is often called Syriac, and who regard themselves as, in some sense, heirs to the culture and empire of ancient Mesopotamia (thus permitting one character to boast, or joke, that he is an "Ancient Assyrian"). Both the terms *Syriac* and *Assyrian* are, however, rejected by some members of the community, many of whom prefer to refer to themselves as "Suryoyé" (singular "Suryoyo"), just as they may prefer to refer to their language, especially in its modern and colloquial forms, as "Suryoyo". In this translation I have used "Assyrian" where the Arabic has *suryani* and refers to people, "Syriac" where the same word refers to the language, and "Suryoyo" on the few occasions where *suryuyu* is used (where the reference is always to language).

On the eve of the First World War, Tur Abdin and neighbouring areas of south-eastern Anatolia such as Mardin and Amid (Diyarbakir) constituted an Assyrian heartland. Starting in 1915, the Assyrians of the region were subjected to forced relocations and massacres at the hands of regular and irregular (largely Kurdish) troops of the Ottoman Empire; perhaps (the figures are disputed) 500,000 persons died. These events contributed to the creation of an Assyrian diaspora in parts of the Arab world such as Lebanon where they had not formerly had a major presence, as well as in Europe (especially Sweden) and North

YALO

"Mesmerizing . . . it would be hard to think of a more worthwhile endeavour for fiction to embark on."   JAMES LASDUN, *Guardian*

"A highly compelling performance, presented in beautifully crafted, often lilting prose, a tribute to Khoury's authorship in Arabic as well as to Humphrey Davies' translation. This novel is about a corrupted individual in a corrupting time, but it speaks of and to us all."   GUY MANNES-ABBOTT, *Independent*

"It is hard to extricate oneself from the compelling, relentlessly immediate tale. *Yalo* is not an easy book to read; not an easy book not to."   DANIEL HAHN, *Independent on Sunday*

"Most powerful in this evocative novel are the smell of incense, the taste of cherries and the sight of blood, as Khoury unflinchingly chronicles how human beings can turn into savage beasts."   ANITA SETHI, *New Statesman*

"A fabulous journey through the extremes of the human condition . . . the work of a natural storyteller."
DOMINIC O'SULLIVAN, *Irish Examiner*

ELIAS KHOURY is the author of twelve novels, four published volumes of literary criticism, and three plays. Khoury was the editor-in-chief of the cultural supplement of Beirut's daily newspaper, *An-Nahar*, and is a Global Distinguished Professor of Middle Eastern and Islamic Studies at New York University. In 1998 he was awarded the Palestinian Prize for *Gate of the Sun*.

HUMPHREY DAVIES' previous translations include *The Yacoubian Building* by Alaa Al Aswany, voted Best Translation of 2007 by the Society of Authors, and *Gate of the Sun*, for which he won the Banipal Prize.

Elias Khoury

YALO
A NOVEL

Translated from the Arabic by
Humphrey Davies

MACLEHOSE PRESS
QUERCUS · LONDON

*The events, characters, places and names in this novel
are creatures of the imagination. Should any resemblance
be found between the novel's characters and real persons,
or between the places and events of the novel and real
places and events, such resemblance is purely coincidental,
a product of the workings of the imagination,
and devoid of intent.*

First published in Great Britain in 2009 by MacLehose Press
This paperback edition first published in 2010 by
MacLehose Press
an imprint of Quercus
21 Bloomsbury Square
London WC1A 2NS

Original title, YALO, published by Dâr-al-Adâb, Beirut, 2002.
Copyright © Elias Khoury, 2002

English Translation Copyright © 2009 by Humphrey Davies

This book has been selected to receive financial assistance from
English PEN's Writers in Translation programme supported by Bloomberg.

ISBN 978 1 906694 81 4

Printed and bound in Great Britain by Clays Ltd, St Ives plc

10 9 8 7 6 5 4 3 2 1

America. The main characters of the novel, who live in the Lebanese capital, Beirut, are thus connected by a "thread of blood" to Tur Abdin and its environs, and above all to their ancestral village of Ein Ward. A parallel thread links participants in and victims of Lebanon's civil war (1975–90) to the Lebanese Druze-Christian massacres that took place in 1860, such as that described by "Nina the Russian" with reference to her unnamed ancestral village near Tyre.

Readers may find it useful to know that "Mar" is a title of saints and prophets (Mar Afram, Mar Elias the Living, etc.) used by Christians of the Levant, and that *memre* (singular *memro*) are religious poems in Syriac each line of which contains the same number of syllables. Other Syriac terms are explained within the text or may be sufficiently understood from their contexts. "Yalo" is a nickname for "Daniel".

I am greatly indebted to Dr George Kiraz for his invaluable help with the transcription of Syriac, and to him and to Elias Khoury for guidance in the complex area of the terminology of the Assyrian people and their language. If I have failed to understand, or misinterpreted, the information provided, the fault is mine alone.

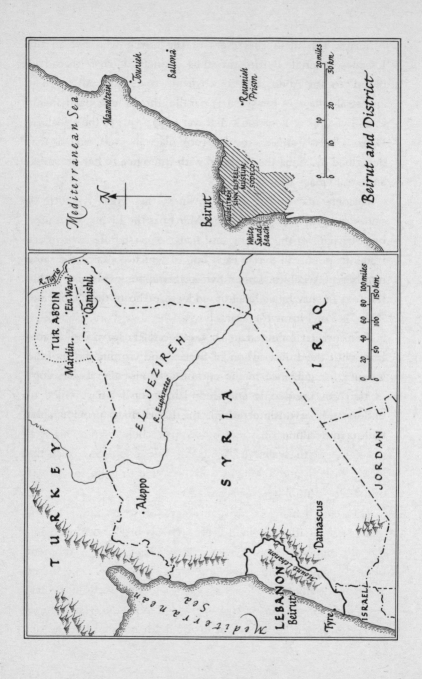

Mediterranean Sea

Touriek

Maameltein

Ballonà

Roumieh Prison

Beirut

AUSEITREH
SINN EL FEEL
MUSEUM
SODECO

White Sands Beach

Beirut and District

0   10   20 miles
0   10   20   30 km

TURKEY

R. Tigris

TUR ABDIN

Mardin.

'Ein Ward

Qamishli

EL JEZIREH

R. Euphrates

Aleppo

SYRIA

IRAQ

Mediterranean Sea

LEBANON

Beirut

Mount Lebanon

Damascus

Tyre

ISRAEL

JORDAN

0   20   40   60   80   100 miles
0   50   100   150 km

Yalo didn't understand what was happening.

The young man stood before the interrogator and closed his eyes, which is what he always did. He closed his eyes when facing danger, he closed them when he was alone, he closed them when his mother . . . On that day too, the morning of 22 December, 1993, he closed his eyes involuntarily.

Yalo didn't understand why everything was white.

He saw the white interrogator sitting behind a white table, the sun refracting off the window pane behind him, his face drowning in the reflected light. All Yalo could see were the haloes of light and a woman walking alone through the streets of the city, stumbling over her shadow.

Yalo closed his eyes for a moment, or so he thought. This young man, with his joined eyebrows, his brown oval face and his tall, thin body, was given to closing his eyes for a moment before opening them and seeing. Here, however, at the police station in Jounieh, he closed his eyes, and afterwards all he saw were lines intersecting at two lips which moved in what seemed to be a whisper. He looked at his cuffed hands and felt the sun that had erased the interrogator's face beating down on his eyes, so he closed them.

The young man stood before the interrogator at 10.00 in the morning on that cold day and saw a sun refracting off the glass and blazing off the head of the white man who opened his mouth, which formed questions. Then Yalo closed his eyes.

Yalo didn't understand why the interrogator was screaming at him.

He heard a voice screaming at him, "Open your eyes, man!" He opened them and the light entered their depths like blazing skewers, which is how he discovered that he had had his eyes closed for a long time, and that he had spent half his life with his eyes closed, and he saw himself as a blind man sees, and he saw night.

Yalo didn't understand why she had come, but when he saw her he collapsed onto the chair.

When he entered the room, there wasn't that young woman who had had no name. He entered stumbling because he couldn't see in the sunlight refracting off the glass. He stood inside the whiteness, his hands cuffed, shivering with sweat. He was not afraid even though the interrogator would write in his report that the accused had trembled with fear. But Yalo was not afraid; he was shuddering from the sweat, that was all. The sweat was pouring from every part of him, and the strange-smelling fluid coming from his pores stained his clothes. Yalo felt as though he was being stripped naked inside his long black coat, and the smell he smelled was not his own. He discovered that he did not know this man called Daniel, whom they nicknamed Yalo.

That girl who had had no name came. Perhaps she had been there in the interrogation room, but he hadn't seen her when he'd entered. He saw her and he collapsed onto the chair, his legs betraying him. A slight giddiness took hold of him, and he could no longer open his eyes, so he closed them.

The interrogator screamed at him, "Open your eyes, man!" so he opened them and saw a phantom that looked like the girl who had had no name. She had said she had no name. Yalo, however, knew everything. He had left her dozing near her naked, dainty body. He had opened her black leather bag and written his name, address, telephone number, everything.

Yalo didn't understand why she'd said she had no name.

Her breathing shuddered, the air round her face seemed to stifle her, and she was unable to speak, but she'd managed to say, "I have no name." Then Yalo bent his head and took her.

There in the hut, below the Villa Gardenia that belonged to *Maître* Michel Salloum, when he had asked her her name, she had said in a voice full of airless gaps that stop the lungs, "I have no name. Please, no names." "Fine," he had said. "My name is Yalo. Don't forget my name."

But there she stood, her name beside her, and when the interrogator asked her her name, she didn't hesitate. "Shireen Raad," she said. She didn't tell the interrogator, "Please, no names," and she didn't stretch her hands out in front of her like she did there in the hut where Yalo slept with her after she stretched out her hands and the smell of incense arose. He took her hands and closed his eyes with them. Then he started kissing her white wrists and smelled the smell of incense and musk. He smelled the smell of her black hair, buried his face in it and felt drunk. He told her he was drunk on incense, and she smiled, as though the mask had slipped from her face. Yalo saw her smile through the shadows the candle's light cast on the wall. It was her first smile on that night of fear.

What is Shireen doing here?

When he opened his eyes after the interrogator screamed at him, he saw himself in Ballona. He said to her, "Come," and she followed him. They left the pine wood that lies below the church of Mar Niqula and climbed the hill to the villa. The girl fell to the ground, or so it seemed to Yalo, so he bent over to help her. He took her hand and they walked, and when she fell a second time he bent over again to carry her, but she avoided his hands. She stood up, grasped the trunk of a pine tree and just stood there, panting loudly. He offered her his hand and she took it and walked beside him while he listened to the sound of her breathing and that terrified panting.

When they reached the hut, he left her outside. He went in, lit a candle and tried to tidy his scattered clothes and belongings but discovered that the task would require some time, so he went out and found her leaning her head against the open door and making weeping sounds.

"Don't be frightened," he said. "Come. You'll sleep here. I'll make you a bed on the floor. Don't be frightened."

She entered hesitantly and stood in the middle of the room as though looking for a chair to sit on. Yalo leapt to pull his trousers off the chair and threw them on the end of the bed, but she did not sit down. She remained standing, not knowing what to do.

"Would you like some tea?" he asked, but instead of answering she stretched out her hands like someone seeking help, and when Yalo took her hands and saw the fear turning into intersecting rings in her small eyes, he drew back. He said he'd been afraid; later, he would say that he felt fear, but at that instant he didn't know because he didn't feel that he'd felt fear until he wrote the word down. He said the word, then felt it, then wrote it down. Today, when he remembers her small eyes in the shadows cast

4

by the candle's light, when he sees how the pupils started to contract and turn into intersecting rings, he feels fear and says he was afraid of her eyes.

As he drew back, he saw her coming towards him, her hands suspended in the air as though she were asking him to rescue her or seeking his help. He went to her, took her hands, closed his eyes with them, and she went quiet. He took her hands and felt a shudder pass through them, as though the lines of fear pulsing inside them had become like the arteries that transmit a tension throughout the body. He put her hands on his eyes and saw the darkness and felt how her body began to become calm and go quiet, and the smell of incense arose.

"What's that nice smell?" asked Yalo, pulling away. He sat down on the chair and covered his face with his hands as though he was tired. He didn't move. The candle flame swayed, shuddering in the breeze that rose from the pine forest, and the girl who had no name was standing next to him, recovering the breath that fear had stolen from her when she had seen the black shadow coming up to the car parked at the corner of the pine wood below the Orthodox church.

Why is she wearing her short skirt and showing her thighs? The girl is sitting before the interrogator in her short red skirt, her legs crossed, and talking as though she is swallowing all the air in the interrogation room.

Yalo had told her not to wear short skirts. "What's this? No way!" But she hadn't answered. She'd looked where he was looking, at her knees, and the wisp of a smile had sketched itself on her lips, and she'd shaken her head. In the morning, they'd gone out together. He'd found a taxi going to Beirut and then returned to his hut.

But now she is sitting and wearing the same skirt, or one

5

like it, and crossing her legs and speaking without stuttering or stammering the way she did there.

They had been like two shadows in the car. Crouching high above them, Yalo had seen only the man's grey hair. Yalo shone his torch at the car as though firing a gun. Stealing through the pines, carrying the Kalashnikov and his torch, he felt like a hunter. The cars were traps for his prey, and, like anyone who hunts, he knew and loved the seasons. He tried to explain this to the interrogator. He said that, for a hunter like him, it wasn't the robbery or the women, it was the pleasure. The pleasure of hunting stolen love in cars with closed windows, the pleasure of the first instant, when the light fell on the two faces, or on the hand reaching towards the thighs, or on the head bending towards the breasts as they emerged from the dress.

When Yalo shines his light, it hits its target immediately. Yalo didn't play around with the light; he hit the target on the first try, and when he didn't, the adventure was to be counted a failure, and he would retrace his steps, or hide and wait for the car to leave and then quietly withdraw, dragging his failure behind him.

First hit or nothing; that was his creed when hunting. And the loveliest thing, as far as he was concerned, was the grey hair when it lit up beneath the light. The loveliest moments were when he saw the men's heads covered with white hair as they bent over a breast or a thigh. The torchlight would pierce that white hair, ignite it, fix it in place. The light would penetrate the inclined whiteness and draw a circle round it. Then the light would move off the white hair and go the other way and trace the eyes, and the woman's eyes, opened onto a mixture of fear and desire, would leap out.

The light draws closer and the phantom descends after

turning on the torch and allowing it to play over the car. During the first moments of the hunt, Yalo would focus the light and make it sharp and narrow like a thread. Afterwards, once the eyes had been fixed in place, he would widen the beam, scattering the light everywhere, and come down. He would approach the closed window, tap on it with the barrel of his rifle, and the window would be opened in alarm. The phantom's head would approach the man's window, but he wouldn't let the woman's eyes leave his, which were like those of a hawk, opened onto the depths of the darkness. He could see in the dark and would scatter the light, and the shadows would rise up. From the midst of the shadows he would approach, tap on the window with the barrel of his rifle, and order them to open up. He would look into the woman's eyes and observe how they widened in fear, the pupils disappearing. Then he would withdraw quietly, bearing his harvest – a watch, a ring, a gold chain, a bracelet, a few dollars. Nothing else. Though one time he had asked a man to remove his tie because he felt that fear was strangling the man with it as it dangled over his undone belt like a hangman's rope; and once he had asked a woman to give him her yellow shawl for no particular reason. But he didn't want more; more came to him without effort or trouble. Yalo didn't go running after more but took it when it came because he'd learned from his sufferings in the city called Paris not to refuse God's blessings.

But with Shireen, things had been different.

Why is she saying he raped her in the forest?

"Me, I didn't," said Yalo, but he heard the interrogator screaming, "You confessed, you bastard, and now you say no? You know what happens to liars?"

But Yalo wasn't lying. True, he agreed that what he'd done might be called rape, but . . . but that night wasn't the point.

Shireen hadn't filed a complaint against him because of that night but because of the days that followed.

With her, there, things had been different, and Yalo didn't know the right words to tell her that the smell of incense that rose from her wrists that night had spread above him like a white cloud, then descended to lodge in his spine.

Three months after the incident in the forest, when he'd told her that he loved her "from his spine", she'd laughed till tears fell from her eyes, and kept blowing her nose. He'd thought she was crying, so he'd bent over the meze-strewn table at Albert's in Ashrafiyeh, but when he was close to her he'd discovered she was laughing.

"I'm laughing at you," she said. "You're stupid. All that height and nothing to show for it. What kind of dumb talk is that?" And she started talking to him in English: "*Finished. You must understand. Everything is finished.*"

He said he didn't understand English, so she said in French, "*C'est fini, M. Yalo.*"

"What is it that's *fini*?" he asked.

"This," she answered.

"You mean you want to *fini* me off?"

"Please, M. Yalo. I can't go on like this. Please leave me alone. Let's come to an understanding. Tell me what you want and I'll do it."

She opened her bag and took out a handful of dollars.

Why did she tell the interrogator that Yalo had slapped her because she'd refused to eat?

No, he hadn't slapped her because she'd refused to eat the little birds, which is what she pretended had happened before the interrogator.

"You can't eat music!" she'd said when she'd seen the plate

8

of small fried birds swimming in a lemon-and-garlic broth.

"I don't eat little birds. It's wrong," she'd said.

Yalo wrapped a small bird in bread, dipped it in the broth and brought it to her mouth.

"*No! No!* Please!"

But the hand that held the bread-wrapped bird remained there and then began moving towards the mouth and hovering round it before plunging towards the closed lips. The girl opened her mouth and began to chew, her facial muscles working.

She swallowed the bird and stopped eating and talking.

Yalo took another sip of arak and looked at her face. Her face was as small as a white moon suspended above her long neck. He wanted to talk to her about the moon. He wanted to tell her how he'd discovered the moon, the stars and the Milky Way, which looks like a smear of milk in the sky, there in Ballona, below the villa to which fate had led him from Paris. But he was afraid she'd laugh at him.

"It seems you're the type that doesn't speak Arabic or like Abdel Haleem Hafez" was what he said to her, or something like that. But she didn't reply. The small white moon remained unmoving atop the long neck, and then the tears gushed from her eyes. She took a paper napkin and wiped her eyes and blew her nose, but the tears didn't stop, so he started telling her about the "Dusky Nightingale", and about Soad Hosni and Shadia and the song "Tyrant of Love" which he liked so much.

He told her he'd learned to love the poetry of Nizar Qabbani courtesy of Abdel Haleem Hafez, and that "Letter from Beneath the Waves", about a man who drowns in the waters of passion, was the most beautiful poem he'd ever heard, and that he'd only accepted the fact that Abdel Haleem didn't write his own lyrics when he'd read it in a newspaper.

"How can that be, Shireen? The words melt in his mouth like sugar, he makes the words come out like spun threads, so it couldn't not be him that wrote the poem. But I believed the newspaper and then I bought a book called *Drawing with Words*, but I couldn't understand it. Poetry only sounds right when Abdel Haleem is singing it. Don't you like Abdel Haleem?"

The moon remained silent, swept by spasms, and he saw the small eyes suspended on the white round surface.

Before he'd come to Albert's, Yalo hadn't noticed that her eyes were small. There, in Ballona, he'd seen but hadn't seen, because the smell had overwhelmed him and stopped him from seeing.

"Remember how . . . I don't know what you felt there, but I felt as though I was drowning. It was the smell of the incense, and I couldn't see anything. Look right at me so I can see the colour of your eyes."

Shireen had chosen the restaurant. They went there together in her white V.W. Golf. He sat next to her and couldn't think of anything to say. She'd told him on the phone to wait for her in Sassine Square, in front of the statue of Bachir Gemayel, at 1.00 in the afternoon. It was raining while he waited, but Yalo never budged. He used the monument as a shelter against the ropes of rain. He didn't duck into the Chase Café nearby. He was afraid she wouldn't find him, afraid she wouldn't recognize him, afraid he wouldn't recognize her car. She'd said she'd come in a white car, so he stood in the rain waiting for the white car inside which she would be sitting, and when the car showed up, he didn't see it. He stared at all the cars, but he wasn't seeing. The car stopped next to him, she opened the door, and she gestured to him. He saw her and fell onto the leather seat and the floor was covered with drops of water falling from his long black coat.

"You're still wearing that coat?" she asked.

He couldn't think what to say. He'd worn the coat for her, to remind her of that night. But he was lying even without saying anything, because he could not be parted from his coat. He'd worn it in Beirut and he'd worn it at the barracks near the Ministry of Justice and he'd worn it in Paris and he wore it in Ballona, and he couldn't bear to take it off, to the point where he hated the summer because of it. Even in summer, the coat was always with him on his hunting trips in the forest. All the same, he couldn't think what to say. The spine idea came into his head, and he wanted to tell her about the love that shatters one's back, but he didn't say anything and waited in silence until they got to Albert's. She parked and they got out. She went in ahead of him. She found an isolated corner where they sat down, but before he could open his mouth to tell her that he wanted her, as he'd planned to do as soon as she agreed to go with him to the restaurant, the waiter came over and asked what they wanted to drink.

"Arak," said Yalo.

"Arak," repeated Shireen. "Why not?"

Yalo started ordering meze, and Shireen seemed not to care what the dishes were or not to be listening. Yalo had been sure that her agreeing to have lunch with him would lead her back to his house in Ballona or him to hers in Hazmiyeh.

When, at 11.00 that morning, he'd bathed and put the green shampoo on his hair and stood under the hot shower and closed his eyes, he'd seen Shireen. The water gushed over him and his love gushed too. He felt as though everything was slipping from his shoulders, that his whole life was slipping away under the hot water, and he felt a strange intoxication. He masturbated without realizing it, and everything slipped away and he went to her. He left desire behind and went just as he was, without desire and naked. He stood under the shower and the business was done, and he left his desire at home and went to her with love. "Just love," he said to himself. Love for its own sake, as in Abdel Haleem. A love he didn't know how to speak but that he would speak, because, ever since his first meeting with Shireen, he hadn't stopped listening to the songs of Abdel Haleem. He had, it's true, continued his hunting parties, but he'd embarked on them without real desire. As for Mme Randa, he'd stopped sleeping with her. He'd only slept with her three times in the past six months, and each time she'd put on a sex video so he'd only slept with her via the film.

Shireen said she'd drive by Sassine Square and pick him up, so he parked Madame's car on the corner by the Lala chicken restaurant and walked towards the square.

Yalo had thought that Shireen didn't own a car, because when he'd been hunting her with the grizzled man whose grey hair was bent over her neck, he'd thought she couldn't own a car. The grizzled man had gone off in his own car and left her shivering in the forest, and Yalo had taken her to his hut because he had no alternative.

Why did she tell the interrogator that he'd ordered her to get out and told the man to leave?

"She's lying, sir," he said.

When he said she was lying, the palm landed hard on his right cheek, and he felt little white circles coming out of his eyes, and everything went cloudy.

What, in fact, had happened?

Yalo would spend many long days in his cell trying to reconstruct the incident exactly, but he would fail.

When the light fell on the two victims and he ran towards them, the sound of his plastic shoes hitting the ground filled his ears. That's how it always was. When he went hunting, his footfalls would grow louder and he would hear nothing else.

He shone his torch at them and moved forward, and when he reached the car, he saw the grey-haired man raise his head in alarm before getting out of the car and standing in front of Yalo. Yalo looked at the girl and motioned with the barrel of his rifle. His gesture hadn't been meant as an order to get out of the car, but the girl opened the door and got out, so Yalo turned and walked towards her, and at that moment the grey-haired man jumped into the car and reversed at high speed. Then the car turned, its wheels squealing as the earth flew up around them. Yalo raised his gun and pumped it as though he was about to shoot, or that was the impression he gave, but then he heard the girl weeping. He turned and saw the girl kneeling on the ground and gasping as she wept. He lowered the rifle, stood next to her, and silence fell between them.

Yalo led the girl to his hut, after asking her to take off her high-heeled party shoes. He had taken her hand and helped her get up. Then he'd made her walk, and when he discovered that she was stumbling because of the high heels, he looked at the shoes and the girl understood and took them off without his having to ask. With the shoes in her hand she walked by his side. But she stumbled again and nearly fell. She doubled over as though she was falling, so Yalo bent over, but she recovered her balance and stood up, so he took her hand and led her to the place where the smell of incense blazed out of her lovely white wrists.

Why did she lie to the interrogator and say she'd been with her fiancé?

Yalo can't remember if he'd told her that her wrists smelled like rice pudding, but there in the restaurant, and after he'd slapped her, Yalo ordered rice pudding. Shireen smiled because she remembered that he'd told her that her wrists smelled better than rice pudding.

No, he hadn't slapped her because of the birds, as she claimed before the interrogator, but because she'd offered him money, and he despised money. He ate a dozen fried birds and drank half a bottle of arak before slapping her because she'd wounded his pride.

No, what she'd said wasn't right. He hadn't ordered her and her fiancé to kneel. She'd knelt after the grizzled man had left. And she wasn't with her fiancé. He knew that because this young man sitting in the interrogation room wasn't with her there in the forest.

She'd told the interrogator he'd ordered them to kneel and pointed his gun at them and that he'd wanted to kill her fiancé, Emile Shaheen, but she'd begged him to let Emile go and he'd done so.

"You're Emile?" asked the interrogator.

"Yes. Right. Emile Shaheen," answered the young man.

"Do you have anything to add?"

"Shireen has told you everything," answered Emile.

She said he'd ordered Emile to say his prayers because he was going to kill him in front of his girlfriend. "That's when I started pleading with him and crying. But he went on like a stubborn billy goat, and the rifle was pointing at the man's head, so I screamed. I don't know where I found the strength. Emile jumped into the car and got away, thank God. My fiancé ran away, and I was left in the clutches of this con man."

"What do you say to that, Daniel?" asked the interrogator.

Yalo knew he would stammer and couldn't speak. The pebble returned to his mouth; his mother had put a pebble under his tongue to make him talk without stammering, but he forgot about stammering when he saw the blood. That's what he would write if he were able to look back at his life in the mirror of days, but instead he was standing there, feeling his mother's pebble under his tongue, and could find nothing to say.

"Why didn't your fiancé report the incident immediately?" he'd say.

"Why was he grizzled and in his fifties, and today he's suddenly a young man?" he'd say.

"Why did he leave you and run away?" he'd say.

But he didn't say, and the interrogator didn't insist. He considered Daniel's silence an answer and a confession.

"Is this the man who raped you and then found you again and blackmailed you and took money from you?" asked the interrogator.

Shireen nodded her head yes.

Emile looked at his watch and asked the interrogator if they could go now.

"Of course," said the interrogator, "of course," and he accompanied them to the door of the police station.

But at Albert's, no.

He slapped her and she shut up. Then when he ordered rice pudding, she smiled, and he told her he loved her.

"I'm engaged, Yalo," she said.

"I love you," he said.

"Please," she said.

The waiter brought the bill, and Yalo paid it and ordered another glass of arak. He sipped the arak and looked into the girl's eyes before closing his own for a long time.

"Please don't go to sleep," she said.

"Don't talk," he replied. "I'm speaking with God."

But the girl began talking, and Yalo listened to her with his eyes closed.

"I respect your feelings, but I'm engaged and I can't," she said.

"To that piece of shit who left you in the forest and ran away?" he asked.

"No, no. I left that one. To someone else."

And the girl told the story, and Yalo listened.

"It was like in an Egyptian film," he said. "Like a film with Fareed El Atrash."

She said she'd listen to Arabic songs for his sake. She said she respected him highly and was sorry, and that he was right to slap her because she'd hurt his feelings when she offered him money.

"Stop talking like that!" yelled Yalo.

He thought of the scene where Fareed Shawqi slaps Hind Rustum in *Maid of the Nile* and the actress kneels and says, "I love you, you brute."

"That's how I want you to be," he said. "You have to love a real man, not shits like those – one of them old enough to be your father and the other frightened of his mum."

"You're right," said Shireen. "But what can I do? I love him. We were students at the American University and we slept together. I was on the pill, but that day I forgot, I don't know why. Then when I told him I was pregnant and we had to get married, he said he was afraid of what his mother would say, so I took care of things. I became depressed, and a girlfriend took me to Dr Saeed, who did the abortion and fell in love with me. He said he fell in love with me because I cried so much. I got to his clinic and I started crying. I couldn't speak. I sat there and put my head in my hands and burst out crying, the tears pouring from my eyes. The doctor didn't say anything. He let me cry and sat there watching me; later he told me that he'd sat there watching.

16

He said he'd fallen for me "for the sake of those tears" – that's how he put it, speaking formally. "For the sake of those tears" and my foolishness, he said. I cried for I don't know how long, and then he told me, "Get up and come into the other room." I went and I could hear him telling me, "Take off your things." I took off my skirt and stood there. He said, "No," and pointed to show that I was to take everything off. I took everything off and he stared at my chest. I felt, I don't know what, but it was like his eyes were boring into my chest like needles, and I heard him say, "Very nice," but I didn't say anything. I was trembling with fear. I told him, "I'm cold, doctor." He said, "Lie down," so I lay down on a funny bed, a half-bed. I lay down on my back with my legs dangling. The nurse came in with a needle in her hand, and he kept staring between my legs and his eyes were kind of weird. I was afraid that there was a problem. I tried to speak, but my tongue had gone heavy in my mouth, like a bit of rubber. Then I don't remember anything. No, before I lost consciousness I told him, "I'm cold. Please give me a blanket." I was afraid and ashamed, and his eyes looked like they could see something, and then when I opened my eyes everything was over. I heard the nurse saying, "Everything's fine. Get dressed and the doctor will see you."

Shireen told her story. Her tongue was suddenly freed. She spoke and cried and blew her nose, and Yalo handed her Kleenex and was set on fire; everything within him was set on fire. The half-bed set him on fire; the doctor telling her to take her clothes off set him on fire; the nurse giving her the anaesthetic injection set him on fire.

She said she took off all her clothes, and she drew something like semi-circles round her small breasts and he smelled nakedness, but he felt paralyzed. She spoke and he listened, and his eyes felt as heavy as they did in sleep. She told him about the haemorrhage she'd had two days after the abortion and about how Dr Saeed El Halabi had taken her to his private clinic, where she'd stayed for three days until she was better, and how she'd fallen in love with him on the third day.

"I let him sleep with me without feeling any real desire. Well, he didn't sleep with me properly."

She said that on the third day, when the clock was pointing to 6.00 p.m. and she was alone, overcome with drowsiness and in need of a cigarette, he came to her room. The twilight was colouring everything with a greyness before which the daylight fled and he entered the room, his ashen hair shining. He sat on the bed, said, "Okay, you're fine. You can go home now," pulled back the bedcover so she could get up and took her hand.

"When he took my hand, I felt that I loved him," she said.

She said it was his hand that made her love him. His fingers, long as a piano player's, entwined with hers and she felt love.

"He put one hand on mine and buried the other one in his white hair, and I fell in love with him." She said she fell in love with him and wanted him to take her in his arms.

"I told him, 'I don't want to go. I've become fond of you, doctor.'"

Shireen spoke about that evening. She said that the night had slid over them and she didn't know what had happened then.

"I don't know what happened. I don't remember. You know I don't remember things like that – not just Dr Saeed, not anybody really. I don't remember with you, I don't remember with Emile. Okay, I remember the room and the doctor next to me, and that I slept with him, but I don't remember the details. I don't know what happened. Why do you think that is?"

"How should I know?" asked Yalo.

"It's strange, I really don't remember anything," she said.

"You mean now you don't remember sleeping with me?" asked Yalo.

. . .

"Don't you remember the second time, how you said that you could smell the scent of pines, as though the trees had come into the room?"

"I said that?"

"Of course."

"I can't believe it."

"You were talking about the scent of the pines, and I felt as though my spine was breaking into bits."

"I didn't say that," said Shireen. "I couldn't have. When I was with you, I was dying of fear, and anyway, please, let's forget it."

Why had she forgotten everything?

She'd forgotten how she'd told him at Albert's about Dr Saeed and about her new-old fiancé Emile. She sat there like a stranger, and something that reminded Yalo of the young men's savagery on that day he had decided to forget, and had forgotten, came out of her eyes. That day when they'd taken the three men to the cemetery and made them lie down under the cypress trees in the cemetery of Mar Mitr as though they were being crucified. They'd crucified them on the ground before shooting them, and then they'd started cursing and spitting, the terror inhabiting their eyes. Yalo had vomited and then wept. Then he'd gone home. Then . . . no, no, he didn't want to remember that now, so he shut his eyes.

She said she'd kissed the doctor. She'd lifted her head a little so her lips could meet his, and she'd fallen in love with him.

"I let him sleep with me even though I didn't feel desire, but he didn't really," she said.

The doctor told her that full intercourse was not a good idea just then.

"He made love to my chest," she said, crying and blowing her nose.

"What do you mean?" asked Yalo, his voice shaking.

"Like this," she said, tracing the line between her breasts with her finger. "And I didn't feel anything. Well, I felt something hot."

She said she'd had a long relationship with the doctor and that he was not normal and always slept with her "that way".

"What way?" asked Yalo.

"Here," she said, tracing an imaginary line between her breasts.

"Like that all the time?"

"Mostly," she said. "He said he liked my tits."

"Don't use that word," said Yalo. "It's not nice for women to use words like that."

"What word do you want me to use? I'm just telling the truth."

"Say 'sahro'."

"What does 'sahro' mean?" she asked.

"You've forgotten? I taught you that word when you were at my house."

"I told you, I don't remember anything."

"You asked me then what it meant and I explained it to you."

"Okay, so explain it to me again."

"Not now," said Yalo. "But don't use words like that."

She said that the doctor didn't sleep with her properly even once. He used to satisfy himself with words of love and then "things like that". "He used to tell me he was afraid to sleep with me properly because we were at the clinic. I told him, 'Fine, let's go to a hotel.' He said everyone would know and he was a married man, so we started doing it sometimes at the clinic and sometimes in the car. At Ballona, the time you raped me . . ."

"Me, rape you? What are you talking about?"

"I mean the time you took me to your house and slept with me, we were in the car and he told me, 'Put your head down.'"

"Maybe he saw me."

"No, he didn't see you. He wanted me to . . ."

"Wanted you to what?"

"He wanted me to go down on him, and then you were so kind as to turn up and we died of fright, and I don't know how I managed to get my head up or how he managed to rearrange his clothes."

"I'm an idiot," shrieked Yalo. "A stupid idiot."

"Keep your voice down," said Shireen. "Please, the restaurant's full of people. Do me a favour and don't raise your voice."

Yalo said in a low voice that he was a stupid idiot.

Where's the smell of incense?

Why didn't Yalo smell incense when he saw her sitting in the interrogation room?

At Albert's he'd smelled it. Her incense was stronger than the arak and the fried birds and everything else. Here, though, in the interrogator's white room, he could smell nothing. Or at least his nose was filled with a rubbery smell. When, later, the interrogator forced him to write the story of his life, he would write about the smell of imprisonment and say that the smell of the prison was like that of wet rubber, a smell of petrol and heating oil and rubber, burning and smoking.

When he saw her before the interrogator, he fell onto the chair and closed his eyes, seeking the smell of incense. He saw Emile seated at her side, he saw her slim, naked thighs revealed by the short skirt, he saw the roundness of her small breasts, and he waited for the incense. But the smell of incense did not rise; in fact, the other smell became very strong, more like that of wet rubber, and the sun burned everything and made it impossible to see.

And Shireen said.

She said and she reached out and took Yalo's hand, in the restaurant, before taking hers away again and saying, "Please."

"Please let me go. I want to go back to my house and my life. I don't want anything from you. I apologize. Forgive me and let me go."

"Where do you want to go?" asked Yalo.

"I want to go back to my house and my life," she answered.

"So go. Am I stopping you?"

"Yes, you're stopping me. Please let me go. I'm grateful for everything, but you have to understand that it's over, it's all over."

Yalo felt a desire to slap her again, but he didn't. The slap had been logical when she'd opened her purse and taken out a handful of dollars and pushed them at him, leaving her purse open on the table, and asked him to leave her alone.

"Take it all," she'd said, "and if you want more, I'm ready to pay. Just leave me alone."

At that moment Yalo had stood up and slapped her. He heard the sound of footsteps approaching, so he thought that someone from the restaurant was coming over. He put his hand into his pocket, feeling for the knife, and got ready to fight, but the footsteps clattered away again. He sat down again and drank the whole of his glass at one go, and the silence was broken only by Shireen's coughing and crying.

He gave her a Kleenex and she put the money back in her purse. Then he gave her a bite of *kibbeh nayyeh* and the conversation returned to normal.

He told her about the Egyptian films he loved because Madame had made him watch them. She would ask him to go down to Beirut once a week to get her Arab films from a video store in Sodeco and she'd spend her mornings watching them. Sometimes she'd invite him to watch with her. He didn't tell Shireen about the other films, though, since he didn't know where Madame got them, but she only watched those at night. Daytime was for the Arabic films and night-time for the other films, which she watched with a bottle of Black Label whisky, and Yalo didn't want to talk about those other films because since Shireen he'd begun to see life with new eyes.

Why didn't Shireen believe him?

Why did she persist in the belief that he was blackmailing her and that his love for her and the songs of Abdel Haleem Hafez meant nothing?

In the restaurant, when she told him about her relationship with Emile, he felt a need to slap her again. She said she'd started to think Dr Saeed didn't love her.

"I mean . . . how can I put it? I don't know, I just felt he didn't love me properly."

She said her relationship with the doctor had come to an end after that hellish night.

"It was like all the doors of Hell had opened. I went to see him at the clinic around 6.00 in the evening, as usual, so that we could spend a little time before he went home. We sat and talked. He reached over to me. He reached over to undo the buttons of my blouse and he asked me about Emile. I'd started seeing Emile again. I was sick of the secrecy and the lying and the unfulfilling dates. And he would only make love to me the way I told you. So I went back to Emile. I can't tell you how happy Emile was when I agreed to speak to him again. He said that he felt guilty, and that this and that that, and that he was going to get his mother to come and ask for my hand. I didn't tell Dr Saeed about Emile. I don't know how he found out. Or I told him that Emile had phoned but didn't tell him I'd gone to the cinema with him and that we'd slept together."

"You slept with him?" asked Yalo.

"So what? He was going to be my fiancé."

"You mean you were sleeping with two men at the same time?"

Shireen didn't answer. She bowed her head and said nothing.

"Why don't you say something?" he asked.

She said she could no longer understand him. He'd raped her and kept pursuing her with telephone calls and forcing her to meet him in cafés and waited for her in front of her house and at work, and he was blackmailing her and threatening her, and now he wanted to give her lessons in morals because she'd slept with two men?

"And how many of the women from the forest have you slept with?" she asked.

"No, I'm not like that," he answered.

"You're not what? Who are you? Why in God's name did I get involved with you?"

"And?" asked Yalo.

"And what?" asked Shireen.

"You told him about Emile, and then what?"

"Oh. You're asking me about the doctor."

She said she'd been astonished by Dr Saeed's reaction. When he asked her about Emile, Shireen decided the time had come to tell him the truth. And when he heard that, after they'd watched *Scarface*, she and Emile had gone to the Italian restaurant for dinner and that then she'd gone with Emile to his flat and spent the night, the doctor didn't get angry and throw her out of the clinic as she'd expected. Instead, he started gnawing his fingernails, and then he touched her chest.

"'No, no,' I told him. 'No, I don't want that any more.'"

"I know what you want," he told her, and he started tearing at her clothes. Then he led her over to the sofa, took off all her clothes, helped her take off his, and the hell began.

Shireen said that she didn't know what happened, whether he'd slept with her or not. He'd had an erection and she'd taken him in her hand and he'd entered her, but she didn't know. Perhaps he'd come quickly, but there wasn't any sign of it. Perhaps he'd suddenly gone soft so he'd pretended that he'd finished. And then he'd started again. He'd been right there, as though he was making love to her, but he hadn't . . . Then he'd said he couldn't, because she'd castrated him. "You're one of those women who castrate men," he'd said.

Shireen asked Yalo, "Does that make sense?"

Yalo said he didn't understand exactly what had happened.

"Nor do I," said Shireen.

"I just hope it doesn't happen with me!" said Yalo, laughing.

"You mean he was right, I castrate men?" asked Shireen.

"I don't know about the others, but I'm ready to try you out right now," said Yalo.

"Look at you. What a thing to think of!"

"What am I supposed to be thinking of?" asked Yalo, drinking some arak.

Shireen said Dr Saeed had got up, put on his clothes and left her alone at the clinic.

"I put my clothes on quickly, without having a shower. I was afraid he'd locked me in, but when I tried the door it opened. I picked up my things, went home and that was that."

"That was that?"

"No. Afterwards the thing at Ballona happened. He pleaded with me and I went with him, and what happened happened and that was that."

"And Emile?" asked Yalo.

"No. No, Emile didn't know anything about my relationship with Dr Saeed, and anyway, what kind of a relationship was it? It had no taste."

She said that with Emile too she didn't taste anything, but she was going to marry him. She'd sleep with him without feeling any desire, but she felt tenderness, especially since he carried his guilt round on his shoulders and was always bent over, as though under the weight of his fear for her.

Shireen said she was going to marry Emile and that she wanted Yalo to understand her position and stop phoning her because the engagement was getting closer.

"The engagement? What engagement?" asked Yalo.

"My engagement to Emile," said Shireen. "We've decided to get engaged. I'm begging you, it's over."

"The truth is out!" screamed the interrogator.

Why did the interrogator say that the truth was out? Was it because she'd come with Emile and lied? Is that how the truth comes out?

The interrogator said that the truth had come out "and there's no point in lying any more."

"Yes, sir," said Yalo, and he wanted to confess. He bowed his head, closed his eyes and could feel the confession; he could hear his grandfather the *kohno* saying in his hoarse voice that was swallowed up by his throat, "Confess!" Yalo had been frightened when his mother said that her father swallowed his

26

voice. He'd get frightened and stop swallowing his saliva so that he wouldn't swallow his voice and become like his grandfather.

"Confess, boy!" the *kohno* screams.

All Yalo can see is a white beard from which a strange smell emanates.

"That's the smell of incense," said his mother. "Your grandfather, my son, is a *kohno*. He chews incense and musk before leading the prayers, and you too, very soon you'll grow up, God willing, and be a *kohno* like your grandfather."

"I hate all *kohnos*," said Daniel.

But his grandfather, the priest Afram (as his name became after he entered the priesthood), forgot everything. He forgot the first name he'd had, Habeel, and his second name, which the Kurdish mullah had given him, and forgot how he'd worked as a tile-maker in the workshops scattered around Beirut, and forgot his mother, who'd died in a faraway village called Ein Ward, and forgot his wife, who'd been killed by a long illness.

All that *Kohno* Afram remembered about his mother was the long black hair in which spots of blood had congealed, like open eyes. Afram chewed pine resin, perfumed his beard with incense and was afraid of open eyes.

"Close your eyes, boy, and confess."

"That boy's eyes scare me. Why are his eyes so big and his lashes so long? Where did he get those eyes? We don't have big eyes like that in our family."

Yalo didn't know how to answer his grandfather the *kohno*'s questions, but he would close his eyes and confess that he'd lied and stolen an apple or not done his lessons or anything else he happened to think of. When the *kohno* listened to his confession, he was transformed from a *kohno* receiving the Sacrament into a grandfather, and instead of preaching to the boy who stood before him, head bowed and eyes closed, he'd start beating him with a cane.

"I don't want to make confession with you, Grandpa."

"I'm not Grandpa, I'm Father Afram, and if you don't confess, you won't be allowed to take Communion tomorrow."

He would force Yalo to confess and then start beating him, and the boy would be frightened of that rasping voice paving the way for the whine of the cane over his naked feet.

Yalo didn't cry. His saliva would dry up, and he would tremble with frustration before his grandfather.

He called him "Black Grandfather", and this square-built man, with his honey-coloured eyes and his large nose, whose white beard filled his face and reached down to his chest, was the master of the small family made up of Yalo and his mother, Gaby. Yalo didn't have a father, because his father had emigrated to Sweden long ago and all trace of him had been lost, and he didn't have any brothers or sisters.

"Just us three," Yalo told the interrogator when he was asked about his family.

"We are a family of just three people – *Abo*, *Bro* and *Rohoqadisho*. I'm *Bro*."

"What are you talking about? Do you think this is a joke?" screamed the interrogator.

"No, sir. It's just that my Black Grandfather used to talk like that. He was an Assyrian, except I think he was a Kurd. I don't know how it all got so mixed up. That's how we are – Father, Son and Holy Ghost, my mother being the Holy Ghost. That's what I was taught when I was small, but my grandfather stopped calling me *Bro*. He said I wasn't a good *Bro*. *Bro* is Christ and I was turning out like Judas, pathetic and useless. That's why he started calling me Yalo, and when he heard my mother calling me *Bro* he'd tell her not to and yell at her."

Why didn't Yalo tell the interrogator these things?

When he asked Yalo about his family, Yalo didn't know what to say. He closed his eyes as though he couldn't hear.

"Confess!" screamed the interrogator.

Yalo decided to confess, and the confession came and he said, "Yes, but it didn't happen like that."

"How did it happen? You tell us and we'll decide."

Yalo said that the man in the car with Shireen wasn't Emile but another man.

"Liar. Why didn't you say that when M. Emile was sitting here?"

And the silence fell.

Yalo felt the silence spreading to every corner, an all-embracing silence that swallowed him and swallowed his voice and ears. He had felt the same when he had arrived at the villa. The lawyer had told him, "Come," and he'd brought him there from Paris, and there, in the village of Ballona, Yalo had heard the sound of silence and became accustomed to it, and it had become part of him. And he'd discovered that night had a body, and the body of night fell upon him and covered him.

A night like a black coat and a silence like silence, and stars that spread above him as though opening onto eternity, and an eternity that took him into another fear.

The lawyer, Michel Salloum, said he'd taken Yalo there to guard the Villa Gardenia. He said he'd brought a Kalashnikov and a box of ammunition, and shown Yalo the hut below the villa where he would live.

"Right, right," said Yalo.

"Go down to your house, get yourself sorted out, and then come back up here so I can introduce you to my wife, Mme

Randa, and my daughter, Ghada."

"Right, right," said Yalo.

"Take a shower, the water's hot. Change your clothes. I've bought you new ones. Then come back up here to me."

"Right, right," said Yalo.

"And I don't want any hooliganism, understand? The rifle's only to be used if anything should happen, God forbid. I don't want anyone to see it, and I don't want my wife to know."

"Right, right," said Yalo.

"My wife's afraid of dogs or we'd have got a guard dog, to help you I mean, but she's afraid. That's why there isn't going to be anyone else for you to rely on. You're going to have to rely on God and on yourself."

"Right, right," said Yalo.

Yalo went down to the hut below the villa belonging to *Maître* Michel Salloum and felt as though he was now the owner of a palace. The house was small and beautiful, thought Yalo when he found himself alone in his new home. It was a large room, about sixteen square metres, rectangular in shape, with white walls and green carpeting. On the right there was a wide wooden bed covered with a blue woollen blanket, and on the left an old pink sofa and, next to that, a wooden table and three cane chairs. A naked bulb dangled from the ceiling, and on the left there was a metal cupboard, which Yalo opened, finding inside three new pairs of trousers, a number of old shirts, clean and ironed, and an olive-green woollen pullover. To the left of the room was a kitchen that contained a small refrigerator, a three-ring butane-gas cooker, a small table and a white cupboard with dishes and saucepans, and next to this was a small bathroom with a white toilet, a shower, a clean mirror, a white box for medicines with the Red Cross symbol on it, and an electric water heater. Yalo turned on the heater, went back into the room and lounged on the sofa. Then he saw a spider's web in the right-hand corner of the room and noticed that the paint was flaking just below the ceiling on the left, but still he felt like a king. He went into the bathroom and took a shower, though the water wasn't yet hot enough, and then he put on a green shirt and grey trousers. He discovered that the trousers were too short, as were the three other pairs hanging in the cupboard, so he decided to put his old trousers on again and buy a new pair the next day.

For the first time in his life, Yalo thought, he was going to live in his own house, and he thought that he could bring his mother there. Then he dropped the idea because 'Mme' Gabrielle had said she wanted to go back to her old house and that she hated Ein El Roummaneh, where she'd been forced to take refuge after being expelled from the Assyrian quarter in Museitbeh at the start of the war.

She'd said her clients were waiting for her to return and take up her work again because she was the best seamstress in Beirut.

She'd said that she couldn't put up with this life any longer and missed her old neighbours, and that the civil war was over, or ought to be.

She'd said that her father had died in Ein El Roummaneh like a stranger. Father Afram had died alone, and she didn't want to die there too; she wanted to die in her own house.

She'd said and she'd said. She'd stand in front of the mirror for long periods and talk, and Yalo began to be afraid of his mother. The mirror began to terrify him, so he decided to leave. He'd left two years before and not gone back. Fate had taken him where it wished, and there, in the metro station in Paris, the lawyer Michel Salloum had stumbled across him and brought him back to Lebanon.

Yalo hadn't visited his mother since his return, and he couldn't explain this to the interrogator as there is no convincing explanation for a man's not visiting his mother.

"I saw your mother," said the interrogator. "She said she didn't know anything about you. I went all the way to see her in her house in Ein El Roummaneh and asked her about you."

"She's still in Ein El Roummaneh?" asked Yalo.

"Why? Don't you know where your mother lives?"

"No, I do, I do. I just thought she'd gone back to Museitbeh."

"You mean you haven't visited her since you came back from France?"

"No."

"Why?"

"I don't know. I didn't want to. There wasn't any need."

"Why did you do that?"

"Do what?"

"You know."

Father Afram would swallow his words when he said, "You know," and the interrogator swallowed his words too, as though he was choking on them. He took a sip of water from the glass in front of him and asked why Yalo hadn't visited his mother.

And Yalo knows that, in spite of everything, his mother wasn't a problem. He hadn't visited her because . . . he didn't know why; or because he was sure she'd gone back to their old house and he didn't like their old house, where all he'd find to look at was the picture of Black Grandfather hanging on the wall.

But Yalo had never once confessed his real sins to his grandfather because he was convinced that there was only one, which he committed in spite of himself and without meaning to, for he'd find himself alone with the sin and he'd go into the bathroom and grab hold of the sin and see stars.

He'd told Shireen he loved her because he saw stars. This feeling of the stars that opened like eyes in the body of the night was something he'd never felt again except with Shireen, there in the little house below the villa; the others, the women of the forest or Madame or the girls during the war, not with them.

"I love you because of the stars," he'd told Shireen in the restaurant, but she hadn't understood. She'd said she was ready to give him all the money he wanted, at one go, on condition that he left her alone and it was over and she could find some peace.

She'd said, as she wept, that she was begging him and that she'd become afraid of him and didn't love him; in fact, she loved another man, whom she was going to marry. So he slapped her. He'd talked to her about the stars and she'd thought he wanted money.

Before he'd left the restaurant, he'd looked at the bill on the table in front of him. He wanted to pay it, but she beat him to it and paid.

"You're my guest," she said.

"It's not right, you paying every time."

"Never mind. Let me do it one last time," she'd said.

She'd paid and left without giving him a lift to Sassine Square, where he'd parked his car. She got into her car and didn't open the passenger door. She started the engine and left, and Yalo remained standing alone on the narrow pavement. She said she was in a hurry and had to get back to work, but that was rude, as Yalo would tell her the next day on the phone, after which he heard, instead of her answer, the sound of her putting the phone down. He called her again dozens of times and never heard anything. Yalo was sure she was hanging up as soon as she heard his voice so he started dialling the number and then, when she picked up, saying nothing and trying to hold his breath, but she wouldn't even say hello. She'd leave the silence dangling from the receiver and then put the phone down. Yalo spent three days on this silent telephone game, and then the sound came back and Shireen started talking to him again, and agreeing to meet up with him, even though she still kept trying to invent excuses.

Why did she say he'd come on the night of her birthday and frightened her out of her wits?

Yalo hadn't done anything. Later he would say that he hadn't done anything. He'd just stood beneath the street light in his long coat and not moved and she'd seen him. She couldn't not have seen him, because he had lit up his eyes and shone them at her bedroom window.

Yalo could swear he hadn't done anything except aim his large black pupils at the glass pane of her bedroom window. He'd stood rigid and unmoving for hours, and then Shireen had opened the window and steam had billowed out. Yalo didn't know what they were doing inside, but he saw white steam coming out of the window, and it changed into a cloud, and he saw Shireen. Her head formed a circle in the midst of a halo of white steam coming out of her window.

"Is that true, you bastard? Is it true that you stood beneath her window on the night of her birthday?" screamed the interrogator.

Why did she say he was carrying two torches and that he stood beneath the street light shining the torches at her bedroom window?

Why did she lie and say he was carrying a Kalashnikov, and

that he'd leapt towards her window just as he'd done on that night in the forest of Ballona when he'd attacked her and her fiancé wearing his long black coat and his shoes that crunched in the dust and pebbles and his white balaklava that hid his face and the blinding light of his torch?

Why did she tell the interrogator that he'd stood beneath her window carrying a rifle and two torches?

The rifle was impossible. Who'd dare carry a rifle in the street and in Beirut once the war was over? As far as the torches were concerned, Yalo never ever carried more than one, and it was the best torch in the world. Madame had given it to him when the electricity was cut off – a slim black torch that emitted a fine ray like a bolt of lightning. That night Yalo hadn't used his torch, and he hadn't stood beneath her window in a threatening manner, and he hadn't tapped on the pane with the barrel of his rifle.

He had, it's true, stood there, and the torch was lying in his coat pocket next to the knife he always carried, but he hadn't been carrying his rifle.

He'd been standing there and his eyes had lit up with love.

"It was love, sir," Yalo wanted to tell the interrogator.

"Love and abjection, sir," he wanted to tell him.

"Love like the Cross, sir," Yalo wanted to say.

But Yalo didn't know how to say these things before the interrogator, because when he spoke he heard the voice of his mother, Gabrielle, or Gaby, coming out of his throat. She would stand in front of the mirror and say that her face didn't look like her face any more. She would weep and then turn on the tap and wash the tears from her face. She would stand for hours in front of the mirror and say she was washing the years of her life from her face.

35

"Only water washes away the years, my son."

He left her, her face washed with the water of years traced in his eyes, and her voice, with its slight huskiness and the lisp that made her words sound like other words, trailing after him.

"How can you understand the way your mother speaks?" asked his friend Tony, who would later take him to Paris.

"Everyone understands her," said Yalo. "They understand what she's saying from the expressions on her face, not from the words."

Yalo wasn't making this up, because even though he only knew a few words of Syriac, he understood everything from the movement of his grandfather's tear-filled eyes and would answer in Arabic, the only Syriac word he used being *Lo*, meaning "No".

He wanted to tell the interrogator to leave him alone, but Shireen had hurt him. Why did she say those things? Why did she look at him as though she hated him?

When Yalo entered the interrogation room, Shireen pointed and said, "That's him."

In that instant Yalo saw her naked thighs and saw the man sitting next to her, so he fell onto the chair that had been placed in the centre of the room for the accused to sit on and where he could be the target of everyone's eyes and under the surveillance of the stern interrogator.

He fell beneath their eyes and closed his own. He heard nothing Shireen said. She'd told the interrogator everything before he'd fetched Yalo and when he came in she said only a few things. She sat silently behind the whiteness of her slim thighs revealed by the short red skirt. She hid behind the whiteness just as she had disappeared behind the white cloud that had billowed out of her bedroom window.

"I went and stood beneath her window so I could tell her I loved her," said Yalo.

"I wanted to surprise her on her birthday. I went at 10.00 at night and stood beneath the window, and I went on standing till morning. I thought that when she woke up and saw me unmoving like the street light, she'd be surprised and understand how much I loved her."

Yalo didn't say this, though. The interrogator's words stunned him like a whip lashing his face.

The interrogator said that Yalo had been carrying two torches and a Kalashnikov and had stood beneath Shireen's window and kept shining the torches at the window. Then, when she'd opened the window, she'd seen him raise his rifle and aim it at her, and when she'd screamed, he'd run away.

The interrogator didn't say "run away". Instead he spoke an entire sentence. "And when she screamed, he took off on the wings of the wind."

"What does 'took off on the wings of the wind' mean?" asked Yalo.

"It means you ran away, you coward," answered the interrogator.

Yalo imagined himself clambering onto the wind and escaping, and he smiled.

"Why are you smiling?"

"No reason, no reason," answered Yalo, and he saw himself clambering onto the wind and he saw the words. That was how it was with words – he'd hear them and then see them. The words would embody themselves before him in real material objects, and he'd feel he was crashing into them rather than hearing or reading them. He was afraid of his Black Grandfather because he was afraid of his Black Grandfather's words. He would hear

37

the words "Come here, *Bro*", and he'd feel a pair of scissors hanging above his head, and he'd cover his head with his hands and go over to his grandfather while the scissors swung this way and that as though they were going to attack the hair on his head. And when his mother told him, "Go to school," he didn't see a school in front of him but scantily clad girls running about behind the nuns, and he'd feel the saliva rising to his lips. And when his grandfather asked him to fry some eggs, he'd see a plateful of stray dogs. That's how he'd been all his life – hearing a word and then seeing a thing, but that didn't mean he didn't understand what was said. He still went to school, and knew that "*Bro*" meant "son", and that his grandfather's requests had to be obeyed because a *kohno* could not be refused.

The *kohno* went to his death in a strange manner. First, he stopped eating meat and started eating only eggs, milk and vegetables. Then he gave up eggs and started devouring great quantities of fruit and vegetables before being stricken with the wandering disease.

Gaby said her father was wandering, and Yalo believed his mother and started to see Black Grandfather in a maze of intersecting lines. The man no longer knew how to get out of the bedroom or the bathroom. He'd enter a place and get stuck inside and only come out when *Bro* went in and got him. At the end, *Bro* had to go out searching the city's byways for his grandfather every night and bring him home.

When the interrogator said, "he took off on the wings of the wind," Yalo saw himself clambering quickly into the air and felt as though the sleeves of his coat had turned into the wings of a bird and that when he'd stood beneath Shireen's window he hadn't looked like himself but like a hawk with a long beak. Yalo raised his hands as though he was about to fly and heard the interrogator screaming, "Put your hands down, you bastard, and confess. Were you carrying an automatic rifle or not?"

"No. I wasn't," said Yalo.

"And the torches?" asked the interrogator.

"No," said Yalo.

"Why did you stand beneath the window and shine the torches at Miss Shireen Raad's house? Is it true you wanted to kidnap her? Is it true you wanted money? Is it true you told her you wanted to marry her and take her to Egypt? And why did you keep terrorizing her?"

Why had she lied and said that he'd forced her to buy him an air ticket to Egypt?

She'd bought the ticket and given it to him with a thousand Egyptian pounds, saying, "This is a present." She thought he needed a change of scene and she couldn't take time off to go with him. She hadn't said anything about her fiancé Emile then and she'd persuaded Yalo that she was beginning to love him, and it never occurred to him that when he accepted the ticket and the money that he'd fallen into a trap and was no longer capable of seeing things for what they were. He told her to come with him to Egypt. He told her he'd take her to Luxor, where she'd see God, but she said she couldn't. He'd put the ticket in a drawer, and it was still there. The thousand pounds he'd hidden in the hope that Shireen would change her mind he'd had to change later into Lebanese currency and spend, but he'd accepted the present. He'd accepted it as a present and as a down payment on love, not for its own sake, so he could say with confidence that he hadn't taken any money from her. The interrogator, using Shireen's words, said he'd been blackmailing her to get money.

Why did the interrogator scream, "Which is the truth?"

Should he have replied that truth is love? How could he convince the interrogator about love?

"Love is abjection, sir," said Yalo. "I loved her and I still love her. Well, now, after what happened, I don't know. But the point is I loved her, and I was ready to do whatever she wanted me to do."

"And the money?" screamed the interrogator.

"The money, sir? There wasn't any money. Money has no meaning."

"Was that why you terrorized her and forced her to pay you, you liar?"

"I swear I'm not a liar but . . . I don't know . . . "

How is Yalo to convince the interrogator about love when the interrogator is holding a thick wad of papers which he says have in them information about Daniel and the members of the gang and everybody? Yalo understood that "everybody" meant Mme Randa and her husband, Michel Salloum, the lawyer, so he decided to refuse to answer any questions related to that subject. What could he say about the wife of the lawyer who had rescued him from hunger and homelessness in Paris and brought him back to his own country? No, he'd say nothing. True, he was a scoundrel, as Mme Randa had said when she found out about his nightly raids into the forest of lovers, but not such a big one that he'd confess to his relationship with Mme Randa and sully the reputation of the good-hearted man who'd saved him. Even if he were to confess, the interrogator wouldn't believe him. Even her husband wouldn't believe him. What was certain, however, was that Mme Randa at least would never be able to say he'd raped her. Shireen might, if she wished, talk about rape because her situation was different, but not Mme Randa. Shireen had come to the interrogation room, sat down next to her fiancé and said he'd raped her in the forest.

Why did she say in the forest, and not in the hut, or the house?

The forest was better for rape, thought Yalo. There it would be the real thing. What did the poor girl know about rape? But that other woman – God bless them all! – now that was a woman! A woman in her forties who tasted like cherries. When Yalo took her behind a huge oak tree, her friend sat on the ground with his head in his hands. He'd caught her by accident. That night, when the road was overflowing with the cars of people fleeing the heat of Beirut for the mountains, he'd been sure he wouldn't find anything. He'd put on his long black coat, crossed the road that divided the Villa Gardenia from the forest and sat down in the darkness of the pines, waiting and not waiting. He'd dozed a little, or so it seemed, because he didn't see the car approaching the trap. He woke up when the wheels came to a stop. He opened his eyes, still heavy with sleep, and saw the woman. He felt for the torch in his pocket and stood up quickly. Yalo would never be able to describe how he'd succeeded in standing up and shining his torch on his victim in one and the same movement. After that, things speeded up. He went over to the car and gestured with his rifle. The man got out first, then the woman. He gestured to the woman so she followed him and he took her there, beneath the oak tree, while her friend sat on the ground with his head in his hands. All Yalo could remember was the taste of cherries, because he was half asleep. He put his rifle on the ground, went over to the woman and took her in his arms. Then he put his hands round her bottom and she lowered herself to the ground. She didn't take her clothes off and neither did he. He didn't even take off the coat. He felt as though he had entered water. In all his life,

Yalo had never experienced anything like it. The woman's water poured out pure and drenching. And she was trembling with pleasure. Everything was trembling in a man and a woman wrapped inside a black coat and making love next to a rifle on the ground and an extinguished torch. And when Yalo finished, after she'd squeezed out his soul and his trousers had filled with woman-water, he'd tried to withdraw but couldn't. The woman gripped him fiercely and he felt pain, and the scream started gathering in his throat and he was about to begin again when he saw her hands pushing at his chest and forcing him out of her. He stood up, zipped up his trousers, picked up his rifle, and went back to his hut. He didn't wait for them to leave. He needed a cup of hot tea so he went, and when he turned to look back at the car he saw the woman opening the door while the man started the engine without daring to turn on the lights, and they left.

"But I . . . But not in the forest," said Yalo.

"I didn't rape her," said Yalo.

What had Shireen told her fiancé, Emile?

He sits here in the interrogation room next to her and nods as though he knows everything, but he knows nothing.

Had she told him the truth, or had she lied to him?

Did she say she'd gone to Ballona with her lover the doctor and that they'd had sex there in the car? Or did she say she'd gone on some blameless errand with him and a wild beast wearing a long black coat had pounced on them and raped her?

Why did the fiancé agree to play that role? Did he think he was being manly? If he'd been a real man, he'd have settled things differently, thought Yalo. Why hadn't Emile contacted him and settled things with him man to man? He could have invited Yalo to the café and talked to him and said that he loved her too and suggested that one of them give her up, as it was meet that noble men should do, and as *Kohno* Afram had done with the tailor Elias El Shami when he found out that his daughter had gone back to her old lover.

Kohno Afram told his grandson the story. Then Yalo had understood nothing, but now he understood everything.

At the time, the grandfather had concluded the story with manliness, and he had told his grandson the story to teach him manliness. "Life is a word you speak, which is then carved into the earth," said the grandfather.

When Gaby found out, she went crazy. Yalo asked her about the tailor and about where his father was, and she went mad. She went to her father and started shouting insults and dragged him roughly from his room. The *kohno* was wearing white pyjamas with blue stripes. As his daughter dragged him out by his hands he stumbled as though beseeching her, and she ordered him out of the house. He swallowed his words and said incomprehensible things and swore by all the saints that his intentions had been honourable and that he had only wanted to explain to his grandson the meaning of keeping one's word. Then suddenly the *kohno* fell to his knees, stretched out his arms as though he was crucifying himself, and his tears poured forth.

The story buried itself deep in Yalo's memory and was only extinguished here, in front of the white interrogator with his snub nose and deep-set eyes. The interrogator pointed at Yalo's face as though he wanted to say something, and perhaps he did say something, but Yalo was not listening to what he said. Yalo was asking himself the question that was written out in front of him as though he was reading from the school blackboard.

Why hadn't Emile done the same thing as Afram?

Afram was brave. He told his grandson he'd castrated the

man. "He came in here all puffed up like a cock and he left crowned with shame. He came in a cock and he left a hen. I did nothing. I just raised the weapon of words in his face. Before the word, my son, a man is weak. That is why God the Father could find no name to give His son but the Word. What does God's Word mean? It means His essence and His truth. Your son is your Word. You are my Word, my son, just as the Son was the Word of the Father."

Afram sent for Elias El Shami. The tailor thought that the *kohno* wanted him to make the priest a white cassock ahead of his being promoted to the episcopate, for he was always saying to his congregation, "Any day now – in a year, in two, in three – you'll be calling me 'Your Grace'!" The years passed, but the *kohno* kept waiting, for from the time when his wife died, after that trip to Homs in search of a cure from Mar Elyan, he had told everyone that this was God's will. He hadn't shed a tear at his wife's funeral. He'd stood receiving condolences and instead of responding with the traditional words – "Your wellbeing is my compensation" or "May you live long" – he uttered the single phrase "Christ is risen", expecting the mourners to respond, "Truly, He is risen." The *kohno* said that God had been testing his slave – meaning the poor woman who had died of cancer – because there is a wisdom of which we slaves are unaware. A catastrophe is a test and God tests his children with catastrophes, and this catastrophe had been, perhaps, a special kind of test, as though God had had something in mind of which we were ignorant.

Naturally, no-one took Afram's words seriously, since God, Great and Glorious, was not so short of options as to make someone like him a shepherd of His pitiful people. Nevertheless, despite the scornful looks, *Kohno* Afram continued to dream of becoming a bishop. His hair turned white, old age got its claws into him, and he devoted himself to prayer, always waiting for the moment that would come.

The tailor arrived. He thought he'd be joking with the *kohno* about the business of being made a metropolitan but found himself facing the most difficult examination of his life. The tailor Elias El Shami was about sixty and tried to give an impression of eternal youth, sucking in his belly to make himself look slim and smiling broadly so that people could see his clean white teeth, the tailor being one of the earliest of the residents of Museitbeh to discover the Armenian dentist Noubar Bakhshijian and, instead of false teeth, having fixed bridges made, which gave the impression that he had all his own teeth.

The tailor sat down before the *kohno*, who'd said, "Come, my son. Sit down before me." He bowed his head, his hair dyed red with henna, and kissed the hand which resembled the dry limb of a tree. Then he listened to the strangest request and responded with the strangest answer.

"You love the girl, right?"

The tailor did not understand the question, or pretended not to understand.

"What girl, Father?" he said.

"You love Gabrielle – my daughter, Gaby – and I know everything."

The tailor didn't know what to say. If he were to deny it, he would make himself look base to this aged *kohno*, who could see his only remaining daughter sliding towards destruction due to her relationship with the tailor. And if he said yes, he couldn't imagine what the *kohno* would ask of him. So the tailor contented himself with looking at his feet, leaving the *kohno* to deduce whatever he wished.

"So take her."

45

. . .

"I'm telling you, take her. What are you waiting for?"

"What?"

"Take her, my son. I'll take care of the legal side. I'll divorce her from her husband because he's been away ten years. That way you'll be able to marry her."

"But I am married."

"I'll get you a divorce too."

"Me?"

"Yes, you."

"But that'll be tough, Father. You know how long these things take for the Orthodox."

"I'll make you an Assyrian. That way I can get you a divorce in twenty-four hours."

"Me? Become an Assyrian?"

"Why not? The Assyrians aren't good enough for you?"

"I have every respect for the Assyrians, Father, but . . ."

"But what?"

The *kohno* told him to take her, and the tailor bowed his head for a long while before answering, "Take her where, Father?"

"Take her to your house and live with her as decent married folk. Decent, indecent, it really doesn't matter; you just have to find a way of taking her. It's what's going on now that's indecent, and it can't continue."

The two men fell silent and remained so until Gabrielle entered the parlour with the coffee tray.

"Sit, my daughter," said the *kohno*.

Gabrielle sat, every limb trembling.

"I told him to take you. I told him, 'If you love her, take her.'"

Then he looked at Elias and asked him, "What is your decision, my son?"

46

"I don't know," answered Elias after he had sipped his coffee and orange-blossom water.

"What don't you know?" asked the *kohno*.

"I don't know, Father. No. Take her yourself," answered Elias in a voice like a rattle from the depths of his throat.

"What did you say?" asked the *kohno*.

"Really, I don't know what to say."

"No. Repeat what you said. I didn't hear you."

. . .

"You said I should take her? Me?"

"I can't," said Elias.

"You said I should take her? She's my daughter! What are you talking about? Get up, you piece of shit! I thought you were a man and you've turned out a piece of shit. Get up and get out of here, and don't you ever, ever come anywhere near my daughter again or I'll smash your head in."

Yalo doesn't know how the visit ended or how Elias El Shami left the house, but he imagines him leaving with his back bent and stumbling.

"He came in a young man and he left an old one," he would tell Shireen, but Shireen didn't listen to the story of his mother. When he met her, she would be in a hurry and frightened and wanting to go home. He wanted to tell her that it was the man's duty to take the woman he loved. If Emile had been daring enough to say, "Take her," Yalo would have taken her; how could he have left her? Someone tells him to take her and he won't? Out of the question. And now, if the interrogator told him, "Take her," he would take her. But the interrogator said that he knew everything, and "everything" meant he knew about Mme Randa. That one he could never take. He imagined the lawyer Michel Salloum. He saw Michel Salloum sitting with him in front of the stove in the Villa Gardenia telling him to take Randa, to which Yalo would say, "*Lo*. No. You take her. I don't want her."

Shireen, however, was something else. No-one would ever tell him to take her because when you love the woman, things don't happen like that. But there in the villa, when *Khawaja* Michel came, Yalo would become frightened and feel Elias El Shami's trembling in his hands. *Khawaja* Michel would come back from his journeys to France or other countries and ask Yalo to come up to the villa. Yalo would go, bent over like Elias El Shami and frightened that those words would slip from his boss's mouth, because he was sure he wouldn't be able to take her, just as he knew he didn't want to. All the same, he went to her when she called and he slept with her when she wanted him and he felt when he was with her that he was inside moments that would carry him off to a world whose real nature he was unaware of, and when he came to try to write those moments down, in the cell, when all he had in front of him was a pile of sheets of white paper given him by the interrogator, he wouldn't know what to write. Should he write that he felt as though he'd entered a bonfire of emotions that was baking him to a crisp? Or should he lie and say that he didn't like having sex with her? Or what?

Yalo would toss and turn in Madame's fire and become sharp and pointed, like a spear, and she would scream at him to pierce her with his spear, and he would stagger and blaze and howl like a frantic wind, and she would moan and tell him to say her name – "Say Randa! Say Randa!" – and he'd repeat after her as she spoke. He even started calling sex "randarizing". He would randarize his way to her and he would randarize while waiting for her and he would randarize on his own and he would randarize in the bathroom.

"Don't come up here unless I call you," she told him.

He would go up when she called him and wait when she didn't call him, and she would come to him when she felt like it and say, "I yearn for Nature."

"I fancy sleeping with your smell," she told him when she came to him in his little house the first time, and she randarized in his bed just like she did in her own and said his smell was what had bewitched her and that she loved the smell of thyme mixed with pine. And he would randarize her and spear her and ask her, "How about changing places? You come live down here and I'll go live up there," and she'd laugh and say that he was sweet and she loved him because he made her laugh. Then she'd leave. She'd go up to the villa, to the tank full of hot water and the soap, and he'd stand under the shower, shivering from the cold, in his hut.

"How did you come to start sniping at people?" asked the interrogator.

"I never worked as a sniper in the war, sir," said Yalo.

"Stop pretending butter wouldn't melt in your mouth. I'm asking you about the forest and the cars and the women. How did you come to start stalking cars?"

Indeed, come to think of it, how had he started?

How can he answer a vague question like that?

"I started just like that, by accident. I saw a car and I went down there."

"Alone?"

"Yes, alone."

"And later on?"

"Later on I was still alone"

When Yalo tries to remember, he sees himself alone and he sees night. How had the night started? Who can ask the night how it became night?

He wanted to tell the interrogator that the sniping he was asking about was like the night, but his throat felt dry and he couldn't find the words. And that's how it had always been: he would be missing the words when he wanted to speak, and his mother would say that her son's tongue was heavy, though Yalo couldn't feel the heaviness of his tongue. The words just got stuck in his throat, and instead of "getting them off his chest" like everyone else, he would swallow them, and the pebbles and the prayers and the vows did no good.

When Yalo remembers those days, he sees another person. He sees a child wearing the words of his mother. He sees him in her words, which slide round him while he is incapable of speaking. The word starts to form itself in his mouth, he feels that it's whole, and then he tries, but it slips back down inside his throat and doesn't come out, and he strains till the veins in his neck stand out and his mother urges the word on with her eyes, then sees how it has slipped back down inside and will only come out in bits, and she starts in on her sermon: "Come along now, dear, come along. I told you. I explained to you how you have to bring it up. Try spitting. Go on, spit. See how all the spit comes up? It's the same for a word. It has to come up like when you spit. Go on, try."

And he would try. He would swallow his words and his saliva and would feel like he was going to be dumb when he grew up.

There, he spat them out.

In the barracks, near the Museum, when he yelled that he was a billy goat now. Tony had told him to spit them out, and he spat them out and learned how to spit.

"War is about us spitting," is what he would say, were he to be asked to define war.

But he doesn't know how to say these big words or to write

them. He knows how to spit, and when he spat, the words didn't stick in his throat any more. He spat and turned into a billy goat, meaning a hero. True, he'd gone back to swallowing his words after that, but he knew why, so he wasn't afraid of being dumb. His stammer came back after he and Tony stole the barracks money and fled to Paris. There Yalo tasted exile and homelessness and longed to be the animal he once had been. Yalo didn't agree that war was an animal act. In essence, it was heroism, but heroism was impossible without something of the animal. Military training can't happen without waking the wolf inside.

"You're wolves," said the trainer.

"No, we're billy goats!" yelled Tony, who was standing in the first row of the training line-up. And they turned into goats. It wasn't Tony who gave the name "the Billy Goats" to their battalion, which was based near the Museum. It was the people who, for some reason Yalo didn't know, called them "the Billy Goats", so they turned into billy goats.

Yalo felt that something like a spear had awakened inside him, but Mme Randa didn't understand what he meant, or didn't care, and when she asked him about his spear, that thing that never left him would awake and he would turn into a billy goat, or a wolf, and spear her. And when M. Michel Salloum found him in the Paris metro and took him home to the 16th arrondissement, he told him not to be a lamb; "It's a shame. You're a young man. Why are you behaving like that, like a lamb?" But Yalo hadn't been behaving like a lamb, he felt he'd really become one and that he'd lost his inner spear. Suddenly he'd found himself in a strange land. Tony, who spoke French, had stolen the money and disappeared from the hotel in Montparnasse where they were staying, and Yalo had found himself an abandoned lamb. He didn't know the language, and he didn't have any money. Suddenly he'd become a beggar, and dumb, so how could he not behave like a lamb? His grandfather had told him that animals were "without speech", which was why the Arabs had called those who didn't speak their language "those who have no speech" – i.e., dumb people.

In that distant country, Yalo had felt that he was a dumb person, like an animal, and that he could no longer spit out words the way he'd learned to in the war, and even when M. Michel brought him back to Lebanon and gave him the job of guarding his villa in Ballona, Yalo remained almost incapable of speech, and words would come only with the torch that lit up his night with desire.

Yalo saw his mother, Gabrielle, or Gaby, only in prison. She came to visit him two years after he'd been arrested, but instead of bringing him cigarettes and food like the other prisoners' families did, she stood behind the iron bars and wept. Then she told him about the room she'd rented and how poor she was and how she was afraid of going hungry. She took a little mirror out of her purse and said, "Look. I can't see myself in the mirror any longer. What kind of a way is that to go on – the mirror eating up my picture? What kind of a way to go on is that, my son? Look in the mirror and tell me what you see." Then she left.

When Gaby opened her little purse, Yalo thought she was going to take out a packet of cigarettes, and his mouth watered at the thought of smoking like the other prisoners and not having to wait till one of them offered him half a fag or he could smoke one rolled by lame Shahadeh, who specialized in collecting butts, unpicking them and rewrapping them into small "recycled" cigarettes.

Gaby didn't take a packet of American cigarettes out of her purse. She took out her little white mirror and began speaking, and Yalo felt a need to run away.

Yalo tried to explain to the interrogator that he'd gone to France because he was afraid of his mother, but the interrogator didn't understand.

He said he'd gone to France because he'd started to become frightened, so the interrogator thought that the defendant had fled Lebanon because he was afraid of going to prison. Lots of young men had left after the war; Yalo was one among many. No doubt he was mixed up in some crime.

The interrogator asked Yalo what he was afraid of, and Yalo didn't answer because he couldn't think of a way to tell him about being afraid of the mirror. Should he say? What should he say?

There was the night, and there was the woman. There was a power cut and the woman lit the house with three candles. How old was the woman? "How old is my mother?" Yalo had never asked himself that question, for mothers didn't have ages, and when the *kohno* spoke about his own mother, and how the red eyes spread over her hair, stiff with blood, he would become like a little child, even to the point that his shoulders would go up, the way children raise their shoulders to make you think they're taller than they really are. Now, when Yalo remembered his mother, he would raise his shoulders and see a woman full of years carrying a candle, coming to her only son's room wearing a long blue nightdress, her hair covering her shoulders. Yalo opened his eyes and saw the long chestnut hair curling on her shoulders and asked where her *kokina* was.

"Where's your *kokina*, Mummy?"

And Gaby seemed not to hear. She mumbled tremulous words, and he understood that she was asking him to get up.

"What's the matter, Gaby?"

"Come with me, please."

Yalo got up and followed her to the bathroom, and she stood in front of the mirror and brought the candle close to her face and asked him what he saw.

"How should I know?" he asked. "What's going on, Mummy?"

She said she'd undone the *kokina* and let down her hair because she'd become frightened, because when she looked in the mirror she couldn't see herself.

"I look in the mirror and I don't see my face. The mirror's swallowed it. Can you see anything, my son?"

Yalo looked in the mirror and saw his long brown face and his mother's round white face next to it and her curly chestnut-brown hair.

"Go and put your hair up. You look like an ogress," said Yalo.

"Can you see my face?" asked his mother.

"What are you talking about? You woke me up for that?"

The woman brought the candle close to her face and stood unmoving in front of the mirror.

"Take a good look. Can you see anything?"

"Of course I can see something. I can see myself."

"I can't see myself," said Gaby. "Gaby's all gone. The mirror's swallowed the picture of my face as though I'd disappeared."

"Stop this nonsense and go back to bed."

Yalo went back to his room, but his mother stayed in the bathroom. Then she took to spending the nights in front of the mirror, and Yalo began to be afraid of her. He didn't understand what had happened to his mother. During the day she'd be normal and not talk about her face in the mirror. In fact, she'd stand in front of the mirror and comb her hair. At night, though, the mirror turned into the great concern of both of them, and her face would disappear and horror would strike the woman.

Gaby went on coming to her son's room almost every night and waking him and questioning him, claiming that all she could see in the mirror was a white spot.

"My face has turned into a white spot. Oh my God, that means I'm going to die," she'd say, and he started to be afraid.

Fear led Yalo to agree to run away to Paris with Tony.

"I went with Tony. Yes, we robbed the barracks and went abroad."

The interrogator didn't believe anything he said, though, so how could Yalo tell him about his mother?

Why had his mother said that he'd run away from Beirut?

The interrogator said his mother had told him everything, but he didn't say what she'd said. And anyway, what could she say when she'd didn't know anything? And there wasn't anything anyway. And what did this man want, wallowing in the sunlight that hid him from Yalo's closed eyes?

"Yes, sir. I confess I raped her."

. . .

"Yes. Yes. I took her money from her."

. . .

"Yes, I used to phone her every day."

. . .

"Yes. I used to wait at her flat. Then when she came out, I'd follow her to work and wait. Then I'd follow her back home."

. . .

"No. I wanted her to see me. I wasn't hiding. I wanted her to know."

. . .

"I was wrong, I know. But she was wrong too. Why did she go to Ballona with that man who left her and ran away like a rabbit?"

. . .

"The men are all afraid. The women are braver than the men, sir. I've seen how they abandon their women the moment they see the rifle. But the women are different. No . . . No . . . I didn't rape her because I'm a coward. Whatever you say, sir, whatever you say."

. . .

"I'm ready to confess to everything I've done."

. . .

"That's not right. Love slew me and dragged me through the mud and humiliated me. If it hadn't been love, if she hadn't known that I loved her, she wouldn't have dared to file a complaint."

. . .

"It never crossed my mind, sir. She kept hinting that there was hope for us. I wanted her. I don't know what I wanted from her. She's the one who made me feel that way."

Yalo smiled.

He didn't say anything because you couldn't say these things in an interrogation, but he smiled at the idea that he was on the verge of saying them. Anyway, he said them to himself.

Tony would become angry and ask him about all sorts of things, and Yalo would answer that he'd already told him about them, so Tony would get even angrier, and Yalo would enter the trance of someone convinced that he said what he said and that his friend, by claiming that he didn't hear, is simply refusing to listen.

Then Yalo discovered that Tony was right and he hadn't said. Or at least, he'd said the things to himself and just thought he'd said them to his friend.

And when Tony ran away from the Paris hotel and left him on his own and he felt the choking that made him swallow his words when he was speaking to *Khawaja* Michel Salloum, when he was like a lonely lamb, he imagined Tony telling him, "But I told you I was going to get away with it. I had no choice, pal. Do you hear, pal? Forgive me, pal."

"Stop calling me 'pal'! You rip me off and still call me 'pal'?"

But Tony didn't say anything, and neither did Yalo.

Yalo stands alone, wishing his image would disappear, wishing he could become like Gaby and be hidden from these people who are gouging his soul with their questions.

"Sir, I've confessed, so stop it. Put me on trial and let the court decide whatever it likes, but stop it."

The interrogator, however, was deaf to Yalo's entreaties.

"We want to know everything," said the interrogator. "Do you really think we're stupid enough to believe that it's just about playing the peeping tom and doing your dirty business? We want all the information about the network that's been planting bombs and wreaking havoc around the country."

"Me?"

"Yes, you. Do you really think you can fob me off with the story of your love life, which I know so much about now? We want to get to the bottom of this. Listen carefully. I know there's something at the bottom of this. Spit it out and you'll feel better and we'll feel better about you."

"The fact is I loved her and I apologize. I did her wrong. I raped her and I loved her and I apologize and it's over. Now I've stopped loving her. Please, sir."

Why did the interrogator ask about the sea?

"Yes, sir. I took her to White Sands Beach."

. . .

"Yes, I combed her hair for her and asked her not to cut it again."

. . .

"Yes, I told her I could walk on water like Christ."

. . .

"Yes, I walked on the water and didn't drown."

. . .

"She said she saw me walk on the water as well."

. . .

"Yes, I put her hair up for her and made it into a *kokina*."

. . .

"That's what we call it in Syriac."

. . .

"No, really, I just know a few words I heard from my grand-father."

. . .

"Yes, I told her I'd bury her if I found out that she'd cut her hair."

. . .

"Bury her . . . Yes, I said I'd bury her."

. . .

"No, it wasn't a death threat, it was talk. I mean, the way people say things."

. . .

"Yes, yes. All that's right. But no, no boat. We didn't see a boat flashing its lights across the sea."

. . .

"Me, no. I did have the torch with me, but no, I didn't use it to signal."

. . .

"She said that?"

. . .

"She's crazy, sir. I'm telling you, she's a madwoman."

. . .

"What's it to do with me what she thought? I wanted her to learn these things and understand the meaning of life and be convinced that love can perform miracles."

. . .

"Yes, yes."

. . .

"Then she wanted to go, but I told her it wasn't allowed."

. . .

"She's a liar. I didn't take money from her."

. . .

"She put a hundred dollars in my pocket and ran off, and I discovered the money at home and was very upset. I said to myself, 'One day soon I'll marry her and I'll spend the money on her.'"

. . .

"Yes, yes."

. . .

"No, there wasn't any boat."

. . .

"I was wearing my black coat because I never take it off."

. . .

"The torch was with me because I always keep it in my pocket."

. . .

"It's a habit I picked up in the war, sir."

. . .

"Right now, for example, I feel I'm missing something. Not

59

just because you took the coat away from me and said it was evidence. I'm lost because the torch isn't with me. I feel like a blind man even when there's electric light. I only see properly when I have the torch turned on."

. . .

"When your boys came and nabbed me, the torch was by my bed."

. . .

"I swear it's just a habit of mine, sir, just a habit."

. . .

"No, no. I didn't mean to."

. . .

"It's how I am. All my life I've been like that, and I never wanted anything. I swear I don't want anything from Shireen. Even if she wants me, I don't want her now."

. . .

"My idea was . . . Well, what I wanted was . . . "

. . .

"I don't know. I don't know."

Yalo tried.

He listened to the questions and answered them. Or he tried to answer them, but the interrogator kept on insisting about the torch and was amazed at the story about making the girl drink seawater and said it wasn't a human being before him, just a monster in the shape of a human being.

"I've seen it all and heard it all, but never have I come across a monster like you before. I want you to tell me everything and why you did all those things. It's not enough to tell me you put the fellow in the boot and slept with the girl, and it's not enough to tell me you took the watch and the money and told them to get lost, and I don't want to hear the story about that other character who kept begging you to sleep with his girlfriend, and I don't want the story about Bernadette, who you discovered was a prostitute and who pretended she was hitching a ride and when you got to the forest and the fellow tried to get it into her started yelling she wanted money, and how you made him pay her and you and she divided the money and laughed like hyenas, and that other poor fellow, what was his name? . . . I've got his name written down somewhere. Remind me, what was his name?"

The interrogator started searching through his papers, but he couldn't find the name.

"Go on, say his name. What are you waiting for?"

"I don't know his name, sir. You told me his name was Nabeel Hayek and he was a lawyer. I didn't know his name. In our job we don't ask people's names. Names don't mean anything. But then there was her. I wish I hadn't found out her name. I don't know what came over me."

"What came over you? Now you want to go all innocent on me and say it's nothing to do with you? I'm not interested in those stories. I want to understand about the torch, what's it for, whom you kept flashing it at at White Sands. Plus, can you explain how anyone can drink and make other people drink saltwater?"

How is Yalo to answer? What is he to say?

He said there was no boat, and he said the torch was part of his character, just like the long black coat, but what could he say about the seawater? Should he tell the interrogator about the beach at night and Father Afram and Epiphany Eve? Should he tell him about Gaby and her hair that turned to gold in the moonlight as she stood beneath the hands of her father, who undid her long hair and wet it and combed it through while young Daniel stood between their legs, bent over the sand and shivering with the cold?

The *kohno* would take his small family to the beach to wait for the Spirit, which moves as it wills. At White Sands Beach, after night had fallen and the small stars that pierced the clouds over the sea had scattered themselves about, the *kohno* would bend down to the water and drink. He would walk out into the cold water and rising waves, take his grandson's hand in his right hand and his daughter's in his left, and they would walk into the sea. When the waves reached the child's waist, the *kohno*, mumbling strange prayers in a strange language, would bend over and fill his hands with water and drink. He would give the mother water to drink first, and then her son, then he himself would drink, and after each one of them had drunk three times, they would walk backwards to the shore. If Yalo's hand slipped out of his grandfather's and the child twisted away and ran back to the beach, shivering with the cold, the *kohno* would run after him and drive him back into the water.

"You mustn't turn your back on the sea, boy! What sort of person turns his back on the Spirit?"

When the three reached the sand-dry beach, the mother would open her bag and take out a big white towel with which she would dry Yalo after making him take off his trousers, and she would give him new trousers, and the boy would turn blue with the cold, the fear and the salty taste that filled his mouth and his guts.

"The water has become sweet and good to the taste," would say the *kohno*.

"Amen," would say the mother.

And "Amen," would say Yalo, waiting for the piece of Turkish delight whose sugary smoothness would blend with the roughness of his salty tongue.

Gaby would stand on the shore before her father and begin to undo her *kokina*. She would pull out the pins and place them on a woollen blanket that she had spread on the sand, and she would tell Yalo to sit on the blanket while she stood awaiting the *kohno*'s comb.

The *kohno* would go to the sea and cup a handful of its water in his palms and sprinkle it on his daughter's hair. Then he would begin combing. The long hair flowed over her shoulders and down her back, fell to her waist and reached her ankles.

On Epiphany Eve, the eve of the day of the baptism of Christ the Saviour, Gabrielle, daughter of Afram, would unloose her hair and spread it beneath the light of night for the miracle to colour, and the long hair, which consisted of twisted lengths that fell unbound beneath the *kohno*'s comb, would begin to turn to gold.

Yalo said that his mother's hair would become gold, that it would dissolve beneath the water and the comb and turn golden and shine. The *kohno* would make his grandson keep his eyes open so that he could see how his mother's hair became charged with gold.

"See the miracle, my boy," the *kohno* would say.

And Yalo saw the miracle and felt the taste of the salty sugar and saw colours emerging from the *kohno*'s lips, edged with his large white beard. The *kohno* would shake the comb, and the dim light that penetrated the darkness of the shore would trace spots on his hands and eyes, and the comb would rise and fall unceasingly. Yalo the Child would sit on the woollen blanket, shivering with the cold, and enter the miracle of the water and the golden hair.

Should he tell the interrogator that he'd been looking for the miracle?

On their return home, his mother would say that she had witnessed the miracle. Shireen, though, had said nothing because she had understood nothing.

The *kohno* would finish the combing, and Yalo's mother would start gathering up her golden hair from her feet, her shoulders and her back. She would gather it in twisted lengths which she fixed in place with the pins Yalo handed to her while she stood with her back to him looking into the distance, to where the sea was, the *kohno* beside her.

Yalo didn't ask his mother why she turned away from him and looked towards the sea for he knew his mother was using the sea as a mirror. Once a year, the sea would become a miraculous mirror, and the child would see his mother and see her hair stretched out over the salt waters that reached to the edges of the sky.

That was what the *kohno* told them.

He said that the sea ended at the sky. "The sky is the extension of the sea, my son, and the sea is the mirror of the world" – for Afram, despite being convinced that the earth was round and of the truth of the scientific discoveries that Yalo studied at St Sawirus's in Beirut, insisted that there was a special relationship between the sea and the sky, or how else were we to interpret the fact that the Spirit of God had moved upon the waters? And how else were we to interpret the story of the prophet Yunan, who had spent three days in the belly of a whale before returning safely to the shore?

Afram used to say that the story of the prophet Yunan was simply an allegory of the death of Christ and His resurrection, but the allegory would not have been possible without the special relationship between God and the sea.

"In the beginning God created the heaven and the earth. And

the earth was without form, and void; and darkness was upon the face of the deep. And the Spirit of God moved upon the face of the waters."

The *kohno* would go to the sea with his little family for the sake of the Spirit that moved upon the waters, believing that the miracle would take place only on that day in January when the Spirit meets with the salt waters and they become sweeter than honey.

Yalo didn't, however, see in the houses of his neighbours and other boys of his age that unction of the Spirit that radiated through his own house on the following morning, when his mother prepared rusks with milk and fried doughnuts.

In that small house, in whose garden were planted seven cassie trees for shade, crowding round a huge china-bark tree standing like a sentinel at the entrance – only there did the miracle occur and the hand of Christ anoint their heads with honey and gold.

Yalo remembers nothing of the return from the beach to the house, for he would come back wrapped in the woollen blanket and sleeping. He would get up in the morning and smell the oil and the halva, and see the *kohno* sitting chewing incense before going to the church.

Yalo didn't see the Spirit's anointing of his fellow-students, and he didn't ask them about their journeys to the beach – whether they went there too and drank the saltwater that turned sweet. His grandfather, when he put his hands together, scooped up the seawater and raised it to his mouth, would say that it was "like honey", and Yalo would drink, shivering in expectation of the piece of sugary Turkish delight, which he would eat sitting on the woollen blanket covered with the hairpins from his mother's *kokina*.

Was this a widespread custom in Beirut? Or a special family tradition the *kohno* had brought with him from his distant village?

Yalo doesn't know the answer to this question, and it never occurred to him to ask his grandfather, for he is imagining the scene now in prison, where he lives within the silence, the voices of the other prisoners coming to his ears as obscure murmurs that carry no meaning, and he is trying to write so he can bring to an end this business that has gone on so long.

He sees the scene by the sea, where dozens of women stand on the white sands and fan their hair out across their backs, and behind each woman stands an old man holding a comb, and with each stroke of the comb, the tresses become charged with gold; combs sliding down, dozens of combs gleaming with gold, and the Spirit of God moving above them all.

Yalo feels the cold penetrating his bones and hears the *kohno* lecturing him, telling him that the reason he always feels cold is because he is tall and thin: "There's no meat on your body to protect you from the cold."

Yalo feels as though the air has penetrated him, as though his body is full of holes. He shivers and covers himself up in the woollen blanket, and the hairpins dig into him everywhere.

Dozens of women comb gold and drink the water of the sea, then pick up their sons and daughters, wrapped in woollen blankets, and set off home to Beirut to prepare rusks with milk and doughnuts in celebration of the baptism of Christ in the River Jordan.

"Listen, my son," the grandfather says in the morning before going to the church. "Join me in half an hour and don't be late for mass and don't you dare put anything in your mouth. You must take Communion on an empty stomach. It doesn't do to eat and then take Communion. It's not allowed. I know everything that goes on, and God knows everything."

But Yalo would steal rusks from the food safe and eat them and then clean his teeth to get rid of the smell before going with his mother to church, where he would sink into a deep sleep. Yalo wasn't present for a single mass in his life, for the instant he entered the church, his eyes would glaze over at the smell of the incense and he would slip into a doze next to his mother and take the bread and wine and taste the blood on his tongue.

During the war, when he was wading in blood up to his knees, he would taste the same taste, the taste of salt mixed with the sugar of Turkish delight, and he would smell a sea smell filled with white spume, and it would make him drunk and he would not wake up.

Whenever he returned to the house, he'd hear his mother saying she smelled blood. She'd hold her nose as she kissed him and say, "I hate the smell of blood, and you are in blood up to your knees."

He'd answer that the taste of blood was like the taste of honey.

"Why are you frightened of blood? Didn't your papa, God rest his soul, fill the cup each Sunday with blood and drink, and give it to the people to drink during mass?"

"Be quiet! God forgive such talk. That, my son, wasn't blood. It was a symbol."

"And this too, Mother, isn't blood. It's a symbol."

"God forgive us both, my son."

"I'm like my grandfather, Mother. I fight with symbols."

"You know nothing about your grandfather or symbols or life. You think life's a joke, you and your friends. God protect us from you."

Yalo didn't think the world was a joke, as his mother said, but, in this city whose name was Beirut and which was doubled up over its own death, he smelled a smell like the smell of the sea, salt and incense, and he kept imagining his grandfather chewing incense and drinking saltwater. He didn't tell Gaby about this, however, because he was afraid for her. He was afraid she'd believe that her son was going to die, for Gaby had learned from her father that those who look on the dead will die. Her mother had died after she'd seen her aunt's ghost calling to her, and on the night that he died the *kohno* said he had gone back to Ein Ward, where he saw his mother putting her blood-speckled hair up in a *kokina*.

"My mother's *kokina* was red, and she was laughing. Maybe she didn't die, maybe the Kurd carried her off," said Afram before closing his eyes onto the eternal darkness.

Gaby told her son not to speak of blood. "What do you know about blood? My papa told me that the blood was there, at Ein Ward. The blood started brimming out of the well after the massacre, and the walls of the church oozed blood."

Yalo used to sleep in the church, sitting next to his mother, closing his eyes and going to meet the "Dominion of Sleep".

When his grandfather said that "the Dominion" had left him, Yalo, who was then ten years old, took it to mean that the *kohno* was going to die.

"My grandpa's going to die," he told his mother.

"Shush, boy! God forbid!"

"The Dominion has left him," he whispered to his mother.

The *kohno*'s night became a torment for him and for his little family, because it turned into a perambulation through the house. He would go to bed at 10.00 in the evening, get up less than two hours later, recite his prayers and keep up an unceasing racket, burning incense to drive away the evil spirits and coughing.

"My grandfather went on coughing until it killed him, because the Dominion had left him, but as for me, the Dominion's still with me," he told Shireen. "Come to the beach with me so that I can show you the Dominion."

Shireen didn't understand the reason for this insistence on going to the beach at night. She was accustomed to Yalo's daily phone calls and his insistence on meeting. She would make sure that the meetings were in the afternoon, and at the Bistro in Ashrafiyeh. He would come wrapped in his long black coat, walking on tiptoe and looking left and right as though he was afraid, before finding his table in the far corner of the café, where he would sit down, swallow and order a glass of beer.

"You're so tall. Why don't you play basketball?" she would ask him before sitting down herself.

"So here I am. Tell me what you want," she would say.

"Nothing, I just wanted to see you."

"You've seen me. Now what?"

"Nothing."

"May I go?"

"When are you going to have dinner with me at home?"

"Where?"

"At Ballona."

"Ballona! Never again! *Jamais!*" And she laughed.

Yalo tells her endless stories and makes up the story of his girl cousin whom he'd killed in the war.

"You killed her?"

"Who else?"

"You killed your uncle's daughter?" she asks fearfully.

"I killed her and threw her into a field."

"Why?"

"Because she wanted to marry a Kurd."

"That's a reason to kill someone?"

"It wasn't just that. She slept with him and got pregnant, so I had to defend the family honour."

"The family honour!"

"Of course. My uncle couldn't see any more. He asked me, 'Where can I hide my head from the shame?' He told me, 'We must kill her.' But he was a coward. He asked me, 'What do you say, boy? You have to do this for me.' I said, 'If that is your command, Uncle.'"

"And you killed her?"

"Like falling off a log. I put the gun to her head, one shot, and it was over."

"Over?"

"Of course it was over."

"And that way you saved the family honour?"

"There's nothing more important than honour," he said.

"Some honour!" she said.

He told her stories to see her looks of admiration, but instead of admiration he saw two small eyes emptied by fear.

He told her about the tailor who raped his mother.

"He raped her?"

"She was young, sixteen years old, and she worked for him, so he raped her."

"And you killed him too?"

Yalo smiled and showed his large white teeth. "No. That one was killed by my grandfather the *kohno*."

"Your grandfather the priest killed a man?"

"Of course he killed him. Was he supposed to let the girl be dragged through the mud?"

"A priest who kills?"

"No, you understood me wrong. He didn't kill him the way

70

you think. He didn't use a gun or a knife. He killed him with words. He talked to him and the tailor couldn't bear what he said, so he died."

Shireen laughs. "Talking's the only thing you're good at."

"Give me your hand," he said, and he reached across the table.

"Not here, please."

"Give me your hand while I tell you something."

"Okay. Put your hand underneath."

Yalo put his hand underneath the table and Shireen reached out her small white hand and took it. Yalo raised his own hand a little, pulled her towards him and put her hand on his waist, and the girl felt the coldness of the metal running from her fingers up to her shoulders. She pulled her hand away quickly and asked, "What's that?"

"It's a gun. Would you like me to take it out now and put it on the table? I'd do anything for you."

Why did she say that when he met her at the Bistro he put his gun on the plate in front of him?

He heard the interrogator reading about the revolver and the plate, and he couldn't believe his ears.

"He put the revolver under the plate and then lifted up the plate and said, 'Look,' and I almost died of fright, but he was dying of laughter."

The interrogator read this sentence from a large notebook in front of him and then asked Yalo what he had to say.

"How should I know?" asked Yalo.

"Is it true you put the gun under the plate and threatened her with the plate?"

. . .

"Is it true that you told her you wanted to play the gun game with the plate?"

7 1

. . .

"What game is that? Explain it to me so I can understand."

. . .

"Is it true you told her that she'd have to get used to the plate?"

. . .

"You were carrying a gun, in front of everyone, as though you could do whatever you liked?"

. . .

"Wouldn't that be wrong?"

"You mean me, sir?"

"Who else? Me?"

"I can't believe it."

"What is it you can't believe?"

"Myself. All I did was tell her about the plate but not like that."

Why did she tell them about the plate? Yalo only said he could put the revolver on the plate in front of everyone to make her believe in his love, and now he said he'd put the revolver on the plate to frighten her, and that she'd begged him to stop, and that he'd laughed as though he didn't care, showing his large white teeth, towering over the rest of the customers, who sat whispering in Arabic and French.

. . .

"I forced her to speak Arabic with me?" Yalo asked in amazement.

. . .

"She said she liked seeing me so she could speak Arabic, and anyway what have I got to do with Arabic? Arabic's not my language, sir. Our language is dead. When I want to speak, I feel like there's something dead on my tongue."

Yalo wouldn't have said this even if he had been able, in this

72

difficult situation, to remember his grandfather's words, for he was unable to form sentences in this way.

The grandfather, at the stage when the Dominion of Sleep had abandoned him, would say that he could feel his tongue dying in his mouth. He would stand beneath the icon of the crucified Christ and say to it, "Your language has died, O my God. How could you let your language die? I feel the taste of death under my tongue. After me, who will pray the way you used to pray?"

"Abun d-bashmayo nethqadash shmokh tithe malkuthokh nehwe sebyonokh aykano d-bashmayo oph bar`o hab lan lahmo d-sunqonan yawmono washbuq lan hawbayn wahtohayn aykano doph hnan shbaqn l-hayobayn lo ta`lan l-nesyuno elo paso lan men bisho metul d-dilokh hi malkutho whaylo wteshbuhto l`olam `olmin. Amen."

"How do you want us to pray, O Jehovah, if the words are dying? I feel worms coming out of them, as though my mouth had become a grave. Your language is dying and you do nothing. To whom do you think you will talk at your second coming? There's no-one left in the whole world who can understand you except me, and I have been abandoned by the Dominion and my death is nigh. Tomorrow, when your slave Afram has died, what will you do?"

Yalo told Shireen that he wanted her to go with him to White Sands Beach after Christmas, but she said no. This made Yalo angry. He took her hand, made her feel the revolver at his waist and said he was prepared to put the revolver on the plate, in front of everyone, to make her believe in his love.

"But, no. No, sir," said Yalo. "I didn't force her to go to the beach."

Yalo phoned Shireen more than ten times that day, and she kept saying that she didn't want to go to the beach and preferred to meet him at the café, but in the end she was convinced. He told her he would show her the miracle and speak to the fish in Syriac, so she agreed to go, insisting that their rendezvous be short because she had a date for dinner. The rendezvous went on till midnight, however, not because Yalo forced her to stay and drink the wine, which is what she told the interrogator, but because the miracle really happened.

They walked on White Sands Beach. Then he asked her to go with him into the water.

"It's cold. Please, stop this nonsense."

He left her standing and dove into the waves without removing his clothes. Then he came back, carrying saltwater cupped in his hands, and asked her to drink. He drank and gave her water to drink, and the water had become sweet, like honey. Then they sat on the cold, wet sand and he took a bottle of red wine and a loaf of bread out of his coat pocket.

He drank from the bottle and gave her to drink. He ate of the bread and fed her.

"The wine's so sweet. I don't like sweet wine," she said.

"It's the water that's sweet, not the wine."

Then he stood up, went down to the sea and walked on the face of the waters. He left her sitting on the sand and walked on the sea, and found that he was seeing himself with her eyes. He saw his back, covered by the black coat, and his shadow, which extended to the sky, and he walked. And when he returned to her, soaked, his teeth chattering with the cold, and he saw her sitting with her head on her knees, he lifted up her head and kissed her and tasted tears.

She wept and said she was going to die there.

"I beg you, let me go home before I die."

Why did she say he'd forced her to eat the bread, and that

she'd vomited up the saltwater mixed with the sweet wine? The water had become sweet, like honey, but she hadn't understood, and now, when Yalo stood before the interrogator, who appeared to him through the sunlight burning his eyes, he discovered that he'd understood the secret of the bread.

He wanted to tell the interrogator he was sorry. Suddenly, he'd understood the secret of the bread, and the whole story with Shireen seemed laughable and not worth talking about. To the interrogator's astonishment, Yalo dissolved into laughter. He laughed out loud, then shrank back into himself and stopped responding. What was he supposed to say? Should he say that the bread . . . should he say that everything was humbug, except for the bread?

"Don't tell me the world has changed, my son," said the grandfather. "Whatever has been and will be, nothing changes. The only real thing that man has discovered is bread. Bring me an invention other than food and then I'll believe that the world has changed. The world hasn't changed because it's round, like a loaf of bread. Everything, my son, is as it was, except for the taste in my mouth. I don't know how it happened, even though I chew incense and pine resin every day. It's because the Dominion has left me. My son, life holds only two things – sleep and bread. Such is our faith. Christ is the grain. He died that He might rise and turn death into sleep. Man sleeps each night so as to become accustomed to death. And when the Dominion of Sleep starts to leave you and you cease to long for bread, at that moment true death has drawn nigh. But what difference does it make? There is no difference. It's like dreams – when we sleep, we dream, and when we die, we shall dream."

Yalo wanted to say to her, he wanted to tell her, but she was weeping. How could he tell her about his mother's hair, sparkling with gold amid the white sand, when Shireen didn't dare to look but rested her head on her knees and wept?

"I beg you, let me go home," she said.

"Did you see the miracle?" he asked.

"I saw everything, but I want to go home."

"When will I see you again?"

"Phone me tomorrow and we'll set a time, but let me go now."

He saw her disappearing into the night. She took off her shoes and ran across the sand. Then the darkness swallowed her up and Yalo remained on the beach alone, with an empty bottle of red wine and leftover bits of bread.

He walked on the beach alone and didn't tell Shireen about his mother. He had wanted to tell her how his mother would drink the saltwater, open her eyes and let down her hair. He had wanted to tell her that he had seen dozens of women standing on the beach beneath their hair, drunk on the golden light of the little moon that tottered between the clouds, each cloud swallowing it then spitting it out at another, the light diving down and swooping up, the long hair covering the child who sat shivering on the woollen blanket.

Why did she say he'd forced her to eat the bread and drink the wine and then stolen the entire contents of her purse? Why did she say that, whenever she had a date with him, she'd deliberately put no more than a hundred dollars in her purse? Why did she say that every time they met he'd take a hundred-dollar note from her?

"But she's not telling the whole truth, sir," he told the interrogator.

"And what is the truth, pray tell us," said the interrogator.

"The truth is that no-one knows the truth but God," answered Yalo.

Yalo was no longer sure about anything, but when they'd met he'd felt that Shireen was melting before his eyes, as though she wanted him to take her but something was preventing her from expressing her feelings, as though she was attached by an invisible string to another world she didn't want to abandon while Yalo reached out with his gaze so she could climb up it and come to him.

"Come to me here," he says.

"Where?" she asks.

"To my heart," he says.

"Sure, sure," she answers.

But she was frightened. Now Yalo understood that she'd been frightened, and fear is a deceiver. Fear makes you believe in things that don't exist. Then – in the torture chambers, that is – Yalo understood. Confession under torture is like a lover's confession to his beloved. Suddenly the lover loses the power to hold his tongue and says things that destroy his love.

Now Yalo was convinced he was wrong. He shouldn't have told the girl about the truth as he'd lived it, but he had told her. And when he'd told her about Mme Randa and how he would randarize with her, and when he'd told her about Mme Randa's daughter, Ghada, and how the jealousy would stream from Madame's eyes as Ghada told him about her boyfriend at university who'd gone to Canada and whom she was soon going to join there, and when he'd told her of the adventures in the forest and about how sorry he felt for *Khawaja* Michel Salloum, he'd fallen into the trap of words, and his game had been discovered.

If he hadn't told her that he'd become convinced that Madame was going to file a complaint against him with the police, the girl with no name would never have dared to go to the police station and file a complaint against him herself.

It was the sickness of truth that afflicted him when he fell in love.

He told her he didn't know why he felt the way he felt, and why he was no longer capable of lying. He told her everything, and when love flowed onto his tongue, he found himself at the police station and he saw her, in her short skirt and with her slim white thighs, identifying him as a criminal.

Yalo said as much to the interrogator, or he wanted to say as much but found himself struck dumb and saw how he fell from her eyes and dropped into the abyss. The truth that had swept him up when love possessed him made him fall from her eyes into the mire of her contempt. He had told her stories about his mother and her relationship with the tailor Elias El Shami. When he saw himself falling from her eyes, he saw in her tiny pupils his image tumbling to the ground, and could do nothing.

How can one save an image that falls from the eyes?

And instead of stopping talking, and reassembling his image, he watched as his words were transformed to mirror his fall. He saw, as if looking into a mirror, how he fell and how his image broke into tiny slivers, and he felt that he was drowning, and all a drowning man can do is flail on into the depths that will swallow him.

Such was Yalo. He drowned when love stripped him naked, and he fell to the ground when he spoke.

"I swear I didn't kill her, sir."

Why did the interrogator ask about his cousin whom he hadn't killed?

Yalo had lied to Shireen when he'd told her about a crime that existed only in his imagination. He was trying to rescue his image, which was tumbling and drowning, so he made up a lie about a crime, and now the lie was transformed into a truth he had to recount to the interrogator.

Why did the interrogator say that he'd send an investigative committee to Qamishli to look for the Jalao family?

"There is no Maria Jalao, sir. I swear she doesn't exist. All it was was I was just trying to show off to Shireen. I don't have a cousin because I don't have an uncle, not on my father's side and not on my mother's. Or at least, I have an aunt on my mother's side called Sara. She went to Sweden a long time ago. I don't know her. My mother told me that she married and went abroad and became Swedish. Then the war came and we lost track of her. That's what my mother said."

"And what about your father's side? I'm asking about your paternal uncle, your father's brother."

"I don't know. Really, I don't know. He may have had brothers and sisters, but I don't know them. I don't know my father. I've never even seen his picture. I asked to see it, but my grandfather would never let me open that whole business."

Why doesn't the interrogator believe Yalo, who stands before him with trembling hands, long eyelashes, a stoop, a stutter and words that emerge broken from his lips?

Yalo knew that no-one would believe him, which is why he said whatever he wished, because in the war no-one had believed anyone. But the war was over, or so he told Shireen. He said, "Believe me." He told her he'd hated the war because of all the lying and that when he'd met her he'd believed the war was over because he'd stopped lying, and that he wanted to begin his life over again, and that he loved her.

No, he'd decided to emigrate before the war was over. The idea came from his friend, Tony Ateeq. Yalo didn't know whether Ateeq, which means "ancient", was the family's real name or a nickname that had attached itself to Tony, the way nicknames did during the war, replacing people's proper names.

Tony used to say he was ancient.

"I'm an Ancient Assyrian," he would say, and then he'd tell lots of stories about his heroic deeds, but Yalo didn't believe him. "How are you supposed to believe words and disbelieve your own eyes?" Words are eyes, though. He tried to explain to his friend that words are like eyes, but Tony was blind in the face of words. He said what he wanted to say and no-one believed it and it didn't bother him. He'd talk and we wouldn't believe him, but he'd go on talking because words beget words.

"Words are eyes," the *kohno* told his grandson as he opened the book to teach him the Syriac alphabet.

"Look well at the words, my son, and you'll discover why men become absorbed in reading, and you'll understand that it's the words that are looking at us, because they can breathe and see."

The war, however, taught Yalo to believe his own eyes, not those of words, and he would only make his peace with words again in prison, when the interrogator told him to write the story of his life, all of it, from beginning to end, over and over. Then he discovered that his grandfather had been right and that words, when written down, look at their writer and hold conversations with him, and impose what he has to write.

The war, though, made words flow the way it made blood flow. Blood flows and words flow, and people stop believing anything any more, whether blood or words.

Yalo only believed Tony Ateeq once, when Tony convinced him that they had to rob the safe at Georges Armouni Barracks so they could run away to France, where they'd start a new life.

Yalo robbed the safe, having first broken it open, and Tony got hold of tickets on the boat to Larnaca in Cyprus, and from there on a plane to Paris.

At the luxurious Paris hotel, Tony disappeared with the money and left Yalo on his own with nowhere to go except the metro station at Montparnasse, where he could feel a little warmth in the midst of the biting Paris cold. Yalo found himself in a strange country with no money even to buy himself a crust of dry bread, so he sat in the metro station and begged, which was when *Khawaja* Michel Salloum had seen him and taken him to Lebanon, and the rest of the story was known because it took place between the interrogator's room and the prison cell.

Yalo said he lied to her to make her admire and love him.

He said it was love.

He said that Shireen made him wait a whole year for her in torment. A year when all he saw in her small eyes was a promise. A year he phoned every day and waited beneath her window or in front of the Araysi Advertising Company, where she worked. A year when he moved like a ghost through the Beirut night looking for her and her lover, the old doctor, and then for the young man with the thin moustache who was her fiancé, she said.

Yalo wrote that he had been taken unawares by the young man when he saw him sitting next to Shireen in the interrogator's room looking through his thick black glasses as though he couldn't see. Short, well built, white-skinned, rosy-cheeked, sitting silently with his fat thighs in the interrogation room, and Shireen next to him, proud of her future groom, and looking with malicious pleasure at Yalo, who almost fell to the ground when he saw her and steadied himself with the chair before sitting down.

"Stand up, arsehole! Who said you could sit down?" screamed the interrogator.

Yalo stood up shakily and closed his eyes, and then the

interrogator let him sit down. And the rain of questions started to pour down on his head.

Yalo wrote that when he pulled himself together and opened his eyes and saw the young man, he felt a need for his torch. This man wouldn't stand up to even a single spot of light. He'd fall to his knees, crawl around on the floor and tell Yalo, "Take her, sir, and let me go!"

But the fiancé is sitting in the sunlight coming through the window, emerging from behind the interrogator's head, and has his little nose in the air as if disgusted with this business and the whole country.

Later Yalo would write that when he saw Shireen sitting next to her fiancé, he faced the third shock of his life.

His first shock had been his mother with the mirror that swallowed her face and made her disappear, or feel she was dead before she'd died.

His second shock was Tony Ateeq, who'd disappeared in Paris, taking the money and the French language, which he knew, and leaving Yalo on his own without money or language.

And his third shock was Shireen.

When they arrested him at his little house, he never thought of Shireen. He thought Mme Randa must have denounced him, because he'd noticed hatred in Madame's eyes some time before. Even when he slept with her, he felt that she wasn't making love with him but had started using him to make love.

As he put up his hands before the rifles pointed at him, he said to himself, "It's Madame," and laughed inside. He'd disgrace her and tell everything about their relationship and enjoy watching how the truth would carve lines into *Khawaja* Michel Salloum's face.

"My husband doesn't suspect me for an instant. I don't know

what would happen to him if he knew about you. My husband's crazy about me, and it would never occur to him that you could have seduced me."

Yalo decided that he wouldn't be questioned at home. He put up his hands and let them search the hut, confiscate the automatic rifle, the revolver, the box of ammunition, the coat and the torch, and waited in silence. When he was there, at the police station, he'd blow everything up in their faces, and instead of telling them about his adventures in the lovers' forest, he'd tell them about Mme Randa.

He imagined her the way he'd seen her the first time.

Khawaja Michel brought him to the villa at Ballona. Yalo went down to his hut, had a shower, put on clean clothes and then went up to the villa. There he saw the most beautiful woman he'd ever seen. Randa was tall and brown-skinned and had short black hair. Her neck was long, her lips thick and fleshy, and her eyes green. When he entered the villa, he saw her taking her husband in her naked arms. Then she seemed to notice Yalo, so she stepped back. Yalo felt that the woman's eyes had fallen on him from above, as if they had gone up and up and then shone themselves at him, and he saw a smile escape from the side of her mouth, so he felt embarrassed, as though his feet could no longer carry him, and he closed his eyes, fell onto a chair, then stood up and tried to leave.

"One moment, one moment," said Madame.

Yalo stood by the door at a loss till *Khawaja* Michel gestured to him to sit down. He sat on the soft red couch and saw that Madame had disappeared. Then *Khawaja* Michel disappeared too and Yalo was left alone in the spacious sitting room, which was filled with Byzantine icons.

When they came back, Mme Randa was wearing a blue

dressing gown over her blue dress and carrying a tray with a pot of Turkish coffee and glasses of cognac, and she offered these to the men and then sat down. She crossed her legs and her brown calf appeared and he saw it rising and falling with the smoke from her American cigarette as she puffed away at it.

Yalo drank his coffee and his cognac in a hurry and went with *Khawaja* Michel to his hut, where it was made clear to him that his job would be to guard the villa and Madame and her daughter, and that he mustn't openly carry a weapon by day or by night, and that his monthly pay would be three hundred dollars plus food, which would be sent down from the villa.

But Yalo had been in the wrong. Later he would write that he had been in the wrong, and during his long imprisonment he would experience moments of regret about Madame. Or rather, in truth, his feelings of regret about Madame started when he saw Shireen's slim thighs trembling in the interrogator's room. All of a sudden things got muddled in his head, and he tasted thorns, and he imagined Madame's calf, to which he had sung so many love songs before being captivated by Shireen's small eyes.

Yalo had done wrong that night, two months before his arrest, and he could neither justify his foolishness nor explain it. Madame was wearing a white nightdress and had draped herself over the sofa in the sitting room, her large breasts almost escaping from the nightdress and the scent of Madame Rochas perfume rising off her. Yalo was sitting in his usual place on the floor next to the sofa. He told her he was tired and that his eyes were hurting, but she wasn't convinced. She poured two shots of whisky into two tall glasses and told him to drink. She picked up the remote, turned on the film and began playing with the hair of the young man seated in front of her. That night, Yalo didn't wait for the end of the film, or for her to begin her

84

fondling, or for the slow sexual ritual she insisted on. He twisted round and took her on the sofa and heard her calling for help, saying, "Not like that!" But he didn't stop. He'd never slept with her there before. She would take his hand and go into the bedroom, and there she would take off her clothes slowly and call him to her, and when he took her she would ask him not to come right away and twist and turn as she watched her naked body in the large mirror at the foot of the bed, while Yalo drowned in the smell of the perfume and worked his way like a snake between her thighs and over the parting of her large, hard breasts. At a signal from her eyes he would come closer, and at a signal from her hands move away; then, as he heard the sound of her final sighs and drowned in the water that gushed from her, he would be annihilated, feeling that he had shot his whole soul into her and that he wanted to fall asleep on her shoulder. But Madame would change with amazing rapidity, covering herself with the quilt, her large pupils starting to circle inside her eyes, and say that she was afraid her husband might come. Yalo would laugh and go back to her, but she would push him away violently and he would understand that he had to go. He would put on his underwear, then his crumpled trousers that had been tossed at the foot of the bed, feeling that his legs were as crumpled as his trousers, and make his way on his trembling legs to his hut, where he would drink a bottle of red wine and fry three eggs, then have a shower and sleep like a dead man.

That night, Yalo felt nauseous and had no idea how he managed an erection or where the desire came to him from. He was convinced that he wouldn't be able to make love to Mme Randa, but he suddenly got an erection and felt proud because he'd had been afraid he'd humiliate himself and had wanted to ask her to forget it, but she hadn't understood his signals. He'd sat like a dog on its backside and watched the film, which was like all the films; all porn films are alike yet they possess an unceasing power to arouse. He swallowed his drink at one go, jumped onto Madame, took her in a few seconds and stood up. He didn't remove his clothes, he just undid his zipper and threw himself on top of her and came. Then he zipped up his trousers again, sat down on the other couch, poured himself another glass and lit a cigarette.

Mme Randa stood up. She wrapped her naked thighs inside her nightdress and stood up. She left the film on and went to her room, dragging her feet. At that moment, Yalo saw how Madame's eyes came falling down and broke on the floor. Leaving his drink unfinished, he put out his cigarette and went back to his hut.

In the days that followed, she'd told him things and he'd told her things. She'd reproached him and he'd reproached her, but she'd never once uttered the words "I love you". She had never once told him that she loved him, not even when she spilled her water in front of him. Rather, she would hover above him like a ghost, then sit cross-legged on the bed, her eyes swaying and circling above her neck before going up and away.

During that long week, she didn't say those words. Her broken, pleading eyes spoke and didn't speak, and Yalo felt a mixture of shame and pride. He would see her at the entrance to the villa and feel the ecstasy of that night, and he would follow her as usual to help her carry her things, but she wouldn't look at him.

One night she invited him to the villa, so he went up, grumbling, sure he was in for another scolding session. He found her on her own in the sitting room drinking whisky. She indicated that he should come and sit down. He sat on the floor next to the sofa and put out his hand to pour himself a glass, but she said no. She didn't reach for his hair, she didn't . . . She drank and drank, and he sat where he was. Then she pointed to the door. Yalo left, falling over his own feet, and it came to him as he slammed the door behind him that everything was over. He also felt that his days at the villa were numbered and started to prepare himself for a new twist to his life, but he didn't give up Shireen. He phoned her every morning, waited in front of her building, and then followed her to work, stood at the entrance and only returned to the villa at night. His hunting parties came to an end, and he no longer felt any desire to stand under the oak tree at night waiting for his lovers to fall victim to his torch. Ghada returned the books he'd stolen for her from the Ras Beirut bookshop on Bliss Street. Thereafter, Yalo lived sad and alone, forever buying tapes of Abdel Haleem Hafez and passing the night with "Her Sweetheart". He thought about writing to Shireen but discovered he only knew how to write Arabic and doubted that the girl was capable of reading it. His meetings with her became frequent or few and far between, depending on circumstances.

So he told the interrogator.

He told him it was only by accident that he'd encounter Shireen.

"And the phone calls every day, you bastard?" asked the interrogator.

Why is he asking him about the phone calls as though he doesn't know the answer? People make phone calls because they feel lonely. Yalo wanted to tell the interrogator that he made phone calls because he didn't have any friends. Yalo didn't have anyone to whom to tell the story of his love for Shireen because he didn't live with anyone. Since Tony had left him in Paris, he'd lived alone, him and his shadow, him and his rifle, him and him.

Yalo had discovered his loneliness with Shireen there, when she'd left him after their lunch at Albert's and he'd taken just the hundred dollars from her, refusing the larger sum she'd offered him. There he'd realized his loneliness and felt a longing for his friend, Tony Ateeq.

Why had Tony done that to him?

Why had he left him in a city where he didn't know anyone and didn't know the language? Why had he left him alone with no money and no language?

"There, sir, there – if you'll permit me to inform you – it was cold. It was the real cold, sir, when everything in you shivers, every muscle, every quiver of your eyes, everything. They have cold there that makes you blue with fear and loneliness."

Yalo told Shireen about the cold. He tried to tell her, but she laughed at him. "You're the biggest flimflam artist in the world," she said, and refused to go up with him to Ballona.

That was a week after the Ballona night. He'd telephoned her flat in the morning. Her mother had answered in a yawning, drowsy voice and he'd heard her yelling to her daughter that someone called Yalo wanted to speak to her. Then came the delicate sound of Shireen's voice, and suddenly her delicate voice became broad and deep.

She said hello in a delicate voice, and then her voice broadened out. It slowly stretched and extended, as though it was coming from an old tape recorder.

"It's me," he said when she asked, "Who's speaking?"

"Who?" she asked.

"Yalo."

"Hello. Hello. Hellooooo."

"How are you?"

"Fiiiiiine, thannnnk yoooooooou."

"I've missed you."

. . .

He said he wanted to see her that very day. She said she was busy. He said he'd wait for her in front of the Araysi office at 9.00 in the morning. She said no. He said he'd be there anyway.

"Of course, of course," she responded.

"I'll be waiting," he said.

"No, not in front of the office. Meet me at the News Café."

He said he didn't know where that was. She said it was near the Clemenceau Cinema.

"Okay, in an hour. I'll be there at 9.00."

"No, no. I can't be there before 5.00."

"Fine. I'll wait for you at 5.00. Mind you come."

"Okay, okay," she answered and put down the phone.

And when he met her at the café and they'd had tea, he told her about the cold, and she laughed and said that he was "the biggest flimflam artist in the world".

Yalo went to the café at 4.00. He sat in a corner away from everyone and drank a glass of beer and waited. When the hands of the clock drew close to 5.00, he felt anxious because he was afraid he wouldn't recognize her. He gathered his expression into his eyes and waited, slowly drinking his beer, but as soon as he heard her footsteps, he recognized her. Then he smelled the smell of incense radiating before him. He half stood up while she sat down opposite him. She didn't offer him her hand. She pulled in her chair and sat in silence. When the waiter came over, she ordered a cup of tea, so Yalo ordered tea as well.

She drank and he drank.

She said and he said.

Yalo can't remember what he said or how the time passed so

fast, and suddenly it was 6.30. Shireen looked at her watch and said she had to go.

"Would you like me to see you on your way?" he asked.

"No, thanks. I have my car."

"Why don't we go to the mountain?" he said.

"Where?" she asked.

"To Ballona," he said.

"I beg you, M. Yalo . . ."

"You remember my name."

"I beg you, as a favour to me. I'm very grateful to you. You behaved like a gentleman with me. Please go on being a gentleman."

"Why? What did I say?" he asked. "I wanted us to have an outing, to get some air."

"Please, let's forget all that," she said.

Then she asked how he'd found out her name and phone number, and he told her he knew everything about her. He knew where she lived and described the tall building in Hazmiyeh where she had her flat, and he knew where she worked, and he said that he loved her.

Yalo doesn't remember when he spoke of love, whether it was at their first or second meeting. He remembers that when he arrived at their first appointment he'd been stammering and that when he saw her in the café and she was trembling, he once again felt like the hawk he had been. He waited for an hour, feeling as if there was water shimmering inside his chest, arms and legs, making him shake as he sat there, and when she came over and sat down opposite him and he saw her delicate lower lip, covered with pinkish lipstick, trembling, and when the penetrating smell of perfume mingled with that of the incense wafting from her arms, he recovered his hawk self and, instead of stuttering, also recovered his speech and could say whatever he wanted.

But he didn't say anything.

He left her to the trembling of her lip, lit a cigarette, sucked in the smoke and blew it out in widely spaced rings. He pursed his lips in an "O" and the smoke rings came out and collided with Shireen's eyes and stole between her lips.

Was that when she said she was afraid of him, or was that at their second meeting?

Yalo doesn't remember the exact sequence of events, but she probably said it at their second meeting.

She said she'd started to be afraid to answer the phone, or open her bedroom window, or go home alone, or . . . because she saw his ghost everywhere and was afraid.

He said he saw her all the time in his imagination and that he'd had her image before his eyes ever since their meeting at Ballona and that he smelled the smell of her body on his and couldn't forget her and loved her.

She begged him.

He begged her.

When she started to get up after paying the bill, he took her hand, which was resting on her purse, and he felt everything within him quiver, and the softness of her hand flowed into him and he felt drunk. Later Yalo would write that there, in the café, he had discovered the softness he hadn't known and regretted that he hadn't discovered it at his hut in Ballona. There, the woman had felt light, as though she was flying to the rhythm of the desire that had exploded inside him and not been quenched. He said he hadn't been aware of her softness because he'd been drowning in the smell of the incense that wafted from her arms. In the café, however, the indescribable softness had flowed into his bones, as though her cold fingers were made of silk and sewn onto her hand.

Why were her fingers always cold?

Once, when they shook hands, he told her that her fingers were as cold as ice and that when he touched her hand he needed a glass of whisky so he could put the ice of her fingers into it and drink it and get drunk. She laughed. When she laughed at him or with him, she seemed like someone trying to stop herself from laughing. The laugh would pop out from between her lips and then return to them. Then her lips would shrink and the thread of sadness would emerge from her eyes.

She taught Yalo to read the sadness in eyes.

She told him once that she could read the sadness in his eyes. They were standing at the entrance to the building where she worked. It was 5.00 in the afternoon, and the sunset was filling the light with spots of darkness. That day he'd waited for her for two hours. He'd gone to Beirut and found nothing to do there. He'd phoned her and they'd told him that she was in a meeting, so he went to the building when she worked and stood outside without moving. He stood without moving for two hours or more, not noticing the time passing, when she peeked out from behind the door she caught sight of him and gestured to him to follow her. He walked behind her without greeting her, and when they got to her white Golf and she bent over to put the key in the lock, she raised her eyes a little and saw that his eyes were wandering. She told him this and he got in next to her and they went to the Chatila Café on the beach and drank beer. Yalo couldn't think of anything to say that day. He felt the sadness coming out of his eyes and saw himself alone and decided that he would visit his mother. They drank beer and Shireen said she was in a hurry and left. She didn't offer him a lift and he couldn't think of anything to suggest doing so he let her go, and she took the coast road and in the mirror of his eyes he saw himself enveloped in sadness.

He had learned from Shireen, he wanted to tell his mother, how to read the sadness in people's eyes, but he didn't tell her anything. He walked to his car in Ashrafiyeh, got in and went to his mother's house in Ein El Roummaneh. He doesn't know why he didn't go in. He saw his mother through the window. She was sitting in the kitchen eating bulghur. He didn't go over and speak to her. He saw the sadness coming out of her eyes too. He forgot what happened after that. All he could remember was the dish of bulghur cooked with tomatoes, and the taste of the hot peppers that swept over his tongue, and the sadness gathered round his mother's eyes, which were covered with rheum, as though she hadn't washed them in days.

When he returned to his hut below the villa in Ballona, he looked in the mirror for a long time and saw how the sadness formed circles round his eyes and pictured Shireen's small honey-coloured eyes and discovered that the sadness in her eyes was different from the sadness in his. His sadness formed circles round his eyes, while hers took the form of fine threads that came out of her pupils and splintered. And he decided to marry her.

Before he met her at the Chatila Café, he hadn't known. He'd go to meet Shireen as though he were playing a game he'd started, not knowing where it would lead, and he'd feel a love for her that emerged from between his ribs and got caught up in his lungs so he couldn't stop choking and needed air. After he'd left her and was driving away, his pocket full of dollars, he'd experience a choking sensation. He'd open the car window and take deep breaths, and when he reached the Ballona turning, where the land was covered with pine trees, he'd stop the car and get out and greedily suck air into his lungs. It was as though this love, which had come to him he knew not how, was cutting off his air supply, so he'd gulp the piney air, drink the air and drink again, till his thirst was quenched and the spiral movement returned to his blood, at which point he'd go back to his car and continue on his way, trying to forget. After the meeting at the café by the sea, however, he made his decision: Shireen would be his wife.

When Yalo realized that whenever he was with her he'd have a longing for fish, he invited her to the Sultan restaurant in Maameltein. He told her about the restaurant on the phone, saying he'd been to it once with *Khawaja* Michel and Madame, and that it served the most exquisite fish, especially red mullet, which was without peer among all the fishes of the world, and squid cooked in its own ink. He told her that the squid wrote in its ink under the sea, and that this sea creature was the world's first writer.

She agreed. They met in front of his house and she drove with him to Maameltein. That day, Yalo became convinced that she loved him. It was the first time she'd agreed to leave her own car to go somewhere with him. He'd felt that she'd never in all her life agree to let him drive her. On that summery day in May, though, she agreed.

She got in next to him and they went to the Sultan restaurant and ate fish and drank arak.

After they'd eaten, they went down to the pebbly beach, and he made her see the bay with new eyes. She told him that. She said he'd given her a new pair of eyes with which to see the world, and she laughed a lot and let him steal a kiss, but when he put his arm round her waist to fold her inside his kiss, she slipped out of his embrace and said no.

94

Anyway, she ate the red mullet and didn't hold back the way she had before with the little birds. Yalo told her to eat the small fish whole – "Cover it with *taratur* sauce and eat all of it" – and when she asked him about the head and the bones, he smiled, took a fish, covered it with sauce and ate it, so she did the same and said it was the first time in all her life she'd eaten fish that way.

She ate with unusual appetite, drank the arak, licked the *taratur* from her long, cold fingers and laughed. Then the squid came, and Yalo announced that now the real food had arrived.

She said she'd never put her hand into that black broth full of the sea creature's tentacles.

"Don't," said Yalo. "I'll feed you."

He took a morsel of bread, dipped it into the ink and ate, saying, "Before we get to the squid, we have to taste the ink."

"You drink ink?"

"Ink is the best food there is. Taste it."

He took the knife and fork and cut off a small piece of the sea creature, then placed this in a mouthful of bread, dipped it in the ink and offered it to Shireen, who opened her mouth without resisting. When she started chewing, she closed her eyes and began to hum.

With that first mouthful, Shireen was initiated into the squid ritual. She licked the garlic- and lemon-flavoured ink off her lips and thanked Yalo for having made her taste the best food in the world, and she behaved tenderly in his car, letting him hold her hand on the Dbayeh Highway after the Dog River Tunnel, and when they found themselves in front of her house in Hazmiyeh, she permitted him a long kiss before getting out of the car, bending over by the door and telling him goodbye.

That day Yalo became certain he would marry her.

While shaving the next morning, Yalo said to himself in the mirror that he would marry Shireen. He would buy all the squid in the world and eat it with her and live in her house. He didn't say "her house", but when he thought about the marriage and the house and the children, he saw the entrance to her building and beheld the sycamore-fig tree on the pavement opposite and imagined himself playing ball under the tree with a fair-haired child who spoke French! And he thought of his grandfather the *kohno*. How would the grandfather talk to the boy, and in what language?

During his final days, the grandfather stopped speaking Arabic, returned to his maternal language and took to spending his time alone in his room, papers piled in front of him. He would copy out the poetry of Mar Afram the Syriac, say that Mar Afram was a great poet, and bemoan the fact that his only grandson was semi-literate and the only language he knew was Arabic and he could only sound out the Syriac letters with difficulty.

"Come, I'll teach you, my son. I want you to be a writer like me."

Yalo laughed to himself and said, "But Grandfather, you're not a writer. You're copying the poetry of Mar Afram, you're not making it up."

"But I am Mar Afram," the grandfather answered, and he smiled because his grandson was such an idiot that he didn't know that all the writers of the world are merely copyists and that there is only one, hidden, book on the face of the earth, a book not written from human inspiration, and that when people write literature or poetry, parts of this book are revealed to them and they copy them down and rearrange them.

Yalo went over to his grandfather and tried to read.

"Do you understand?" asked the grandfather.

"*Aloho hab yolfono*." Yalo strained to read the words. "Kind of," he answered. "But why bother, Grandfather?"

At this, the *kohno* would start in on his philosophy of books, which he believed were like icons, windows that we open onto the eternal and through which we glimpse the other world. "Of course, we don't see everything. We just see bits, as though we were peeping."

"People don't peep at books, Grandfather. People peep at women!"

"Books are more beautiful than women, my son. What do you know about books, or women?"

With his black robe that covered him from head to toe, and his bottle of ink on the table next to him, the grandfather resembled a sea creature exuding the smell of ink.

Yalo wanted to tell Shireen about his grandfather who resembled a squid and about peeping at books and the women who resemble books that have been opened and through whom one could peep into the other world, but he didn't. The ideas flew out of his head when he was with her. He'd start to speak, then forget, and then he didn't know.

This was the story of his life.

What would happen was that he wouldn't say anything. He would trip over his tongue before this girl, go back to being a small, stammering child, and forget and hesitate. His stammering frightened Shireen. She would listen to him and feel she couldn't gather the words together into proper sentences, and she'd hear the words flying and never coming to settle next to one another on the branch of telling.

"Why do you talk like that?" she asked.

"You don't like what I'm saying?"

"Okay, okay, that's not what I meant. I don't know."

"You don't know what?"

"I don't know anything."

She said she didn't know anything.

"And I don't know anything either," Yalo would respond later, but at the time he didn't say that.

She beat him to the announcement of her complete ignorance, so he didn't know how to announce his own. That's how Yalo was. He'd speak to her without knowing what he was saying, so he'd stagger among the words, tripping over his tongue and falling into the emptiness.

And in the cell too, when he sat down alone to write the whole story of his life, he felt the emptiness being dug out around him. He saw the sheets of white paper and the pens, and he yearned for the smell of ink in his grandfather's room and understood the essence of the secret of the squid, which the ancient Arabs called the "Inker". It came to him that this sea creature was the first to discover writing because with its ink it wrote its defence and its resistance to death. It misled its enemies by releasing its ink into their faces and disappeared into the black thicket its ink had traced within the waters of the sea.

Yalo is alone in his cell. He has to release the ink onto the sheets of paper. He is like the squid. All he possesses to squirt and mislead the fishermen and escape death is the weapon of ink, but alas if the sea creature should fall into the fishermen's net, for then they will cook it in its ink. It occurred to Yalo that he would be cooked in the ink he was writing with, that the black ink that flowed across the sheets of paper would kill him, and that he was incapable of misleading the fisherman, who was waiting for his writings so that he could wrap him up in them and kill him and eat him. He wrote and wrote like a squid going to its death.

"You, you monster!" screamed the interrogator.

. . .

. . .

How had the interrogator found out that he called himself a hawk?

Had Shireen told him?

Had he told Shireen that he was a hawk?

Yalo hadn't told her about the hawk, so how did she know? And what had she said? He hadn't told her; it was his secret, so how had she found out?

He was like a hawk. He hid in the forest waiting for the right moment to swoop down on his victim, and when he saw it, he would hesitate, decide to attack and pause, and then his black coat would fill with air. The long black coat would puff out and the sleeves would expand. Yalo would stretch out his arms, which had become like wings, hover on his puffed-up belly, put his rifle over his shoulder, barrel dangling earthwards, switch on his black torch and descend.

He would feel as though he was descending from a great height, and when the light caught the victim, he would begin his swoop towards the ground.

He was a hawk. A long black coat, a thin beam of light like a thread shining at the car the night had swallowed, two feet trotting in rubber shoes, a large nose to smell the smell of the perfume-enveloped victim, and two wide eyes that saw in the dark.

"You're a hawk, you piece of shit?"

Two men grabbed him by the arms to stop him. He felt as though he was flying, so he closed his eyes.

"You used to tell women you were the 'woman hawk'?"

They carried him by his arms. He stretched out his arms like wings, and the words started to rain down on his face and beak.

"So you think you're clever, you shit, and you're going to escape justice?"

The hawk was beneath the feet, which were crushing it.

"You told Shireen you loved her and wanted to marry her? Do you know who you are and who she is?"

They stamped on his face and broke his beak. The blood began.

"So do you still think you're a playboy?"

He saw the boots through his closed eyes, and there was reflected sunlight, and there was pain.

"We want you to confess about the gang and the explosives. Do you hear?"

Blood was. The hawk was. Pain was. Then suddenly the body left its owner and went to a place of pains too many to number. He saw it moving away and plunging into the pool of pain. He saw it go, but he couldn't call out to it: his beak was broken and his voice was hoarse and his blood covered the ground. The body went to its pains, and Yalo felt as though he'd taken off the hawk and donned the tentacles of the squid, and the pain stopped. He observed how he had sprouted eight hands, and how seventy million optical cells had been distributed throughout his body, and he saw his mate. It was Shireen, swimming beside him in the depths, so he stretched out his fourth hand from the right, which was his sexual member, and he inserted it into the heart of the female emptiness, and touched the eggs, and fertilized them and slept inside.

The hawk was beneath the feet, and the squid was having sex with its mate, who swayed around it playing its beautiful, exotic games. His fourth hand was inside her, and the thousands of eyes with which he saw dissolved into a world of uncountable colours. He saw what was within the blue; he saw colours that have no names because humankind cannot see them. The ink was coming out of all parts of Yalo, who had been transformed from his hawkish state into his marine state. He dove into the depths, stretched out his eight hands and flew through the water, and when he saw them, and he saw their shoes, he squirted his ink to mislead them, and the ink came out the colour of blood.

The hawk stood up.

They stood him up and bound him with blood, and he saw the face of the interrogator, bent by the rays of the sun, and he saw the colour red like haloes that generated themselves round his head and went out through the window and flew. The interrogator came over and spat in his face. Then he slapped him, and his hand filled with blood. He wiped the blood off on the hawk's coat and ordered them to take him away.

The hands pulled at the wounded hawk as though they were going to drag it along the ground. The hawk was pulled along quietly, and the red lights penned in its eyes. Yalo closed his eyes and immediately felt the tears and tasted saltiness spreading through his body. Yalo became salty. He wanted to tell them that he needed a little sweet water. He wanted to cry and leave his body to shiver and moan and for the heat of death to leave it before he died, but he fell into a vast abyss. He felt as though the valley had swallowed him up and that he had become a pine tree; he smelled the resin and began chewing. The blood welling up in his mouth had the taste of toasted pine nuts. He ate his pine nuts and wrapped himself round his tall body and saw himself leaving the interrogator's room and dragged to the jeep, where they sat him in the midst of a group of policemen whose bellies hung down over their leather belts.

Yalo knows not what, or where, or how.

Did he drink?

Did he eat?

Did he speak?

Did he?

Afterwards he wrote that he found himself in a pool of water. He was standing, leaning against the wall, the water was rising towards his chest, he was purchasing air with his gasps, and the colours were blending into smells. His body mingled with the smells of his blood and faeces and urine, and it stretched out to its full length in the water and then contracted, and he began to drown. Yalo remembers that a voice came out of his insides, remembers that he became a voice, and that he felt a mouth howling in his mouth, and that he doesn't remember.

Yalo wrote that he doesn't remember.

When they took him back to the interrogation room and he saw the interrogator's head between him and the window, and saw that the sun had disappeared into the glass, Yalo wanted to ask the interrogator where the sun had gone. He wanted to see the light that hid vision but brought illumination. He wanted the light, but the interrogator asked him what he thought.

Why did he ask him what he thought?

"What do I think about what, sir?"

"What you think about what happened to you," asked the interrogator.

"Why? What happened to me?" asked Yalo.

"The bath," said the interrogator. "Tell me if you enjoyed the bath."

Yalo realised that "the bath" was the name the interrogator gave to those mysterious memories of blood, water and fear.

Yalo lowered his head even further and saw the interrogator's hand reaching towards him. He pulled back, but the hand, with the sheets of white paper, came closer.

"Here," said the interrogator, and he gave Yalo a number of sheets and asked him to write the story of his life from beginning to end.

"Write the story of your life."

Yalo tried to say that he didn't know how to write.

"I want everything. Don't overlook even the smallest detail."

. . .

"When I read, I want to understand and know. Don't write riddles. Write things the way they happened."

. . .

"I don't want you to make anything up. Clear your head, sit down, remember and write it the way you remember it. I want the story from beginning to end."

Yalo tried to say that he didn't know where it began or where it ended and that he couldn't write, but the blood prevented him. The blood was dripping out of his nose and the air around him had disappeared. He tried to open his mouth so that he could breathe, and he closed his eyes.

Yalo was unable to write a single word. He found himself in an isolation cell and saw the sheets of white paper spotted with the black light that spread round him, so he closed his eyes and decided to sleep.

"Write, arsehole!" screamed the man.

He picked up the pen and he saw the circles of darkness shot through with a silver light that came from the depths of his eyes, and he couldn't write. He threw the pen down on the small table they had put in his cell, and he heard the voice screaming at him again. The voice started to vibrate inside his head, as though it had been suspended within the winding passages of his ears and turned into endless echoes.

Yalo said.

Later, when he had finished writing, Yalo would say that those echoes were his constant companion during that long year of ink.

They brought him a fountain pen and a plastic inkwell and ordered him to write.

He wrote because he loved life and was waiting for the end

of that long tunnel of torment so that he could leave the prison and take revenge.

Despite the terrible pains of the torture, Yalo felt a strange pleasure, and this pleasure was his imagination. While being beaten, or "on the spit" or suspended by his hands, he would imagine himself in the torturer's place and imagine his victims – Shireen, Emile, Dr Saeed, Mme Randa, *Maître* Michel Salloum, Tony Ateeq and everyone else.

No. He used to imagine these things *after* the "party", as they called the torture session, was over. During the party, he would imagine the cell, and then in the cell he'd have his own party. He'd be thrown into the cell, utterly exhausted, and the only means he could find to recover his body and his strength was his imagination, and the reversal of roles. He would turn his mind inside out and imagine things the way he wanted them to be. Then he'd recover something of his strength, and the shadows of the hawk's glance, which spread terror through the bones, would return, and he would put his body back together again, piece by piece. He would rip the pain from its parts and throw it on the bodies of the others and see how the agonies would leave the tips of his fingers and toes and take possession of his victims.

Then he would doze.

Yalo's sleep, after torture, was his revenge. He would make up his dreams as he liked. In his imagination, he would have the instruments of torture brought, making sure he had forgotten nothing, and then allow his eyes to close to the rhythm of the chains and the sounds of screaming, or to the electric cables, and watch how his victims fell beneath his torture, which was now theirs.

Even the final torture, which, when they performed it on him, made him feel that his soul was asking for death and his body for the earth, even this final torture he distributed among the others, falling asleep to the sounds of their death rattles and cries for help.

That was at the "Big Party".

At this party, which he first named "the Big" and then gave many other names to, Yalo was so terrified that he couldn't open his mouth, so he put up his hands as a sign of surrender and the tears poured from his eyes and he entered into an animal-like moaning before the officer ordered them to untie the sack from round the prisoner's waist.

Even this torture Yalo took to his imaginary world, where he decided to dedicate it to Dr Saeed, who had left Shireen on her own in the forest and fled in his car, its wheels squealing loudly as the gravel flew round them.

At the beginning, Yalo decided that he would forget the sack and exclude it from the memories of his imagination, but he found himself presented with the scene of the sack when he closed his eyes, which were wet with tears. He heard the cat's yowls, and saw the bamboo cane, and felt the claws savaging him.

That was the moment of the torture that led Yalo to offer all his confessions.

Why are they asking him to write the story of his life? Why haven't his confessions satisfied the officer?

That same day, the day that entered Yalo's imagination as the "Day of the Sack", they took him from his cell at dawn and put him in something like a small room. His eyes and hands were bound, and he felt his way along the corridor with his bare feet, trying not to fall. When he reached the small room, he fell to the floor because a hand pushed him forwards and made him fall, so he fell. He heard a voice telling him to take off his trousers.

He tried to stand, but he tripped over his feet and rolled on the floor. He heard guffaws and felt a hand helping him to get up, so he stood, and the hand started to undo the buttons of his trousers. He reached down to the buttons and a blow landed with a noise on his neck, and then the hand removed the blindfold. At first, all he could see was darkness. Then after a few seconds a tall man with broad shoulders wearing a khaki suit loomed before him and ordered him to take off his underpants too.

Yalo looked with his exhausted eyes and saw three men with bulging muscles next to the officer. They were wearing waist-coats, and black hair shone on their chests and hands. He decided that he was surely going to be raped. The world went hazy and he froze.

"Take off your pants, arsehole."

He felt for the wall and tried to bury himself in it. He remembered his grandfather's story about the metropolitan who moved back and back and then the wall split asunder and swallowed him up.

It was the legend of Constantinople. "When Constantinople fell to Mehmet the Conqueror, the metropolitan entered the wall, and they're waiting for him still," the grandfather said with a smile. "Those Greeks have the minds of children. As though they didn't know that they themselves caused the disaster!"

"Did the wall really open?" asked Yalo.

"That's what they say," said the grandfather.

"And what was the disaster?" asked Yalo.

"The disaster was that they went into the wall and they're still inside the wall."

Yalo sensed that the hand that had undone the buttons of his trousers was going to reach for his underpants and pull them off, so he bent over and took them off and then stood in front of them, naked from the waist down, humiliated, waiting for them to order him to bend over so they could begin raping him.

Behind the smoke of his cigarette, which filled all the space in the room, the tall officer was smiling, sending a nauseous shudder through Yalo's soul.

"Let's go, boys," said the officer, and Yalo pulled back in terror and stuck his back against the wall, shivering with fear and cold. Two men came forward carrying a sack. The first was holding the opening of the sack, while the second had his hands underneath it.

"Come closer, come closer. Don't be frightened," said the officer.

Yalo went rigid and stuck his backside even harder against the wall.

"I told you, don't be frightened," said the officer. "Come over here and take the sack from the boys and put it on."

"How can I put it on?" asked Yalo in a low voice.

"Put your legs into it like it was a pair of trousers," said the officer.

"Trousers?" asked Yalo softly, without taking in what was being asked of him, staying where he was because he didn't know what to do.

He leaned his head against the wall and closed his eyes. The third man pounced on him, seized his shoulders and pulled him into the centre of the room. Then he went round behind him and put his arms round his chest, pressing up against him till he was joined to him in a total, form-fitting embrace. The two men with the sack now came forward and bent over while the third man lifted Yalo and forced him to put his legs into the sack. The first man then half raised Yalo's body and tied the sack round his waist.

The three men stood back, and Yalo was alone in the centre of the room. He felt something strange moving between his naked legs, but he only caught on to the game when the officer, a bamboo cane in his hand, came forward.

"Will you confess, or shall we begin?" asked the officer.

"I swear, I swear by Almighty God, I swear by Almighty God, I've confessed everything, but I'm yours. I've told you everything, but I'm ready to say whatever you want, whatever you like."

"I think you're still bullshitting us," said the officer.

"I told the truth. I swear, I swear, I am not, I am not bull-shitting."

The bamboo cane described an arc from the officer's hand and fell on the sack between Yalo's legs and the torture journey began. The cane stung what was in the sack to life, and the yowling and clawing and that awareness of the abyss began. The cane stung the animal a second time, and the cat began to lash out and twist in the space that separated the bottom of the sack from Yalo's crotch. A cat that quivered with savagery, that jumped and jumped, as though trying to climb Yalo's penis, gnawing and clawing. And it had whiskers. Yalo didn't see the whiskers yet he saw them. They gleamed in a kind of light. The cat's two eyes flashed in the darkness and its whiskers gleamed and Yalo fell to the ground. At first, his mind didn't take in what was happening. He heard scrabbling and yowling, but he only caught on when he heard the officer ordering the cane to make the cat jump up, and he understood that he was at the mercy of a savage cat.

"Kitty kitty, up up up," said the officer.

So Yalo fell to the floor. Faced with the cat's attacks, he squatted down, and the animal's ferocity increased. It leapt and seized his testicles, and it was then that Yalo saw it and saw its whiskers and felt that his testicles were exploding and that his penis was dripping blood. He stood, in an attempt to get some help, but the officer's cane kept stinging the sack as he repeated "Kitty kitty," at which the cat would quiver and jump and jump and Yalo would fall.

Inside the sack, Yalo discovered how pain is eliminated in the face of fear, and how that valley which runs all the way to the depths of the earth had opened up in his belly.

The officer had the cane that whipped in his hand; Yalo had the sack that leapt at his crotch; the sack had the cat that gnawed and clawed and moaned and muttered. The cat's yowling was like the crying of a thousand babies, and Yalo was like a lonely baby who had lost its ability to scream.

And when Yalo put up his hands and his tears poured down, he confessed to everything.

"I'll confess now," he wanted to say, but he didn't say. His voice came out like a hoarse yowling, and he fell, and he saw himself entering the forest of savage cats that gnawed at his limbs. He was like someone swimming; later he would say that he was like someone swimming in cats, and he named the sack the "kitty pond" and he saw himself diving down into blood, clawing and yowling.

And he saw his tears.

For three days and three nights the tears fell and covered his eyes and his face, and he did not wipe them away. He left them to fall, take paths and make furrows, then drop onto his neck and cover his body.

In the end, the kitty pond baptized him in tears.

"The true baptism, my son, is the baptism of tears," said his grandfather. "I am now being baptised, so leave me. No, I am not upset. The tears fall of their own accord."

Gaby would order her son to go to his grandfather's room to cheer him up. "I don't know what's happening to your grandfather the *kohno*. Go to his cell and tell him something to cheer him up. Go on, *Bro*, there's a good boy."

"What am I supposed to talk to him about, Mummy? Now he's started talking Syriac and he tells me off."

"Your grandfather's sick. Go to him."

Yalo entered the small room where the black garments made a pile in a corner that had become known as the "weeping corner". The grandfather was sitting on the ground like a bundle of clothes, his body emaciated, his bones thin; he sat in a heap in his corner, and the tears poured from his eyes.

"*Shlomo*," said Yalo.

"*Shlomo*," said the *kohno*.

"How are you?" asked Yalo.

"*Shafir. Tawdı ımoryo*," said the grandfather.

"What, Grandfather? What's wrong?" asked Yalo, and the grandfather didn't answer.

The boy sat down next to his grandfather, and the *kohno* covered his face with his veiny hands covered with black spots and went on with his quiet sobbing, the tears seeping out between his fingers. The boy was paralyzed, and he crouched where he was and listened to the ringing of the silence broken only by the sighs that issued from the depths of the man sitting in his weeping corner. After a long while, the man took his hands away from his face and told the boy not to be afraid of him, and told him of the tears of baptism.

"Would you like to know why I'm weeping?" asked the grandfather.

The boy nodded.

"Man, my son, is baptised twice in this life. The first time is when he is little, when he is baptised with water. The second time is when he has become an old man, when he is baptised with tears. I know that I am now being baptised before going to where my mother is."

"I hope you get better soon, Grandfather."

"I don't want to go, but I'm going to go, and this is the sign, this is the sign of Ismail, my son. Ismail is the grandfather of both the Arabs and the Assyrians, but the Arabs know nothing. Ismail was the first man to be baptised. He was abandoned in the desert, he and his mother, Hajar, and he was baptised with tears, and God sent the water and didn't let him die of thirst. Do you know why? Because he wept. The water came from the tears, and water is life. 'And we have made from water every living thing', as it is written. I didn't know these things, but a Maronite priest called Joaquim told me about them. He used to visit me so that he could speak Suryoyo with me. He said that there was no-one left in this country who knew the language of Christ, so he would give his tongue a workout with me, and I'd listen to his stories. Dear me, what stories he knew! You know, I was a tile-maker by trade, and I studied and finished theological college, but he was a different sort of thing altogether. He had studied in Rome and he knew more stories about the Messiah than are written in the Gospels, and he told me about the baptizm of tears. He said that the Muslims too were baptised in the tears of Ismail, and this put my mind at rest about the mullah. God bless him, he told me that he wanted me to go back so I could inherit. Who wants to inherit blood? He wanted to make me inherit blood, but I refused. And then afterwards he put my mind at rest; Father Joaquim told me the mullah's father had been baptised too, and that baptizm is the path of forgiveness, which means that God had forgiven him too."

"Your papa was a Muslim?"

"*Lo, lo.*"

"What was your papa's name?"

"I was telling you about the tears. Father Joaquim said that baptism was only complete if there were tears. He was an old man, like your grandfather is now, and when he spoke Suryoyo with me his tears would flow and I would feel like laughing, but now I've discovered the truth, and when you grow up, you, like me, will discover the importance of the baptism of tears."

The *kohno*, whose face had been devoured by his long white beard, was drowning in his final baptism, and Yalo didn't understand, and he didn't dare to approach any closer to the secret that the greatest event in a man's life is his death and that the *kohno* was weaving his shroud with his tears as he raved about how the mullah had wanted to make him inherit blood and that the priest Joaquim had revealed to him that humankind's common inheritance is its tears.

Yalo asked his mother about the tears, but the woman, who was watching her father die, told him to keep silent. "Don't you dare start talking about such things. Now isn't the time for us to be asking questions. Now is the time for us to help your grandfather, and that's all." Yalo told his mother he didn't understand, and she said, "Later. Soon you'll grow up and you'll understand more." And he grew up, but he didn't understand.

On 6 January, 1975, on the eve of the war, when Yalo was twelve years old, his mother asked him to help her take the *kohno* to White Sands Beach. At first Yalo refused and said that the man wouldn't be able to withstand the cold and might die, but in the end, at his mother's insistence, he agreed.

"You still believe in those superstitions?" he asked her.

"Be quiet or he'll hear you," she answered. "Go on, take his hand and follow me."

And they went, and it was night, and winter. On the beach, beneath a bitter rain like bullets, the woman let down her hair and took her father's hand and walked with him into the sea. The old man stumbled and fell into the waves and swallowed water and salt and cried a lot. Then she gave him to drink. Gaby cupped her hands and took a little of the sea water and gave the *kohno* and her son to drink, and she said that the water had become sweeter than honey.

"Did you see the miracle?" she asked. "Behold, my hair has turned the colour of gold."

"The water has become sweet and more delicious than honey," she said.

"The Lord Christ, peace be upon Him, says that you will become well, Father Afram," she said.

But the *kohno* was tottering. His legs were no longer able to hold him upright, so Yalo and his mother carried him to the road and took him home in a taxi.

"Don't die, I beg you!" his daughter screamed at him.

Afram lived for a year after the visit to White Sands, when he was taken with a fever for an entire week, but for the rest of her life Gaby was reproached by her conscience.

"I killed him," she said. "I killed the *kohno*. After that outing, he couldn't walk any more. He crumpled, the weeping consumed him, and his eyes started getting smaller, as though he didn't have eyes any more, as though his eyes had been wiped away and all that remained were two small black points, like springs full of tears. And he started to bathe in tears, and he died."

And Yalo now – which is to say there, when he came out of the sack and drowned in his tears – Yalo, there, now, discovers that, like his grandfather and like Ismail, he has passed through the baptism of tears and is drowning in his eyes.

He placed a sheet of paper in front of him and decided that he would write, but he couldn't. There was no escape, however, for the interrogator was waiting, and so was the fear. True, Yalo suffered agonies on the days when he had to write, but there was no torture in the world to compare with that of the kitty pond that had crawled over his crotch and cast him into a deep valley, and the sack remained in his memory. As he wrote he imagined two sacks – a sack above and a sack below.

The first sack wasn't a problem, because it was the sack of war, and the fighters, of whom Yalo had been one, had been the sack's masters. That was why he hadn't been frightened by the first sack, with which they'd covered his head when they'd arrested him. He'd closed his eyes inside the sack and gone off with them. Of course he'd fallen to the ground and felt that his legs had become invisible, but he hadn't been afraid. He'd known that the game of darkness was part of the game of war, and that he was now entering another one of the pranks of a world he had come to know well. Later he would say he'd fled Beirut for Paris because he'd got fed up with the war and sick of the screaming of the victims, though in fact he didn't speak those words. He was a son of war, which didn't lie because it didn't speak. At the barracks Yalo had entered when he'd been fourteen, he had learned not to speak. The war hid what it wanted to say behind what it said, and words were thrown to the ground like banana skins, and people slipped on them, and the sacks were masks that covered everything. He put on the first mask after his two weeks of training in the forest near a mountain village whose name he could no longer remember, and he got used to it. Later, he discovered that speech also has its masks, which was something he would live with when he came to write the story of his life in accordance with the honourable interrogator's request.

But the second sack was different. The sack below wasn't a mask, it was a probe and an exposure and a sorrow. Yalo awoke from what seemed like a coma and didn't find the sack that covered him below and beheld himself in the midst of his urine and faeces. He put his hand between his thighs and felt a strange familiarity, and the warmth came and the tears spurted and he thought of Shireen. At that instant, he understood the meaning of love and felt her tears in his eyes, the trembling of her lip in his, her small, warm knee in his. He grasped his knee and the ghost of his smile came to him, and he saw how he'd reached for her small knee and taken hold of the kneecap and rubbed it with his palm.

"What are you doing?" she asked.

"I'm soaping my hands. When I see you, I have to be clean, and the best cake of soap is your knee. What do they call the kneecap? What's its name? Answer me."

She looked at him with her small eyes and faked a half smile before answering, "They call it 'the cake of soap'."

"The knee is a cake of soap and I'm soaping my hand. What's the big deal?"

Yalo laughed and Shireen asked him to remove his hand from her knee because she was afraid someone would see.

"I don't care about other people, I only care about you."

"Okay, take your hand away for my sake."

He removed his hand, rubbed his hands together and passed them over his face as though putting soap on it and washing it, and Shireen yelled at him not to take his hands off the steering wheel, and he raised his hands in the air, letting the car swerve on the Jounieh Highway before taking the steering wheel in his left hand and leaving the right one reaching across the seat waiting for hers.

Yalo swam in his wastes, as he would say later, affecting disgust, but there, in the midst of the pond in which he found himself, he felt he could curl up into himself, so he did, and became a child. He grew so small it was as if he had returned to his mother's womb; he enwombed himself and put out his hand. He was hungry and thirsty, and he put out his hand and licked. He closed his eyes and swallowed the sticky fluid and wanted to sleep. He saw his mother's face and Alexei's face and vanished into his tears.

In the kitchen Gaby was pulling her long, pleated hair and weeping because her son had sucked her life up and then gone to war and ruin. Yalo was standing by the kitchen door and telling her he didn't want to study to become a kohno like his grandfather. His mother had put him into the Atshaneh School near Bikfaya to be rid of him and his torments, but he'd run away from the school and returned to their house in Ein El Roummaneh. From Ein El Roummaneh he'd gone off with Tony and joined the war.

Yalo stood at the kitchen door listening to the woman telling the story. Why was she telling this story and saying that she'd eaten shit?

"For your sake I ate shit, you shit. What an idiot I was, damn it! When you were a child I ate your shit and now you want to make me eat shit again? I spit on you!"

Why did she say, "I spit on you!" when he stood at the kitchen door trying to calm her down, saying, "Relax, Mother. I'm like that because all young men are like that"?

Yalo's childhood had been full of his mother's story of how

she'd sworn an oath so that God would send her a boy child. She'd gone to the church of St Sawirus and sworn an oath. She was pregnant and had a feeling that her husband wasn't going to stay with her. Her husband was like a phantom, "and I knew he was going to take off and all I wanted out of this world was to have a son. I knew from the start. From the moment we got married there was something fishy about him. He said he wanted to go to Sweden and that he'd send for me. I worked it out for myself that he was not going to come back and I swore an oath to the Lord. My father the *kohno* was at home and heard me as I stood beneath the icon of the Virgin and swore my oath. He cursed me and said this was blasphemy, the very essence of blasphemy. It wasn't blasphemy, it was despair, the very essence of despair. I swore that if God would give me a boy, I'd eat his shit. And God answered my prayer, so I ate it."

When she told this story, Gabrielle would describe the taste of milk. "The taste of the shit was the taste of milk, and it had something of my own smell. I breastfed you, and when I ate and fulfilled my oath, I smelled milk."

Yalo doesn't remember the story as words; he remembers it as a yellow picture. A woman standing before a child in its bed bends over and puts her finger into its nappy and then licks it. And after she's finished bathing her child and before offering it her breast, she smells her breasts and becomes drunk with the two smells – the smell of her son and the smell of her milk. The woman didn't abandon this ritual until the doctor told her that the child needed solid food – fruit and vegetables and eggs. She fed him these and lost him, for after he'd eaten, the smell of his faeces would become mixed with new smells, and she became aware of the distance between herself and her son and started to smell the smell of shit, and it was no longer possible for her to fulfil her oath, so she decided to ignore the doctor's instructions and to feed her son nothing but milk. But the new smell had invaded the child's body and faeces, and she couldn't bring Yalo back, and she felt that her son had been separated from her.

Yalo sees himself now, meaning in that place, and sees the weeping. He is swimming in the liquids that have come out of him and he sees the tears that spurted from his eyes when he saw Alexei. How does Alexei come to be in this waking that resembles sleep?

"Blond Alexei", as they called him, was tall, well built and fair-haired. He left the barracks to do body-building training at the Sanharib Club in Ashrafiyeh. He was accused of sodomy and of having suspect relationships with the young boys he brought to the barracks on the excuse of giving them weapons training. He denied the charges, though, and all he talked about was relationships with married women. He used to say that married women were "polished": "A woman has to be rounded, so you can pluck her like you pluck an orange." He'd put out his hands and cup them as if he was cupping two small breasts that he'd plucked, and he started to eat and lick his lips as though the juice of the oranges was still on them. Yalo didn't believe Alexei's stories about married women, but he didn't tell him about Thérèse.

Why, in fact, when he listened to Alexei's stories about women, would he see Sister Thérèse as though she was part of his story, and forget the shop that smelled of wood around which the blind man's eyes roamed? He would take Thérèse to a distant hotel, where Engineer Georges had taken her, and discover first love with her and first sex. Sister Thérèse's face was like a white light that leapt out from among the folds of her black habit and gathered Yalo to itself. Her soft white hand would steal under his short trousers and make the world the size of a fist holding the cylinder of life, and the cylinder would be bursting with desire. Thérèse became his story and he didn't tell it to anyone, and the secret that he hadn't experienced became his personal secret in which he revelled without turning it into words.

Blond Alexei was mad, and he couldn't keep a secret, and Yalo didn't know how Thérèse's name slipped onto his tongue in Alexei's presence, with the result that the blond Russian took to calling Yalo "Thérèse's boy", and, when the young men would ask Yalo about her, he'd say nothing, as though he was guarding a great secret. Then the name slipped out again in Shireen's presence, but Yalo wouldn't write about Thérèse when he came to write the story of his life. Once he told Shireen that she looked like Sister Thérèse and she asked who Thérèse was, and he said she was a nun who'd taught him at school and that he'd been attached to her and enchanted by her beauty, and he never dared to tell Shireen the true story.

Alexei was like a madman that terrible night. He must have snorted a huge amount of cocaine or he wouldn't have made the man do it. Yalo told Tony their first night in Paris that God wouldn't forgive them because they'd forced the old man to eat his own faeces. Tony laughed and said he didn't believe Yalo, and then he disappeared. He disappeared because he didn't believe anything. He stole the money and the language and left Yalo alone in that city.

Alexei turned up, the cocaine dust etched in red on his bulging eyes, and told Yalo to come with him. They went to a yellow building close to the Hôtel-Dieu, descended some steps, and Alexei unlocked the basement door. There Yalo saw a solitary man, blindfolded, kneeling in the dark. Alexei shone his torch at the man's head, and he turned towards the light without speaking.

Alexei then began his game. He fired his revolver in the basement, and it made a sound like an artillery shell, and the kneeling man began to shake. Alexei went up close to him and put the hot muzzle of the revolver to the man's temple and began threatening him. When Alexei told the man that the hour of his execution had come and that he should get ready to meet his maker, the man trembled, sat back with his feet out in front of him, and defecated. The smell spread with amazing speed. Holding his nose, Alexei went over to the man and ordered him to stand. The man began to cry and plead, but the revolver's muzzle approached once more and the man started to move away, putting his hands on the ground to support himself. And then Alexei saw the shit.

"You shat yourself, you coward!" screamed Alexei, laughing loudly. Then he told the man not to stand up.

"If you can't stand up, we'll execute you in your shit," said Alexei. "And before you die, you must eat."

Yalo doesn't know why the man ate. He was going to die anyway. Yalo saw night and the smell, and the tears dripped black from the cheeks of the man in his sixties, who put his hand into his waste, lifted his fingers to his mouth and licked them.

"You have to finish it all," screamed the blond Russian.

The man ate slowly, as though stealing time from death, and Yalo just stood there. Then suddenly he needed to urinate and a sort of paralysis struck him, and he imagined himself sinking into the ground. He thought he might choke and his lungs tightened and he suddenly found himself running outside. Engulfed by dizziness, he reached his house and began to vomit. He went into the bathroom and thrust his head over the basin, and the yellow vomit came out of his mouth and his nose, and his ears filled with a ringing sound. He heard Alexei asking if he was all right and laughing loudly, and he wiped his mouth with the towel, turned on the tap to get the yellow out of the basin, then ran back outside and went with the blond to the barracks, where he listened with the others while the Russian told the story of the old man they'd kidnapped and forced to eat his own shit.

They called him "the Russian", but he wasn't Russian. He would claim that he was a White Russian and say that the whole of Russia was red and there was only one spot of white in it and that was Alexei. In fact, he was an Assyrian who'd forgotten the language of his ancestors just like Yalo and most of the other young men. He was also a close friend of Saeed Mansurati, who would set poetry to music and sing it, calling himself "Singer of the New Lebanon", the country that was going to be born after the war. Alexei would get a bottle of white wine and Saeed would play his oud and sing, and the boys would get drunk on the rhythms of Andalusian ballads. Saeed composed poetry about Ashrafiyeh and sang it in his husky voice, which resembled that of Farid El Atrash, and the boys would get drunk.

Saeed Mansurati disappeared and Alexei died, and Yalo found himself alone in his pond and heard Alexei's words in his ear.

He said he'd found the man upstairs in an office and that he had a strange accent. "I didn't ask for his I.D. or anything. I caught on that his accent was strange and told him to go down to the basement and left him there for around five hours, kneeling and blindfolded. I swear I forgot all about him, and then, after I'd had my coke, I remembered him, and when I fired above his head he shat himself. What a coward! I told him to eat before he died, and he ate. He knew he was going to die, and he ate, and you, you coward, ran away. I swear if your mother hadn't appeared I'd have given you a beating to remember. I'd have made you shit yourself so bad you'd never have forgotten me for the rest of your life."

"And him? What happened to him?" asked Yalo.

"God rest his soul," said Alexei.

"You killed him?"

"What do you think I should have done?"

"No, seriously. I'm asking you seriously."

"No, I didn't kill him. I left him in the basement and came here. Come with me and we'll go kill him."

"I don't want to go."

Alexei said that the man had died without his having to kill him. He'd left him to get on with his meal, and then he'd fired a shot above his head and the man had died.

"He died of fear, not from being shot," said Alexei. "When people die, they die of death, they die of fear, and you too are going to die of cowardice for sure."

Yalo didn't believe the man died because he was frightened by the sound of the gunshot. He was sure Alexei had killed him for a laugh. And it occurred to Yalo that Alexei was right, so he decided to abandon his own cowardice and laugh himself. He regretted that he'd run home out of fear and vomited all over himself, and he felt a desire to kill everybody, and he filled with laughter. He was at a loss as to why people didn't laugh, and he laughed. He lived the rest of his war on the verge of laughing. Even death was an occasion for laughter and a source of entertainment. Laughter is the highest form of life. Laughter means that everyone is a stranger and deserves to be laughed at. The stranger is laughable because he's a stranger. Even Alexei was a stranger, and they could laugh at him any time they wanted to.

In the presence of Alexei's corpse, the boys were seized by something like a paroxysm of weeping, so Yalo felt like laughing.

Alexei didn't die the way other people do, but he did die, and when they found him, it wasn't him. It was a pile of clothes, stones and bones. Three months were long enough for him to no longer be the man they'd known.

No-one knew how Alexei came to disappear. All of a sudden, the blond Russian wasn't there. They looked for him everywhere and couldn't find a trace of him. Then their leader, Mario, decided that Alexei was a traitor and a coward. He gathered everyone together in the barracks and announced that Alexei was a coward and would be brought before a military tribunal when he reappeared, but the blond didn't reappear, and the mill of the civil war ground on. Mario said that the war was "a mill". He'd bend over, bare-chested, as though he was a mule, whinnying like a donkey, and say he was carrying the mill of war on his back.

"We grind the people and we ourselves are ground."

He'd drink arak and his eyes would wander, and when he'd become drunk, he'd start in on grinding himself and the others. The young men of the barracks would watch Mario the hero-turned-mule and laugh. And he became known as Mario Mill.

Mario issued Alexei's death sentence without a trial. He gathered the boys together and said Alexei was a traitor: "We don't know who he is or where he comes from. He said he was Russian, but he isn't Russian. He said he was Assyrian, but he isn't Assyrian. He said he was Lebanese, but he isn't Lebanese. Anyone who sees him must shoot him without asking questions."

"The bullet is the question," said Mario. "Shoot him and get rid of him, and after he's dead we'll question him. Who does he think he is? Interrogation follows death. First we execute him and afterwards we interrogate him. That's how it has to be."

But how?

How did Alexei melt away, in that distant building?

Alexei's image was to become engraved on Yalo's memory. The face that wasn't a face but a skull that laughed.

It was Mario who recognized him.

A group of the boys came and told Mario they'd seen a decomposing body in the Jreidini Building, next to the French faculty of medicine in rue Damas, so Mario ordered them to get rid of it before they took up position there. But he noticed their fear and hesitation.

"Get rid of it, and no messing about. I've told you, you need to set up a position in the Jreidini Building. You look scared, and I don't like your feeble excuse."

Mario picked up his rifle and walked ahead of them, and when they reached the heap of clothes, stones and bones, their leader bent over the remains and froze, turning, in that partially demolished room, into a bent bow.

Mario was walking ahead when he heard them stammering about the bones. "Follow me," he said, and ordered Yalo to go with him. He ran ahead and bounded up the steps of the building, and when he reached the third floor, he froze. Yalo followed the sound, but he didn't run with the others; his steps were heavy and he climbed the steps slowly, and in a corner of the dark room, with its piles of smashed furniture, he saw everything.

"That's it," said Tony.

Mario looked at Tony with irritation and drew back. He leaned his short, well-built body against the wall before going over and having a look. Yalo didn't know how long the short man remained bent over that way, but he felt that time had frozen over Mario's back. Then the back began to tremble as though a wave had swept over it from the head to the waist, and he saw

Tony go over to Mario and put his arm round him, and he heard Mario saying things he couldn't understand because his voice was stuck inside his windpipe as though it was held prisoner by his Adam's apple, which was moving but producing no sound. The back fell to the ground and Tony fell next to it, and Yalo saw himself moving away with the rest.

"Where are you going?" screamed Mario. "It's Alexei."

Mario's scream mixed with that of the boys, and Yalo wanted to run away. He felt his legs tensing to run, but the voices immobilized him and he saw everyone staggering. The light was black, draped in the darkness that seeped from the buildings destroyed by the war. The shadows of destruction spread over them, and they bent over what seemed to be a skeleton in clothes perforated by rot.

"It's Alexei," said Mario. "We have to move him."

Yalo saw a shredded pair of trousers and an eaten-away shirt on a skeleton. The knees were bent and the bones were covered in black light.

"I can tell by his belt," said Mario. "Come on, lads, let's pick him up."

The leather belt was the sign. The Russian boy had been eaten.

"Who ate him?" asked Yalo, feeling as if he was going to laugh. He wanted to laugh, but he cried like the rest. That day Yalo discovered that laughter lives side by side with weeping, and that to distinguish between them is a matter of the greatest difficulty because they have been mixed together since the beginning of creation. Both are unexpected and paradoxical, and both fill the emptiness felt by the soul.

There, in front of that scene he would never forget, the weeping was like a haemorrhage from deep wounds. Yalo saw himself bent over the pile of bones, whose identity was indicated by a burnt brown leather belt, and he saw his companions stripped of their clothes and their flesh. He saw bones bending over bones, and the laughter that comes from weeping swept over him, and he understood what he hadn't been able to explain to Shireen when he was pursuing her with his love. He understood that the mingling of laughter with weeping is the mark of humanity, and that every person carries two souls within him, the first for laughter and the second for weeping, and that everyone's problem is that these two souls work together, which is why people are never able to define their feelings.

He said to Shireen, as she wept, that weeping was the mark of happiness and love. She looked at him with her small red eyes as though she didn't understand why he didn't understand.

"Please, Yalo, understand me."

Before she stood up, she asked him to understand her. Shireen would stand up in the middle of their dates as though she was preparing to leave, and he'd look at her with his small eyes and she'd sit down again without saying anything.

Later she would tell the interrogator that she was afraid of his eyes and his long, thin eyebrows that met in the middle. She would say she didn't know why she went out with him and that she'd been afraid of him and that she'd only agreed to meet up with him in order to convince him to end their relationship.

The interrogator asked her why she'd agreed to meet him the first time, before things had really got going. She said she'd wanted to end it.

"And afterwards? You saw him the first time, so why did you keep going back to see him?" asked the interrogator.

The girl stammered and said she didn't know, but she was afraid of Yalo and felt pity for him.

She would go to see him determined to leave after a few minutes, but his eyes would change and she'd find that she'd sat down again. Shireen believed that Yalo possessed two faces and that each one had different eyes. When they met up, she'd see the first face with its sleepy, half-closed eyes, and she'd make up her mind to go. She'd stand up to say, "Enough," and the other face, with its wide-open eyes, would appear and stop her where she stood and compel her to sit down again. She'd cry and listen to his voice speaking words of love.

Shireen didn't understand because she hadn't seen Alexei as a clump of bones covered in his shredded clothes, the young men round him transformed into skeletons and tears.

Yalo pulled back and saw how man eats himself. This was the second truth of humanity. The first truth was the mixing of laughter with weeping, the second that people ate themselves. On the third floor of the Jreidini Building, Yalo understood that the last banquet that a man holds for himself is his death.

The voice was Tony's, but the question was everyone's.

"Who ate him?"

Yalo looked round him, searching for a wild animal or a dog. In those days dogs were lords of the city that the war had reduced to ruin. Yalo believed a wild dog had devoured Alexei – one of those that roamed the streets and that the fighters amused themselves by shooting at on the line that separated Beirut from Beirut.

But no.

Mario said Alexei had died of an overdose of heroin. "The bastard started needing drugs all the time, and he started using needles. He must have been upstairs with one of his boys and shot up and died. No-one killed him. Who would have killed him? It must have been the needle, but I'd like to know who was with him. And how he could have left him like that . . . Damn it, we've become worse than animals."

Mario's decree that Alexei had died of an overdose ended the debate, but Yalo saw something else. He saw Alexei eating himself. He bent over his death and his last banquet began. He ate himself with himself. That was death. It was the final banquet, when the dead man becomes both banquet and guest, and eats without food because he has become food, and when the food is finished, he finishes with it, and all that is left is what cannot be eaten: a skull, white bones and a laugh. That was what Alexei had become — a collection of bones proclaiming themselves the leftovers from a feast. After Alexei had finished eating himself, he had devoured his teeth, and the laughing skull was left, the mouth empty of everything but laughter and death.

The skull laughed and Mario wept and drank his tears. All of them drank their tears and started coughing, as though the tears had stuck in their throats and they could no longer swallow them or get them out, so they had to go on sobbing and coughing and standing around impotently in the presence of a corpse that didn't look like other corpses.

"How are we supposed to pick him up?" asked Tony, and he tugged at Yalo's hand to ask him to help, but Yalo didn't move. He remained immobile, imagining the banquet that Alexei had made for himself in this room with its missing doors and windows. Alexei had refused to hold his banquet in secret. He hadn't entered the grave so that he could eat himself in the dark, he'd gone back to being a child eating its insides, as would happen to Yalo after the night with the sack, when he would lick his wastes and drink his tears in search of warmth.

Gaby, however, hadn't understood the meaning of the last banquet. She'd taken her son's hand and dragged him to the bathroom so that she could show him how her face had disappeared, and Yalo had told her that the mirror had eaten her face: "In other words, your face is eating you, Mother," he'd told her.

"What does that mean?" she asked fearfully.

"How should I know? Go to sleep, Mother, and forget about it. What business do you have with mirrors?"

But Gaby remained frozen there, just as Mario had over the bones stretched out inside the remains of the blue trousers and the khaki shirt.

"Don't be afraid, Mother. Go on, get to bed."

"No, no," she replied. "Look carefully. Can you see my face in the mirror or not?"

"I can see you, Mother. Your face is clear. Get these black thoughts out of your head and look."

"I can't see it," she said. "Please, I don't know what's happening to me. Perhaps . . . I don't know. Please, my son, tell me what to do."

"Get on with you! What did I do to deserve this? Leave me alone and go back to sleep."

Yalo told the interrogator that he'd run away because he was afraid of her and her words. "I ran away, sir, from her and her mirror. I was afraid she'd kill me with her stories. I was afraid she and the war and this life would drive me mad, so I decided to run away. Tony told me, 'Go,' so I left with him for France."

"And what brought you back to Lebanon?"

"I told you, sir. Tony stole the money and left me on my own."

"And then what?"

"Then it was Ballona. From France to Ballona, and you know the whole story, sir."

"No, I don't. I want the true story."

"I told you the whole story about Shireen, and I confess I'm guilty."

"You think you can make fools of us? I want the story of the explosives. I want details about the gang – who was in it, who funded it, who gave the orders."

"It was nothing to do with me, and I know nothing about it," said Yalo.

"It looks like your memory's bad and needs refreshing. It seems you won't talk till we've torn your body to shreds. Let's go."

He said, "Let's go," and they took him to the sack place and there, in the middle of the pond of his spilled guts, he opened his eyes and saw Alexei's mother. How had the woman got to the prison?

The woman was fat and white, and she sat next to Yalo on the ground, wearing the same silly smile she had worn since she'd seen her son in his coffin.

Mario and his companions, Yalo among them, went to her house behind the Azariyeh Convent, in the long, winding street that looked out over the cemetery of Mar Mitr in Ashrafiyeh, and the woman saw death, and the grimace of tears inscribed itself on her face. Mario told her that they had found Alexei dead, and that the burial would take place the following day. The woman said nothing. She didn't ask where they'd found him or how he'd been killed or who'd killed him. She slumped in her seat and apologized for not being able to make coffee for her visitors because she couldn't stand up.

Mario said they wouldn't be bringing the body to the house, and she raised her eyebrows in refusal and said that her son would go to the cemetery from his home.

Mario tried to explain, but it was as though she couldn't hear, and she only agreed when Mario said that it was the orders of the leadership, which no-one on earth could disobey.

"If that's how it is, then do what you want," the woman said. She said she'd meet the boys at the church and that there was no call for them to come to the house to escort her.

Mario said they would print up the obituary notices.

Alexei's mother said there was no call for that as she had no family here.

"He was a martyr," said Mario. "We can't not print an obituary notice, and a poster too."

Mario gave the woman some money in a small envelope, and a smile sketched itself on her face. When she tried to get up to say goodbye, Yalo noticed her swollen legs with their blue veins and her obese body almost bursting through her clothes, which, though loose, seemed tight. But she couldn't get up.

"Please don't get up, madame. There's no need," said Mario.

"What do you mean 'no need'?" said the woman angrily. "Kindly help me up. I'm afraid I may have lost the use of my legs."

Mario put out his hand. She took it and pulled herself towards him. Mario almost fell over, but the woman still couldn't get up. It was as though she'd become stuck to the chair, and her face turned red with effort. Yalo went over and placed one hand under her elbow and took her hand with the other, and they tried. Mario was holding her on one side and Yalo on the other, and the woman had her arms stretched out but didn't budge, as though she had surrendered to gravity and was welded to the chair. Mario asked her to push with him — "Push, madame, push" — and the woman pushed and her groans grew louder — as though she was giving birth, thought Yalo. She pushed and gasped with three young men around her trying to help, but it was useless, and then, all of a sudden, she shot out of the chair and landed on her backside, her legs in the air.

"I'm fine, I'm fine," said Nina the Russian. "Leave me alone. I'm fine."

Yalo doesn't know why he thought that the child must have fallen out between her thighs, but he was overcome by the need to laugh. He let go of the woman's hand and left the front room, swallowing his laughter, and stood waiting for his comrades.

And there, while the boys were bending over the heap of bones, where the weeping was, Yalo swallowed his laughter and stood waiting.

"Pick him up!" screamed Mario.

"How are we supposed to pick him up?" asked Tony, his voice sounding as though it was coming from behind a cloth tied over his mouth.

Mario put his hands under the trousers and shirt in order to lift Alexei as one would a child, but Alexei came to pieces. Mario picked him up and the bones began to fall.

"Leave him, Mario," said Tony in a voice covered with fear and whiteness.

Tony bent over and gathered the bones that had fallen through Mario's arms, and Saeed Mansurati appeared carrying a wooden box like a coffin into which he put Alexei's pieces, and Alexei was carried to headquarters at Georges Armouni Barracks at the School of the Good Shepherd, and there was no smell.

Alexei spent that night in the barracks, in a room that no-one entered. Tony suggested fetching two large candles and putting them on either side of the box as is customary, but everyone ignored his suggestion. Thus Alexei spent his last night in a dark room whose light no-one could be bothered to turn on.

The following morning, Tony brought a real coffin, brown in colour and with raised designs resembling roses, and a notice was stuck on the front of it reading "Martyr Alexei, 1963–1988". The boys carried the coffin to the church of Mar Mitr, where the mother was waiting, swathed in black. The bier was placed in front of the altar between two large lighted candles. When the priest had finished his prayers, the bier was carried to the Strangers' Cemetery, as they call the graveyard that belongs to the church, not to any of the Beirut families, and which is set aside for the poor. It was then that the thing happened that imprinted itself on Yalo's imagination. The coffin was opened so the priest could sprinkle a handful of earth over the corpse, say, "Dust to dust," and give permission for the burial. All the priest could see was a white sheet covering something, so he drew the sheet aside to sprinkle the earth on the face of the dead man, and Alexei's laughing skull popped into view. The priest drew back in terror and the handful of earth fell from his hand, so Yalo closed the coffin and asked the gravedigger to lower it into the grave. At that moment, Nina somehow got between the priest and Mario, saw the skull, screamed, "That's not my son!" and started shouting abuse. The insults, to which there was no end, balled up inside the mouth of the standing woman, her face turned a whitish yellow, and she screamed, "That's not my son! Why are you doing this to me? Where's my son?" Mario tried to calm her, but she lunged at the coffin with the idea of overturning it and scattering its contents. Mario and Tony, however, were able to push her away, and the coffin was lowered into the grave.

Yalo can't remember what happened next. A sort of black veil fell over his eyes, and everything was erased from the screen of his memory. But he heard the story from his comrades. He heard how they tried to carry the woman to her house, but she refused to leave the cemetery, and how later she was taken to a home for the elderly in Atshaneh but refused to live there because the old women spoke only Syriac or Turkish and she didn't know either. After that, she was taken to die in an Orthodox home in Ashrafiyeh, close to the Greek Hospital. The workers at the home were convinced that the woman was insane: she couldn't be Russian, as she claimed, because she couldn't speak a word of Russian, and her son wasn't a saint and hadn't been transformed into a skeleton at the moment of his death, because that was impossible, not to mention that one of the signs of sanctity is that the saint's body is preserved from dissolution after death. So how could Nina claim that her son had cast off his body as a man casts aside his clothes, and been transformed into a clump of bones?

Nina died alone and sad, having herself come to believe the old women in the home who said she was insane when she told everybody her story of her son who'd cast off his body. Nina would try to re-enact the scene and start taking off her clothes and screaming, which would bring the nurses running to calm her down and then restrain her while she tried to convince them to allow her to cast off her body so she could become a saint like her son, Mar Alexei.

Nina believed she was insane and went to the church at the home to ask the young priest who conducted mass every Sunday morning for the members of Beirut's small Russian community to cast the devils out of her, just as the Lord Christ used to do. The priest pushed her aside as he made his way to the sanctuary to begin the dawn prayer that precedes the mass, and Nina fell to the ground and there was a big commotion. Male nurses and porters were summoned and she was carried back to the home, where she died two days later. She was buried in the Strangers' Cemetery, next to her son.

It wasn't the priest who killed her, as Sister Pelagia, who supervised the home, hinted to the mourners. Sister Pelagia hated the White Russians and didn't like their style of chanting, and she used to say that the only acceptable form of prayer was that performed in Greek to Byzantine tunes because that was how they prayed up there in Heaven.

It wasn't the priest's fault. The woman had come to the church to die, and there were no devils to exorcise, so all the Russian priest found to cast out of her was her soul. She went where everyone goes in the end, and that's all there was to it. No-one believed the story of her son the saint, which stated that he had been shot in the chest; the saint had leaned on his comrade Yalo and told him that at the moment of death he would cast off his body because he hated the idea of puffing up like normal corpses, which were devoured by insects and worms; then he had bowed his head and given up the ghost. When his friend bent over to pick him up, he found him not; what he found was a skeleton.

Nina said that when Yalo saw the skeleton he was struck by terror and ran to tell his comrades of the miracle. By the time they arrived, the area had come under fire from the enemy, so they couldn't get to where Alexei had cast off his body and was laid out in the form of a skeleton. So they left him. "And when I found out what had happened, I went and brought him back to the house. His bones were white as snow, as though they'd been washed with soap and water. I went on my own under fire to fetch him, and his comrades refused to go with me because they feared for their lives. I used to think they were the White army. What cowards they turned out to be! I spit on them. I went on my own and brought his bones back so as to preserve his name. His grandfather was an officer in the Tsar's army, and

I'd hoped he'd turn out like him. Damn it, they let his flesh fall from his bones. They left him alone, and no-one beheld the miracle. Even that tall Assyrian boy, Yalo, Gaby's son, the one who himself beheld the wonder, just stood there like a dumb ox. 'Tall and stupid' — what else can one say? Alexei's grandfather told me that miracles like that used to happen in Russia at the time of the civil war. He told me that when an officer died, he'd turn into a skeleton and the bones would be white as snow, and that's what happened to my son. In Russia they'd beatify the officer whose body had fallen away at the moment of his death and proclaim him a saint. But they left Alexei because they're cowards and don't believe in the Holy Trinity. I consigned him to the keeping of the Trinity. His father died when he was young, and I had no-one but the Trinity and that boy."

Sister Pelagia listened to Nina and wanted to believe her, but Nina started making a spectacle of herself by taking off her clothes, and her body, in front of the other old women, so the nun became convinced that she was mad and told her such thoughts were the Devil's work.

Why did Nina return from the old people's home in Atshaneh cursing the Assyrians? Sister Pelagia knew that Nina's son was Assyrian, like all those boys, and that his family came from Mardin. Where had Nina got the story of the grandfather who was an officer in the White Army?

The sister decided that Nina was mad and ordered that she be given sedatives, which put her into the coma that may have caused the obsession with the Devil that led to her demise.

Yalo remembers nothing of what happened at the graveside. The scene was wiped from his eyes and the woman shrouded in a sort of fog. He went home and decided to leave the boys and the war and everything.

At the beginning, Yalo saw himself as a hero. The war had come to teach him the secrets of life, or so he thought at the training camp where he became a billy goat. He and his comrades from the poor of the Assyrian quarter became lords of the streets. Yalo had never understood much about the complications and twists and turns of the war that made talk about them seem like straw. He believed he was defending the existence of a people who had melted into the darkness of history, as the *kohno* would say, describing the never-ending migrations that had led him from Ein Ward to Beirut. "We walked in the darkness of history and we shall remain in darkness until the sun of justice rises." When Yalo asked him what the "sun of justice" was, the *kohno* replied that it was Christ. "We are waiting, my son, for the kingdom of Christ, and He has said that His kingdom is not of this world."

Yalo didn't understand Lebanese politics and the language of the war, but he did feel that he was a stranger to it all. He saw his shadow emerging from the darkness of history and living with his comrades, most of whom had come from the area around El Jezireh in Syria to die in defence of a homeland that wasn't theirs.

Yalo would have liked to forget about the war and treat it like a game. He made out that he was acting in a film, and when he took part in a battle, he would feel like a hero. After a time, however, the feelings of heroism disappeared, and when he heard his mother's words, mimicking the *kohno*, about the pointlessness of the war, he felt sad. "We must be yeast. We don't make war, my son. The yeast doesn't fight with the dough. On the contrary, it enters into it and leavens it so that it may become bread. Give up war and go to school. You must become a *kohno* like your grandfather."

Yalo feared the image he saw in his mother's eyes: himself transformed into a miniature of his grandfather the *kohno*. He was afraid of the white beard and the boredom. No, it wasn't the bones covered in shredded clothes that made him frightened, it was the boredom. War becomes monotonous when it becomes real. The idea of war is seductive and gives you feelings of heroism, but war itself is a tedious and wearisome thing.

Saeed Mansurati dreamt of becoming a singer. Ah, the pity of his disappearance! No-one ever found his bones. This was why Yalo agreed to go to Paris. He beheld his own phantom in Paris before he ever became a phantom of the Ballona night with its pine trees and lovers' sighs. When he found himself in prison, with the sheets of white paper in front of him, the whole thing seemed like a joke. He hated writing, and he'd never liked composition homework, and now he had to write a long short story entitled "The Story of My Life"!

Yalo wasn't an outstanding student at St Sawirus's. He was ordinary at everything. He studied, passed and moved up from class to class, but he hadn't got what his grandfather called the "flame of the spirit". He was outstanding at Arabic Language because of the books his mother brought home and never read herself, but that was it. All the same, Yalo didn't hate school. Because he was tall, he'd sit at the back, and the teacher, *Malfono* Haleem, would say he was as beautiful as a girl.

"Me a girl, *malfono*? That's weird," said Yalo in the head-master's office, to which the *malfono* would often invite him to give him books to read. The *malfono* placed his hands over his student's large eyes and told him he had a mouth like cherries.

In those days, Yalo didn't understand sex, but he saw some-thing burning in the eyes of the *malfono*, who taught them Arabic and Arithmetic. It wasn't true what Saeed Mansurati had said, that they all passed through Haleem's hands, that he could never get enough. All Yalo remembered were the *malfono*'s hands on his eyes and lips. But the boys said something else: they spoke of the *malfono*'s cunning and would trace circles on their thighs with their fingers.

"Ah, Haleem! Good old Haleem!" Tony would say, pouring himself a glass of arak. "I swear no-one had fingers as clever as his!" And he'd take hold of his penis and pull on it, repeating "I swear there's no-one like him." The strange thing was that they seemed to think *Malfono* Haleem had had sex with all of them.

Yalo's memory tells him something different. Things didn't go beyond innocent touching. The *malfono* would sit behind his desk and tell his pupil to come nearer so he could show him his spelling mistakes, and when the pupil approached the table, the *malfono* would ask him to come round next to his chair, and the *malfono* would place his hand on the boy's thigh.

"I swear there was no-one like him," Tony would yell. "Where are you now, Haleem? Where are you now?"

"Don't say 'Haleem'," Saeed Mansurati would say. "We all called him '*Malfono* Haleem'. Ah, how sexy he was! The way he played with his hand was amazing. I've never felt like that with anyone else."

"What did you feel?" asked Yalo.

"Listen to him! He pretends he doesn't know. He must have done the same thing to you," says Saeed, laughing.

Yalo doesn't remember anything.

"You were the girl," said Saeed. "He used to say you were prettier than a girl, and once, I swear this is true, once while he was stroking me, he started talking about you and how beautiful you were, and that was probably the time I got horniest."

"Because of me?!" asked Yalo.

"Yeah, you. We all passed through Haleem's hands. He'd say it was how the philosophers discovered life. It was what Plato did with Socrates and Ahmad Shawqi with Muhammad Abdel Wahhab, what all the geniuses did."

Malfono Haleem would say that Yalo was more beautiful than a girl and reach for his hips, taking the boy to the ecstasy that welled up inside him. They called him the "mellifluous *malfono*", "because pleasure flowed mellifluously from his hands," as Tony put it.

But Yalo doesn't remember anything, or what he remembers is that he was more beautiful than a girl, a statement he attributed to his mother.

Yalo experienced small adventures with girls that resembled instants of stolen pleasure. He discovered a connection between the stealing of pleasure in war and his robberies at Ballona because in both cases he would feel he was plucking a flower curled up at the top of his thighs. He would caress the tip of his flower and recall the sensation that *Malfono* Haleem's fingers inscribed on his lips and his neck and his thighs.

Why now?

Why does the *malfono*'s ghost come to him as though to awaken him from his death and restore him to a life Shireen stole from him and crushed beneath her feet?

The feeling itself – the feeling of being curled up and bent like a bow – that feeling began with Elvira and then continued with all the other women; even his "randarizing" was a part of the same bow that was pulling him towards a kind of death. And when he thought of the flower curling up on itself between his thighs, he would remember Maroun and see the pain radiating from his eyes, and he would bend over Elvira and discover the pain traced on her white thighs.

"War erases names," he would tell the interrogator later. No, he didn't say that. He said it was the war, and he hadn't asked for names.

"And in the forest?" asked the interrogator.

"No, sir. Not there, ever. I never once asked for a name."

"What about Shireen?!"

"Shireen's different."

"Didn't you make her get down on her knees, threaten her with the rifle and ask her her name before raping her?"

"Me?"

"Yes, you. Who else?"

"Me?!!

"Why did you make her get down on her knees and ask her her name? Why did you rape her under threat of force?"

Yalo doesn't know where the interrogator could have got that story from. He wanted to say that when he was with Shireen he forgot the pain, but he didn't dare. How could he talk about the pain that gushed from his guts? And about his flower that had wilted under torture? How could he talk about his grandfather *Kohno* Afram, who would sit opposite him and open the Gospel and read from the Apostle Paul — "a thorn in my side" — and then close the book and say, "Pay attention, my son: the thorn is sin, and sin hurts. Beware of your thorn."

Yalo didn't know how a man was supposed to pay attention to his thorn and also beware of his thorn when the thorn moved every day between his thighs.

"Maroun was the one who got me going," he told Tony while they were guarding Georges Armouni Barracks at night and talking about women, and Tony was boasting about his adventures, lying and believing himself.

He told Tony about Maroun. After chewing on his cigarette

and taking a long drag into the deepest part of his lungs, he said that Maroun, the son of Salma the cook, had showed him his thorn. Yalo was ten when he went with Maroun to the chicken pen in the garden at the cook's house. Maroun sat down on a stone, took out his penis, grasped it and started repeating the name Mary. "For Mary. Come on. Get it out and join me." Yalo was astonished at the size of Maroun's member, which was long, thin and uncircumcised. Maroun, who was fourteen, held his long thorn and pleasure spread across his face. He took it in his hand and jerked on it, yelling out the name of his neighbour, the widow Mary. Then he stopped and looked at Yalo with contempt. "What's the matter? Scared? Show me your willy." Yalo undid his zipper and took out his thing. It was small, fat and stiff. Maroun looked at it and said, "Still small. Don't worry, it'll get bigger soon. Come on, join me, for Mary." Yalo joined him. He sat down on a stone facing him, started jerking on his penis, and felt the pain. The pain may have come from the chickens, because the sight of the black hens standing terrified in the corner of the pen disgusted Yalo. But Maroun didn't stop. He was yelling the name Mary and moaning and moving his shoulders. The name started to get faster and with it the movement of his hand, and then Maroun went slack. His hand was filled with sticky white and he yelled at his companion, urging him on. To Maroun's shouts of the black widow's name, the pain erupted in Yalo's hand. "For her," yelled Maroun. "For her," said Yalo, his hand speeding up. Then something suddenly erupted from within him and his hand started to convulse to the rhythm coming from his penis, but the convulsions were beating against a thick wall that wouldn't let them through. They went off in bursts in Yalo's hand and then were extinguished, and the white fluid didn't come out.

Maroun laughed and started singing, "*Qaddishat aloho, qaddishat hayltono, qaddishat lomoyuto*." He told Yalo not to worry because he was still young, and when he got older he'd be watering women's bellies with his fluid, which contained his soul. "Man shudders because the soul is there, in the middle of the white," said Maroun.

Yalo waited for his soul, and eventually it came to him. The waiting caused the pain that would be his companion in his relationship with his soul, for the thorn would be transformed into a flower but would go back to its thorniness whenever the white fluid began to erupt, and would be walled in by pain.

"My thorn hurts," said Yalo as he stood alone in front of the mirror in the bathroom. He beheld Mary, swathed in black and carrying her son, making her way to the house of Edward the taxi driver. He took his thorn in his hand and screamed in pain. The woman hadn't taken off her black dress since the unexpected death of her husband, the young man who'd worked on the electricity grid and suffered a stroke with which the entire Assyrian quarter of Museitbeh reverberated. He'd been forty and Mary, his wife, twenty-nine. They'd had their first child, Najeeb, six months before the man died.

"Heart failure," said the *kohno* to his grandson.

"How can a heart fail?" asked Yalo.

"It can stop speaking," said the *kohno*.

"Stop speaking?" asked Yalo.

"The heart speaks by beating. A man's heart keeps on beating and never sleeps, but when the heart does sleep, it means the man is dead," said the *kohno*.

Yalo felt the pulse at his neck and asked his grandfather if he was afraid of death.

"There is no death," said the grandfather. "We call death

'slumber', meaning 'sleep'. The dead man sleeps. He casts off his body and sleeps, and then he wakes up, up above, with Abu Eesa."

"Who's Abu Eesa?" asked Yalo.

"Abu Eesa is God, my son, the father of Jesus. Christ is the son of God, which is why we call God Abu Eesa."

Edmond's heart went to sleep, leaving behind his young wife, who swathed herself in black and took her child, Najeeb, in her arms.

The wife, who found herself with no-one to provide for her and no-one to turn to, went to work for the tobacco company rolling cigarettes, or so they said, and became the mistress of Edward the taxi driver, who related the wonders she performed.

She would knock on the door. Edward, who would have just prepared a table groaning with good things, most notably a bottle of arak and fried whitebait, would open it and she would drink, eat and dance. She wore an Oriental Dancer's costume and danced to the songs of Umm Kulthoum, and Edward knelt and sang.

The image of Mary engraved itself on the minds of the boys of the quarter as that of an Oriental Dancer coiling to music like a snake and never tiring – an image attributable to the stories Edward told in front of Abboudi's shop after he'd had a beer with the boys and was discussing horseracing.

She would come carrying her son in her arms and, before eating or drinking, would put a little arak on her finger and give it to her son to lick, and the boy would go to sleep and she'd put him in the bedroom. She'd start drinking and her body would begin to radiate light. Edward recounted everything. He said that at the beginning she'd refused to take her black dress off and had slept with him wearing her clothes. Then little by little she'd started to feel comfortable, "and then she undressed, boys. Ah God, what whiteness! She was wearing a red blouse and red brassiere, and said she was allergic to black. She was all red and white, and it was time to dance. God, how beautiful she was! White as milk, white sifted with white, white on white – and I'd melt. Then she left. God, I miss her! I told her from the beginning that I couldn't. The truth is, I was afraid. It's true I'd decided I'd stay a bachelor, but then I said, 'Why not?' I don't know what happened to me, but I thought I'd marry her. Then I said, 'No, I can't.' It must have been her who murdered her husband. Who could tame a filly like that? I'd never seen anything like her. I only had to approach her to feel the water rise up inside her. A well! I swear to God, she had a well inside her that never ran dry. God, how delicious she was! But I got scared. She told me that everyone knew about us and we had to make things decent, meaning we had to get married. I told her I couldn't. I was afraid she'd murder me the way she'd murdered her husband. A hundred times I asked her how he'd died, and a hundred times she didn't answer. No-one, lads, ever saw the man in the living room. They said he died in the living room after asking for a cup of coffee and some water. We ran to the house when we heard the screaming and found ourselves in the bedroom with the dead man stretched out on the bed and covered with a white sheet. He was wearing a white shirt and no-one saw if he was wearing anything else. Mary was standing next to the bed with her hair in a mess. When the doctor came, he ordered us out of the room except for Mary. One minute later, he came out and said, "Heart failure. Long life to you all," and looked like he was smiling. What does that mean? It means it had nothing to do with a cup of coffee. A hundred times I asked her, and she'd smile like the doctor and refuse to answer. The arak would make her belch, and something like fire would come out of her chest. What does that mean? It means – that's right – that he died because he couldn't cope with such beauty. And you expect me to marry her and die?!"

The stories attributed to the taxi driver came after Mary and her son had left for an unknown destination. It was said that she'd gone to the village of Choueifat, where she lived in a hut close to the tobacco factory. Whatever the truth of the situation was, Edward's stories fascinated Yalo and his comrades.

Mary's fascination derived from her whiteness, made even more beautiful by a mole on her neck – a woman in her thirties, her white face sprinkled with freckles down to her throat, of medium height, her long black hair put up like a hat, carrying a child and walking, lust keeping pace beside her.

Yalo and Maroun and all the boys of the quarter continued to masturbate in her honour even though she'd disappeared from the neighbourhood. Maroun would spurt his white, and Yalo would do it with the thorn that had sprouted between his thighs, screaming out her name and the pain.

Beginning with Mary, Yalo looked differently at women. He became haunted by sex. He'd see a woman walking down the street and he'd imagine that she'd just got out of bed. He'd see her naked and next to her a man with obscure features and closed eyes. Those closed eyes had sex with every woman in the streets of Beirut. Yalo's imagination also started taking him to faraway places, where he could no longer distinguish between young women and old ones. In his imagination all of them became naked women lying on the bed of his closed eyes. Even his mother came into the picture. He would see Gaby, her hair up in a *kokina*, sitting at the sewing machine in her pale yellow shirt while the tailor Elias El Shami hovered round her and made love to her. All Yalo could see was a world clotted with desire, as though all the women were one woman with multiple heads. He would be walking in the street or playing with other boys and when a woman appeared everything would be wiped away and all that would remain was the image of white.

And when the white erupted in his hand, Yalo was alone, and it wasn't Mary, it was Elvira. On that spring morning, Yalo had woken up to find himself awash in fluid and with an idiotic smile on his lips. Years later, when Shireen asked him why he was smiling, he would answer that love made the lover an idiot, and ask her when she would be smitten with idiocy like him.

When had he said that to her? And when did she answer that he made her laugh? And when had he felt an overwhelming love for her that devoured him from the inside and made him masturbate before seeing her, so that he would come to her transparent and pure with love?

Here, cast down alone and cut off, it is difficult for Yalo to work out how to organize his memory. It is difficult because things come to him all together, the images running together in his head and the times running into one another in his consciousness, as though he was an old man. The *kohno* said to him once, as he trembled over his papers, that the last stage of life was a long dream, and that Mar Afram the Assyrian had awakened from the dream of death when he had succeeded in transforming his body into clay and become like our grandfather Abraham before God breathed His spirit into him.

"And how did they bury Mar Afram?" Yalo would ask.

"They broke him into pieces. They couldn't bury him until they had broken him into little pieces, and that was how they lowered him into his grave."

. . .

"And I'm the same," said his grandfather. "When life is coming to an end, a man becomes like baked clay, and he can't distinguish real from unreal and past from present any more, and he becomes like a little child."

The grandfather smiled as he told his grandson about how Mar Afram's body had turned to baked clay, and Yalo saw the silliness traced on the face covered with white hair, and he saw the clay, which extended to the two hands that emerged from the folds of the black robe. Old age had left its mark on the grandfather's hands by turning them into clay fired by the sun, with black spots and thin fingers, and by making his bones an underlying clayey layer, and giving him the smell of earth, and when rheumatic pains started to torment the grandfather and stiffness began to afflict his hands and feet, Yalo was frightened, and saw the grandfather as an earthenware statue, and started imagining himself breaking the clay body to put it into the coffin.

Yalo's nights became filled with his baked clay obsession. He saw his grandfather in multiple forms. He saw him as a huge corpse, inflated with earth fermented by the sun. Then he saw him as little pieces strewn across the bed. Or he would see himself holding a huge mallet and hammering the clay body and smashing it, blood flowing from its hands and clothes.

When he stood over Alexei, of whom nothing remained but his white bones and shredded clothes, Yalo saw his grandfather's face as he expressed his disgust at how his daughter fed his grandson bits of raw sheep's liver to cure his anaemia. The grandfather would hold his nose against the smell of the blood on Yalo's lips, Yalo himself being incapable of resisting the hands of his mother as she cornered his lip with a morsel of raw liver accompanied by fresh mint and onions.

The grandfather would leave the table repeating his theory

about the grave: "A man's belly isn't a grave," the grandfather would say. "Why, my daughter, do you do that to the boy? A man's belly shouldn't be a grave for dead animals. Man is made in the image of God. What savagery is this? We kill animals and bury them in our bellies and become like graves walking the roads. A man becomes a big graveyard. The stomach is the grave, and the head and eyes are the grave markers. And then, when a man dies, the grave that's in his belly eats him. A man's belly becomes his grave. When man eats the animals he's killed, he's just building the grave in his belly. The bodies of the saints don't rot and the worms don't eat them because they don't eat the flesh of the dead. What is man? A graveyard?"

The grandfather would talk of graves, and Yalo would imagine his belly as a grave for animals and cry at the sight of his mother's implacable hand that had had no mercy on the little sheep whose liver had become little pieces she crammed into the mouth of her emaciated son. At the age of eight, Yalo went on strike against meat, and the mother had to play tricks on her son, cooking the meat with bulghur and lying to him, saying it was potato rissoles. Yalo lived off the faked food, or so his mother told him later on, until he started going to the Sanharib Club and doing athletics and body-building, at which point he started eating only meat and became interested in food only for the protein he needed to overcome his emaciation and build up his muscles.

The war made Yalo forget about body-building, but it didn't make him forget his grandfather's stories about the stomach-grave, or his life with the Kurds and the sight of the sacrificial animals hung at the entrance to the house, and the smell of blood as the mullah lifted his robe and stepped over the blood and picked out the pieces of meat, which he would eat raw, his women and children around him.

"I used to eat like them, attacking the slaughtered animal and reaching for the blood, and I was always hungry. My brothers, that is to say his sons, called me the 'Christian woman's son' and stole the food from in front of me, and I was always deathly afraid of hunger. When I ran away . . . no, I didn't run away, my uncle came and offered to buy me, but my dad, which is to say the mullah, refused to sell me. He spat on the ground and said I was free to do as I liked, and then suddenly I found myself with my uncle in Qamishli, which is where I felt I'd made a mistake, so I ran away to Beirut and worked as a tile-maker, and then the call came and I became a *kohno*. I was kneeling in front of His Grace the Metropolitan and he was blessing me, and I saw my whole life. Don't they say that at the moment of death a man sees his whole life like in a film? Beneath the hand of Our Lord the Metropolitan I saw my whole life, and I saw the blood. I saw the sheep and the calves hung up in front of me, and I began to weep. I felt blood falling from my eyes in place of tears, and everything tasted salty, and I saw the calves weeping. The calf, before being slaughtered, weeps like a little child. I felt as though I was being slaughtered. I finished the prayer and remained kneeling. I was supposed to go on into the sanctuary and take part in the mass, but I couldn't get up. I felt my legs freeze, so I stayed kneeling and weeping. Then the metropolitan, God rest his soul, took hold of my shoulders and said, 'Afram,' and I'd forgotten that they'd named me Afram – my name is Habeel Abyad – so I said, 'Who is Afram?' and he said, 'What's wrong with you, my son? Come on, stand up. Your name has become Afram by the power of the Spirit. You must forget your old name. Spit on Satan and get up.' I got up, and that day I decided to stop eating meat. My wife would trick me, like your mother used to trick you, and I wasn't master of my own fate till your grandmother died, God have mercy on her dust. She would mix the meat with anything there was and tell me, 'This is vegetarian,' and I, simpleton that I was, believed her. Then I realized, because after she died the smell of my body changed and the rankness left me, and I decided that I had to become baked clay and eat only of the plants of the earth. The basic food must be herbage, and the most important herbage is *khubz al-arab*, 'the bread of the Arabs', which is to say *khubbayza*, 'little bread' or mallows. Eat plants and nothing else. Why have you become like this, my son? When you were small, you were like a saint. Now you've turned into a monster and your belly into a graveyard."

Alexei became his own graveyard, and all that was left of him was a clump of bones and shredded clothes around which gathered the terrified exclamations of his comrades.

After the Alexei night, Yalo saw himself as a grave. He saw his death as screams mingling with the gnawing that ravaged his lower parts, and he felt that death was a mercy. The laughter of the officer holding the bamboo cane was like the echo of voices coming from beyond death. Yalo tried to scream, but his voice came out as a faint yowl, and then the giddiness took him into the quiet. There, in the silence, he licked his wastes, unaware of what he was doing, as though he had started to eat himself before going to his grave.

That day, Yalo confessed to everything.

What did he say? He no longer remembered, but he heard his voice shaking as he knelt and told the officer that he was ready to kiss his shoes. He bent over the shoes and kissed them and didn't see how the muscles of the officer's face convulsed with self-esteem and pride. The officer was savouring his victory over this man who lay in front of him, transformed into a clump of shit and urine.

"You're shit," said the officer. "Did you hear me? I asked you what you are."

. . .

"Answer the question."

"I'm shit," said Yalo.

The officer's bursts of laughter stretched out in the emptiness of the room with its rotten smell and started to feel like the stinging lashes of the whip that rained down on Yalo's back.

Yalo discovered that a man is capable of everything. That was what Mme Randa had taught him. With her he'd discovered his body as limbs detachable for pleasure. Then she'd taught him kissing. No, kissing was the first lesson he'd been taught by Elvira, who married Eesa, the director of the Banco di Roma branch in Hamra Street, even though she loved Yalo. The women of the war, though, had made him forget that kiss till Mme Randa came along and randarized his lips.

Elvira told him she loved him but was going to marry Eesa because he was rich. And Yalo didn't mourn. It's true he loved this girl who was five years older than him, but when she said she was going to get married, he felt as though he'd heard the same thing somewhere before and that he'd been waiting for that moment for a long time. He looked at Elvira with sad eyes and then lifted her skirt to cast one last caress on her brown thighs.

After Elvira, Yalo forgot about love in his immersion in the war and its women. Where did they come from? And why was the love like killing? And why did everything taste of wood?

The first kiss was at the government school for girls. Yalo and his comrades would ogle the girls there as they played volleyball. They wore short shorts which left their thighs exposed. The boys' eyes sneaked through the screen door, causing the convulsion that creased trousers and making the thorn that had to be broken off stick out. Elvira, with her polished brown thighs, used to jump behind the screen. Elvira taught Yalo everything there. She'd return to the Assyrian quarter with him, looking over her shoulder as though she was afraid. He would wait for her every Saturday afternoon behind the school door, and when games were over she'd put on her short dark-blue skirt and find him waiting for her, and they'd go from Raml El Zarif, where her school was, to her house in the Assyrian quarter. She'd take Yalo's arm and say, "You're five years younger than me. I'll really catch it if Aunt Gaby finds out I've snagged you!" When he told her that he loved her, she patted him on the back and said, "Go play with girls your own age" and squeezed his elbow, and his thorn lit up with desire and he tried to kiss her neck. "Not in the street," she said, and in front of her house she invited him to come up, and he hesitated. "Come up. I want to show you something," she said. He went up the stairs with her and found the house was empty. He sat in the living room and she asked him to wait because she had to take a shower. After the shower, she appeared in a billowing white dress and sat down next to him and kissed him on the lips, so he bent towards her and put his lips on hers and pulled, imagining that he was doing what they do in films. Elvira pulled away and said, "Not like that. Close your eyes and don't move." He closed them and felt something clambering around his lips, which he pressed together again.

"I told you, not like that. Sit still and don't move."

She asked him to close his eyes, so he closed them, and her lips started to climb his face. Then he felt a lip going in between his and the taste began to steal into his mouth, and he felt her tongue on his tongue and began to feel dizzy. The lips withdrew and he heard Elvira's voice telling him to open his eyes and kiss her the way she'd kissed him. She closed her eyes and leaned back against the sofa, and his lips approached her face and started slowly climbing up it. They reached her lips and he tried to insert his upper lip between them, but he couldn't. He felt as though he was about to eat the two red-coloured lips, opened his own, took her lips inside them and felt her hand pushing him back. He didn't withdraw, though. He took her whole mouth and then felt with his tongue, and the lips started opening and entered into the game of the kiss. He kissed her and wasn't satisfied till the pain started spreading through his lips, while Elvira awaited his kisses, her head resting on her hand and her eyes closed, inviting him to the banquet.

"Ouch!" said Yalo. "My lips hurt."

She got up and said she was going to make tea. Yalo stood up and hugged her, and at that moment, while his body clung tightly to hers, the fluid spurted out, and Yalo shook with the pleasure that came before he had begun. He felt the pain of his thorn and continued to cling to the girl, who whispered to him begging him to back away a bit.

"Please. Please. My dress'll get wet."

He backed away and saw the spots on his trousers and shadows of the fluid on her dress. She kissed him quickly and asked him to go before her mother came home and saw him in that state.

"What am I supposed to do?" he asked.

"You don't have to do anything," she said. "Walk around a little before you go home and your trousers will dry."

Walking became a compulsory sport with Elvira. He'd accompany her to her house and hug her behind the gate, then he'd walk for a whole hour to dry the fluid before he went home.

Everything changed when Elvira took him to a discotheque called Quartier Latin, in the White Sands district near the Egyptian Embassy. There they sat in the dark and danced the tango, and while he was dancing with her he felt his thorn and she told him, "No. Not that way," and went back with him to the dark corner where they'd been sitting. She asked him to undo his zipper and took the thorn in her hands and put it between her thighs, and there in the dark he saw her. He saw the short shorts and the girl who jumped with the volleyball, and his heart opened and he wanted to scream. She put her hand over his mouth and told him to come. "Come, my darling," she said. When he heard the word *come*, everything exploded and his white blood went everywhere over her thighs. She took a Kleenex and wiped off the gushing fluid. "What's all this, big boy?" she asked. She wiped the thorn and put it back in its place inside his trousers.

Yalo picked up the glass of wine in front of him to have a drink, but she said, "No. Not now. Give me your hand." She took his hand and put it under her skirt and started moving and moaning and asked him to kiss her ear.

"No, not like that. Take it between your lips."

He took her earlobe between his lips and licked it and heard Elvira's stifled cry, but he kept on moving his finger.

"That's enough," she said. "Take your finger out. You're hurting me."

He withdrew his hand and drank the glass of red wine at one go, and he told her that he loved her: "I love you more than anything in the world."

"You're too young for love," she said. "We can have fun now, and later on we'll see."

They started going to the discotheque every week. She'd finish sports and he'd wait for her at the Café Jandoul. She'd go home, bathe and come back, and they'd go to the darkness of the dance club.

One time he practised that type of love with her in the light, on the day she informed him of her decision to marry Eesa.

"But he's a lot older than you," he said.

"And I'm older than you," she said.

She asked him to put his trousers back on and go home. He went home without having to walk the streets; he went home aware of his tongue. That day he'd kissed her breasts and licked them all over and discovered the map of her body, but she left him to get married and he went home to his mirror, trying to remember the black widow and burning with the flames of jealousy over a man he didn't know.

Yalo came to his senses in the presence of the shoes. He put his hand to his crotch to make sure that his privates were still there and that the cat hadn't devoured them. He bent over and kissed the shoes to announce his readiness to confess everything.

"Do you confess to rape?" asked the officer.

"I do."

"And that you and your gang were Israeli agents?"

"I do."

"And that you took your orders from Abu Hamid El Naddaf?"

"I do."

"And that you placed explosives in Antalyas and Ashrafiyeh?"

"I do."

"And that you personally were in charge of the network in Beirut and Mount Lebanon?"

"I do."

"Excellent. Now that you've confessed everything, we'll transfer you to the prison, and I'm sure the court will take your cooperation into account and will find mitigating circumstances."

"Thank you, sir."

"Sign your statement and you can start the real sessions."

"There are still more sessions, sir? I've confessed to everything the way you wanted."

Yalo said that he wanted to confess everything now, to be done. He said, "Let's get it over with," and tasted rubber in his mouth and said he was thirsty and hungry.

"I'm thirsty, sir, and hungry. May I have a drink?"

"You ate everything and you're still hungry?"

"I'm hungry, but whatever you say."

"You may eat and drink," said the interrogator, "but first you have to sign these papers. We'll read you your confessions and if you agree to them, you'll sign them and then everything will be fine."

"I'll sign whatever you want, there's no need to read them. I'll sign everything."

A voice began reading. Yalo heard his name and his father's name and his mother's name. He heard about Ballona and Shireen and Emile Shaheen and about the explosives gang. He heard the names of his victims and nodded his head yes.

The officer bent over him, gave him some papers and said the real sessions would be the ones he would spend on his own, because he had to write the story of his life from beginning to end without leaving anything out.

In the cell, Yalo was incapable of writing. He felt as though he had fallen into a well and could no longer breathe, for after the exhausting interrogation sessions that had ended with his confessing everything, he could no longer remember. Also, he didn't know how to write, so what was he supposed to write? In the Paris metro, he had written a large sign and sat next to it like a beggar, beneath the slaps of the eyes of the passers-by. There he had felt the savagery of language. French words whose meanings he didn't understand rained down on his head like the lashes of a whip. He yearned for his mother, and he yearned for someone with whom he could speak Arabic, the only language he knew. In the metro, Yalo cried when M. Michel Salloum spoke to him. He cried because he heard Arabic and smelled Lebanon. Here, however, in solitary confinement, he felt he didn't know how to write.

They read him his confessions in formal Arabic, and the tall, thin young man signed in colloquial. The first time, he signed his name ܝܠ. The interrogator took the piece of paper and raised his eyebrows. He raised them again at the Jounieh police station and then again at the prison, where he visited Yalo a number of times to ask him to redo what he'd written. This meant that things weren't going according to plan, and that the interrogation was going to take Yalo off course and into further torture.

"What's that?" the interrogator screamed.

"It's my signature."

"What? Are you trying to make fools of us? You think you're smart?"

When Yalo explained his signature, the interrogator exploded angrily. "What? You've come here to teach us Syriac? You said you didn't know Syriac."

"I don't, but that's the way I sign my name."

"No, this won't do," said the interrogator, looking round and raising his eyebrows. This convinced Yalo that torture was on the agenda so he said he was sorry for his unintentional mistake and ready to sign any way they wanted him to sign. The interrogator ordered the clerk to rewrite the last page so Yalo could sign it in Arabic.

Yalo took the new sheet of paper with trembling fingers and

signed it "Yalo". Once again, the interrogator cursed him.

"What's this shit? Why don't you write your real name?"

"That is my name," said Yalo.

The interrogator couldn't think what to do until in the end he asked the clerk to write the accused's full name and, next to it, "styled 'Yalo'".

"Take him away," said the interrogator.

They took him up to a lorry that took him to an isolation cell. This was a small room, four metres square, with an iron-grilled aperture high in the wall, an iron bed with three woollen blankets on the right, and, in the left-hand corner, a green Formica table and a white plastic chair. On the table had been placed sheets of white paper, a fountain pen and an inkwell, and it was Yalo's assignment to write, on this table, the story of his life.

Had he been a poet, he would have written that he had drowned in the well of words and embraced night, and that his ink had become blacker than night.

Had he been a novelist, he would have written his memoirs to a consistent rhythm, and called them *Ein Ward*, starting with his grandfather as a young boy and how he lived through the massacre of his village in Tur Abdin and how his feet had led him to Qamishli and from there to Beirut, and how he'd been transformed from tile-maker into *kohno*, and from someone who knew no Syriac to someone who sought to revive a dying language in his own mouth.

Had Yalo been a storyteller, he would have sat in the prison and told of Yalo who fought like no-one else ever had, who was a knight and a hero, and who then joined the Migration to the West that his grandfather had begun, and emigrated to France, whence he had returned to become a master lover, who, like all lovers, had been deceived.

Had he been.

But he wasn't.

Yalo was a young man trying to read in the whiteness of the paper his own story, which he didn't know how to tell, and his language, which he didn't know how to write, and his memory, which he didn't know how to articulate. He beheld himself as a wild ass lost in the plains.

Hadn't his grandfather the *kohno* told him that Ismail was the grandfather of the Arabs, the Assyrians, the Christians and the Muslims?

"'God hears.' 'Isma' Il' means 'God hears', and God hears only the language of tears. We are the children of Ismail. We were baptised in tears. Christ came and took us to the baptism of water.

"'He shall be a father unto a people, and he shall dwell in the plain like a wild ass'," said the *kohno*. "Remember this verse from the Old Testament, from the Book of Genesis, and commit it to memory, for you too are a grandson of Ismail, and you too are going to be a wild ass."

Yalo writes about the wild ass. Then he tears up the sheets of paper and starts writing again, and drowns in the whiteness of the page, which rises up before him like a vast desert.

My name is Yalo; Daniel Jalao, son of Georges Jalao and known as Yalo; from the Assyrian quarter in the district of Museitbeh, Beirut. My mother is Gaby, Gabrielle Habeel Abyad. I am an only child, with no brothers or sisters. I lived with my mother and my grandfather. I don't know my father, and my grandmother died before I was born, which means that I don't remember her at all. My father I don't know in any way because he went abroad when my mother was seven months pregnant. That's what they told me. They said he emigrated to Sweden, and that my grandfather threw him out when he found out he wasn't Assyrian. That's all I know. I know that my grandfather *Kohno* Afram Abyad agreed to my mother marrying him to solve a big problem. My mother was in love with a married man twenty years older than her. She worked for him at his tailoring shop, and his name was Elias El Shami, and he's a well-known tailor. I don't know him well. He visited us a few times at home and took me on outings with my mother, and I remember his spectacles and his eyebrows, which were thick and grey. I was afraid of him and his black spectacles. Then his visits suddenly stopped after my grandfather discovered that my mother had gone back to her relationship with him. My mother swore to my grandfather that I wasn't the son of the tailor but of Georges Jalao. My grandfather didn't believe her, but what difference does it make? Whether this one or that one was my father doesn't change anything in my life because my real father was my grandfather the *kohno*.

My mother married my father when she was twenty. In other words, my mother is only twenty-one years older than me, and I love her a lot. My grandfather found out that Georges Jalao was a liar, and when my father decided to emigrate, my grandfather refused to let my mother go with him. He told him "Go and get yourself set up, and then send for your wife. Your wife's pregnant and has to look after herself." So he went and never came back. Some people said he didn't go to Sweden but back to Aleppo, because he's from Aleppo, from a family that was rich and then became poor. They used to work as joiners, and then the craft declined. My father came to Beirut and worked in the shop of Saleem Rizq the Blind. Saleem was a friend of my grandfather, but my father stole from him. That's how my grandfather found out that my father was a Greek Catholic from Aleppo, like *Khawaja* Rizq, and a thief and a liar. When my grandfather would get angry at me, he'd say I was turning out like my father and that I'd grow up to be a thief like him and that I'd better go to Aleppo and look for my roots, because I didn't have any worth mentioning. Then he'd be sorry and tell me I was his only son and that

God hadn't granted him a son; he'd granted him two daughters, my mother and her sister, Sara, who married Jacques Kassab and went with him to Sweden, and my grandfather said that there they spoke Suryoyo in the streets and they had radio and television in Suryoyo, but none of that mattered because a language outside its own land dies. And that God had made up for it with me. He'd sent my grandfather Georges Jalao so that the boy would come, and he'd been struck dumb like the prophet Zachariah before my mother gave birth. He went three days without speaking, and then, when my mother was in labour, my grandfather spoke and said it would be a boy, and that he'd seen the prophet Daniel in a dream, which was why he named me Daniel and I came to be called Yalo.

My full name is Daniel Georges Jalao, born 1961 in Beirut. I studied at the St Sawirus School in the Assyrian quarter in the district of Museitbeh. In the summers I worked at *Khawaja* Saleem's shop. Then the war began. We had to move to the Ein El Roummaneh district, Mreiyeh quarter, and I went to school in Atshaneh. Then I trans-ferred to the Progress School, near the Centre Mirna Chalouhi in Sin El Feel. In 1979, I joined the Lebanese Forces and became a fighter, and I stayed a fighter till the end of 1989. I took a number of military training courses in the Dahr El Wahsh area, but I didn't go to Israel for training because I didn't qualify for the parachutists' course – I was too tall. I am very tall, 191 centimetres. Some of the boys from our battalion, which was called the "Billy Goats", went there and trained, it's true, but not me. My friend Tony Ateeq took me to the training session and told me that *Khawaja* Nabeel Afram was enlisting boys from the Assyrian community and that we'd have control of the largest barracks in Ashrafiyeh, which was the Georges Armouni Barracks.

In the war, I got to know lots of the kids, especially Assyrian boys who came from Syria and whose motive in joining in the war was to get Lebanese nationality. We fought, and a large number of us died, and we stole a little, as everyone does who fights, but we were afraid, especially the Syrian boys because their dialect wasn't Lebanese, and there was a danger they'd get caught at our checkpoints, and this took up a lot of the time of Mario, the battalion leader.

Towards the end of 1989, I was in despair about everything. Tony Ateeq was the one who had the idea of emigrating to France. Tony and I stole the barracks money box and ran away to France. We travelled by sea from Jounieh to Cyprus, and from Cyprus we took a plane to Paris. It was the first time in my life that I'd been on a plane. I had a great time on the plane, but Tony drank a lot of whisky and then he started throwing up and we got into big trouble. Still, being on a plane is beautiful. And in Paris, Tony left me at the hotel. He pocketed the money and ran away and left me on my own. I didn't have a single franc. He was the bank and the bank disappeared, and I don't know French. I left the hotel and became a *clochard*. That's what they call street people there. I became a *clochard*, and I didn't have the money to buy a crust of bread. In other words, I became a beggar and slept in the tunnel at the metro station of Montparnasse.

At the metro station I came across *Khawaja* Michel Salloum, God grant him every blessing. He took me to his house at 45, rue Victor Hugo, let me have a bath and new clothes and fed me, and when he heard my story, he offered me a job in Lebanon. He said he didn't like the militia boys, but he saw something different in me, someone from a decent family, and he said that it was my grandfather the *kohno* who'd interceded with him on my behalf. I flew back to Cyprus and had a great time and only drank one glass of whisky because I was afraid the same thing would happen to me that had happened to Tony on the plane. At Larnaca I met up with *Khawaja* Michel and we went back together by boat to Jounieh and from Jounieh to Ballona, and I worked as a guard at the Villa Gardenia and lived in a little house below the villa, and that's where the hooliganism began.

Yes, hooliganism. I say it and feel sorry, and I ask God to forgive me, and I pray to my grandfather the *kohno* to intercede with God for me because I fornicated with other people's women. I'd sit and watch the lovers who'd come to the pine forest to have sex in their cars. My grandfather used to tell me I was turning out like my father and I'd become a thief like him, and that's what happened. The fact is that my purpose was just to watch and I didn't want to rob anyone. I enjoyed watching the sort of sex they had in cars very much, and I'm embarrassed now to write about such scenes, which must offend the honourable reader's eyes and drag him into sin.

Satan seduced me and I began the hooliganism. I began with robbery. I'd swoop down on the cars with my electric torch and the Kalashnikov that belonged to *Khawaja* Michel, and when they saw me they'd be scared of the scandal and of dying and they'd offer me everything they had so I'd let them go. I started with robbery and then I moved on, and here I'd like to say that it wasn't all my fault. It was theirs too, because if they'd resisted I wouldn't have done what I did. It was never my intention to kill anyone. Which is why, I don't know . . . but I would have backed off. The main thing is, sir, that the first time I raped a woman it happened by accident and without any planning or forethought, but the man who was with her ran away and she just stood there. She was shaking with fright, so I went over to her and had sex.

I'm not lying. I promised the respected officer that I'd write the truth, and the truth is that I misunderstood the meaning of her shaking. I thought she expected me to do it, so I had sex with her, and I was wrong. My feelings were wrong because the way I was was wrong, and when I had sex with her she began to cry. She put her hands over her eyes and started crying, but instead of stopping I went on. I felt a strange pleasure, as though I'd become a monster. I swear I don't know what happened to me, and now — after falling in love with Shireen, that is — I've understood that that's a dishonourable feeling and that it's what they call rape.

After the first time things got easier, and I started mixing robbery with rape. Sometimes, though, I'd satisfy myself just with robbery and feel I was being chivalrous, especially when I saw how the woman would thank me with her panic-stricken eyes because I didn't do more than steal. I would feel I was being chivalrous and noble, and that gave me back some of my self-esteem.

I accept whatever retribution the court may hand down. God, Glorious and Almighty, has already exacted retribution for my dreadful deeds, and I have been subjected to torture I deserved, and I now proclaim my repentance.

In Beirut, Heikal, who was with us at the Georges Armouni Barracks, seduced me with money. He gave me five hundred dollars and said they were from Abu Ahmad El Naddaf and asked me to hide some things in my house, or hut, below the Villa Gardenia. I hid them. I didn't know Abu Ahmad El Naddaf and I hadn't met him, but Heikal took part in a parachute training course in Israel and got to know El Naddaf there. The things I hid in my hut were ten kilos of gelignite, twenty fuses and five grenades. Then we began.

Heikal came and said that the work had begun, and they started taking the explosives and going I don't know where. I didn't give the matter any thought. My first concern was Shireen. I would make dates with her and chase her from one place to the next and love her. Don't ask me, sir, why I fell in love with her. Love comes from God. I fell in love with her and she became the light of my eyes and the warmth of my heart, and she loved me too in some way. I could feel her love for me and how she'd have fun with me, but she was afraid of me and I now know she was right, because my behaviour was, well, not up to her standards. But that she'd go and make a complaint against me and ruin my life the way she did, that I can't understand. All she had to do, sir, was ask me, in a serious way, to break off our relationship, and I would have broken it off. Can anyone force anyone else to love them? But she didn't ask clearly; I could feel that she wasn't sure, and that's what pushed me to continue. My intentions were honourable. I wanted to marry her and have done with the dog's life I was living. When my grandfather got angry at me, he'd call me a son of a dog, to remind me that my father had left me in my mother's womb and gone off I don't know where. And *Khawaja* Michel told me that he wouldn't get a dog to help me guard the villa because Mme Randa was afraid of dogs, so he put me in charge on my own, and I felt like a dog. I thought, I'll work with El Naddaf, get a little money together, marry Shireen and live with her in a beautiful little house in Hazmiyeh. But before that I had to get some capital together to open a joinery shop. When I was young, my grandfather sent me to learn mortise-and-tenon joinery with *Khawaja* Saleem, and that's how I learned the basics of the craft.

But then I was arrested.

I now confess before God and before the judiciary, and I ask for mercy on my soul, for I have decided to repent and follow the path of my grandfather, God rest his soul, and to look after my poor mother and never get married. I have decided against marriage and to give up Shireen and love and everything. I have also decided to stop eating meat.

This is the whole story of my life, from the moment I was born to now. I wrote it on my own in the prison in February 1992, and God is my witness that I have told the truth in everything I have written and that I am ready to repeat my statements before the court.

Yalo reread what he'd written and felt depressed. It had taken him more than ten days to write these pages. He'd wept and suffered and felt he could never write anything. The respite he'd been given would end in twenty more days. The officer had given him the sheets of paper and told him he had a month, no more: "You have one month. You must write the story of your life, and woe betide you if you leave anything out."

Yalo lived in his little cell and pummelled his brains and tried. He wanted to listen to Fairouz or Marcel Khalife, to have a break and feel that he was human, but they wouldn't give him a radio. The guard told him he had to remain in total isolation so he could concentrate and write.

"But I don't know how to write," Yalo said.

"Whatever you say. I'm just telling you, watch out. The person who was here before you didn't write anything, and if you knew what happened to him . . ."

"What happened to him?" asked Yalo.

"They kept beating him till he started bellowing like a bull, and they didn't stop beating him till he died."

"Died?!" said Yalo.

"Of course not," answered the guard. "It's just an expression. It was like he died."

"And then what?"

"Then he wrote. He sat down at the table and wrote about fifty pages."

"Fifty pages?!"

"Of course," said the guard. "Everyone has to write the whole story of his life. Of course, a man's life needs at least fifty pages."

"And how long did it take him to write it?"

"A month. Here they only give a month. Sometimes if the story's important and the prisoner's writing, they increase the time, but normally they only give a month, and the ones who don't write are done for."

"Which means I'm done for. I can't. There's no way I can write without a radio and cigarettes. I can't write without smoking."

"I'll fix the cigarettes," said the guard. "Give me some money."

"I don't have any money. They took it all."

"Give me the receipt and I'll take out whatever you need."

"They didn't give me a receipt."

"That's not possible. Here they give prisoners receipts for their money, their watches and rings and everything," said the guard.

"I told you, they didn't give me a receipt," said Yalo.

"Perhaps the receipt's with the lawyer. Ask to see the lawyer. He's bound to have receipts, and we'll be able to fix everything. Don't worry."

"But I don't have a lawyer," said Yalo.

"Impossible. Here they appoint a lawyer. If the accused doesn't have any money on him, they appoint one."

Yalo felt bad.

Now he remembers that the interrogator brought a lawyer to him after the night of the sack, but Yalo refused to talk to him and said God was his only defence and that he didn't need a human being to defend him.

The lawyer signed the statement without reading it or speaking to the accused. He conferred in whispers with the interrogator, signed the statement and left.

It occurred to Yalo that he might ask for the lawyer so he could request his help with the writing, and he asked the guard to contact the lawyer, whose name he didn't even know, but the next day the guard gave him a single Marlboro and said he couldn't do anything for him and he'd brought him the cigarette out of pity. "Maybe the cigarette will help to get your mind working. Honestly, I couldn't fix anything more. Put your faith in God, take a few puffs, and try to write."

Yalo put his faith in God, smoked the cigarette, having first had breakfast, and felt a superb giddiness. It had been months since he'd tasted tobacco, and through this cigarette its true taste was revealed. Tobacco was better than hashish – it took you to shuddering ease and the vertigo of things – but people treated smoking with contempt by making it a meaningless habit. Yalo decided that when he left prison he'd smoke one cigarette a day and get drunk on it.

He went back to his pages. He read them again and discovered that they wouldn't do. When the interrogator read them, he would surely think that Yalo was putting one over on him and send him to suffer the bull's fate the guard had told him about.

He hadn't asked the guard his name, for he had learned, in this isolation cell, to listen to the sound of the silence ringing in his ears. The short hunch-backed guard with his white pock-marked face directed not a word to Yalo. He'd open the aperture in the cell door and put food through it twice a day, at 8.00 in the morning and 5.00 in the afternoon, and he'd open the door at 10.00 in the morning and gesture to his prisoner to follow him to the bathroom, and he must have been wearing rubber shoes because Yalo never heard his footsteps. Silence formed round the cell like a solid black wall, so much so that Yalo didn't dare to cough or talk to himself out loud. He'd whisper something and then look round for fear that someone might have heard him. The silence remained unbroken until the day when he finished writing the story of his life, which was short and which wouldn't do and which he didn't know how to rewrite. That was when he longed for music and tobacco, and, without knowing where he found the courage, he spoke to the guard and asked for his help, but the result – a single cigarette and the story about the bull – wasn't worth the effort.

Yalo read what he'd written and decided to tear it up. He oughtn't to have written about his father and *Khawaja* Saleem Rizq the Blind because that way he'd make trouble for himself. The interrogator would tell him he wasn't Lebanese because his father was a Syrian from Aleppo, and this charge would be added to those of theft, rape and the explosives. He'd be accused of forging his nationality because his father, Georges Jalao, didn't have Lebanese nationality.

"But I'm Lebanese," he would reply to the interrogator. "It's written on my identity card."

Therein lay the problem.

At the interrogation, they hadn't believed him when he'd said that Georges Jalao was his father and *Kohno* Afram his grand-father. What was written on his identity card was something different, because his grandfather had registered Yalo as his own son. So on his card he was the son of Habeel Abyad and Mary Samho, and his mother, Gaby, was his sister. Of course this was not true. *Kohno* Afram was known as Habeel in civil life and hadn't changed his name on his identity card following his entry into the clergy, at which point the metropolitan had named him Afram. The *kohno* had registered his grandson as his son so that he would have Lebanese nationality, since Lebanese law does not permit a woman to pass her nationality on to her son even if the father has died or disappeared or divorced her, or left the country never to return.

When he was asked at the interrogation whose son he was and answered truthfully, he was treated as an imposter and a liar, and took a savage beating before the interrogator was convinced.

"Okay. On your I.D., you're the son of Habeel Abyad!"

"Right," said Yalo, "but the truth is that Habeel is my grandfather. My father's name is Georges Jalao."

"That's forgery," said the interrogator. "We'll have to get M. Habeel in for questioning."

"M. Habeel is a priest now, and his name has been changed, so he's Father Afram," said Yalo.

"Then we'll summon the priest Afram Abyad."

"But he died about ten years ago, sir, and it wasn't my fault. What business is it of mine? I'd barely been born when he forged my nationality. Let's pretend that he adopted me and the problem's solved."

"That's what we'll assume," said the interrogator.

"So when I'm asked my name, I have to say Daniel Abyad, right?" asked Yalo.

"Quite right. But."

"But what?"

"I told you that's what we'll assume for the moment. In other words, I'm not going to consider you a Syrian citizen with a forged Lebanese identity; I'm going to consider you Lebanese for the time being, and then we'll see."

"Whatever you say," said Yalo.

"No, whatever *you* say," said the interrogator. "Meaning, if you cooperate and confess, we'll forget the matter."

"I'm at your service," said Yalo.

"But if you don't cooperate, you won't just be beaten up and tortured, you'll lose your Lebanese nationality too."

"What should I write?" wondered Yalo.

Should he write about his real father, of whom he knew little, or should he write his name as it was on his identity card? If he ignored his real father, someone might come along and accuse him of lying or hiding the truth, so what was he to say?

The safest solution was to make no reference to the subject whatsoever. He must never, ever write his name in full. Having eliminated his father, he would have to eliminate any references to *Khawaja* Saleem Rizq, who had been the cause of his father's origins being shown up. He would write that his name was Yalo. He'd have to get rid of his family name, and he'd have to eliminate *Khawaja* Rizq from the picture. But how could he explain his passion for Arabic calligraphy, Oriental art and the woodcraft that had driven him into the arms of Mme Randa?

The blind carpenter who had seen with his eyebrows and read with his fingers occupied a large space in the conversation of the *kohno*, who wanted his grandson to learn this craft and sent him during the summer holidays to work in the blind man's shop near the Hotel Saint Georges, where he sold the most beautiful, authentic Damascene wooden doors, which the rich of Beirut used to adorn their homes under the influence of the

Orientalist style that swept Beirut in the early '70s.

The grandfather wanted his grandson to learn that a man had to suffer and work hard, that you "earn your bread with the sweat of your brow".

Yalo worked in Rizq's shop for three summers, and he grew to love the craft and looked forward to the end of the school year so he could return to his work with wood. Yalo decided on a career in joinery, and that he didn't need any more learning, he just needed to be able to read and write, which he already knew how to do. At the same time, *Khawaja* Saleem's son, whom they honoured with the title "Engineer", discovered Yalo possessed a talent for Arabic calligraphy and began training him to write Koranic verses in Kufic script, which was much in demand in those days.

"I'm an artist," Yalo told his grandfather, repeating the words the Engineer had said as he taught him how to hold the pen and write the Throne Verse, whose words still rang in his ears.

In the summer of 1974, however, when Yalo was thirteen, he didn't go to work at the shop. His grandfather told him there was no longer any reason for him to work during the summer. "The summer's for rest. You have to read, study and prepare for next year, when you begin the preparatory stage, which is a difficult one, and needs to be got ready for."

Yalo only worked out why his grandfather hadn't sent him to the shop years later, when he put together the stories his mother would tell about *Khawaja* Saleem's death, and about the Engineer and Thérèse.

Gaby said that the Engineer's wife didn't go to the funeral of her paternal uncle, her husband's father. She shut up her house, went with her parents to the Mountain, and, shamefully, did not perform her duties.

"And where was the Engineer?" Yalo asked naively.

"As though you didn't know," said his mother, and continued with her intermittent elegy for the blind man who had faced his son's sin with nobility and courage.

"I shall think of you as my daughter," the blind man told Thérèse. "Come and live with me. What more can I do?"

The son disappeared. It was said he wanted to seek forgiveness for his sins and went to Aleppo, where he decided to build himself a pillar like that of Mar Simeon and sit on top of it practising mysticism and renunciation. So they arrested him and sent him to a mental hospital.

Khawaja Saleem recounted the story to his friend the *kohno*, and *Kohno* Afram, whose friendship with *Khawaja* Saleem was deep, going back to when he'd arrived in Beirut, where he'd worked as a tile-maker before being called to the priesthood, told his friend he should find a way to protect his honour: "and shouldst thou be afflicted with calamities, then protect your honour." He also offered to use his influence with the abbess of the Khinshara Convent, but the abbess refused to receive him when she learned he'd been sent by the Rizq family.

The *kohno* didn't like nuns and believed in the total separation of monastic and civilian life. "What's this nonsense? Calling themselves nuns and living like ordinary women? A nun's place is in the convent, not among the people. They ought to be put back in their boxes," Afram told Saleem Rizq as he recounted how the abbess of the Khinshara Convent had refused to receive him.

The thing that ruined Yalo's career started when Thérèse, who was a novice working as a teacher at the Tabarees School, came to Rizq's workshop to place an order for some icon frames and expressed amazement at the beauty of the joinery created there without a single nail. She asked the school's headmistress for permission to take woodworking lessons from the Engineer and started coming, with another nun, Sister Rita.

What happened then, and why did Sister Thérèse claim that she was going to visit her family in the village of Ein Dara and then disappear with Wajeeh for three days at the Grand Kamel Hotel in the town of Souq El Gharb before returning to the school?

It seems that when, in the room at the hotel, Engineer Wajeeh saw how her long hair covered her shoulders, he promised to marry Thérèse. But why did the novice nun confess her sin and come to the shop with the abbess four months later, at which moment Wajeeh exited stealthily through the back door? *Khawaja* Saleem then found himself faced with a scene the like of which his eyes had never beheld, in the days, twenty years ago, before they had closed.

After hearing the confessions of Sister Thérèse and of her decision to leave the convent and marry Wajeeh, who had taken her virginity, Saleem said he didn't know what to say.

The tall, fat abbess, who was over sixty, said that Thérèse had received the convent's harshest punishment. She had been sent to Khinshara and imprisoned for three months in a vault beneath the convent which in the past had been used for nuns who had entered into relationships with the Devil. "We left her for three months in iron chains, with only bread and water, and then we decided it was enough. We asked her what she wanted to do, and she said she wanted to come here, and I've come with her so that we can reach an understanding with Engineer Wajeeh."

"But Wajeeh is married," said the father, who was then overtaken by a fit of hysterical laughter. "You bastard, Wajeeh. You've turned out more of a prick than your father. Can you credit it, *ma soeur*? I swear I can't."

The blind old man went over to Thérèse, whose brown face was quivering with fear and humiliation, and reached towards it, then took her small, sweaty hand and told her that she should come and live with him, and he was willing to do whatever she wished.

"Come closer, Thérèse, my daughter. What can I say? We're Greek Catholics, and we don't have divorce. My son Wajeeh is married and has two boys, God protect you and them. Just tell me what to do and I'll do it. Come and live with me. My wife is dead, I live on my own, and I'm blind. I'm prepared to make good my son's misdeed. If you want it, that is, and if it be God's will."

"You?" shrieked the abbess. "You want to marry this virgin, this bride of Christ? At your age, and blind, and you still have no shame?" He tried to explain to her that he didn't mean marriage, albeit marriage would preserve the decencies for the lovely girl and draw a veil of propriety over the scandal.

"Why? Can you see, even, to tell whether she's pretty?" asked the abbess, stifling her shriek in a voice tense and staccato.

"Yes, *ma soeur*. I see beauty because beauty sees me" – and he pointed to the masterworks in wood with which the small shop was filled. "Do you see those? Those are me. To this day, I'm still the one who designs the difficult items. I read with my hands, *ma soeur*. And now I'm . . . what was it you called me? God, how did I get myself into this mess? I have only good intentions. I didn't have to say anything. What's it got to do with me? It was Wajeeh, and Wajeeh's not here. We'll do whatever you wish."

The abbess said that they'd come back at 10.00 the next morning and that he was to "tell the gentleman to be waiting for us". Then they left.

When Wajeeh returned to the shop and his father confronted him, he denied everything and said Thérèse was mad, that she'd made the story up and that they didn't have a relationship.

"Don't worry," said the father. "We'll find a solution. Just tell me how you managed to sleep with her. I mean, how could she agree when she's a nun? Tell me what you did with her in the hotel."

At first, the son persisted in saying that Thérèse wasn't a nun, just a novice, and there was a big difference, and that she was a bit mad because she'd invented the story from beginning to end, but when his father told him that the abbess would be coming the next day, he went to pieces and confessed to everything, and said he didn't know what to do.

"Don't worry, my son. If you can't take her, I will."

"You, you filthy old man, you think you're going to marry a nineteen-year-old?"

Saleem told the *kohno* how his son had hit him and kicked him and how Wajeeh had turned into a different person, as though a devil had emerged from within him. "The boy disappeared. Disappeared, Father! I swear I wasn't going to marry her because I wanted to. As though I still had anything I could do anything with! And anyway, she's a child. I thought, that way I'll keep her decent, and my son too. And why did the abbess talk that way? Wajeeh told me it wasn't him that took her virginity, she'd already lost it. I don't understand anything any more."

Wajeeh disappeared. They said his wife threw him out and he went to live in a cheap hotel on Burj Square before fate led him to the lunatic asylum in Aleppo.

Yalo didn't sleep the night his mother told him fragments of this story, and about how the novice nun would come to the shop every morning at 10.00 before she disappeared and all trace of her was lost. Wajeeh's wife had a nervous breakdown, then asked Saleem Rizq for her husband's share of the business and broke off all ties with the Rizq family.

The scandal made it all the way to the family's hometown of Aleppo. Wajeeh went to build his pillar next to that of Mar Simeon and was arrested and sent to the mental hospital. The father, however, was unable to find any trace of his son either with his relatives there or at the hospital, so he made up his mind that Wajeeh had put out the rumour about the pillar so he could escape his wife and live with his virgin nun.

Yalo didn't sleep that night. He imagined the beautiful brown-skinned nun and played the character of Wajeeh and took her to the Grand Kamel Hotel in Souq El Gharb, where he breathed in the smell of the long hair that covered her shoulders and drowned in the smell of the incense that rose from her neck. They stayed for three days without leaving the room, to which food was brought and where they bathed and ate and slept together. She told him she loved him and loved the Lord Christ. She asked him to kneel beside her so that the Lord might bless their love. And Yalo, or Wajeeh, drank his youth, which welled up in droplets of arak that seeped from her pores into his, and chanted prayers with her, and took all of her, just as she possessed him.

Yalo didn't see the virgin blood either.

"Where's the blood?" he asked.

She pointed to the covers with their pink designs on top of the white sheet and he took her in his arms and told her that she would remain a virgin for ever.

Yalo has to be careful not to refer to *Khawaja* Saleem and his son the Engineer in his life story, but how else can he explain his passion for mortised wood and Arabic calligraphy?

"I'm an artist," he told his grandfather when the *kohno* suggested that he join the seminary. "No. I don't want to be a *kohno*. I'm an artist, and when I'm older I'm going to work as a calligrapher."

He did not, however, become a calligrapher. His grandfather died a year after they left West Beirut during the war, and Yalo enlisted at the barracks and became a fighter like the thousands of young men who left their studies and went to the fate the war had fashioned for them.

How will he explain to the interrogator his beautiful handwriting, his passion for wood and his relationship with Mme Randa?

It was true that the name Randa hadn't been mentioned throughout the two months of interrogation that Yalo had spent in torment, but who could guarantee that the forty-year-old wouldn't appear at any moment and claim he had raped her? And how was he to explain his knowledge of the art of joinery if she were to confess to her relationship with him?

In that village in the district of Kasrawan known as Ballona, which witnessed a major building boom during the Lebanese civil war, Yalo lived alone. Ballona was like many of the villages of Kasrawan, the heartland of the Maronites in Mount Lebanon, in that it was barely touched by the war and became a refuge for those fleeing other parts of the country. The Greek Orthodox who left the Museitbeh quarter built a district for themselves there just like their old quarter in West Beirut, and they founded a church which they named St Nicholas and which became known as Mar Niqula, and whose officiant was Father Serafim Azar. There the Beirut accent, which emphasizes particular letters as if spitting them out, and the Kasrawan accent, which twists Arabic and mingles its letters in strange combinations, met.

Yalo lived alone in a hut, boredom his constant companion. One day, Madame called for him. The *khawaja* had gone to France to see to his business there. She wanted Yalo to help her fix one of their valuable inlaid chairs, which had been knocked over and had broken one of its legs. She asked him to carry the chair to the car so she could take it to the carpenter.

"Why a carpenter?" said Yalo. "I know how to fix it."

Yalo sat on the ground and began mending the chair, and when Madame saw him working and asked him why he didn't use nails, he explained that this kind of woodwork didn't require nails.

"How do you stick it together? Do you use glue?"

Yalo told her about mortise-and-tenon joinery, about how one could turn wood into male and female joints so that when they entered one another the parts were bound together for ever.

"What do you mean, 'male and female'?" she asked.

"Come and look, madame," said Yalo.

The lady bent over the young man's lean back bent over the wood, and a smell of jasmine wafted from her.

"That's what they call joinery?" she asked.

"Yes, joinery," said Yalo.

"You mean wood's like people, who join with one another?"

"Wood is better than people, madame, because when it's joined, it remains joined for ever."

"And the bits don't get fed up?" she asked, and laughed. Then she left the room. At that moment, Yalo had a glimpse of "randarizing", and later he would call that year the "joinery year".

She said she fell in love with him the moment he joined the pieces of wood, and that she wanted him to take her the way wood takes wood, and stay inside her for ever.

He was going to have to eliminate *Khawaja* Saleem, his son

and the joined wood from his story. True, he had spoken to Mme Randa of blind Saleem and of his infatuation with calligraphy, and of how Engineer Wajeeh had forced him to memorize entire verses from the Koran so he could engrave them on the wooden doors, but what was he to do? If he wrote the story, he might lose his Lebanese citizenship, and if he didn't, he might enter an endless labyrinth.

Yalo was consumed with desire for another cigarette and put the end of his pen between his lips and started sucking on it and expelling its imaginary smoke into the narrow cell. He stood up and paced back and forth, trying to organize his memory. "I must find a thread that ties the story together," thought Yalo, and the thread of blood that stretches from Ein Ward to Beirut sketched itself before him. "That is my thread," he thought. "I started there with my grandfather the *kohno*, all the members of whose family were killed in the massacre. Who can pass judgement on a man whose throat has been cut? I will write that I am a man whose throat has been cut. I am Daniel, scion of the slaughtered. My grandfather was born in blood and drank blood on Sunday with every mass he celebrated, and I have been intoxicated with blood. Is that my fault? Did I start the war? Everything you say is true, but I'm right too, and anyway, there weren't any explosives. Those stories about the explosives, or about Heikal or Abu Ahmad El Naddaf, are baseless. I've been framed. They forced me to confess to the explosives to stop the sack torture; I had to confess I'd been a member of the explosives gang or it would be the cat waiting in the sack to eat my crotch. Either I agreed or I ate shit. And I ended up agreeing and eating shit too."

Yalo sat down at the green table, pulled out the cigarette-pen from between his teeth, looked at the white paper and wrote down his story all over again.

My name is Daniel and I am known as Yalo. From the Assyrian quarter in Beirut. Born 1961. An only child, no brothers or sisters. We moved from the Assyrian quarter in Museitbeh in 1976 because the war had got worse and we were frightened by the communal tensions, which had greatly increased. Our house was large and surrounded by a garden that contained every kind of tree – loquats and almonds and cassie and china-bark and dates. We left our house without taking anything with us, and we went to the Mreiyeh quarter, in the Ein El Roummaneh district, and there my mother rented a furnished house from one of her clients. My mother is a seamstress, and the client set us up with a house for 250 lira a month and said it'd only be temporary. I transferred from St Sawirus's to the Progress School. My grandfather the *kohno* was no longer able to work because in the new quarter where we lived there were no Assyrian families. My grandfather died of grief and my mother had less business in Ein El Roummaneh so she started going from house to house and working by the day. In other words, she'd go to a house, stay there all day, do whatever sewing they wanted – lengthening clothes, letting them out, patching, tailoring – and get a day wage rather than a piecework wage. Our circumstances became very difficult, and I wasn't comfortable in the new school. The classes were all mixed together, and most of the pupils were refugees from Damour. I left school and joined the war. Tony took me to Ashrafiyeh, and there I got to know a young man named Alexei, a White Russian who was a leader of the Billy Goats Battalion. Alexei asked me if I wanted to become a billy goat and I said no. They told me I had to fight to defend my country and Tony started laughing at me and said I didn't understand the language of war. He said to me, "Say you want to be a billy goat," so I said I was ready to become a billy goat, and I became a fighter and I made war.

I made war because my grandfather had urged me not to emigrate. He told me that emigration killed a man's soul and made him feel lost, and he told me about his migration from Ein Ward to Qamishli when he was fifteen years old.

My grandfather told me not to emigrate. But I emigrated to France, and that migration was the cause of all my woes. The truth is I got tired. I got tired of the war and I got tired of the poverty and I got tired of my mother. My mother had become like a madwoman with her mirror and the phantom of my late grandfather, which she saw every night in her dreams. Emigrating was Tony's idea, and I got very enthusiastic about it. On my identity card my name is Daniel Habeel Abyad, but people call me

"Jalao's son". I was born in Beirut in 1961. I work as a guard at the Villa Gardenia, which belongs to *Khawaja* Michel Salloum, in the village of Ballona, in the district of Kasrawan.

I started my new job after the war. I went with my friend Tony Ateeq to France. We ran away after we'd stolen the money from the Georges Armouni Barracks in Ashrafiyeh. In Paris, we stayed in a small hotel in Montparnasse. The hotel was excellent, and it was the first time in my life that I'd had a room to myself. At home, I would sleep in my grandfather the *kohno*'s room. My grandfather decreed that when I reached the age of fifteen, when he ordered me to move from my mother's room into his, and said there had to be a strict order in the house – the men in one room and the women in another. So I moved in with him, even though I'd slip into my mother's room and sleep in her bed almost every night.

We lived in the hotel for about a fortnight. We didn't do anything. We'd walk around Paris and eat in the restaurants and drink French wine. Once we went to the Pigalle quarter, and there the French woman, the prostitute, forced me to sleep with her using a condom. I hated it and I nearly went soft which is something that had never happened to me before. I hate wearing a condom, but in France they make people do that because they're afraid of A.I.D.S.

I began to feel anxious because we weren't working, but Tony reassured me. He said he'd contact some friends and ask them to find us jobs, but we weren't in a hurry because the strong box Tony had was full of money.

Then Tony ran away.

I don't know how or why. I didn't even notice that he

was getting ready to trick me. I was following him blindly, and suddenly I discovered that he'd gone. I found myself alone in Paris, without a single franc to my name.

The woman who owned the hotel, a respectable French lady, took pity on me. She spoke with me using a few words of English and sign language, and she made me understand that before Tony left he'd given her money for two extra nights for me. She said she was prepared to let me stay a third night without charge and give me breakfast. After that I'd have to find a solution for myself.

Tony knew French, but I didn't. When the lady started talking to me, I felt as if she was throwing stones at me. That feeling stayed with me till I returned to Lebanon. In France I came to realize that words are like stones and that when you don't know a language it's like being stoned or tortured. It's different with Syriac. True, I don't understand it, but I feel it and I know how to slip in among the words and the sentences and snatch something of the meaning. My grandfather would speak to my mother in Syriac and she'd reply in Arabic and tell him to stop speaking Kurdish, and he'd get very annoyed. My grandfather was Kurdish. No. How can I put it? He wasn't Kurdish, but he spent his childhood with the Kurds after the massacre of Ein Ward, and he spoke their language. Then he emigrated to Beirut and worked in the tiling trade like many of the young Assyrians who had gathered in Museitbeh. And in Beirut he started speaking Syriac. He didn't study the colloquial Suryoyo that ordinary people speak; he learned the formal language in church, and when he became a *kohno*, he started speaking the formal language. But with me, he'd speak colloquial Arabic studded with a few Syriac words. When my mother called him a Kurd, he'd get annoyed, especially in his last days when he was given to long bouts of weeping and my mother would despair of being able to comfort him.

After my grandfather became a *kohno*, he stopped eating meat. Then his wife died of cancer and he became very puritanical and impossible, especially in matters of food, hygiene and morals.

My grandfather's puritanism created a huge problem in the family. I didn't give the matter any thought, but my grandfather told me how he'd castrated *Khawaja* Elias El Shami, which made my mother go berserk. Not because my grandfather had castrated him, which was nothing to do with her, but because he'd told me and shamed her.

I don't know why, but when I heard the story I felt as though I'd heard it somewhere before. *Khawaja* Elias was present in my life, even though he didn't visit us very often. My mother, though, would take me to the funfair, and he'd be there. I'd ride the Vortex all the time. I'd sit in this spinning machine and leave them below and spend an hour, or two hours, looking at the sea and the city from above. The world spun and they'd be sitting drinking coffee and talking.

Once I got lost. I remember things now as though they happened to someone else. I used to think that the idea of the other person who's like me was part of my childhood. I mean that when I remember my childhood, I feel that the child I was then was somebody else. But now, after experiencing imprisonment and torture, I've started to see Yalo's whole life as that of somebody else. I don't know how to describe that feeling, sir, but it's a true feeling.

I look at myself in the mirror of myself and I see another man, and I'm afraid of him and his thoughts and actions. No, I'm not saying that to avoid my responsibilities. I know that I am paying the price for my mistakes, and I seek forgiveness from God, Glorious and Mighty.

I do not seek forgiveness from people, and I'm not writing this as a way of winning the sympathy of His Honour the judge. Life no longer interests me. I know that I will be condemned to death on a charge of planting explosives and killing innocent people, but I am innocent, I swear it – despite which I will accept the sentence with no hard feelings and say that this was my fate from before I was born and there was nothing I could do about it. I see my grandfather weeping before me and I ask him to intercede for me with Mar Afram the Assyrian, and all I seek for myself is mercy and peace in the next world.

I got down from the Twister, or the Vortex – I don't know what the ride's proper name is – and I couldn't find my mother or *Khawaja* Elias, so I began to cry, and people gathered round me and asked whose son I was and where I lived, and I couldn't tell them the way to the house. I told them my family were the Abyads and that our house was in the Assyrian quarter, but that was all I could say. People stood round not knowing what to do, and I cried. Then someone recognized me and said, "He's the priest's son," and took me to our house in his car, and there was my grandfather, and the scandal, which became associated with me, came about because my grandfather realized at once that my mother was still having an affair with the tailor.

I was very frightened in Paris. Suddenly I found myself

on the street, in a city whose language I didn't know and where I had no friends. So I resorted to the art I knew. On a piece of cardboard that Mme Violette, the hotel owner, gave me, in beautiful *naskh* script, I wrote the following: "I am a young Lebanese, homeless and alone. I ask for your sympathy because I can't afford even a loaf of bread."

I sat in the Montparnasse metro station, along with my piece of cardboard, for several days, during which all I ate was dry bread given me by a homeless French *clochard* who drank wine straight from the bottle and stank. *Khawaja* Michel happened upon me there and saved my life. He brought me back to Lebanon and gave me work in his house and treated me generously, may God be generous to him, and I betrayed his trust. This is my great sin. My sin is the betrayal of trust. A man put me in charge of his house and his wife, and I did not deserve his confidence. Rather than becoming his dog, as he asked me to, I became a street dog and went into business on my own, playing the peeping tom using the forest below Mar Niqula as my base.

I want to tell the truth so that I can clear my conscience. In the beginning I didn't want to steal or to rape women. That only began when I came upon the cars parked in the forest. I watched them so I could protect the villa. I thought that maybe there was something suspicious going on and it was my duty to know everything. But it was just sex and dirty business. At a distance I couldn't see much, but what I did see, the silhouettes of the men on top of the women, set my imagination on fire, sir.

My story began with a love of watching dirty things, no more and no less. Then I decided to move in closer to see more clearly. Why did I do the things I did later on? I don't know.

I know that the first time I went down, I was carrying the Kalashnikov and the torch, and I saw how fear touched the lips of the man in the car and I discovered that fear begins with the lips. I rapped on the window with the barrel of the rifle and the man opened the window and tried to say something, but the words wouldn't come out and his lower lip was trembling. Then he put his hand into his trouser pocket and gave me a handful of dollars and Lebanese lira. I hadn't planned to rob him. I hadn't had a plan at all. I'd only wanted to watch. He held out the money so I took it and stayed where I was, so he took off his watch and ordered the woman to take off her watch and gold chain and cross and he gave them to me. I took them and stayed where I was, and the woman said, "I beg you, sir, forgive us." I don't know why I replied, "Shut up, whore!" Instead of her getting upset and the man becoming angry and getting out of the car and tangling with me, he bowed his head as if he was agreeing, and the woman smiled as though she was frowning. That was when I wanted her, but I didn't do anything. I got amazingly excited, but I went back to my house below the villa and I heard the car's tyres screeching as it turned round.

After that, things followed their natural course. I went hunting once or twice a week, not more, because I wasn't greedy. I was afraid if I made too many hunting expeditions, people would stop coming to the forest, and I always picked the last car, by which I mean the last car to come on a given night.

I witnessed indescribable things. It taught me a lot

about human nature and made me understand my mother's madness. My mother was a woman to be pitied. Her crime was to fall in love with a man who didn't deserve her, and she took her love to the limit. I'm like her that way. True, it's shameful to compare my idiotic behaviour and despicable desires with the nobility of a woman who became a sacrifice to love, but God made it my fate too to become a sacrifice to love and to end my life the opposite of how it started. I began with the sin in the forest and ended with love. I'm both the opposite of my mother and her extension. She drowned in her mirror and I have no need of a mirror. She could no longer see her face in the mirror, and I can see mine without one.

I saw, sir . . . what can I say? Some of them would come in broad daylight, though these were certainly a minority. One of the men would come at 10.00 in the morning. He must have been the most shameless man in the world. He would park close to the huge sycamore-fig tree and have sex with the woman, and I'd see her big breasts through the branches. He wouldn't undress her completely; he'd undo her blouse and get out her breasts and have sex with her on the seat. He'd sit on the passenger seat and she'd be on top, her breasts bouncing. They'd arrive, her next to him in his red Peugeot. He'd get out of his car and undo his trousers, and she'd open her door and get out. He'd sit on the passenger seat and then she'd get back into the car and sit on top of him.

One of my first experiences was with that woman. I saw her open the door and stand there waiting for him and I couldn't contain myself. The sun was everywhere and I found myself picking up the rifle, putting on my balaklava and running. I didn't rob them. I got to her before he did. He saw the rifle and froze. I waved him away and he didn't resist. I sat on the passenger seat and ordered her to climb on top of me the way she did with him. I undid my trousers and uncovered her breasts and took her the same way he did. When I went back to my house, I saw the man climb into the car and leave.

Things began to take on a new shape, and to my original pleasure — watching people and taking their money — a new pleasure was added, and so it continued till God decided to make me fall victim to love.

I read a lot of the books I found in my mother's room, but the book that had a special impact on me was *Lovers and Their Tragic Ends*. This is the only book I've read many times. On the first page there is a dedication in red ink: "To My Little Darling, That She May Know", followed by an illegible scribble. I don't think my mother read the book because she didn't like reading; she didn't even read the newspaper. And I believe that the scribble is the signature of the tailor who loved my mother and didn't marry her. I used to tell Shireen that I was a tragic lover, and she'd laugh because she doesn't understand the meanings of words. I told her about lovers who died for their love, and she laughed at me and at them. The tailor likewise, or so I imagine, would tell my mother the stories in the book, and she too would laugh because she didn't understand.

My tragedy was that this girl made a complaint against me and I was sent to prison. When I saw her in the Jounieh police station, I thought that revenge must be her way of proclaiming her love, something that happens a lot in love stories. In other words, she could only get rid of me through an act of revenge. This increased my infatuation. However, when I saw Emile, her fiancé, that dumb idiot of a boy who knows nothing of the truth, I understood that our love had come to an end. I'm sure that wasn't Emile with her. When I took her to my house it was another man who was with her, the fifty-year-old doctor whose name I can't remember, but he's a well-known physician. Why don't they bring him in for questioning so he can say what really happened? Then my innocence will be obvious to all. I did not rape her, at least not really. Honestly I don't know. But I confess before God and before you that I used to rape women, because you call it rape, and because after I became enamoured of Shireen I discovered that it *was* rape compared with the beautiful, fantastic sex a person can have with the woman he loves. I only slept with Shireen a few times, but I made love to her on every one of our dates, and it was something beautiful and huge and not to be compared with the sex I had with the forest women. Love is a human thing, like you are praying, but the sex in the forest was like war, so now I'm persuaded that it was rape. I confess that I used to be a rapist, and I ask for clemency and for mercy on my soul, for the sake of my mother, who lives alone and greatly needs her son. I promise to dedicate the rest of my life to her.

I confess that I robbed and plundered and raped, and I'm convinced that God will hold me to account through you.

The last chapter of my life is the strangest chapter of them all, sir, because I don't know how I got involved in the business. Heikal — I don't know his family name — got in touch — he'd been with us at the Georges Armouni Barracks — and seduced me with money. He gave me five hundred dollars, told me the money was from Ahmad El Naddaf and asked me to hide the stuff in my house so I hid it. I didn't know this El Naddaf, but I had heard of him because he was famous in the border zone occupied by the Israelis and was responsible for explosives training, and lots of our boys got trained by him. Heikal gave me ten kilos of gelignite, twenty fuses and five grenades to hide, and then we began. Heikal came to say that the work had begun, and they started taking the explosives and going off with them. But I didn't give the matter any thought. My only concern was Shireen. I'd make dates with her and chase her from one place to the next and love her. I wanted to marry her and be done with the dog's life I was living. When my grandfather became angry with me, he'd call me a son of a dog, and *Khawaja* Michel told me that he wouldn't get a dog to help me guard the villa because Mme Randa, his wife, was afraid of dogs. I thought, I'll work with El Naddaf, get a little money together, marry Shireen, and we'll live in Hazmiyeh. But before that I had to get some capital together so I could open a joinery shop. I'd learned the craft in *Khawaja* Saleem Rizq's shop when I was young.

I now confess before God and proclaim my repentance and that I shall follow the path of my grandfather, God rest his soul, and look after my poor mother. Likewise, I have decided not to marry, and to renounce everything. I have also decided to stop eating meat.

This is the whole story of my life, from the moment I was born to now. I wrote it myself in the prison in February 1992, and God is my witness that I have told the truth in everything I have written and that I am ready to repeat my statements before the court.

Yalo read the pages he had written and put them aside feeling a deep sense of comfort. He had succeeded in writing the story of his life in its entirety, and when they summoned him, he would say he'd confessed to everything and had written everything and left nothing out.

He had written about his childhood, his youth, the war and *Khawaja* Michel. He had written about his mother, her lover the tailor and his grandfather the *kohno*. He had written about Shireen, whom he'd loved, and about hunting at Ballona. True, he'd had to concoct a story, the one about Heikal, El Naddaf and the explosives, but that fabrication was something he couldn't get out of. Yalo felt he was cleverer than the interrogator because he'd mentioned the names of two men no-one would ever be able to trace. Heikal had committed suicide in November 1991, when it was said that he'd hanged himself because he couldn't get hold of cocaine any more. And El Naddaf had emigrated to Brazil, where all trace of him had been lost. Yalo had confessed to what they wanted him to confess but without opening up any loopholes that would allow them to abuse his body and soul again. The interrogator would read those names and look for those men. Then he'd decide to close the file because he'd be unable to pursue the matter with two men who couldn't be found.

Yalo sat on the floor of the cell, rested his head against the wall and felt hungry, as though the words he'd written had created spaces inside him that only food could fill. He imagined a fish and his mouth started watering. He would have said to Shireen, if Shireen had been there, that he'd stopped being afraid of anything when he'd discovered the blood in fish.

He had told her, or had been going to tell her, about Munir Shammo, who brought the big sea bass to the house while it was still flapping away its life.

What happened that day?

As Yalo was recalling the story for Shireen, he felt that stories could be told only through love. When he became a tragic lover, he became aware of the taste of words. Words are full of flavour when they come through love. True, he didn't love her any longer, and true, he felt capable of killing her because she'd broken his spirit with the betrayal that had traced itself on her naked thighs in the interrogation room, but as he sat there then, in order to write, he became aware of her and remembered how he'd become a book open before her. He'd tried to seduce her by talking, by making up stories that had or had not happened, but she wasn't interested. He had written his life in her presence, but she had refused to read. She was always in a hurry and unfocused, as though she didn't understand, or didn't want to understand.

Now, here, it is as though she is sitting next to him in the cell and listening to the story of the fish. However, his thoughts were distracted a little by her lipstick. She started eating, pulled back her lips as though she wanted to put the food into her mouth without having it touch the red, and then, when she felt it wasn't going to work, took a paper napkin to wipe off her lipstick and Yalo screamed, "No!" and desired her lips and imagined himself rubbing his lips on hers and licking off the lipstick that had come off on his lips. He knew she didn't like Arabic songs or poetry, but he couldn't contain himself, so he told her to listen and Shireen put the napkin on the table and looked at him, waiting for him to speak.

"Listen to this poem," he said. "Mansurati used to spend time with us in the barracks and sing, and we'd sing along with him. From the beginning, he bewitched me. Mansurati bewitched me with his voice and his oud. I've never been able to carry a tune. But Mansurati! When he picked up his oud and started singing, I sensed the world's unreachable soul. Don't you feel like that when you listen to music?"

She replied in a kind of mumble that the music that captured the soul of the world was classical music, and that she loved Bach and thought that popular songs were an abuse of music.

"Don't you like Nizar Qabbani?" he asked.

"I'm not talking about Arabic poetry," she said. "But even Jacques Brel . . . Do you know Jacques Brel?"

He nodded his head yes, but his ignorance showed in the way he knitted his eyebrows to give the impression that he understood.

"What are you talking about?" he asked.

"I was saying that even with Jacques Brel, whose songs are complicated, it makes me feel as if he's lowering the tone when he puts words to his music."

"But you don't know what I'm going to tell you," he said. "What I'm going to tell you is the most beautiful song in the world, more beautiful even than Abdel Haleem Hafez. Listen."

He said, "Listen," threw his head back, put his right hand to his temple and then began reciting the poem:

In Ashrafiyeh when you were there and so was I
My soul to your lips close hewed.
I tasted then their fruits, which a flavour, if not
Of luscious grapes, then of their sister, did exude.
But for the softness they held and my tenderness
In love, I would have munched on them and chewed.

And he started warbling, "chewed, chewed, cheeeeeeeeewed" and then said, "It's beautiful, isn't it? That was our song at the barracks. We'd sing 'and chewed' and each of us would change it the way he wanted to. Alexei would change the 'ch' into 'scr' and then Mansurati would get upset. He was a fantastic musician. I don't know what happened to him. He said he was sick of the war and wanted to be a musician. All of us were sick of the war, but not everyone, of course, who becomes sick of war becomes a musician, right?"

Yalo laughed, thinking he'd made a joke, but when he saw no trace of a smile on her lips he went back to being serious and told her about the fish and the war.

When he thought how he'd remembered this story, he was struck with amazement. The fish that was full of blood had sunk deep into his memory and become as though it had never been. When the girl tried to wipe the red off her lips to avoid contaminating the food, the fish awoke and became a story.

He recalls the fish's head, which was taken up by two silvery eyes and a large mouth that opened and closed as though it wanted to say something but couldn't. Munir Shammo, the *kohno*'s friend, who, having retired as a tile-maker, did nothing but fish, came early that Saturday morning carrying a fish in his basket. He put it in the kitchen and left. Gaby, when she entered the kitchen proclaiming how lucky she was that she was going to have to clean the ugly black fish that Munir Shammo usually brought, a fish full of bones called "Bolsheviks" in Lebanon, saw the big sea bass on the floor and screamed. The fish had leapt out of the sink and was slithering around and flapping. The grandfather came running when he heard his daughter's voice and saw it too.

"The fish is speaking with God," said the grandfather, and he knelt down and tried to pick it up, but the fish slipped out of his hands. The fish was about a metre long, and its grey skin, glittering with white spots, was slithering across the floor and its eyes were shining with life. Afram knelt, bent over and took it in his arms as though he were picking up a baby, and he said he was going to put it back in the sea. But the fish fell through his hands so the *kohno* said he'd summon the fisherman. Yalo couldn't remember where his mother had disappeared to, but he found himself alone with the fish in the kitchen. He went over to it, slipped, fell, bashed his head, and the blood flowed. In the midst of the coffee grounds that his mother put on his head to stop the bleeding and the massacre that took place in the sink, the memory that stood out in Yalo's mind was that of the grandfather weeping over the fish whose blood was spattered over the sink and wall.

"You slaughtered it?" screamed the *kohno*. "What sort of person, my daughter, slaughters a fish?"

Gaby had slit the fish's belly, ripped out its guts and started to remove its scales with a large knife by the time the *kohno* had returned with his friend Munir Shammo.

The slaughtered fish, its blood flowing from its guts, was flopping in Gaby's hands, and Gaby was busy scaling it and saying it was the best fish she'd ever seen and that she'd get three meals out of it: she'd fry one half for lunch, grill the other half on Sunday, and then cook the huge head with "fisherman's rice".

"God bless you, Uncle Munir. You're invited to eat fish with us three days in a row!"

The grandfather, repeating what he'd said about the slaughtering of the fish, left the house with his friend and didn't return till evening, when he announced that he'd given up eating fish.

"And that was how my grandfather came to give up eating fish. He even stopped eating squid, even though the squid is ink; its veins are an inkwell, and it doesn't have a drop of blood in it. Did you know that in France they eat blood?"

"What?" asked Shireen.

"I'm telling you that in France they eat blood. *Khawaja* Michel gave me a dish called '*boudin*' to eat. He said they stuff a pig's intestines with blood and eat it."

"Did you eat it?"

"Of course. What of it? Then I lived in a house where we used to drink blood almost every day."

"You drank blood?" she asked, looking disgusted. She turned as though she didn't want to look at the person who was speaking to her, then picked up the paper napkin to wipe the red off her lips.

"No! Don't take off the red. I love the red."

She was looking at her watch – and when Shireen looked at her watch, it meant she'd decided to leave – when he surprised her by asking if she believed in God.

"Of course," she said. "Of course."

"And do you go to the *atado*?"

"What?"

"Do you go to church?"

"Not always, but certainly, you know, at Christmas and on Good Friday, like everyone else."

"And do you take Communion?"

"You know. Sometimes."

"And when you take Communion, what do you feel?"

"Why all the stupid questions? Let's go."

"No, let's not. I'm asking you a question. Answer me."

"Very well. I open my mouth and I eat the Host."

"And drink the blood!"

She said it was just a symbol, that the wine was only symbolically transformed into blood at the mass.

"Not true," said Yalo. "The mass is a blood offering, which means a slaughter. That's what I know."

"You know nothing," she said.

She said she didn't like talking about religion, because she didn't understand anything about it, but she believed in God, and that was enough.

"Of course it's enough," said Yalo. "But I was telling you about the *kohno*. My grandfather pretended he was a vegetarian, but every day he drank blood."

"Drank blood?"

"Of course he drank blood. He was a *kohno*, and at the mass he drank the blood of Christ. He'd put sweet wine and water into the cup and drink blood."

"That was wine. You scared me. I don't know why I still believe the things you say."

"No. It wasn't wine. It had become blood," said Yalo. He told her that he'd been afraid of the mass. He would close his eyes and open his mouth to take Communion, and he'd taste the blood and become dizzy. He wanted to tell her about his grandfather's miracles and about the Kurdish mullah's miracle and about Alexei and his Muscovite mother, but he felt that talking to Shireen opened up an infinite number of gaps inside him and that he was incapable of explaining this to her. When he was with her, he felt that speech flowed from him and then he discovered that he hadn't said a thing because he was incapable of conveying a clear and simple sense of his love for her.

"But you don't know me," she said.

"I know everything," he answered, for love is the greatest knowledge. He wanted to tell her that her smell never left him and that he was ready to transform his life for her sake, and that he wasn't just a tramp or a villa guard but a victim of circumstance and that he was going to open a joinery workshop. But he didn't say any of this, for talking calls for something else, something Yalo wouldn't learn until he was in the isolation cell. Talking calls for trickiness, and the trickiness only came to him there, when he found himself penned in by walls – the grey wall of the prison with its peeling paint, filled with cracks and holes that took on human shapes at night, and the wall of white pages that had been put in front of him so he could write the story of his life. Yalo was unaware that this technique for extracting confessions was the one most widely employed with political prisoners in the Arab world, where it was the custom, following the traditional torture parties, for the prisoner to find himself forced to sit, naked, on an empty cola bottle, and where, if he survived death by blood poisoning or haemorrhage, he'd be given a pile of sheets of white paper and asked to write his life story. This was when the real torture began, when writing was transformed into a murder weapon and a form of suicide, the words coming to resemble knives stabbing their owner, who would descend into an abyss he dug for himself, slipping on the letters and falling into the blood that took on the colour of ink, smelling his own blood.

Yalo hadn't smelled his own blood before he'd gone to prison. Even when he'd been in the presence of Alexei's bones, from which the flesh had departed, and listened to the stories of Nina the Russian, he hadn't smelled what he smelled in the cell when he tried to trick death by writing his own death's story.

Nina's image returned to him in the cell as though leaping out of the wall.

"Are you Russians, Auntie?" he'd asked her, drinking sweetened rosewater, which the Muscovite prepared in a special way.

"This is for the feast of Mar Elias the Living," said the woman, gesturing towards the rosewater. "We drink iced rosewater not because . . . not because the feast falls in July, when it's so hot. No, because Mar Elias is the prophet of fire. He went up to Heaven in his chariot pulled by horses of fire. The crushed ice is because of the fire. I would never make rosewater before the feast of Mar Elias. Rosewater, my son, is the essence of the red damask rose, whose colour is that of fire. We put the fire with the ice and we drink to the feast of fire. Drink, my son."

"Thank you," said Yalo and sipped the magic drink that refreshed the heart. He hesitated a little before returning to his question.

"Are you Russians, Auntie?"

"Did you ever tell me, son, where you're from?"

"From here."

"No. Before here, where are you from?"

"We're from Ein Ward. That's what my grandfather says. It's a hamlet in Tur Abdin."

"Alexei's father, God rest his soul, was from Mardin," the Russian woman said. "That's why he didn't speak Syriac. Mardin people speak only Arabic. When he came to ask for my hand, I told him I wouldn't accept an Assyrian, and he told me he was

Assyrian and not Assyrian, so we got married."

"So you're Assyrians?" Yalo asked.

"They were. My husband's family. Not me."

"So you're a Russian?"

"That's what they say. They call us 'the Muscovite woman's children', but we're Arabs. One day I'll tell you the story of my grandmother's grandmother. She was the Muscovite woman, and the name stuck, which is why I called my son Alexei. His father wanted to call him Alexander. I said, 'No. Alexander means Alexei. That way we can give the boy a Russian name, like the tsars. What's more beautiful than the tsars?'"

Yalo creeps inside the mantle of sleep. He wraps himself up in himself on the iron bed in the corner of the cell, closes his eyes and sees the ghost of the pregnant woman running, her long robe stained with blood. The woman emerges from a place in the wall and he sees her. The image starts with her belly, which is smeared with red, a belly swollen with a foetus in its sixth month. The belly emerges from the cracks in the wall in its black robe spotted with black blood.

The image starts with black. Then the black disappears and white takes its place. The robe turns white and the blood spreads over its swellings as though tracing the head of the foetus and its face, astonished at the sight of death. The woman's face, on the other hand, isn't clear but seems to be overlaid with a pale yellow smudge.

The woman emerges from the wall and starts running through the narrow streets. Suddenly the streets disappear and the woman finds herself alone on the plains, and then she reaches the outskirts of Tyre. She stands before a walled building. She knocks on the door and a nun opens it, then closes the iron door in her face. But the white robe spotted with blood raps again and makes a sobbing noise like a nursing child. The nun opens the iron door again, takes the woman by the hand and leads her into the convent.

Fragments of the story Yalo heard from Nina the Russian transformed themselves into an image stuck onto the wall of the cell. At night, the image emerges from the wall and sets off running, looking for the convent of the Muscovite nuns in Tyre, which will take it in along with its belly swollen with the foetus crying inside it, and save her life and its life.

Yalo can't remember the story in a coherent form. Nina said the name of the village and told how the man had been butchered across his wife's belly, but Yalo didn't remember the name and didn't know how to explain what had happened in 1860, in the massacre that inaugurated all of Lebanon's massacres. They said that when the Muscovite nun heard the crying of the foetus wallowing in blood inside the pregnant woman's belly, she was amazed and could not stop herself opening the door again and allowing the woman into the convent, where she gave birth to her only daughter.

"That daughter was my grandmother's mother, and they used to call her the 'Muscovite woman' because she'd come into this world in the convent of the Muscovite nuns in Tyre, and her children and grandchildren became known as the 'children of the Muscovite woman', and that's how it came to be our name."

What had happened on that hot day in July 1860?

Yalo drew an image of the village in his mind and called it "Nina's village". There, in that village drowsing on the flanks of Jabal El Sheikh, the massacre began, in the house of the woman who was six months pregnant.

A man came in carrying a rifle and said to the husband of the pregnant woman that he would cut his throat because he was his friend and he wasn't going to let anyone torture him before he died. He rested the man's neck on the belly of his young, pregnant wife and cut his throat as though he were a sheep. The blood gushed and penetrated the guts of the woman, who had lost the power of speech, and she ran from her house and found herself at the convent of the Muscovite nuns in Tyre, and there she had her child.

Before getting to the point in the story where the rich man asks the abbess for the hand of the orphan daughter, only to die and leave her and her only son great wealth, certain issues ought to be clarified, but Yalo didn't dare tell Nina that the placing of the man's head on his pregnant wife's belly prior to slitting his throat was difficult to believe, or that the things that were said to have been said more closely resembled a scene from a novel or film than they did reality.

Yalo is convinced that in this latest war the Lebanese were grubbing up the history of their earlier wars to justify their insanity, and this is what made it impossible to talk to them. True, he behaved like any other Lebanese during the war, and he was Lebanese and hadn't allowed the interrogator to play around and threaten him with his father who wasn't his father, or whom he didn't know. Yalo had fought under the flags that had been raised and had swallowed everything that had been said. However, when Nina the Russian recounted the story of her grandmother, he felt as though his belly had become distended with stories, and he couldn't take any more. Nina told the story as though she had witnessed the incident herself; she even repeated the words the murderer had spoken as he was committing his crime.

"You are my friend and I am the one who will kill you. Do not be afraid. A wasp's sting. You will feel nothing. Just a sting like a wasp's."

She said the killer had said, "A wasp's sting," and that he'd come to the victim's home the night before and assured him that nothing would happen in their village and that everyone was committed to living in peace. So the man slept despite the smell of fear that enveloped the place. In the morning, he heard a knock on the door, opened it and saw the face of death. Horrified, the man didn't utter a word. He placed his head on his wife's belly and died.

The killer said, "A wasp's sting," before taking a knife and slashing through the other man's neck, across the belly of his pregnant wife, who was not more than seventeen. Then he went away, leaving the woman to her insanity, which set her to wandering the roads and plains for days before arriving at the convent of the Muscovite nuns.

"It couldn't have been like that," thought Yalo as he watched the woman emerge from the wall with her distended belly and start running towards the convent in Tyre.

She knocked, and the nun opened the iron door a crack, and when she saw the rounded belly with the spots of blood, she closed it again hard.

The woman knocked again, and the foetus inside her belly cried.

Nina said that if the Russian nun hadn't heard the sound of the foetus crying from inside the woman's belly, she wouldn't have opened the door again.

"The foetus cried in its mother's belly," said Nina.

"Could that really have happened?" asked Yalo.

"Of course it could have happened, my son. It was a miracle, and the proof is that that nun is now a saint. The other nuns all kissed the hand of the one who'd opened the door because she'd heard a voice that nobody but Elizabeth had ever heard.

Could anyone but a saint hear the voice of a foetus?"

"But maybe the saint was your grandmother, because she was the one from whose belly the foetus spoke," said Yalo.

"No, my son, that wasn't my grandmother. That was my grandmother's grandmother. She didn't hear the foetus that spoke inside her belly because God didn't open her ears. Only divine intervention can open one's ears."

Yalo said he understood, but he understood nothing. The young woman had fled her village and taken refuge in the convent, where she had given birth to her daughter, and the two of them had gone on living there, the mother working as a servant and the little girl studying. When the daughter reached the age of fourteen, *Khawaja* Nakhleh Sadiq, a merchant from Tyre in his fifties who had emigrated to Argentina and returned to Lebanon to marry, encountered her. He saw the girl once in front of the convent and fell in love with her. He asked for her hand, but her mother refused to discuss the matter, saying that she and her daughter belonged to the convent and he would have to talk to the abbess. The abbess summoned the girl in the certainty that she would refuse the marriage, being the daughter of a miracle, and that she would choose to become a bride of Christ. To her surprise, the abbess heard the girl agree to the marriage, though she made it a condition that her mother should live with her and that *Khawaja* Nakhleh should not return to Argentina. The greater surprise, though, was that *Khawaja* Nakhleh agreed to both conditions, and the rich merchant married the girl and she bore him her only son, Musa.

"That's why we're part of the Musa family, though people call us the children of the Muscovite woman," said Nina.

"So you're not White Russians?" said Yalo.

"Our hearts are white, and we love Russia," said Nina.

Yalo saw the girl emerging from the wall, the front of her dress spotted with blood and taking on the form of a foetus in the shape of a girl-child clinging to her mother's belly. The mother runs towards the forest and hides under the first pine tree. Then she gets up and runs towards the convent of the Russian nuns.

Yalo didn't ask what had happened to the corpse of the man whose severed head his wife had had to push off her belly before gathering her blood-laden dress round her and leaving. Had the woman thrown the head aside? Or had the murderer-friend not severed the head from the body but simply cut the man's jugular? And who had buried the body? Had it been buried, or had it been left to rot in the abandoned house?

The story seems impossible to Yalo, but when he sees the pregnant woman emerging from the wall of the cell and approaching him and wiping his brow with the sticky blood gushing from her long robe, he feels that it would be easier to write this story than to write the story of his life.

How is he to write, and what, when he doesn't know how to put the necessary distance between the word and its image? He writes the name Nina and sees the Christians and the Druze drowning in their own blood. He writes his name and he sees his own image, which has become attached to the name, so that he has to erase the image before he can go on writing, but the name is erased along with the image, and Yalo finds himself in the silence of the black ink.

Tomorrow, when the interrogator comes, he will give him the pages he has written and say that's everything; all his confessions have been written, and it's enough.

"I don't know how to write, sir," he will say.

Yalo had closed his eyes and enveloped himself in sleep when that woman, the one with no face, came and sat next to him and wept, and Yalo became both men, the murdered husband and the murderous neighbour. He put his head on her distended belly, heard the beating of two hearts as they mingled in a strange rhythm, and understood his mother's words about the feelings a man cannot feel.

Yalo's mother would drink coffee in the living room with her friend Catherine. She told what had happened between Elias El Shami and her father and wept. Having humiliated the tailor and thrown him out of his house, the *kohno* pointed at his daughter and said, "Enough. No more dirty games. I think you need to wake up, get a grip on your feelings, and cast Satan out of your body."

She said her father was a man, and men understood nothing. The *kohno* thought she was like him and that her motive in forming this long relationship with the tailor was the satisfaction of desire. Even Elias thought that. "He sleeps with me and finishes and then he looks at me and asks, 'Did you come?' At the beginning, I used to tell the truth and ask myself why he asked when he knew the answer. A woman, when she comes, is like a spring. What was one supposed to say? And when I'd say I hadn't come, he'd get angry and start behaving stupidly, and I don't like that kind of thing. Later on, I would lie to him. I'd say I'd come and he'd be happy. He'd light his cigar and start puffing away, like a cockerel."

"You mean he'd never come at the same time as you?" Catherine asked.

"Of course. I mean a few times. What do you think?" guffawed Gaby. "But it's not like pressing a button."

Gaby said that men knew nothing about desire. They thought it was a ring stuck onto the ends of their penises, which was why men finished before they began and never knew the taste of that wave that mounts from within and takes the body to unknown places with infinite winding ways.

"I wanted nothing from Elias. My dad got everything wrong. It wasn't about sex, it was about tenderness. I knew he couldn't marry me. It's true I suffered a lot, and I hated it when told me about his wife and children. I told him, 'Please don't talk about them, because I can't bear it. Every time you talk about your wife and her illnesses, I hate you and I hate myself.'"

Gaby said she forbade him to talk about his family because whenever he talked about his wife, Evelyn, he'd become a different person. He'd lose his masculinity and his attractiveness and turn into an old man giving off the foul smell of false teeth.

Gaby didn't tell anyone.

How could she say what couldn't be spoken? How could she say that all she remembered of that day was the smell of the man's words, which spread over her body? How could she say that when she undressed for him, she sprang out of the dark and rose like a sun that had been concealed in the darkness of her clothes, which resembled a shroud?

Gaby was eighteen when she went to learn her craft at the tailoring workshop owned by Elias El Shami, and there she saw the world blossom with the love that took over her life.

He told her . . . She remembered that he told her something about her having to sew a new dress. The autumn evening had begun to spread its shadows, but Elias El Shami didn't turn on the light and the two assistant seamstresses had left and Gaby was giving the workshop a final tidy before going home. She became aware of *Khawaja* Elias at her side saying something about her having to make herself a dress and that he'd found a lovely piece of cloth for her.

"For me?" asked the girl.

"Of course for you. I want you to wear a dress that shows off your beauty. It's a shame to see you in these concealing clothes. They seem to be covering you up. Clothes shouldn't cover the body. Clothes should be an extension of the body. That's the secret of tailoring, that's what makes it an art.

"Come closer so I can see you," said Elias.

The girl approached hesitantly. He took the cloth tape measure and started taking her measurements. He took the height and then he took the hips. Then he reached her breasts, and she saw how her dress fell to the ground without her being aware of the hands that had undone its buttons. The dress fell and Gaby stood in her underwear under the tailor's gaze, which crawled over her body and clung to it. She put her hands round her wrists as though she wanted to hide them, but she was really trying to subdue the hair on her body, which was standing straight up as though surrounded by a magnetic field.

He left her standing there and drew her body with a piece of green soap on some tracing paper. Then he looked at her breasts and said, "What an awful bra. Tomorrow I'll buy you a better one." Then he sat down on his chair and asked her to walk towards him.

The bra fell to the floor and Gaby found herself standing in front of the seated man. She felt his breath on her breasts. He put his head between her breasts, took a deep breath and said that he could smell flowers. She felt lips taking hold of her left nipple and then the tailor started sucking the nectar. That's what he used to say every time he took her breast in his mouth: "I want to suck the essence of roses." The girl would feel her breast between the man's lips that crawled and clambered and retreated and advanced, and she would quiver with something that rose up from deep inside her and then subsided.

He pulled away, stood up and went into the other room. Gaby stood there not knowing what to do. Her body was quivering with eruptions and secretions that came and went. She stood unmoving for an endless while. Then she bent over, picked up her bra and put it on, and put on her dress. When she saw him coming back, she said, "Do you need anything, boss? I'm going home," and felt she was hearing her own voice for the first time. Her voice came out like that of another woman. It sounded deep and came from her chest. She asked him if he wanted anything, and he looked up but didn't reply.

Suddenly darkness fell. She bent over to pick up her bra, and by the time she had straightened up again to put it on in front of the mirror, darkness had fallen. She bent over when it wasn't dark and the pale, white light covered everything, but when she picked up the bra and stood in front of the mirror, she saw darkness and couldn't see herself. She dressed hastily and decided to go home. She saw him standing at the door of the room like a ghost. She asked him if he wanted anything, and she heard her voice and left. At home, she went into the bathroom and washed herself, and when she covered her breasts with soap that sensation of a magnetic field that had taken her to distant places returned and made her realize that the *kokina* of hair held together with pins no longer suited the beauty of her nakedness and that she needed her long hair so that there could be shade inside her.

In the days that followed, Gaby felt depressed. Every evening after she'd finished sweeping and tidying the workshop, she'd wait for the green soap and the dress project, but *Khawaja* Elias would treat her as though she didn't exist, as though he'd never taken her breasts in his hands and said that her beauty hurt him. "Your beauty hurts me, but you aren't hurt by it," he would tell her when he rescued her from the evenings of waiting. He'd seen that she was only a child and been afraid for her. "I feel guilty, I swear. You're the same age as my daughter. I don't know what I'm doing."

She waited more than a month before he returned to her, carrying the new dress. She'd finished her work and was getting ready to leave when she saw him coming towards her carrying the yellow dress that shone in the sun.

"What do you think?" he asked.

"God, how lovely!" she said.

She took the dress and turned away from him to take off her old dress and try on the new one, and she heard him say, "No, not like that," and ask her to take a bath before putting on the new dress, and he pointed to the bathroom.

Gaby looked where he was pointing and asked fearfully, "Take a bath here?"

. . .

"But I don't have my things."

He left her standing there uncertainly and came back carrying a towel and underwear and went ahead of her to the bathroom. She followed him as though under a spell. He turned on the tap over the tub and the hot water gushed out and the steam arose. The man bent over and put bath soap in the water. He stirred it with his hand, and bubbles began to form and with them the smell of apples, and Gaby felt as though she was drunk. The steam entered her eyes and wrapped her in a white darkness. Two moist hands removed her dress and her underwear, and she stepped naked into the water. The man knelt at the edge of the tub, took a loofah and began rubbing her body with it. If Gaby had told the story, she would have said she'd seen a man hanging over the water like the branches of a tree. The branches were above her and around her, and her body was slippery with the soap and the smell and undulated to the rhythms of the water. And when he took her hand and helped her to stand up, he started kissing her, working downwards as though exploring with his lips and his eyelashes. He took her out of the water and embraced her, and the water dripping from her body started spotting his shirt and trousers. Gaby didn't see him naked, she had her eyes closed, but she felt him naked, and felt how the man had become part of the water and how, with her middling size, and with her white body and her smell, she had become an extension of the man who stood embracing the body of the woman who had arisen out of the soap and water. He dried her carefully, then dressed her in her new clothes and asked her to look in the mirror. Gaby beheld how her image had been born in the mirror, and she had emerged as a new woman with a new body, new eyes and a new voice. She stood in front of the mirror and undid her *kokina* and let her hair fall loose over her shoulders.

"What's all this?" asked Elias El Shami. "Come, come. I have to bathe you again."

She started repinning her *kokina* and asked him not to touch her hair.

"What are you doing?"

"I'm doing my hair."

"Madwoman!"

He said she was mad and that hair like hers had to be worn loose, and when she tried to explain that she couldn't do that because her hair had to be pinned up like a cake to adorn her head, and that it was never to be left loose except for the night of the miracle – Epiphany Eve – or the night of her marriage, the tailor laughed and said these were superstitions.

"Hair is sacred. Hair is a woman's soul," he said.

She put her hair up again, pinned it with several pins and coiled it round her head, the tailor repeating, "Impossible. Impossible. You should wear it loose," while she said, "Shame on you, shame on you, M. Elias."

She put her hair up and left without a backwards glance but then discovered that her heart had fallen to the ground. She felt a need to bend over and gather it up but pulled herself together around her backbone and went home.

That is how Gaby started. She took off the old Gaby and put on a new likeness along with her yellow dress. In the street that joins Talaat Shahadeh Street, where the tailor's workshop was, to the Assyrian quarter, where she lived, she discovered that the way she trod the ground had changed, and became aware of her hips and the curve of her pelvis, and of her neck, which led her.

Elias El Shami took her to the secrets of the world, where her navel, her "secret place", became itself the secret of life. It was there that he would begin, explaining to his young beloved that the art of tailoring began at the navel, for when humankind tied off the child's cord at the moment of its birth, people discovered that they could also make ties of leather, invent cloth and thread. And he told her the story of the Navel and the Dog, which he said he'd read in the Gospel of Barnabas. When the girl asked her father about this gospel, the *kohno* cursed the Devil and spat, and told his daughter to spit on the Devil.

Spitting on the Devil was one the Abyad family's customs in Beirut, and Yalo took it with him everywhere. Even in prison, when he wrote a wrong sentence or an inappropriate thought came to him, he would feel a strange taste mounting from his throat to his tongue and say, "I spit on the Devil!" and spit. Shireen hated spitting, and her face would contract in disgust when Yalo formed his spit ball. When he tried to explain that he had to spit on the Devil because it was the Devil who had started by spitting on humanity, the disgust sketched in her eyes intensified. But Yalo felt that if he didn't spit he would vomit. Then he realized that he'd been afflicted with stomach ulcers when he was fourteen and that the ulcers had been accompanied by scurf on his head, both conditions being attributable to shock. Yalo doesn't deny that it was during the civil war that he learned to distinguish shock from fear. He never forgot his first night at Sodeco on the Green Line in Beirut when the firing had started and he'd felt he couldn't control his bowels and his legs would no longer support him. He'd crawled away and defecated; no-one saw him – all the boys were busy fighting. He, though, was busy with his shit, as Alexei told him the next day, when the smell reached them. The shit would have stuck to his name too, had the battalion not withdrawn from its position at Sodeco and taken up a new one close to the Museum, where Yalo learned to be afraid without losing control of his bowels. All the same, with each outbreak of firing, he would feel a need to urinate. At first, he'd manage to hold on. Then, when he was on the verge of losing control, he'd joke with the boys that he was going to piss on the enemy, and when he saw their admiring looks, he'd go out in front of the barricades, squat down, and urinate under enemy fire.

"Why do you piss like that, like a Bedouin?" Tony asked.

Yalo replied that it was the proper, human way to urinate: "We should squat and not show off what God has given us," said Yalo, in his grandfather's voice.

In the war, Yalo learned the difference between fear and shock. A fighter feels fear, but the ordinary person suffers shock, which is why Yalo chose to be a fighter. He fought so that he could inspire shock rather than feel it. True, he felt fear, but fear was nothing compared to the shock that paralyzes a man and wipes out his memory.

When Yalo was eleven and the shell fell in the street where he was playing, he wasn't afraid, but he was shocked and froze where he stood. A few days later, a white scurf erupted on his head, and everyone said he was going to go bald, and a smell of burning emanated from his stomach. His mother took him to the doctor, who diagnosed shock and asked Yalo what had happened. The boy couldn't remember, though, for the image of Najwa, the girl who'd been playing ball with him in front of the house when the shell came and who'd been torn to shreds, had been erased from his eyes. Yalo didn't remember the incident. He heard about it from his mother when she told the doctor that her son had been deaf and dumb for two days and had then started vomiting a green liquid and the white patch had erupted on his head.

The physician said it was shock and prescribed a yellow ointment for Yalo's head and a black liquid that he was to take every morning before breakfast for the ulcer. This was also the reason for the small white patch on the right side of Yalo's head which he called his third eye.

"I have three eyes," he told Shireen.

"How did you see me?" she asked.

"I have three eyes," he said, and he pointed to the staring white patch towards the front of his head.

"I have a white eye in the middle of my black hair, and I don't know what's going to happen to it when my hair turns white," he said, and smiled. Shireen frowned before smiling in turn and accepting his invitation to coffee at a nearby café.

She asked him about the eye, which resembled a white hole,

and he told her he didn't remember the incident and that he'd even forgotten what the girl who'd died looked like. He said he hadn't heard anything, not even the sound of the shell. "That's shock," he said. "Shock is when you forget." Shireen lit a cigarette, inhaled deeply, and coughed. Then the cigarette began to jerk between her fingers.

"You mean to tell me that you were in shock, and that's why you don't remember anything about what happened?"

"I told you, I forgot because of the shock. Why won't you believe me?"

"And why won't you believe me when I tell you I've forgotten everything that happened at Ballona? You have to understand, I was in shock too."

"In shock?" He repeated the word a number of times in a low voice. "But you reached out to me, and I smelled incense."

Did Shireen say that, or is Yalo, in his loneliness, his silence and his sorrow, hearing voices that come from so deep a level of his imagination that he is no longer capable of distinguishing between reality and fantasy?

Yalo didn't tell her about the shell and the death of the girl. He said that it was his third eye, and that people only had third eyes if they saw things differently, and then he felt the green coming up from his guts, so he spat on the Devil and asked her to spit, and Shireen stubbed her cigarette out irritably in her cup of coffee and swallowed her saliva and left.

When Gaby told the story about the navel and referred to the Gospel of Barnabas, her father told her, "Spit on the Devil, my daughter." The *kohno* spat, his daughter spat, and his grandson spat. But Gaby was convinced that while the Gospel of Barnabas might all be lies, the story of the navel was not.

Elias El Shami said that God was the first tailor because when

He commanded the angel to remove the spittle from Adam's clay body, he ordered him at the same time to sew up the hole in the first man's belly. Thus the hole was converted into a navel, and the navel became the mark of humankind.

"Do you know, Gaby, what the navel is?" asked Elias.

She was standing naked, the way he liked her. He'd ask her to undress and walk barefoot about the workshop, and then he'd kneel and start kissing her navel before devouring her body with his hands.

"Do you know what 'navel' means?" he'd ask her.

"Of course I know. It's the gut that's attached to the after-birth."

"No. No, Gaby. Listen, my darling. I'm going to tell you, but it has to remain a secret between us, because the navel is humanity's secret."

Elias El Shami got up and went into another room. He returned holding a book with a green cover. He sat down, put on his spectacles and started leafing through the pages. Then, when he reached the place he was looking for, he said, "Listen," and began to read:

Then one day when all the angels were gathered together, God said, "Let all those who take me as their lord, prostrate themselves to this earth," and those who loved God prostrated themselves. Satan, however, and those of his persuasion, said, "O Lord, we are spirit, and it is not just that we should prostrate ourselves to this clay." And God said, "Be gone, accursed ones, for I have no mercy for you!" And as he departed, Satan spat on the lump of earth and Gabriel removed the spittle along with a little of the earth, and for this reason man came to have a navel in his belly."

"Did you understand the story?" asked Elias.

She said she'd understood, but she wasn't convinced. The tailor always treated her as though she was incapable of comprehension. He'd tell her something and then ask if she'd understood, and when she said yes, he'd start repeating it. He'd repeat his words a number of times till the girl felt she was going to burst and look at him with narrowed eyes and he'd understand that he'd overdone it a bit and start condensing and shortening his sentences, so as to bring his explanations to an end.

By this repetitive method, Gaby learned the art of tailoring and the art of love, along with all the other arts the tailor attributed to his Damascene family, which moved to Beirut following the massacre of 1860.

One question of Master Elias's always took his young sweetheart by surprise: "What is the most important thing in life?"

When she replied with an answer she'd learned from having had to reply to the same question on an earlier occasion, she'd discover that the master always had another one up his sleeve. To begin with, the most important thing in life was the art of tailoring. Then it became the navel, then the dog, then she knew not what.

Master Elias El Shami was infatuated with his young mistress's navel. He'd read to her about the navel of Our Lord Adam, peace be upon him, from that forged work that an Italian monk who had embraced Islam in the sixteenth century had written and by means of which he had hoped to solve the intractable problem that human beings had created when they'd divided God up among them. Then the tailor would bend over her navel and hug her to him and kiss it.

"God cannot be divided," said Elias. "That's the most important thing."

He bent over the girl's navel, submerged in the water, a small navel resembling a rosebud in a hairless belly. He knelt and said that the navel was the first icon that God made, an icon fashioned by the removal of the filth of Satan's spittle.

She'd said she understood and felt she had to sit down. She was standing naked in front of him listening as he announced that love was the first lesson a man learns when feeding at his mother's breast. But when he moved closer to her, the chill of fear fell suddenly on Gaby and she said that what they were doing was a sin – the sin of which her father the *kohno* always spoke when he spoke of women, saying, "All God has granted me is two daughters, one of whom has gone to a faraway land and the other of whom is divorced and not divorced, a widow and not a widow, may God save us from sin."

Gaby said that she hadn't gone back to him after her husband had disappeared and had her son because of the navel or the sex. She'd gone back to him because she'd felt lonely and the night was heavy upon her body. She'd gone back to him, and she wanted him, at night. "I told him, 'Just one night. I want to sleep the whole night next to you so that I don't feel that the night is a valley that is going to swallow me up.'" Gaby was incapable of describing her fear of the night to the man, not because she didn't know how to talk, but because speech cannot come if the other person isn't prepared to listen. Without that readiness, it falls into the gap between the one and the other. Yalo learned that from Mme Randa. At first, when he was in thrall to her randarizing of him, she couldn't stop talking, and he'd drink in her words and her love. He didn't talk much because he didn't know how to talk like she did, but what she said would seem to become his. When the talking stopped, so did the love, and Yalo understood that a person can talk only when the other person has become a part of his words. That is why Shireen would leave him feeling sad. He would try to trick her silence with words; he would tell about his adventures and his wars and stories that he had and hadn't lived so as to stretch out towards her a thread by which she could climb up to him, and she would approach the thread, grasp the end and then draw back.

Elias El Shami was different. When Gaby went back to him, he felt that he was awaking from sleep. He didn't lie to her. He told her he didn't want to be like all the other men, who lie. He told her that when she'd married, she'd fallen off the edge of his life and left him. He said he'd forgotten her and felt at peace. "Why have you come back? I was at peace, I'd said to myself, 'It's over.'"

How could she tell him that at 6.00 in the evening she'd felt a gale arise within her and that the gale had commanded her to go to the tailor's workshop? She'd known that the tailor would be there alone and she'd felt the gale in her arms. He'd opened the door and rubbed his eyes as though he couldn't believe what he was seeing.

"Come in, come in," he said in a hesitant voice.

She went into the private parlour where she had stood every day at 6.00 in the evening and undressed in front of his eyes and where he had taken her with his hands. She stood hesitant and stammering.

"You're still pretty, Gaby," he said. He lit a cigarette and sat on the rocking chair without inviting her to sit down. She remained standing, her hands wrapped round her wrists. He said what he did about having forgotten her and having gone back to his normal life and how he'd made things right with his customers. He had returned to the innocent sexual indulgence he permitted himself of lording it like a rooster over the women in the workshop, which cost him no anxiety and meant he didn't have to take his clothes off. He dissolved in laughter: "You know, Gaby, you taught me to get naked. I may have taught you everything, but you made me take my clothes off. I don't like taking my clothes off, I get embarrassed. Even with my wife, I . . . "

"Don't mention your wife," she said.

Gaby didn't know where those old words had come from. In the days of their love, she hadn't allowed him to talk about his wife and three children. And now, even though she'd come for a job, she didn't want to resurrect that business and for the jealousy to drive her insane again, so she returned instinctively to her old words and said she didn't want to hear anything about that woman.

When Gaby had agreed to marry, she'd been like someone throwing herself into a chasm. She saw the man who came to the house and she heard her father say yes, so she closed her eyes and said yes and fell from a great height. She said yes and went to the workshop the following morning. She went to the room of Master Elias El Shami, who was drawing on a piece of cloth with green soap, and told him without preamble that she had got engaged and was going to be married. The man raised his head, looked at her over his spectacles and said, "Congratulations. I can't say anything. Congratulations, my dear. It's the right thing. I have no claim on you. I hope you'll be happy."

She left his room, went to her sewing machine and buried herself in her work. In the evening, she didn't dawdle as before; on the contrary, she was the first to leave. At the door, she heard him asking her to stay behind because one of the dresses needed fixing, and she said, "Please don't mind if I say no. I'm in a hurry. Tomorrow."

She gave up going to work. She told her father she no longer felt any desire to work, and the *kohno* said it was better that way. It never occurred to him that his daughter, who had closed her eyes when she'd agreed to marry Georges Jalao, was throwing herself into the valley of despair, having despaired of her lover.

She said she hadn't come because of the past, because she was a married woman now. She'd come, in fact, to work, and she asked if she could take up her old job again.

"Everything will be just as it was," he said. "You can start work tomorrow morning." Then he moved closer to her and put out his hand as he had done before, but she didn't reach for him.

"Thank you, master," she said, and left.

That "thank you" quickly dissolved, however, and Gaby returned to her old story, and there he was, sitting before her and asking, "What is the most important thing in life?"

Gaby couldn't understand how the man didn't get sick of his own words. She was there because she needed work, and because she was afraid of the night that lay heavily over her life. She wanted just one night when they would go together to a hotel or any place he liked. He would make arrangements for them to go to the Grand Hotel in Sawfar, but at the last minute, and after she'd invented her lie and made her father believe it, he'd tell her he couldn't and they'd have to put it off. And when she became upset, he'd be overwhelmed by sorrow and anger and she'd be obliged to make him feel better, as though it was she who'd made a mistake that had to be forgiven.

"You didn't tell me what the most important thing in life is."

She knew he was waiting for her to give him the same old answer about the navel and the art of tailoring, but he surprised her on the final occasion with the dog. He said the most important thing was the dog, and he went back to the Gospel of

Barnabas so he could read how God had created the dog.

"Listen," he said.

She stood, half-naked and yawning, sure that she going to hear the story of Adam and the spittle and so on.

He began reading:

One day Satan approached the gates of Paradise. When he saw the horses eating the grass, he told them that if that lump of earth were to gain a soul, they would be afflicted with emaciation. Therefore it was in their interest to tread on the lump of earth in such fashion that it would no longer be good for aught. The horses then rose up in anger and started bitterly to attack that piece of earth that lay among the lilies and the roses. God then gave life to that unclean piece of the earth on which Satan's spittle had fallen and which Gabriel had removed from the lump, and He created the dog and it started to bark and the horses were affrighted and fled. Then God gave man his soul, and all the angels sang praises to the Lord, blessed be His name.

"Did you understand?" he asked.

"Enough, I beg of you. I want to go home. I'm tired and I have a bad taste in my mouth."

"You understood that God created the dog to defend man, which is true, but that's not the point. Ask me what the point is."

"Get on with it. What is the point?"

"The point, my dear, is that man and dog are of the same clay, and when sin takes man over, he becomes a dog."

"You mean you and I are dogs?" she said.

"Not at all. Love isn't a sin," he said.

When he spoke of the dog, she felt that everything had

become monotonous and insipid and that she no longer loved him. Gaby told Catherine she no longer loved him. "I stopped loving him, but I stayed with him, and that's the most awful thing – to not love and stay with him without his being your husband. I mean I know – a married woman or a married man, it's her they judge, and the judgement is always in the man's favour, but what does that matter to me? I don't know what came over me."

"And how did you leave him?" asked Catherine.

"I didn't. I stayed with him till the end, even after my father humiliated him that way. I don't know. Things just died of their own accord."

Here Gaby narrated what happened between her father and Elias El Shami, and how she had felt, as she listened at the door to the dialogue between the two men, that her father had devoured the tailor.

"He ate him. That was the first time in my life that I saw how a man can turn into a wild beast. He ate him with his words. I don't know how to tell you. It was like my father was chewing him up, and he, Elias, it was like he was shrinking. I don't know how. But God was kind and I was happy. I pretended to be upset because I was supposed to, but on the inside my sorrow was sweeter than joy."

Gaby said that she was happy when she saw her father eating the tailor with words, as though he was spreading the words out the way one arranges the food on a table before beginning to devour it. The *kohno* started chewing on his words as though he were chewing on the man, and the man shrank and almost disappeared.

The tailor asked her and she didn't know what to reply.

She thought of saying that it was velvet, for the tailor was very fond of velvet. He'd asked her to put on a pair of blue velvet trousers so he could undo the buttons and let his hand lose its way between the velvet of her trousers and the silk of her white breasts.

"Look in the mirror," he'd say when they'd finished making love. "See how beautiful you are. See how love makes you beautiful."

She said it was the dog: "The most important thing is the dog, the dog that came out of man's navel."

He said no, and the little furrow that crossed his left cheek widened. Gaby loved that wound that formed the final landmark of the master's manhood, for he'd been cut on his cheek with a razor by a swindler who'd been playing the three-card trick in Burj Square. Elias told his tale of the three-card-trick player often, and each time the story ended with the blood that flowed down his face and how he'd succeeded in catching the swindler and driving him before him to the police station. Then he'd put his hand to his cheek and say, "Ouch!"

That day, though, she didn't respond, "Poor thing!" because she no longer cared. The love had started to disappear, the expectations had been erased, and all that remained was a killing feeling of loneliness with a man she couldn't leave because . . . she couldn't say why.

When he said no, Gaby decided to go. She turned away from him and went, just as he started on a new analysis of what came first, this time making food the most important thing in the world.

Gaby told no-one that she felt an indescribable yearning for this man, that the yearning began in her arms, that she felt a thrill that ran through her arms before turning itself into a wave that encircled her ribs with a sort of throttling sensation, and that she didn't understand this because she hated him and

230

hated his smell. "Once I started to become aware of his smell, I couldn't stand it any longer," Gaby said, unaware that for all those years she'd been smelling her own smell: when she approached the man, the smell of the female that overwhelms everything would rise from her, and when her desire ceased, she began for the first time to smell his smell, the smell of cracked leather mixed with something rotten.

Unlike Yalo.

In prison Yalo only smelled his own smell when it was mixed with his wastes. Yalo had become convinced that he'd never be able to prove his innocence, and the words he wrote terrified him.

Yalo said that he had to get out of prison to achieve one goal. He wanted to go to Shireen and smell the smell of incense coming off her arms. That was the smell of love, and Yalo wanted to remember love so he could recover the flavour of life. He tried to write everything, but he could only write a little. He read the pages and felt the lashes of the whip and the electricity that tore out his finger- and toenails; the interrogator would take the pages and throw them in his face because he hadn't written the whole story of his life. But Yalo didn't know how. Was it really possible to remember the whole story of one's life? And if he remembered, the time it took to write it down wouldn't be shorter than that of his life. Yalo smiled at the thought. He would tell him, "Yes, sir," and then unveil his theory that no-one in the world could write the whole story of his life. Even Jurji Zeidan, whose books Gaby would bring home and not read, even Jurji Zeidan, all of whose novels about Arab history Yalo had read, had felt obliged to write a million pages about other people, but when it came to his own memoirs he had written nothing.

Yalo can't understand why they tortured him so much and

why a further chapter of unimaginable torment awaits him. Was it because of Shireen and the night cars at Ballona? Why didn't they put the whole Lebanese people on trial? Yalo is convinced that the whole Lebanese people has sex in cars. Why just him? Why didn't they put all the other lovers on trial? Was it because he'd robbed people? Who didn't rob people? His grandfather said they were all thieves and that one of the saints had written that all rich men were thieves since it wasn't possible for one man to get rich without stealing from the rest. "Observe, my son," the *kohno* would say. "Observe well how each puts his hand in the other's pocket. Observe well, my son. You have to look behind things. A man can't see what's behind things unless the blessing of the Gospel be with him. Observe and learn and you will receive the blessing and then you will see, and when you see you will discover that man's greatest curse is his hand. The sin is made present through the agency of the hand. When someone puts his hand in his neighbour's pocket, and his neighbour puts his in someone else's, and so on for ever, then you have a society. That is why the Holy Fathers shunned people."

"And you, Grandfather? Why haven't you shunned people?"

"Because I'm not a saint, I'm a sinner. I'm even . . . I don't know what I am. My life has passed without meaning."

Yalo laughs when he imagines the hand of his grandfather, trembling with the fear of God. Yalo knew that it wasn't like that, for the discovery towards which he had been moving in Ballona was greater than all his experiences during the war. The war had taught him death, but Ballona had taught him that everything was death, or resembled death, and that the hand was the extension of the penis, which is what he'd learned with Randa. Then in the forest he'd discovered the dark, where the differences between the members of the body were erased.

The lovers in the cars had taught him that one could become like a sardine, covered in the oil of sex. The cars were like sardine tins, and the people were like fish floating doubled up in oil. He liked the idea and decided to add it to the first idea, about writing. He took a sheet of white paper and wrote, and this was the first time he wrote outside the requirements of the interrogation.

First he wrote that one could not write one's life and that one had to choose between living and writing. And Yalo chose to live, so he was writing to fulfil the requirements of the interrogation. However, he didn't want to end up like Jurji Zeidan, hidden within other people's lives. On the contrary, he preferred to hide the book within his life, if, that was, they wanted him to write the story of a love unlike any other.

Second he wrote that all people desire all people and that experience had taught him, as he watched the lovers of Ballona, that most lovers practise or accept infidelity, and that even he, even at the height of his passion for Shireen, would betray her when the opportunity presented itself, because "infidelity is the most delicious flavour of all," which was an idea he stole from Mme Randa, who told him when randarizing with him on one occasion that infidelity was the most beautiful thing and that she had started to fear that she was getting used to him and would soon no longer feel that she was being unfaithful with him.

Third he wrote that all ideas are stolen, and that people spend their time stealing each other's ideas.

Yalo was delighted when he wrote these three ideas in the form of the following three statements:

1. No-one can write life.

2. Desires times desires.
3. All ideas are stolen.

– and he felt a strange peace and decided to look again at the story of his life. He would write it in an abbreviated, clear form, and the next day he would present the interrogator with two texts: a first, detailed text, and a summary that would speak eloquently of his life.

He sat down at the green table, puffed on his pen as though smoking a cigarette and began.

Your Honour,

  I would like to add these pages to the story of my life, which you have requested that I provide in writing and which you will find in the file of the accused, Daniel Habeel Abyad, known as Yalo.

I would like, sir, to ask to be excused, for I have discovered over the two months that I've spent in solitary confinement with nothing but sheets of white paper and the Holy Book that I am not Yalo the criminal.

No, no. I'm not claiming insanity the way criminals do to escape the hangman's rope. No, sir. I am no longer the same Yalo. In writing the story of my life, I discovered that I am no longer he. The time I spent under interrogation, and my constant reading of the Holy Book, have caused me to discover that I have been born anew. In this matter, sir, I would refer you to the Noble Gospel and all other holy books. Thus, when they say, "In the beginning was the Word," it means that the word was the first thing, and when I wrote the story of my life, I discovered the word that created me anew. I'm not sure how to explain it to you in good Arabic, but, I don't know, it's as though, when I saw my life from beginning to end, I felt certain that I'd become a new person. In the same way, I became convinced that the old Yalo wasn't aware of what he was doing. I mean, he didn't make his life the way he wanted it to be. It was as though he was hypnotized. It's not just that a person should pay the price for actions he didn't choose to carry out. Yalo, the tall young man who wore a black coat and descended on lovers in their cars, Yalo who laughed while he fought and killed, no longer exists.

I assure you, Your Honour, that I have become another person. I know my story because I wrote it, and I will write it again if you want me to, but I feel, here in prison, that I no longer have any connection to the past. The only thing I have learned from the past is love. Yes, sir. Yalo began his life when he discovered love, but that love was also the cause of his death. In other words, when Yalo stood he fell, and he got fucked when he became a human. Yes, sir. He treated Shireen badly and pursued her, but he discovered love. The human being, sir, is the one who loves; that's what my grandfather the *kohno* taught me, God rest his soul, though my grandfather was the cause of our downfall. He prevented my poor mother from staying with the man who loved her, because that man was married and a coward and didn't dare to divorce his wife. Did my mother have to be deprived of love because her lover was a coward? My mother was deprived of love, and a woman deprived of love cannot give. I believe that that was the underlying reason for the confusion in which I lived.

I ran away from the war, sir, and I didn't run away because I'd stolen the money belonging to the Georges Armouni Barracks. Anyway, I suffered in Paris because Tony, my friend, stole the money and left me on my own.

I ran away from the war because I could no longer understand. No, I wasn't a coward. Not once did I show cowardice. Even when I was afraid, I'd get a grip on myself and pretend I wasn't. Isn't that what courage is? Which means that I was brave, and I left the war because I'd got fed up with it. At the beginning, I was like all the boys. I wanted to defend Lebanon. Then I discovered I was fighting other poor people like me and that I'd remain a stranger whatever I did, because one is a stranger in this world. My grandfather used to say he was a stranger because he was a man. When I discovered I was a man, I fled to Paris, and I suffered, and *Khawaja* Michel Salloum rescued me and gave me a job as a guard at the Villa Gardenia in Ballona.

Everything I wrote in the story of my life is correct, but there is a matter I'd like to clarify, and I do not intend any harm to anyone by this clarification, God forbid. I am now pure and white like this sheet of white paper on which I am writing the story of my life. I just want my conscience to be clear and to put an end to my former life by confessing everything, and this cannot harm *Khawaja* Michel. Anyway, I harbour the greatest respect for the man, but the truth has to be told.

I want to confess to something I tried not to confess to throughout my torture and imprisonment, because I was concerned for other people's reputations. All the same, I discovered that confession is my only means to become a new person and start my life, and I'm sure that you will take my situation into consideration and issue me with a pardon, because it's hardly reasonable that the amnesty law should cover all the war criminals while I spend my life in prison because I slept with a woman, or a number of women.

When I came back from France, sir, and worked at the villa, I was in despair. Everything seemed black and I couldn't see colours any more. Now I wish I could relive those days. I lived in a villa in the middle of a green pine forest and I couldn't see the colours of nature. Is there anyone alive who can't see nature?

Yalo couldn't see the colours. He spent his time with his eyes closed. Yes, sir. My eyes were closed so I could stay in the heart of the colour black. Black became my life, and I lost my sense of living. It was like being in a long dream, I swear it was. Then a woman came into my life, a respectable woman for whom I feel nothing but appreciation. This woman, in whose house I lived and whom I was meant to be guarding, saw that I was poor and alone and felt sorry for me. Then she taught me how to love my body. Without her, my pores, which were closed and black, would not have been opened. The first time she spoke to me, she asked, "Why is your face the colour of indigo?" My skin is wheat-coloured, shading to dark. I was unaware that my colour had become dark blue. When I returned to my house below the villa, I looked in the mirror and discovered that my skin had turned black, like the colour of the things I was seeing. This woman gave me back my proper colour and my sense of life. The sex and the love that I experienced with Mme Randa Salloum is more than that tasted by all the rest of the world's men. Her love brought me back to life, but it opened a well in my heart that nothing could fill. When I stood in the garden and smelled the scent of the pines, I was in a turmoil. Believe me, sir, I became a part of nature, and nature doesn't recognize the boundaries between things. That is what led me to the cars and the problems that came with them. Suddenly, I felt as though I was living in a dream. Up there, the lady was teaching me the arts of love, and in the forest I felt as though the cars were animals that slept with one another all the time, and the smell of sex was everywhere.

I lived at the Villa Gardenia belonging to *Khawaja* Michel Salloum close to the church of Mar Niqula and I only went to mass once, because I missed the icons and the smell of incense. Ballona became like a triangle – the villa, the forest and the church.

Yalo was wrong to steal, but stealing wasn't his goal. He stole by accident. He robbed them because they robbed him, meaning that when he went down so he could see up close, he would fall into the trap of money and the seductiveness of jewellery, and that won't do, sir, not just because stealing is wrong but because money distorts things and makes pleasures too acute.

As for the matter of rape, the truth is I raped, but I didn't know that that was what's called rape. I thought sex was like that: you come to a woman and you don't need to explain anything. And that was idiotic.

Yalo was an idiot because he discovered later, when he was smitten by the sickness of love, that that kind of sex has no meaning. All the same, even love didn't stop him from practising that kind of sex because man is sinful by nature.

I am confused, sir. Yalo was in love with Shireen and thought of no-one but her, but he didn't stop going down to the lovers and having sex with the women when circumstances permitted. Perhaps it was the place. The place, sir. The forest is full of devils that hover round the smell of the pine gum and wild herbs. I don't know. I never lived in the mountains. My grandfather used to live in a village he said was like Paradise, but I've only lived in the city, first in the Assyrian quarter in Museitbeh and then in the Mreiyeh district in Ein El Roummaneh. In our first house there was a garden full of trees, especially cassie trees, which are covered in white and yellow flowers and have a beautiful smell. But the scents of our garden have nothing to do with the scents of the forest of Ballona. The pine trees alone, sir – when the scent of the pine mixed with the scent of Shireen, the place turned strange and my lust was aroused.

I am sure that Shireen loved me. My problem was that I didn't understand her love and didn't know how to treat her. The girl was going through a psychological crisis after her fiancé left her and she fell in love with the doctor who gave her an abortion. Yalo's relationship with her would have succeeded if he'd shown her his real self, but he played the intimidation game with her and was ready to die for her and dreamed of marrying her. In love, when you are ready to die, everything gets out of hand, and that's what happened. Shireen got scared and she was right to be scared. When a person loves something a lot, it escapes. That's what happened to Madame, because I started to feel I was a tool she was using to get something and she could no longer do without me, so I ran away. The same thing happened with Shireen. But she did fall in love with Yalo. I can assure you, sir, she fell in love with me. When we met, she would tremble with love. Now I can see her properly. In the past, I thought she was trembling because she was afraid, so I'd make her more afraid, but now I know that she loved me and was jealous of Ballona. Instead of telling her I was an artist and a calligrapher and educated – in other words, a person of culture – I kept telling her about crimes I'd committed and hadn't committed, which made her despise me, so she decided to get rid of me by any means.

I am certain, sir, that she is in torment now. Shireen and I made a huge error against love, and I want her to know that I am prepared to put it right. I am prepared to begin a new white page with her, and if she wants marriage, I have no objection. I want Shireen to know that I am prepared to marry her whenever she wishes, and she knows that I say this because I love her.

I didn't just sleep with her at Ballona when I caught her in the car with that pathetic doctor, and she wasn't with her fiancé, as she claimed, but I don't want you to interrogate her because I know she is frail and her thin body will not withstand the torture. In fact, I slept with her a number of times after that, in a hotel in Jounieh. Please forgive her for lying and saying she was in the forest with her fiancé, Emile, who is a cowardly youth who trembled with fright the whole time they were interrogating me even though it was me who had been tortured, not him.

As far as the explosives are concerned, I am prepared to

maintain my confession concerning Heikal and El Naddaf if this is necessary, and this, sir, is a sacrifice I make in the service of communal peace in Lebanon.

I hope, sir, that you will find this new information useful and that it will help to close my file and prove my innocence. I place my faith in you, sir, for I am an orphaned youth whose father is unknown to him, whose grandfather is not his father and whose mother is not his sister.

In closing, sir, I want to thank you and thank the interrogator and all his assistants, who have allowed me, during this stay in prison, to come to terms with myself and discover things that had never occurred to me before.

Yalo closed his eyes and spat on the Devil. He was standing in the interrogation room and felt a tremor inside him. The interrogator's face appeared to him through the wan fluorescent light from the ceiling. Yalo stood beneath the light and saw. The interrogator's greying hair had a yellowish tinge, and his small face looked as though it was sprouting from the table as he shuffled through the papers and looked at the tall ghost who blended in with the white fluorescent light.

Yalo closed his eyes and saw with his third eye. He felt a spasm pass through his arms and thighs, and he spat on the Devil. In prison he had learned how to spit in his heart. He no longer pursed his lips and spat the gob onto the ground. Now it was enough for him to say, "I spit on the Devil!" with the promise to himself that one day, when he emerged from this nightmare, he would spit out all the devils he'd been obliged to deal with. He said, "I spit on the Devil" in order to stop the spasm that convulsed his heart and his muscles, but the convulsion spread like a gentle wave that washed over the tall ghost's body from his head down to his feet. Before the short interrogator had spoken a single word, Yalo understood that he had fallen into the pit.

"What's all this, sex king?" asked the interrogator, inserting spaces between his words to indicate that what he said carried a range of threats.

Yalo wasn't afraid, or so he had convinced himself. What did he have to fear after all the things that had been done to him? There was nothing worse than the sack, nothing worse than that sensation of having become a eunuch, curled up and rolling round among their shoes, so why should he be afraid? He put his hands on his thighs to check the convulsing of his body, but as he bent over he heard his neck crack. How had the interrogator got behind him so fast and slapped him? Yalo straightened up again and felt the interrogator standing behind him waving the papers.

"Are you making fun of us, sex king?" asked the interrogator, walking in circles round the tall man, who was at a loss as to where he should be looking to intercept the short, fat interrogator's words. Yalo spat on the Devil and closed his eyes. He thought he might suggest to the interrogator with his fat thighs and round face that he stand on the chair opposite so that they could come to an understanding, but before Yalo could open his mouth, the interrogator delivered a blow to his solar plexus and the air was knocked out of Yalo's lungs and he doubled over, opening his mouth as wide as he could, as though begging for air before he closed his eyes and died.

Later Yalo would say that he had felt death. When he was in the sack or under the whip or the bastinado or in the pool of water, he hadn't felt his final death. But now, in front of the short interrogator who walked in circles round him carrying the papers or punched him in the stomach or kicked him in the backside, Yalo started to think of the implications of death and felt contempt for himself, for his self that was incapable of protecting its own air.

The interrogator returned to his chair behind the table and his head entered the fluorescent white once more, and Yalo found himself trying to link the words he heard coming out of the interrogator's mouth in order to understand their meaning.

Yalo heard the names of Michel Salloum and his wife, Randa, a lot and deduced that the interrogator was asking him about the few pages he had added to his confessions. He couldn't answer the question because he hadn't understood it. He heard the names splintering between the interrogator's thin lips.

"Why aren't you answering, arsehole?"

"Sir, I don't know."

"You don't know? So who does?"

"I wrote, sir, that I was going to start my life over again. Give me an opportunity. Enough is enough, for the love of God."

The interrogator said he understood what Daniel was playing at and that he would experience agonies that would force him to tell the truth.

"You think you're clever, arsehole, and you want to play games with us. We gave you paper so you could write the truth, not make up stories and accuse people and ruin everybody's lives. You, you bastard, you are trying to tell me . . . ? Tell me, go ahead and tell me, that you slept with Mme Randa. Tell me. What are you afraid of?"

Yalo didn't tell, but he felt an urge to dance because the interrogator was letting his phrases drop as though he were singing to a staccato tune emanating from his own throat. A smile traced itself on the lips of the lean ghost.

"You're laughing, you ponce?" asked the interrogator, pointing.

Three giants whom Yalo had not noticed rose up in the room.

The fluorescent light, rippling with yellow, spread across the grey lump of hair that sat atop the interrogator's round face. Yalo looked for a while at this face, and he was struck by a tremor of fear. It was as though the face, from a slit in whose lower part the words issued, was not real. Yalo had never seen a face like it before – a flabby nose that erased the lips, and a roundness like the roundness of a ball. His work in the forest had made him an expert in faces, able to distinguish the good-natured face from the mean-spirited one without difficulty – a large nose meant fear, thin lips mean-spiritedness, a plump face submissiveness and so on. He knew them by their faces. He read them by the light of the torch before deciding how to proceed – whether to employ violence, furrowing his brow and rapping on the window with the muzzle of his rifle, or to be kind, in which case he would lower the rifle and gesture with his head, or to be nonchalant, knocking with the rifle and looking at the ground. Yalo knew all the faces, but this face . . . On previous occasions he hadn't seen the interrogator's face. He was the prey, and the prey doesn't see the face of the hunter. That day, however, and after Yalo had written his story numerous times, the tremor struck him when he saw the face of the interrogator – a flabby nose disappearing inside the round, fleshy surface, lips like threads drawn in green, oval eyes which seemed not to have pupils, and a voice that issued from some obscure place in this ball thrown down on the table.

When Yalo finished writing the story of his life, he was sure that his journey of torment had ended. He wanted the story to end so he could return to the life he'd left behind. When he sat down at the table and was torn apart by physical and spiritual pain, Yalo had discovered that his life was not real. The life he'd written came to him from shredded, incomplete stories, and he saw himself in those stories as though it wasn't him, which was why he hated writing and hated himself. "Damn!" He'd close his eyes and say, "Damn! This Yalo whose story I've been writing will go from these papers to the hangman's rope, stand beneath the gallows and then dangle there like an unreal ghost, and he'll say he wrote everything down and he didn't have anything to add and there had been no call for torture."

Yalo stood before the interrogator to say that he wanted to return to being a real person and escape the trance into which his memories and the story of his life had taken him. He'd become a shadow like his grandfather Habeel Afram Abyad. The grandfather, whom old age had transformed into his own shadow, would say of his life that it hadn't been his life, and Yalo would listen with half an ear. Here in the cell, Yalo discovered that he hadn't been able to hear the *kohno* because he was dying, and the living can only hear the dead if they die with them. Splinters of the grandfather's voice did, however, return to him in his loneliness, and in the isolation cell he heard the words he had refused to hear before, and he lived with the dead, and his story became a shadow of his life. Yalo lived in the shadows and hated the black colour that the ink breathed on the paper and decided that he would return to life.

He stood before the interrogator to say this, but the interrogator wasn't like a real man. He placed his head on the table and spoke in a low voice that could barely be heard, and Yalo felt he was still only ink on paper and that his soul would not return to him, so he closed his eyes.

The interrogator didn't scream at him to open his eyes, as he had done on previous occasions. He left him with his eyes closed. However, the boy felt the three tall men standing directly behind him. He saw them with his third eye, which had suddenly returned to him after it had been extinguished and ceased to see when he'd been arrested. In prison, he'd tried to make it see, as it had in the forest when he'd felt he was a tall tower that looked out over the world in all directions. Was it true that he'd seen himself that way, or had that idea come to him that time in the café in Ashrafiyeh when he'd tried to convince Shireen to believe in him and his love? It was there that he'd told her how his third eye had erupted and how he'd started trying to see with it after hearing the *kohno* say to his daughter that the boy had acquired a third eye, and how he'd started closing his eyes so he could see with the new one. Shireen laughed and her small eyes widened in amazement. There, Yalo turned into a tower; with Shireen he'd possessed three eyes and found he could see whatever he wanted to see. He'd behaved as though he was a tall tower that fell on its victims and was filled with the seeing that blended with his desire to possess all the women of the world.

Here, however, before the interrogator, in this room which the fluorescent whiteness wreathed in yellow light, he saw with his third eye three men standing behind him, smelled the smell of blows, realized that he had not yet escaped the trap and saw how his shadow broke against the wall as it doubled up in response to the blows from behind him.

"Please tell me that you slept with Madame," said the interrogator.

"I . . . said . . . not . . . " answered Yalo.

The blows rained down on the shadow, which Yalo saw with his three eyes. The shadow twisted in pain, and the pain extended itself from the wall to the third eye, whose sight was suddenly extinguished.

"You?" asked the interrogator. Then he stood up and came out from behind the table and walked over to Yalo. The interrogator

stood up and the blows stopped, and Yalo listened to the interrogator reading a message the accused had written and asked the
judge to pass on to *Khawaja* Michel Salloum:

I want to send this note to *Khawaja* Michel Salloum the
lawyer. I feel grateful to that noble man who saved my life
and brought me back to my country, Lebanon, after the
torment I'd suffered in France. I want to apologize to him
for everything. I betrayed his trust and bit the hand that
had been extended to me in charity, and I ate of the flesh of
the man who had fed me and given me shelter in his house
and restored my dignity. Not only did I use the automatic
he'd given me for ignoble purposes, but I used the
7.5-mm Colt revolver he kept hidden in his car for the
acts of assault that I committed. I hid the revolver in my
room below the villa, under the fourth tile to the right of
the entrance, wrapped in cloth and plastic.

I also want to ask *Khawaja* Michel Salloum to forgive me
for my mistakes. I know that he has a kind heart and will
forgive me. But I have hesitated a long time before deciding to confess, and it won't do. This kind-hearted, humane
man has to know the truth; it is my moral duty. I have to
tell him the truth, however difficult and cruel it may be, so
that he may know, and so that I may feel that I have repaid
him in small part for his favours. I slept with his wife,
Mme Randa. The lady seduced me. I'm not saying that
she was wrong and that I'm innocent, for I too am guilty.
I believe that the Devil seduced us both. I ask *Khawaja*
Michel to forgive me and her.

At first I thought that Mme Randa had denounced me
because I'd decided not to go on with this shameful and

immoral thing that we were doing. She threatened and humiliated me and prevented me from talking to her daughter, Ghada, even though my relationship with Ghada didn't go beyond my buying her books. Ghada is an outstanding and well-mannered girl. I used to buy her novels by Agatha Christie, and my relationship with her didn't go beyond discussing those detective stories. I don't like detective stories because they frighten me and I think they're an exercise in intimidating the reader. Ghada, though, finds an intellectual pleasure in them.

I ask *Khawaja* Michel Salloum to forgive me and to take into consideration my life and the morals of this woman with whom he shares a roof. By doing this I have put my conscience at rest once and for all, and I am prepared to receive the punishment he deems to be appropriate. And I ask God to assist *Khawaja* Michel because his problem is worse than mine.

Yalo watched the reading face and was overcome with sorrow. The truth that he had not wanted to be revealed had been revealed. He didn't know why the pen had slipped and written these things. Later he would tell the interrogator that he regretted everything he'd written and that he withdrew his confessions, but he wasn't prepared to write everything down again. He couldn't. The beautiful two-storey villa must have become a house of hell by now. The staircase connecting the living spaces on the ground floor to the bedrooms on the first floor must have collapsed under the weight of *Khawaja* Michel's footsteps, now he'd discovered that his life had been a lie.

"Who do you think you are, you shit? First, we confirmed the existence of the revolver, and *Maître* Michel produced the license for it, so he got out of the shit you tried to drop him in. And then, do you know what *Maître* Michel did when he read that bullshit about Mme Randa? He burst out laughing and said, 'Poor chap. I knew the boy wasn't normal, but it's my fault for taking pity on him. See what happens when you do a good turn?' And he laughed and he laughed and we all laughed. And then he screamed 'Aaaagh!' and fell to the ground and turned red, and we took him to hospital and couldn't understand what he was saying any more, and he kept getting redder and redder, and in the hospital they discovered he'd had a heart attack. However, God saved him from your criminal behaviour, and he had a bypass and he's on the mend, thank God. He refused to bring charges against you, said he couldn't bear to hear your name and begged us to close his file.

"Happy now, arsehole?"

. . .

"Answer."

Yalo heard a moaning coming from his shadow, which lay against the wall. Then the interrogator started reading statements from the interrogations of men who'd reported crimes committed by Yalo in the forest after news of his arrest had appeared in the press. He could hear the interrogator saying he wanted him to write it all again and put in the details these men had confessed to, and write about the explosives network in the minutest detail.

"Listen, arsehole. You must write like this:

My name is Georges, son of Asaad Ghattas, mother's name Angèle. Born 1961 at Ballona, resident there at my father's property, registration number 20, Ballona, Kasrawan. I wish to inform you that on 16/5/91 at around 10.30 p.m., during my passage from the district of Jesus the King in the direction of Ballona in my car, make Mercedes model 220, black, registration number 1713620, and on arrival at Jeita, I saw a young woman unknown to me standing at the side of the road. I stopped, at which point she got into my car and it became known to me that her name was Georgette, full name and place of residence unknown to me. After some conversation, I stopped my car in the district of Ballona close to the Greek Orthodox church and we began to chat inside the car, and approximately five minutes after I stopped the car at the aforementioned place, a person unknown to me suddenly appeared and approached me and knocked on the side window of the car brandishing an automatic rifle, type Kalashnikov, in my face, at which point he ordered me to give him whatever money and jewellery I had. Immediately and fearing that he might do me harm, I gave him the sum of 180 U.S. dollars and 30,000 Lebanese lira that were in my possession. Similarly he took from the young woman who was in my company a pair of gold earrings set with diamonds. He also started uttering threats and insults. He likewise made so bold as to take the girl's watch and, when he had ascertained that said watch was of no value, threw it away from the car and started threatening me with death, and ordered me to get into the boot of the car, which I refused to do. At this, there occurred some discussion between me and the said armed person, who also tried to molest the young woman who was in my company, asking her to undress. When she refused, he put the barrel of the gun against my stomach and said he would kill me if the young woman did not undress. At this, she began to scream that she did not know me and did not know anyone. He then dragged me from the car and kicked me in my testicles so that I fell to the ground from the pain, and I saw the young woman undress. Then everything disappeared as I lost consciousness. When I came to, my head hurt me greatly. I saw that the car was empty and the young woman was not in it and the armed man was not there. I therefore drove back to my house, where I took two aspirin and slept. In the case of my seeing that person a second time, I would be able to recognize him. I also wish to inform you that he is of tall stature and lean build, age approximately thirty years; also he was wearing a long black coat. After being shown by you pictures of the man called Daniel Habeel Abyad, I can confidently state that he is the same person who made so bold as to rob me.

"Now do you understand how you're supposed to write?"
. . .

"Listen, arsehole. I have here all the stories of the people you attacked and raped and robbed. But there are gaps in the stories. I need you to fill in the gaps. You need to write what happened when the man fainted, for example. Got it?"

Yalo said, or tried to say, that he could no longer write. He said he didn't know how to fill in the gaps. He said he'd confessed to everything. He said he didn't know.

"And also," screamed the interrogator, "and also, don't forget the explosives network, and don't you dare go defaming half the world's women. Got it?"

"Got it," said Yalo.

"Now fill in the gaps," said the interrogator.

"What gaps, sir?"

"About Georgette. You kicked the man and then what happened?"

"I didn't kick anyone, sir."

"He's lying. Listen, we know everything."

"If you know, why do you want me to write? Give them to me, sir. Give them to me and I'll sign them without looking at them. Please, just stop."

Yalo saw three men approaching the tall ghost, who tried to protect his head with his hands. Then he saw how the ghost rose upwards. He rose and felt no pain. Yalo became above the pain. He went higher and higher and he saw the world like a circle and he saw his spirit turning inside it and he felt something entering his heart with a single stab and lodging there so that everything turned into a stifled moaning and a stifled weeping and a stifled screaming, and a pain that went into the recesses of the bones and the sheaths of the nerves.

The interrogator ordered them to sit him on the bottle. The tall ghost heard the order, but he didn't understand its meaning. He saw the interrogator carrying a cola bottle in his hand, which he opened. Then he put his thumb into its mouth and pulled it out again, producing a sound like that of a bottle being opened for the first time. The interrogator raised the bottle to his lips and drank a little, then he placed it on the table in front of him disgustedly and said he only liked cola when it was cold.

"And how do you like it?"

. . .

The interrogator came over to Yalo and ordered him to stand up. Yalo tried to support himself on the wall, but his hand slipped and he fell again.

"Help him stand up," said the interrogator.

They stood him up and he stood with two men holding him under the armpits.

"Come over here," said the interrogator.

The two men brought Yalo forward, lifting him by the armpits.

"I asked you how you like your cola. Answer."

"Me?" said Yalo.

"You. Who else do you think I'm talking to?"

"I like it a lot," said Yalo.

"I know you like it, but I mean how do you like it, cold or warm?"

"Normal," said Yalo.

"Fine. Let him stand on his own."

The two men let him go and Yalo felt the pain in his back and shoulders fall to the bottoms of his feet, and he said, "Aaagh!" before straightening his back and finding his balance. The interrogator gave him the bottle and told him to drink.

"Me?" asked Yalo.

"I want you to drink the whole bottle so you don't get thirsty."

Yalo drank, and the reddish-brown liquid descended from his throat to his stomach, causing it to contract spasmodically. Yalo stopped drinking because he felt like burping so the interrogator screamed at him to raise the bottle again and drink it at one go. He became aware of the two men nearby. The first took hold of his shoulders while the second raised the bottle and poured its contents into his mouth. Yalo felt he was being choked and wanted to vomit, but he saw himself and saw that he was now naked from the waist down, and the two men ordered him to sit. He didn't see the empty bottle that had been placed on the elevated wooden bench they called the "throne". The first man grasped the bottle while the two of them sat him on it and he was overwhelmed by spasms that soon gave way to a scream that came out of his throat and mouth without his realizing. One scream and Yalo was on the throne. Bits of glass like splinters came off the neck of the bottle and mingled with his blood, and he started rising higher and could hear only sounds coming from distant places.

When Yalo came to in the isolation cell, he was a clump of pain. He remembered that a doctor had visited him and given him some black ointment. He remembered that the doctor had said that that part of the body was extremely sensitive to pain because a large bundle of nerves met there and advised him to wash the wound.

Yalo lived for a long time with his agony. Visits to the lavatory were the most painful, because the constipation he experienced for the first few days after his descent from the throne gave way to diarrhoea and his life became all pain, when he was unable to sit, or to sleep even on his stomach. Yalo had risen on a column of piercing light on which he moved upwards, so that he found himself outside the prison, from time to time writing, not the way the interrogator asked him to but the way he saw things there with his three eyes, which gave him the feeling that he was looking out from the highest place in the world.

I want to write the story of my life from beginning to end. My life is over. I now understand, sir, that I couldn't write before because I was hanging from the ropes of hope. I had a conviction that it was possible. Meaning that it was possible that something might change – perhaps Shireen, or *Khawaja* Michel or Randa. That perhaps one of them would take pity on me and help get me out of this mess.

Now it's over. Hope is over, and it's up to Daniel Georges Jalao, or Yalo Habeel Abyad, to write his story from beginning to end.

Yalo is on the throne, as though he were a lighthouse, his three eyes lights stretching out to the end of the story. He sits on the pillar, like Mar Simeon Stylites, who sat on his pillar a thousand years ago in Aleppo, the city of my father, Georges Jalao, which I have seen only through the closed eyes of Master Saleem Rizq.

Yes, sir. I see Yalo there and I envy him, which is to say I envy myself, for it is myself that found out how to reach the spirits of the dead and speak with them and discovered that "vanity of vanities, all is vanity." A person lives in vanities and believes vanities and makes of his life one more vanity to add to the rest.

Now I am writing about the Yalo whom you raised on top of the bottle, calling it the "throne". Yalo is on the throne, like the angel of death. Yes, sir, I see him dead, and the dead do not write, because they are dying.

When you asked him to write the story of his life, you were wrong. Yalo couldn't write because he was in another place where they do not write because they have no need of writing. I, Daniel, write, and I shall write everything you want about him and about me and about everyone. But Yalo will not. I want to be frank: Yalo has left me and gone far away. I am body and he is spirit. I feel pain and he flies. I have come down from the bottle, but him, he sits on the throne.

I imagine him before me. I go over and question him, but he does not answer. He said his words no longer understood his words. He mixes Arabic with Syriac with languages I do not know. How then am I to understand him?

I write in Arabic not just because you asked me to do so but because I am an Arab. If my father isn't Georges Jalao from Aleppo, he's Elias El Shami from Damascus; there is no third possibility. I prefer the second alternative, even though the subject is of no importance to me. My mother kept the secret from me. She said many times she'd tell me, but she was afraid of what the shock might do to me, and every time she began the story she'd stop at the disappearance, or emigration, of her husband, and when I asked about the secret she'd yawn. I never knew another woman who yawned like that. She'd hide the secret in her open mouth and cover it with the palm of her hand. Then she'd walk round the house doubled over, as though looking for something she'd lost.

I know that the reason my poor mother was no longer able to see her face in the mirror was because she wanted to wipe out her secret. She believed she had lived in vain because *Khawaja* Elias hadn't asked her to marry him. When I asked her about it, though, she said she hadn't wanted him. She said she'd hoped he'd propose so she could turn him down, but he didn't. Gaby's case is strange. Could the sorrow of her life have been that it didn't give her a chance to refuse?

Yalo didn't pay attention to his mother and her problems because he was preoccupied with the idea of leaving Lebanon. We need to understand him. He's a victim, sir, and the victim will become more savage than the torturer if given the opportunity. The war was Yalo's opportunity. I agree, we must detest the civil war and its chaos, but imagine with me the situation of this boy, whose father was his grandfather and whose sister was his mother. Imagine with me what the war was able to do with him. The war was his opportunity, but he wasted it, and instead of setting himself up for life, like many others, he left his native land and went to France.

I don't agree that the mother's problem was caused by Elias El Shami; Elias was the result. As for the cause, we have to lay that at the door of *Kohno* Afram. Gaby lived with him after his wife passed away, and she was his daughter, wife and mother. A man deluded and obsessed by the thought of death. Gaby knew Syriac, but she preferred to speak Arabic. She told him Syriac was like a rosebud that had opened and become the Arabic language. She would close her five fingers into a fist and then open them as she told her only son not to cry when his grandfather beat him because he hadn't memorized the Syriac words.

When Yalo met Shireen on the mountain, he fell in love with her. I prefer to say "met" her, and I don't like to use the word *rape* which you imposed on the poor boy. Yalo didn't rape Shireen because a man can't love a woman he's raped. Rape, sir, is a horrible business. Ask me because I know. Yalo knew the meaning of rape because he had practised it. He had practised it and felt remorse. But not with Shireen. Shireen I loved because she reorganized my body and my soul.

Gaby didn't believe her son when he told her he'd decided to leave school. She thought it was just a whim. But the boy stamped his foot on the floor nine months after his grandfather passed away and said, "Enough."

The mother lived like a lost woman in her new house after the war forced her to move from West to East Beirut. There in East Beirut Yalo decided to join the war, and whenever he came home he brought with him the smell of blood. Gaby, however, lived alone. She went round the houses of her new quarter to revive her profession as a seamstress, and Elias El Shami disappeared off the face of the earth. She didn't look for him, but she asked and was told that he'd bought a house in Ballona with a group of people from their old quarter who'd left the city.

The name of Yalo's story, sir, is the war.

How can I describe to you, sir, what happened to Yalo after *Khawaja* Michel Salloum came across him in Paris, the return to Lebanon and the job at the villa in Ballona? The day he arrived, Yalo saw the village like a word written on the brow of the ageing tailor. He saw the ghost of Elias El Shami, who had filled his childhood with the smell of his false teeth, which was like rotting mint, and was afraid. Yalo wanted to refuse *Khawaja* Michel's offer, but he had no other option.

The truth, though – which no-one knows, sir, but Almighty God – is that my memory is messed up and I don't know. Did Yalo hear from his mother that Elias El Shami had gone to live in Ballona, or did he hear the name of that village in Kasrawan for the first time in his life from *Khawaja* Michel? In any case, for some reason of which he was unaware, he connected the village with the tailor, and that's how things stood in his head. The mother lost the tailor when she fled West Beirut and went to the Mreiyeh district in Ein El Roummaneh, and she said that she thought he'd gone to Kasrawan, but it isn't clear if she mentioned the name of the village. Why then did Yalo see the name of the village written on the man's brow? And why did his feet lead him to commit his first offence a month after he'd taken his new job?

I have to clarify things so we can understand what happened. When Yalo returned to Lebanon with Michel Salloum and took up residence in his little hut, he lived by night because night was his cover. By day he felt naked, and his long black coat wasn't enough to make him feel decent. He only went out once in daylight, to fetch the things he needed to repair Mme Randa's wooden chair. The mistake that was the beginning of all the others was made in the church. No, sir, the mistakes didn't begin with Shireen. All that happened with Shireen was that Yalo stripped to his ultimate nakedness in the daylight, as though he no longer cared about the danger staring him in the face; love blinds eyes and pencils a touch of foolishness onto faces. The mistakes began at the church. What came over him to make him go, early that Sunday morning and wearing his long black coat, to the Orthodox church in Ballona in search of Elias El Shami? Did he really intend to kill him, the way he claimed when he was telling Shireen about his love of killing? Certainly not.

Yalo would lie to Shireen all the time — lie and believe his own lies. I swear he lied, which is why there was no need for the torture party he was subjected to when he was tied to a chair for three days without enjoying that natural right that belongs to all God's creatures, animal and human, namely the right to go to the lavatory and relieve oneself. That torture was without benefit. I lied to Shireen. I told her that I entered the church carrying a revolver and a grenade because I wanted to shoot Elias El Shami and then throw the grenade at his corpse and blast it to bits. Yalo was carrying a revolver and a grenade when he entered the church, and all eyes turned to him. Entering the church was his first mistake. This mistake was linked to the statement of M. Georges Ghattas, a resident of Ballona, about a man wearing a long coat whom he had seen previously at the church and whom he thought might be the same man who had assaulted him when he was in his car with a woman called Georgette, other names unknown. It had never occurred to Yalo that a resident of Ballona would screw around in the forest near the town in which he lived. And what brought him to the church anyway? "He was screwing around and then he went to church with his wife? What shamelessness!" said Yalo, before becoming the target of a hail of slaps and kicks. "The truth is shameless, sir. What can one do with someone like *Khawaja* Ghattas? I'm prepared to confess to everything because nothing has meaning any more."

The interrogation about the church was fatuous, and forcing Yalo to confess that he'd intended to kill Elias El Shami and blow up the church was meaningless. Yalo went to the church to see the man who might have been his father, but he didn't see anything. He entered the church when the priest was doing the rounds with the censer, so all Yalo saw was the incense, and he started to cough and tears came to his eyes before he crossed himself and left.

Yalo lied to Shireen because he was, how can I put it . . . ?

Because love makes one talk. Love is the wellspring of speech, and without speech love cannot exist. So that the talking could continue Yalo was obliged to make up stories. Shireen spoke only rarely, which forced Yalo to balance alone on the tightrope of speech. He made up stories for her so that love would survive. Speech is love's bedding, on which lovers sleep. That is the truth and that is the reason for the amorphousness into which the interrogation fell.

Yalo is above and does not answer. His three eyes see in all directions – north, south, east, west, past and future. The future is clear to him. It is death, and all Yalo needs is to take a little jump to find himself in its kingdom. It is the past that is the problem. The past frightens him and frightens me too because the events are amazingly mixed up. He says "yesterday" and he means twenty years ago, and he says "a long time ago" and he means last week. This is the perdition that I and he live in. And Yalo's perdition did not start on the throne where he sits now; his perdition started when he failed to be covered by night.

Yalo lived in the Ballona night not because he was afraid but because he was looking for security. And even if he was afraid, where's the crime in that? He had a right to be afraid. Which of you, sir, is not afraid? It was Yalo's right to feel fear or alarm because he had stolen money from the Georges Armouni Barracks and gone to France. This is the truth he didn't tell to *Khawaja* Michel Salloum. At the house in Paris he took a shower, shaved, put on newly ironed clothes, drank a glass of French red wine and told *Khawaja* Michel that his friend had stolen the money and run away. M. Michel laughed and said, "A man who steals from a thief is like a man who inherits from his father – good luck to him!" Yalo tried to explain that he wasn't a thief, but *Khawaja* Michel didn't want to listen and deliberately gave the impression that he understood everything but had decided to turn a blind eye.

The truth is that Yalo covered himself in night because he didn't feel safe. When the war ended, it left a great gap in his life. The war shut up shop and the fighters' vague fear began. The war had been like a barricade behind which they had hidden. When the barricade fell, each one of us felt naked. The most difficult thing that can happen to a person is to find himself stark naked the way God made him. This is something Mme Randa taught me. The lady would take off her clothes when her lust began fluttering its wings in her eyes. She would stand naked in front of the mirror and look at her brown skin that sparkled with lust. And when he'd finished, she'd cover herself with the quilt and refuse to get out of bed until Yalo left the room, because she was embarrassed by her nakedness. And we, sir, were like Mme Randa: when the war had finished, we felt embarrassed by our nakedness and went looking for something to cover us up.

No, sir. I wasn't afraid: the war was over and there was no-one to hold me to account for the stolen money. I stole it and it was stolen from me. No-one can bring a charge against me on that score. I sought the cover of night because I felt naked, not because of fear. Even with Mme Randa, Yalo's relationship ended with his clothes; the relationship ended as it began, with clothes. The first time, she took everything off. He, however, had taken off only his trousers when he found himself coming inside her. That day, Mme Randa stood in front of the mirror looking at the beauty of her nakedness and Yalo discovered the difference between the cooked woman and the raw. He told her she was a cooked woman and she laughed out loud because she thought he was joking. Yalo smelled sun and spices and saw how the woman had been well cooked in her lust, and he began a classification of women that he divulged to no-one.

And now, sir, even as he hangs between earth and sky, the ecstasy flows through Yalo's veins when he remembers the difference between the cooked woman and the raw. The theory was one his grandfather, God rest his soul, invented and that Yalo improved. No, sir, my grandfather wasn't a womanizer. He was a complex person, but he divided food into two sorts – meat and plants. After he had given up eating all forms of meat, he took to classifying plants into three levels – the incomplete, the uncertain and the complete. The incomplete only became properly cooked and fit to be eaten after it had been cooked over the fire, like courgettes, black-eyed peas, okra and so on. The uncertain also needed to be cooked over fire but could also be eaten raw, like aubergine, spinach, broad beans, chickpeas, green peas and so on. The complete was cooked by the sun and had no need of fire because it had fire inside itself. This included all the fruits, of which the most exquisite were grapes, figs and tomatoes. My grandfather chose the complete plants and ended his life eating only raw vegetables and fruit. He even gave up eating bread, and he started getting smaller and more emaciated till his bones turned to baked clay and his flesh became as hard as his bones, and he died trying to turn into pottery or, in other words, earth cooked by the sun.

This was just nonsense, and there wouldn't have been any need to include it in Yalo's life story had not his grandfather's theory about food played a critical role in defining the way the youth looked at women. And I can state that one of the reasons for his obsession with playing the peeping tom was his desire to watch cooked women. Yalo's theory didn't imply the same order of preference as his grandfather's. The *kohno* hated the cooked and preferred the raw, which had been cooked by the sun. Yalo, on the other hand, preferred the cooked. The cooked woman was the one who had been brought to perfection over the fire of her lust. The raw was without fire. The thing he hated most was attempts by raw women to cook themselves artificially by the use of cosmetics or silicone, the latter having become very popular in Beirut after the war.

Despite the fact that Yalo had turned his grandfather's words upside down, he came in the end to adopt their substance without realizing it: the cooked woman does not need fire from outside herself; the sun of her desire is enough to bring her to perfection, and in this she resembles "complete" plants ripened by their inner fire.

When Yalo stumbled onto a cooked woman, he would experience an implacable attack of desire, and on such occasions he wouldn't steal or direct abuse at the man who was with her. He would display a resolute desire, and the man would understand that he must either withdraw or endanger his life.

This is why I can assert without any doubt that when Yalo found himself with Shireen – a raw woman *par excellence* – he felt no desire. The grey-haired man fled leaving the white young girl on her own, and this forced Yalo to take her to his hut. In the hut, his theories, and those of his grandfather, about fruit and women, fell apart. He smelled the smell of incense rising from the girl's outstretched arms and was intoxicated, and he entered the passionate unknown that brought him to his miserable end.

I question him and he averts his face as though he were living in another world. Once he wanted to ask Mme Randa her opinion of men and whether they could be divided into two types, raw and cooked, but he felt embarrassed and didn't ask her.

Yalo never abandoned his theory. He thought of Shireen as an exception and believed that women also divided men up the way he divided up women. Naturally, I believe that I belong to the cooked variety, and I wanted to hear it confirmed by a woman. Yalo didn't ask Shireen about this because she had told him not to talk about sex. Even when they went to the beach and ate fish, and he put his hand in the small of her back so she would bend backwards in anticipation of his kiss, even at that moment when he felt he owned the whole world, he didn't ask because he was afraid of upsetting Shireen, for the girl was young, delicate and easily bruised.

How had that angelic creature been transformed into its opposite?

In the interrogation room, Shireen had worn a mask of cruelty and indifference. The delicacy had disappeared from her eyes, and the little nose that had sniffled when she cried had turned into a thorn stuck into her face.

Why had her nose suddenly got larger?

In his last days his grandfather, God rest his soul, had complained of his nose and his ears. Everything about him had become smaller. His body had become shorter, and he was so withered that his skin stuck to his bones, but his nose got larger and his ears got longer and bigger, and he would look at his face in the mirror with disgust. Once he said he wanted to snip off his nose and clip his ears the way people do their nails. That day he frightened even me, me who never feared anything in my whole life. I feared the *kohno*'s nose and ears because he said the nose and ears were the signs of death. All the parts of a person's body stop growing except the nose and ears. Death was a mercy because if one went on living, he'd become just a long nose and large ears, in other words a cross between an elephant and a donkey.

I believe, sir, that I have explained the circumstances that led Yalo to commit his sins and his crimes. Now I will try to write the whole story from beginning to end. Consider me his voice which he lost when he was sitting on the throne. There he neither complains nor moans. I am certain that he is experiencing an exquisite moment that no others have been granted the opportunity to experience, except those who have risen above the greatest torments.

Do not say that he deserves no credit because he mounted his pillar against his will. True, you forced me to drink the bottle of cola and then sit on it. Yalo's virtue lies in his decision to not come down. I came down. He did not. I suffer pain. He does not. My pains are great, sir, because the fire is burning the door of my body. Nevertheless, I am convinced of the necessity of our writing the whole story so that we can escape this dilemma.

I want to write, but I am lost.

Do I have to write, when I write about my life, about my grandfather and my mother and my father? Or does my life concern only me? I don't know. You want everything from me, especially the stories about Ballona and its women and the explosives. I think the story ought to begin with those events. But I cannot since I . . . Since when? Since the sack and the kitties? No, since I was in the water. No, on the chair. No, under the bastinado. No . . . since the torture to which I have been subjected, I cannot tell beginning and end apart. Which reminds me, I can only congratulate you on the inventiveness of the forms of torture you employ and on your capacity to extract confessions from the accused as easily as extracting his soul, meaning that he feels as though his soul is about to depart and he's going back into his mother's belly, so he confesses everything. However violent torture may be, its physical effects wear off quickly and all that remains is the spiritual effect, which makes you feel that the soul is about to depart. So I congratulate you, sir, especially on the bottle. The bottle is the finishing touch to finish all finishing touches because it is long, by which I mean that it makes time long and endless. I sat on the bottle for about a thousand years, or a thousand times longer than that. You say it was only half an hour and you're right, for you know more than me because you wear accurate Swiss watches. Me, though, what a mess I was! But the bottle changed the meaning of time, meaning I felt I was in eternity, that time had stopped, that I was living the last minutes of my allotted span, and that my allotted span was long, infinite. I wanted it to end so that the pain would end, but there was no more ending, and that is eternity. I will not speak of the pains that are with me still, especially when I go to the lavatory. It's not nice to talk about things like that. But the truth is – and you want the truth – the truth is that the thing that scares me most is the sensation of needing to go and sit on the lavatory. There I feel eternity again and I smell myself and I become aware that pain has a smell. Pain does indeed have a smell, and its smell is shit. That is what I feel, and smell.

All the same, my good fortune has been great, which makes me think that the prayers my grandfather said for me were not wasted. One of the guards here told me that many accused persons have died after the bottle because it broke in their backsides and they got gangrene in the large intestine and everything inside them got inflamed. Thank God it didn't go that far with me. On the contrary, the bottle helped me in many ways. I don't know how to explain it, but your experience with prisoners will surely mean you are capable of understanding what I write; I am not the first to ascend this throne of voluted glass and I will not, of course, be the last.

When I was on the throne and the pain pierced me from bottom to top and from top to bottom, I was certain I was going to die. I ascended and the dying began, which is to say that I began to sense death. Death is violent and has a sound. Something explodes inside you and you hear a sound no-one else can hear. After the sound, your body goes numb and you feel as though you're being dragged across white sleep. You aren't sleeping, you're swimming above sleep. And that's it. Stop. Everything goes dark, and so sorry for your loss. That is literally what happened to me. I'm not lying, I'm telling the truth, sir. Something went bang and then I was above the sleep, meaning I was sleeping and not sleeping, and then I came to.

You took me all the way to eternity and you made me understand the meaning of life because I tasted death and drank it, from bottom to top.

I want to say, sir, that in all these experiences, when I got to the heart of things, I would see him before me. Can you credit, sir, that my grandfather, who is also my father, was waiting for me everywhere, and I didn't want him? I didn't want his story because it had no meaning, but death, sir – when death approaches, it imposes its own conditions. Dying means living things we haven't lived, and stories we've only heard becoming realities. When I came close to death, I became my grandfather and my great-grandfather and the whole human race. I am speaking now based on life experience, which is why my task is very hard. I can't write you all the stories of humankind that I know but don't know how else I can write them. For this reason, I earnestly request the honourable interrogator to be patient with me for a little longer. I will reach my death throes and arrive at the heart of the matter you are searching for, but I have seen another essence, one I cannot ignore, which is why I will write it down in the smallest possible number of words, so that I can be true to myself and to my soul, which is suspended there above the throne of death.

When I thought that the story had to start with my grandfather, I hated it, for I didn't love my grandfather, who was the very soul of cowardice and selfishness. My grandfather was afraid of everything, perhaps because his conscience troubled him greatly after the passing of my grandmother, Mary Samho, God rest her soul, of whom it is said, though only God knows whether this is true, that she died because of him. My grandmother died before I was born, which is why my grandfather insisted that my father – or my mother's husband – live with him in his house. I think the husband was aware of the trick from day one and that's what made him pack up his things and escape with relief from the atmosphere of that unbearable household. He left because he never for one moment felt that he was in his own house. The bed wasn't his bed, the life his life or the woman his wife. My grandfather claimed that he'd found out by accident that my father – or my mother's husband – wasn't an Assyrian but an Arab from Aleppo who belonged to the Melchite church. Fine, but what difference would that make? And what was his crime? And why hadn't the *kohno* discovered the truth before his daughter married the man? My grandfather murdered my father and trampled on his memory. Are you aware, sir, that I do not possess a single photograph of my father? He was even torn out of the wedding pictures. Even his name has disappeared, since I bear my grandfather's name and my I.D. card gives my family name as Abyad. What can I say? To this day I don't know what the difference between an Assyrian and an Arab is supposed to be. A man is a man. All of us are from Adam and Adam is from dust, so what's all the fuss about? I do not understand the anguish of my grandfather, who had made his mouth a grave for the language of Christ. How ridiculous can you get? Did he think Christ didn't understand Arabic, or Greek, or Latin?

My grandfather's fear was indescribable. My mother used to say that his fear stemmed from his childhood and was a result of the massacre in the village of Ein Ward at the beginning of the twentieth century, but I'm not so sure. Maybe my grandmother's death was the cause. I heard about my grandmother from other people, not from my mother. My mother spoke only rarely about her mother, but I was aware of a black cloud hanging over the taciturn relationship between my mother and my grandfather. Sometimes, all of a sudden, this taciturnity would be broken and they'd talk to one another without words, from which I concluded that real dialogue between people took place that way. Words don't say things, they cover them. Now I have worked out, sir, why I find it difficult to write, which is because what I've been asked to do is cover the story up, which makes me feel impotent, for anyone who wants to write has to have a twofold text and dub over the silence with speech. When what is being told is your life, though, you speak silence.

I understand, sir, that you ask people to write their life stories for the sake of the moral, or the lesson, that can be learned from them. But of what use is my story? And why am I telling my grandfather's story rather than my own? Is it because the kohno murdered his wife? Is it true that Habeel Abyad, known as Afram, murdered his wife, and that was why he was afraid of everything?

The kohno used to say that a person's body was the abode of fear, and that God had given the spirit a body of clay in order to quieten its fear of fear, or of God. However, the physical body was transformed into a new cause for fear through sin. People die because they have sinned, and death is their greatest fear. We are afraid of the body, which is why we melt it before it can melt our souls. We have to make it clay once more and pay it no more attention than the potter does the pot. He pours water onto it and puts it in the sun. All the body needs is water and a few plants that have been cooked by the sun. All else is vanity.

At first, the *kohno* tried to defend himself. He said he didn't want his wife to suffer. But when the suffering took up residence after the sickness had spread through her bones, he didn't know what to do, so he had to seek the help of doctors and the woman was transferred to the Greek Hospital in Ashrafiyeh, where she died on morphine, which couldn't alleviate her agonies.

The silence between the *kohno* and his daughter, which constituted their means of communication, was understood by Yalo only when he heard their neighbour, Mrs Mary Rose, threatening that she'd abandon her husband to die like the *kohno* had his wife, without treatment. Yalo pictured the scene, seeing it through the eyes of his mother, and understood how a person can read what has been erased.

In the course of his telling the story of the massacre in Tur Abdin, his grandfather said he had learned to read what had been erased: "We have to learn how to read the words that have been rubbed out. This is our story. We are a people whose story has been rubbed out and whose language has been rubbed out, and if we don't learn how to read what has been erased we will lose everything."

In the past I didn't believe that the *kohno* had the capability to read the books that time had erased and history torn up. Now, though, I have started to believe, because I have seen how Yalo read the silence and erased words.

My mother started speaking what had been erased before her

face was erased from the mirror. She used silence to show the *kohno* that she knew.

Indeed, sir, it does seem that my grandfather left his wife to die. He took her to the doctor, who diagnosed the cancer in her left breast, but instead of putting her into hospital to have her breast removed, my grandfather took her home again, bought a packet of aspirin and left her to die. He told his daughter that the cancer was incurable and the best thing was not to let the doctors cut her body open: "All I care about is that she shouldn't suffer."

But she suffered a lot!

Gaby never said those words, but she looked at her father and he read them in her eyes and his tongue could no longer go on talking. That day, Gaby invented the language of silence, and she tried to speak to Elias El Shami in it, but the tailor did not possess the blessing of taciturnity. Yalo alone learned it, and his relationship with his mother took place in silence from then on. He would come to the house, read the sorrow and the loneliness and her longing for him in her eyes, and he would answer her, without speaking, that he wanted to live his own life and could do nothing for her.

Gaby could no longer taste food. She told her son that the taste was there, in the old house in Museitbeh, and that she could no longer cook because she could no longer distinguish tastes. All foods tasted the same, like bulghur: "This is how my dad was at the end, and maybe I'm at the end now and can't feel taste in my mouth."

Gaby didn't tell her son how she'd answered her father when he said he'd lost his sense of taste because she was afraid the *kohno* would get angry in his grave. The *kohno* had felt slighted when his daughter had told him he was homesick for the taste of

Kurdish food because he was a Kurd. Yalo didn't know why his grandfather was so sensitive on the subject of his Kurdish origins. When the grandfather had fled from his uncle in Qamishli to Beirut, he had spoken Arabic and Kurdish, and he only learned to speak literary Syriac well once he was here. He said he'd forgotten the Kurdish language as though it had been erased from his memory, even though he spoke it when the Kurdish mullah came to their house in Museitbeh, where he was taken by surprise by his son's refusal of his inheritance.

Is that story true? Or did my mother make it up? I don't know.

W hat I've been asked to do is simple and straightfor-
ward. I have to write down the details of the crimes
I have committed, with a short introduction about
my upbringing and my experience in the war.

I shall try, sir, to suppress the details that do not concern the
honourable interrogator or serve the purposes of justice. This
being so, I shall try to focus on just two points – the crimes at
Ballona and the explosives crimes – as you have asked me to do.
When I ask Yalo, though, I find he is silent. What am I to do? I ask
him, and his silence answers me with a question. How can this
be possible, sir? If everyone followed this procedure when
talking, talk would come to a halt!

I asked him, and he asked me whether the crimes in the forest
were graver than those of his grandfather.

Yalo didn't kill anyone. If he'd wanted to, he could have
killed as many as he wished, buried his victims in the forest, and
no-one would have known. If he'd killed Shireen, would she
have brought a complaint against him with the police? Or would
Dr Saeed El Halabi have been daring enough to go to the police

station to file a complaint against a young man who'd caught him in suspicious circumstances with a girl younger than his own children?

Yalo is now a criminal, and that is natural, and his grandfather became a saint in people's eyes, and that's natural too, but where's the justice?

I was discovered, sir, because I didn't kill, and my grandfather became a saint because he killed. Do you call that justice? I don't believe we can justify the *kohno*'s crimes by invoking his good intentions any more than we can justify Elias El Shami's crime against my mother with the fact that his wife was sick so he didn't want to upset her.

Why should my mother die for the sake of the tailor's wife's peace of mind? Why should my grandmother die because the *kohno* was ambitious and wanted to be a metropolitan?

And what about my father? My grandfather claimed that *Khawaja* Saleem said that my father wasn't an Assyrian but was from Aleppo. So what? I worked three summers with Master Saleem and his son Engineer Wajeeh, and no-one said anything to me about it. I believe my grandfather concocted the story about my father because he knew in his heart of hearts that I was the son of Elias El Shami. The tailor was from Damascus, and Damascus isn't far from Aleppo. That makes me the "son of the man from Aleppo" or, in other words, the "son of the man from Damascus". But that's not the point. The point is, how did Georges Jalao come to agree to marry a girl who wasn't a virgin? What did he do when no virginal blood flowed? Or did Gaby cut herself and fake the pain to make the man think he'd deflowered her? Did she behave like a whore to make the man think she was a virgin? I'm not saying that because I've got anything against girls who aren't virgins. I am convinced that there is only one virgin in human history, Our Mistress Mary, Mother of God, glory be to her, so there's no call for virginity because Mary has taken upon herself the virginity of all women. Gaby's false virginity, however, caused Georges Jalao to fall into the trap. The man lived in the *kohno*'s house like a stranger. Even when he had sex with his wife, it took place in secret and with lowered voices, as though Gaby wasn't his wife, as if she was her father's wife. He told her she was her father's wife before he disappeared, and his words turned out to be true, in the sense that I became her father's son. How, though, was the *kohno* able to register me as his son, knowing that his wife, which is to say my grandmother in real life and my mother on my I.D. card, died before my mother was married? The only explanation is that my grandfather set the date of my birth before that of his wife's death. In other words, he made a false statement for which he could be punished under the law. The most likely scenario is that I wasn't born in 1961, as registered, but in 1962. This would explain my backwardness at school, my stammer when I was small and so on. But how did he get away with it? Didn't the registrar of births notice that my grandfather was sixty years older than me? I mean how? Was he the prophet Zachariah, as he claimed when he told everyone that he'd been struck dumb three days before the birth? Where did he get his criminal imagination from?

I said I hated my grandfather, and that is not true. How could I hate him when Yalo has become like my grandfather, his body baked clay, his memory forgotten? He is a spirit, and the spirit has returned to its source and is no longer concerned with stories. I will tell the story from beginning to end, and the beginning is there, with my grandfather who returned to the beginning, stopped eating and began breathing faulty memories. At that stage of his life he told me everything, but I believed nothing. How is one to believe a demented old man who tied the rooster to the fig tree by its feet and then killed it because he hated the way it mounted the hens? This story's unbelievable, and I'm not asking you, sir, to believe it.

We were living in Museitbeh, in a small house with a large garden. My mother raised chickens in the garden to have free-range eggs. We had a rooster and about ten hens, I can't remember exactly how many, but I remember how they died, which is what this is about.

One day, my mother came home from work to find, to her surprise, our old rooster tied up and feeling sorry for himself. He was a large bird with yellow feathers and multicoloured wings, and his crowing filled the world. My mother didn't ask who'd tied up the rooster because she knew. She went over to the fig tree and untied it. The rooster leapt up, attacked the hens, and things took their ordained course. I heard the rooster making a racket, so I rushed into the garden and saw an unforgettable scene – the rooster having sex with all the hens at the same time. I don't remember how old I was. I may have been eight. Naturally, I used to reckon my age according to my I.D. card and was unaware of the false statements made by my grandfather, which I only uncovered here in prison, thanks to your project of making me write the story of my life, which has made me remember things I didn't even know I remembered, which is why I'm grateful to you, sir, for the idea, for writing is the only way to remember. Without it, a man's life would be confined to his present and he'd live without memory, like the animals. I have discovered that when I write, the doors of memory open themselves before me. I know you're asking me for a brief account and so I'll summarize, but I'm awestruck before the memory that has opened up before me and which now embraces my mother, my father, Tony Ateeq, Alexei, Mario, Shireen and all the people I've ever known in my wretched life. My biggest surprise has been the ink. The ink flows without hesitation. The ink never stammers, sir. The ink comes out from between my fingers, as though I'd become like the squid Shireen ate. Shireen is eating me now. I see her devouring the squid, which feels terrible pains that extend from below me to below the world. The ink comes out from between my fingers and teaches me proper Arabic. I write now because Jurji Zeidan taught me language and writing. If it weren't for him, I'd be like so many others who are ignorant of the language and its magic. My mother used to bring home *Hilal Magazine* novels from Elias El Shami's and I would read them. Master Elias was infatuated with history books and with my mother, so he gave her books, but she didn't read them. I found a private pleasure in reading. At first, it was hard. Then the lines, which resembled clumps of ants, transformed themselves into words and entered my head. This is why I was good at Arabic Language at school. I asked the guard here to get me books, and all he brought was the Bible. I have every respect for the Bible, but I want the works of Jurji Zeidan so I can draw inspiration from him. I mean, I know that the story I'm writing isn't historical. Yalo isn't a hero of history, but he is a hero, meaning that there is something heroic about his life, and a hundred years from now the story will have become part of history. Never mind, though; I'll try to write the way I know without forgetting what I owe Jurji Zeidan. This writer revealed to me that the Ghassanid kings were Assyrians, in other words, Monophysites. When I found this out, my grandfather was devastated. I told him that the Arabs too were Assyrians, so there was no need to hold my origins against me, and I wasn't going to study Syriac because the Ghassanids had prayed in Arabic and they were righteous in their faith. When he didn't answer and tried to play the silence game with me, I told him he'd lost *haylo*, meaning in Arabic "his stamina", and he jumped on the word *haylo* and asked me, "And what does *haylo* mean?" and I said, "*Haylo* means *haylo*." He said, "Listen: *qaddishat aloho, qaddishat hayltono, qaddishat lomoyuto*. Translate that into the language of the Ghassanids, my fine scholar!" So I did, though in fact I didn't know I was translating, but I knew the meaning of the words because we pray with them in church every Sunday. I said, "Holy is the Lord, Holy is the Almighty, Holy is He who does not die." He said that *hayltono* came from the Syriac word *haylo*, meaning "strength". "Now you're using a Syriac word without knowing it. Half the words people use are Syriac. Those Ghassanids don't know what they're talking about." And he started enumerating the words, from the names of the months to *qallaya* and *sawki* and *nahlo*, and so on. The only thing he could come up with to defend himself and his dead language was to adopt my mother's theory about the rosebud that had opened.

The rose opens now in the ink that covers my papers. The rose opens inside my body, which rises with Yalo, embraces the spirits of the dead and bends over my mother. I must return her, sir, to her house in Museitbeh. If I am not sentenced to death for the explosives case, which I am going to tell you about in detail, and if I get out of prison, the first thing I shall do will be to take my mother back to her house so she can live in honour and dignity. Then I shall return to my original job as a joiner. I used to think I'd forgotten the craft, but joinery is like swimming – you can't forget it. You have to know how to divide the wood into two types, male and female, and insert them into one another the way the male inserts himself into the female. Nails kill the wood's spirit while joinery brings it back to life by marrying it to itself and restoring its sap, which bled from it when the trees were cut. Engineer Wajeeh taught me that wood never wears out because joinery gives it new life.

Instead of becoming angry with his son, Master Saleem offered himself as a solution to the problem, which is a demonstration of the nobility of blind *Khawaja* Saleem's morals, which were the opposite of *Kohno* Afram's. How, come to think of it, had they ever become friends? Saleem, instead of tying his son to the fig tree, volunteered to defend him and then tried to save the situation, which led to his being maltreated. My grandfather, on the other hand, when he saw that my mother had set the rooster free, yelled at her and said he'd tied it up there because it could never get enough, and we went through three days of quarrels, him tying it up and her setting it free and saying he was jealous of it. On the third day, my mother came home to find the rooster staggering around, still tied to the fig tree. His yellow feathers had fallen out, and he was dying. She asked her father what he'd done and he said he hadn't beaten the rooster to kill it, he'd beaten it to teach it manners and reduce its sexual voracity.

In the end the rooster learned its lesson and gave them its life. The rooster died alone in a corner of the hutch. The following morning, we awoke to strange noises. The terrified hens were hovering round the rooster and crowing. Yes indeed – the hens started crowing like husky-voiced roosters, and the crowing didn't stop until my mother went down to the hutch, pulled out the body of the rooster and buried it in the garden.

After the death of the rooster began the tragedy of the hens, which turned our garden into a charnel house. The massacre occurred after the rooster's death, when the hens started staggering giddily around and falling over. Has anyone other than me seen a lovelorn chicken stumbling as it walks and then spreading its wings to recover its balance and not fall over? I started to fear my mother's return from work, because the evening came to mean the slaughter of another hen. My mother would stand in the garden rolling up her sleeves, take hold of a chicken, twist its neck, slash its throat and then throw it to the ground to wallow in its blood. My mother's excuse was that the hens were sick and would all die of mourning for the rooster so they had to be slaughtered or they'd die as carrion and we wouldn't be able to eat them.

We went for a whole month eating only chicken, and my grandfather would stare at the chicken soup and grumble at the eyes of fat scattered on the surface. I now appreciate my grandfather's position in abstaining from meat; the smell of blood is overwhelmingly rancid. The sole concrete expression of my solidarity with my grandfather occurred immediately after his death, when I gave up drinking wine, because wine made me think of the smell of blood. I know now that my position was incorrect and that giving up wine and concentrating on arak did a lot of damage to my stomach.

Shireen loved wine, but I forced her to drink arak, and that was wrong. I made a lot of mistakes with Shireen, as though a wild beast had awakened inside me, and I interpreted everything the way I wanted to. I took her fear of me to be a lover's timidity and her aversion to eating to be the satiated feeling that goes with love. It was the same when I was Mme Randa's lover. I don't deny that I felt love for her – the woman made me insane, and the reason was her calf, which would appear and disappear through the slit in her long robe. I wanted her constantly, at night and during the day. I would wait for her and burn. I burned most, though, when *Khawaja* Michel came back from Paris. When this happened, she would give me the cold shoulder and muffle her voice in cork and treat me like a servant, lifting her nose as though she could smell a bad smell while I stood before her like a dog.

It wasn't my intention to steal, sir. I was looking for my soul, of which that woman had taken possession. I discovered the lovers' cars by accident and found in them my entertainment and my consolation. I am not a dog that I should accept such treatment. Indeed, I accepted the unacceptable while in thrall to her brown calf, down which flowed the sweat of lust. In the game of the cars in the forest, things began to take a different turn. My life took a turn in the forest, and I gradually began to move away from Mme Randa. All the same, glory be, my lust for her never ended till I fell in love with Shireen.

I know, sir, that you want to hear about three things: what I did in Paris, the women in the Ballona forest and the explosives gang that I joined.

I'll tell you Yalo's stories in detail, because I want them to be a "lesson for those who would learn", which is why, when I sit at the table holding the pen of flowing ink so that I may write, I feel terrified. This ink that fills the pages is my soul. I am not like the squid, which uses its ink to evade fishermen and predators. I do not seek to evade anyone. I know that in the end you will cook me in this ink, but I go to my fate with a cheerful heart.

I am not afraid of death, sir, and I do not use my ink to evade you, but I would be lying if I confessed what you want me to confess. Would you agree to let me leave you a few blank pages for you to fill in as you please, with my consent in advance to whatever you may write? Of course I won't do that because I'm afraid of your anger.

Once Yalo had beheld the world from that towering height, the thought of his being taken down to be tortured became unbearable. I tried to reassure him. I told him not to be afraid because I would write everything and would never again let him taste the agony of the body.

I knelt before the window where he sits on high and I asked him to help me a little. I cannot write these things on my own. Digging into the skull is painful; it makes you incapable of putting the words down in proper sentences.

The *kohno* knew that, so he took the words as they were and copied them out. He copied the poetry that Afram the Assyrian had written, or the *memre* verse written by Hanno of Ein Ward in lamentation for a people driven to the slaughter whose blood became a long thread stretching from Amid to Heaven.

The *kohno* would write the red thread with black ink and say that when he copied the poems and the *memre*, he became their author without doing violence to the words or sentences. How I wish I might have in front of me a book telling the story of Yalo! I would copy it out and be done with this mess. I said in my soul that my soul must remember, but the more I remembered the more I forgot, and I discovered that I had to remember from the beginning and that I was still far from the heart of what I have to write, which is an honest confession of my crimes, a proclamation of my readiness to take responsibility for them and a willingness to accept the just sentence that will be passed upon me.

The truth, sir, is that I didn't do anything in Paris. I spent three weeks there that were longer than a year and during which I knew destitution, poverty and hunger. Had God not sent me *Khawaja* Michel Salloum, I would have died like a dog on a metro platform. I confess that my greatest crime is that I spat on the hand that was offered to me. Instead of making myself a slave to this noble and generous man who saved my life, I betrayed him. Yes, betrayed him, and that was the first of my crimes. I am not referring to my relationship with his lady wife, which was my destiny and which I had no part in choosing. The betrayal happened long before that. The betrayal was committed in Paris and was an act I must spend the rest of my life regretting. It is of no concern to me that *Khawaja* Salloum made his fortune as an arms dealer working between Europe, Lebanon and the Gulf: that's his business, and he is free to do what he likes with his money and good luck to him, not to mention that we here in Lebanon are the last people to have the right to condemn the arms trade. Without the arms dealers, how could we have made war? He's an arms dealer and we used the arms. What's the big deal?

I resided at the home of *Khawaja* Michel in Paris, 45, rue Victor Hugo, for one week, and saw things you wouldn't believe, before I was sent to Lebanon to work as a guard at the Villa Gardenia in the village of Ballona in Kasrawan.

Khawaja Michel rescued me from the jaws of death. I was sitting in the Montparnasse metro station with a piece of cardboard on which I'd written my name. *Khawaja* Michel stood in front of me for a long while before telling me to rise and follow him. I couldn't believe my ears. I heard words in Arabic and I understood. God, how good it was to understand! In Paris, when they spoke to me in that language I didn't understand, I felt that they were using the words to beat me with, and I would put my hands over my face without thinking to escape the blows.

He told me to rise and follow him. First, he asked me who I was, but the racket made by the trains drowned out my voice. He commanded me to follow him and I remembered the words of the Lord Christ to one of his disciples – "Take up the cross and follow me" – and said that I would follow this man to the ends of the earth and never leave him, and would be his slave and his servant.

Khawaja Michel stood on the metro platform and asked the tall, lean young man why he was sitting there like a beggar. Yalo tried to tell his story, but he didn't know what to say, so he wept. Or rather, he didn't weep, but his voice choked with tears. The *khawaja* asked him, "Whose son are you?" and he replied that he was the son of the priest Afram Abyad, and the *khawaja* cried, "Son of a priest, and forsaken here?" Yalo said the priest was his grandfather, and the man said, "Come, come. Your father, or your grandfather, must be weeping in his grave. Come, rise and follow me." And he followed him. Yalo found himself in a luxurious home. He bathed and put on clean clothes and he met Ata. *Khawaja* Michel didn't give his guest a chance to ask any questions. He ordered Ata to bless Daniel the son of the priest Afram Abyad, and a short man with a large belly and small hands stepped forward and greeted Yalo. Then *Khawaja* Michel asked him for some oil, and Ata hesitated for a moment before turning to face the icon of the Holy Trinity, which showed three persons, their heads surrounded by haloes, sitting in a semicircle round a table on which three cups had been placed. Ata went towards the icon, which made him look as though he was standing on his backside: Ata's legs were short and his backside was large and counterbalanced his swollen belly. Standing on his backside, Ata reached out and after a few seconds the oil appeared, oozing from his palms. *Khawaja* Michel cried, "Holy, holy, holy! Do you see the oil, my son? Stand that we may be blessed. Cross yourself and stand." Yalo hesitated but then followed *Khawaja* Michel, who went forward, his head bowed, and took a little of Ata's oil and put it on his forehead, tracing the sign of the cross. Yalo followed his new master and did what he did not believing his eyes, as though he were dreaming. When Ata turned, the oil stopped flowing from his hands. He looked at Yalo, saw the amazement on his face and winked. Naturally, Yalo winked back.

That was when the betrayal began. Yalo didn't tell his master the truth he'd discovered, not because Ata gave him money, but because he was afraid. He was afraid of telling and then not being believed and finding himself back on the street. That was the betrayal that Yalo regretted so much. He had got to know Ata in the alleys of war in Beirut. Ata Ata – that was his full name – worked with the Jehovah's Witnesses, a religious group that spread during the war and then gradually disappeared again. The group claimed to be Protestants, their members abstained from alcohol and smoking, and their women were forbidden to use perfume or cosmetics. Their main message was the need to be prepared, for the end of the world was nigh. Ata distributed religious books to people's homes, and Yalo met him for the first time in Mreiyeh when Gaby threw the missionary with the dark brown complexion out of the house because "God forbid – we follow Jacob the Saddler and Mar Afram the Assyrian, and these people come to proclaim the religion that grew up in our country and speaks our language? What a scandal!" Then Yalo met Ata again in the Karantina Prison, where it was said he was incarcerated because he'd stolen jewellery from one of the houses he'd entered as a missionary, and from which he was released only after he renounced his relationship with the Jehovah's Witnesses.

Yalo returned Ata's wink with an involuntary wink of his own after witnessing the miracle of the oil, which was repeated during the visit of Bishop Mikha'eel Sawaya to the house of Michel Salloum in rue Victor Hugo.

That evening, *Khawaja* Michel was in a dither. Metropolitan

Mikha'eel was coming to visit him to determine the validity of the miracle of the oil that had appeared at the hands of his servant Ata. A French cook came in the morning and prepared dinner, and the Philippina maid cleaned the house from top to bottom. In the evening His Reverence arrived, carrying his staff, and the house was left to the three men.

I was sitting alone in my little room when *Khawaja* Michel opened the door and asked me to come and greet His Reverence. I felt extremely embarrassed. The *Khawaja* was bound to have told the metropolitan my story, and now the questions would begin and I didn't want to talk. I thought of running away. I'd had it up to here with the ghosts of priests, and now there was this conman who performed miracles and on top of everything else the metropolitan had turned up. But could I go? I had worked out, sir, that my grandfather was the cause of my being rescued from the abjection of Paris. If *Khawaja* Michel hadn't fallen under the spell of miracles, he wouldn't have given me a second look. The moment he found out that my grandfather had been a priest, he'd said, "Rise and follow me." I stood up and then found myself on my own in a corner of the sitting room while Ata turned away from *Khawaja* Michel and the metropolitan, who were seated on the sofa opposite the icon of the Holy Trinity. Suddenly, the oil began seeping from the small outstretched hands and the *Khawaja* cried, "Holy, holy, holy!" and the metropolitan made the sign of the cross. Ata began to shrink while the shadows cast on the walls by the candlelight created a strange atmosphere. The electric lights had been turned off on Ata's orders. The lights had been turned off and candles lit, and the shadows had spread across the walls and the oil had begun. Ata's legs disappeared. Yalo shivered when that happened and almost believed the miracle. Then he noticed that the man had gone down on his knees and the oil had started to gush more strongly. Ata stood up and started backing away from the icon. When he reached the metropolitan, he suddenly turned round and bent over to kiss his hand, but the metropolitan took Ata's hand in both of his, raised it to his beard and wiped the beard with the holy oil. At this, *Khawaja* Michel threw himself down on his knees in front of Ata and asked him to place his hands on his head. Ata placed his hands on his boss' head and then raised them in the air, took two steps backwards and stood with his arms folded across his chest.

The metropolitan asked why the oil had stopped, and the *khawaja* answered that the oil stopped when Ata turned his back on the miraculous icon.

The metropolitan stood up and went over to the icon, bent over in an obeisance until he was touching the ground with his right hand, then kissed the icon, cried, "Holy, holy, holy!" and knelt. I heard the metropolitan saying that the icon was seeping oil and then his voice rose and he prayed, "Lord, now lettest Thou Thy servant depart in peace for mine eyes hath seen Thy salvation." Then he stood up and asked *Khawaja* Michel to turn on the lights. The chandelier in the centre of the room shone with light and Yalo saw the three men glistening with oil.

I saw tears in the eyes of the metropolitan as he said he wanted to sit down. Ata took him by the arm and helped him back to the sofa. The metropolitan said he was feeling dizzy and *Khawaja* Michel offered him a little rosewater, but the metropolitan raised his narrow eyebrows in refusal and asked the *khawaja* and Ata to sit down next to him.

I was sitting on my own in the corner, and I could see them though they couldn't see me. It occurred to me that His Reverence must pluck his eyebrows like a woman and I almost burst out laughing, but the metropolitan's voice made my blood run cold. I heard a thick, broad voice that seemed to be coming from his chest: "The Father, the Father. I see the Father. Look, Michel. Look, my children. The Father is seated in the midst of the icon and moving. He is picking up the cup and moving it to His lips. No-one sees the Father but he dies. The Father is calling us to His kingdom and proclaiming the good news of the second coming of the Lord." He said that the Father had raised His cup again and that the icon had been wiped clean. "The icon is wiped clean," boomed his thick voice, before he fell to the ground.

I thought the metropolitan would die. He slithered off the sofa and ended up sitting on the Persian carpet. Then he crawled towards the icon and knelt, resting his forehead on the floor. Michel and Ata knelt, and I found myself kneeling and looking at the icon, in which I could see no change. I don't know how long we went on kneeling, but I felt it would never end. We knelt in silence and could hear nothing but the breathing of the ageing metropolitan, which sounded like snoring and then began to grow quieter. I thought we would kneel there like that for ever and I began to feel pain in my knees and my eyes began to hurt so I closed them, and after a long while I heard Ata's voice saying that dinner was ready. It seems he'd left us kneeling and gone to lay the table. I opened my eyes, found that they had got up and walked behind them into the dining room. The table was laid with five plates, five glasses, a bottle of wine, a glass bowl from which the smell of veal wafted and a bowl of vegetables. After the metropolitan had blessed the food, he turned to the empty chair and asked *Khawaja* Michel if we should wait for someone else before beginning our dinner. *Khawaja* Michel looked at Ata, who said that the empty chair was for Elias, the living prophet. "That's a Jewish tradition," said the metropolitan, and asked that the plate be taken away. Ata objected, saying he had seen the plate in the vision. He said he'd heard the voice of the prophet Elias asking him to leave a place for him at the table. Ata's voice became higher, like the voice of a little girl, as he pleaded with the metropolitan to allow Elijah the prophet to sit with them. Irritation appeared on the face of the metropolitan, who was eating the veal as though swallowing it whole, and he said nothing. Silence reigned. His Reverence took only one sip from his glass, so no-one else drank.

While Ata and I were cleaning away the dinner things, I saw *Khawaja* Michel bend over and kiss the metropolitan's hand and I noticed him giving him something and the metropolitan taking it and saying, "God bless this house for ever." I wanted to tell the *khawaja* and the metropolitan that Ata was a swindler and there was nothing religious about him, but I wasn't sure my voice would emerge from my throat. I was afraid my voice would change like Ata's and come out high-pitched like a little girl's, so I said nothing.

In the kitchen, while we were doing the washing up, Ata finished off all the glasses of wine, saying it was the best in the world. Then he finished off the bottle, smacking his thin lips, and he gave me some money, never once looking me in the face.

Yalo wasn't invited to the supplementary oil sessions that were staged three times during a single week at the Paris flat. He guessed that Ata had decided to exclude him and thanked the Lord for it, because he was certain that if he'd been invited to a second session, he would have exploded with laughter and exposed the whole operation. It was at the villa, however, that the operation was exposed. Ghada told me how Deacon Isam Murqus succeeded in doing this.

Ata exploited *Khawaja* Michel's faith and milked it. Yes, milked it. Ata was a swindler, and thank God his exposure wasn't at my hands. I saw how he left the villa in the February cold. He was naked from the waist up and looked as though he was walking on his knees. I thought he was kneeling and assumed that he must have transferred his miracles from the sitting room to the garden, but I was wrong. Ata stood under the illuminated portico, sheltering from the rain. I shouted to him and he turned round and when he saw me, a frown appeared on his face, which thrust itself forward and became wet with rain. Then he ran into the darkness, which swallowed him up.

Ghada told me that Deacon Isam had exposed Ata. The party was being held as usual in darkness and candlelight, and the oil had begun seeping from his outstretched hands when the deacon jumped up and put his arms round Ata from behind and ordered them to turn on the lights. Before he joined the clergy, Isam had been a professor of mathematics at Bishara College. When he hugged Ata, the poor man was no longer able to move. The electricity was turned on and the deacon told Ata to take off his shirt. Ata refused, but the deacon wouldn't give him room to move. He ripped the shirt off and removed two small plastic bottles of oil from the man's armpits. Then he turned to *Khawaja* Michel and said this chicanery had to stop.

Ghada made fun of her father's naiveté and said that Ata was a swindler who'd got money out of her father and run off, but I didn't tell her what I knew about Ata. I was afraid she'd tell her father and the *khawaja* would think I'd been a part of the operation, even though it had nothing to do with me. All I knew about Ata was that he belonged to the Jehovah's Witnesses, and there were absolutely no ties between us. True, he'd winked at me and given me money to buy my silence, but I would have held my tongue anyway. Our relationship didn't go beyond the fact that I'd seen him, just as dozens of others had, at *Khawaja* Michel's house, and I'd seen how Metropolitan Mikha'eel Sawaya had seen God the Father, which was, of course, impossible. I know from my grandfather that no-one can see God the Father. Even the prophet Moses on Sinai didn't see Him. Only Christ saw Him. No-one has ever seen the Father but the *Bro*, and Christ is the true son.

That's everything that happened in Paris. I know you asked me to tell about Paris because you suspect that my relationship with the explosives gang began there, but I swear to God Almighty that's all there was to it. *Khawaja* Michel had nothing to do with it.

In his earlier confessions, Yalo wrote about meeting Heikal. The truth is that the story of the explosives started with that meeting, which probably took place in Ashrafiyeh when Yalo was outside the Arayis Advertising Company waiting for Shireen.

Yalo ignored Heikal at first, but the gang leader approached him. After the greeting and the hug, the talk began. Heikal blackmailed Yalo and threatened him with exposure about the Georges Armouni Barracks money. Yalo didn't get into a discussion with the man because he was waiting for Shireen. He felt afraid for her so he agreed to everything. He agreed to meet Heikal at the Badaro Inn the following day at noon, said goodbye and left. Yalo pretended to have left but turned back behind the Ampère Cinema and waited for Heikal to disappear. Yalo then returned to where he'd been waiting and stood under the eucalyptus tree shading the pavement. Suddenly he felt a hand on his shoulder, turned round to find Heikal standing there and realized he'd been caught out. Heikal asked for his address, and Yalo couldn't find a way out of giving him the address of the villa. Heikal said he'd prefer to meet Yalo in Ballona, cancelled the Badaro Inn appointment and left, though Yalo was sure he'd hide somewhere nearby and keep him under observation. He therefore decided to leave too. He looked at his watch and shook his head as though he was waiting for someone who hadn't showed up. Then he left.

Yalo went into the café next to the Ampère Cinema, drank a glass of cold beer, then returned to the Arayis building and waited. Shireen did not come out, however. It seems she'd left while he'd been in the café. He looked at his watch again, shook his head and departed.

That, sir, is how Yalo got caught up in the gang. I'm not saying that Shireen was the reason; in fact, I'd say it was just fate and fortune. Yalo got caught up in fate and fortune and was compelled to store the explosives in his hut, but he didn't take part in the bombing operations because he was preoccupied with something else. Yalo was in love, sir, and that was all that mattered.

I made you a promise and I have kept it. I can't, though, make anything better out of the subject of the explosives, or answer that question of yours that cost Yalo so much in various forms of torture and beating, namely, "Where did you hide the explosives?"

After Yalo confessed, in accordance with your urgings related to the explosives, you searched his hut, you turned the villa upside down, and you dug up the garden, but you didn't find a thing. I can't guide you to where they are, not just because I don't know, but because my imagination won't play along with me that far. What I've been asked for is the truth, not imagination. I've said as much as I can about the gang, and I cannot imagine more. Now I am remembering, not imagining, and there's a big difference between the two. Remembering is imagining too, for my memories come to me like my imaginings, and take me into a long night, but I cannot guide you to where the explosives are because I'm not writing a story; I'm writing the truth. I know that if I indicated a specific place, you'd search there, and if you didn't find anything, which of course you wouldn't, the consequences would not be to my advantage.

I swear I can imagine anything you want, but I cannot guide you to where the explosives are because the place doesn't exist. Even the story of my meeting with Heikal in front of the building where Shireen works I could only compose because something similar happened when I met Najeeb Mansurati.

I was standing under the eucalyptus tree waiting for Shireen when I felt a hand on my shoulder. I turned quickly and saw a smiling face, but I didn't recognize it. "It's Najeeb," the man said, but I couldn't remember who this Najeeb was. I thought he must be one of the dozens of "modern-style" beggars who are to be found everywhere in the streets of Beirut. One of them comes up to you and speaks to you politely so you think he wants to ask you something, and then it turns out he's telling you a long cock-and-bull story about his sick mother or wife or son, and the end of the matter is that he asks you for a dollar. The dollar phenomenon puzzled me and I couldn't work it out. Why didn't they beg in Lebanese currency? Even the beggars, sir, have lost confidence in the national currency! I thought he was one of those, so I turned away. But he said my name. He called me "M. Yalo" – and never before had my name been joined to *Monsieur*. I'm plain Yalo or plain Daniel. Where did this young man come up with the *Monsieur* to put in front of my name? I turned back to him and he said he was Najeeb Mansurati, the brother of Saeed, the singer, and he brought his face close to mine to kiss it, so I kissed him. Then he asked if I knew anything about what had happened to his brother. I gathered from him that Saeed had decided to become a professional musician, so when the war ended he had gone back to Qamishli to work as a singer at the Khabour Hotel, which belongs to a Kurd called Muhammad El Heita, and had disappeared. Najeeb told me they'd looked for him everywhere and that his mother had gone to Syria and visited all the prisons but found no trace of him.

Najeeb asked what I thought and I said I didn't know. Anyway, how could anyone who'd been in the Billy Goats Battalion go to Syria to work as a singer? What an idiot!

"They must have chewed him," I said.

"What?" asked Najeeb.

"Forget it. I was remembering the lyric "I would have munched on them and chewed." Remember how your brother used to sing it?

In Ashrafiyeh when you were there and so was I

My soul to your lips close hewed . . .

The brother began humming the song and I almost got carried away along with him, but then I remembered that we were standing in Tabarees Square in the middle of Ashrafiyeh, and people would think we were mad.

I wanted to say, "My condolences," but I don't know what I said. Then he invited me to visit him at home and stood close to me and offered me a cigarette. I said, "No thanks." He lit his cigarette and smoked calmly. He was waiting for me to ask him how he was so he could ask how I was, but I didn't say anything. I wanted him to leave so my relationship with Shireen wouldn't get caught up in my former life. Shireen had to be the beginning of a new life that had nothing to do with memories of the war. Najeeb went on standing there, however, in his long, carefully ironed navy-blue trousers. Through the trousers I could imagine his white, hairless thighs, and I saw him in my mind's eye when he would come, wearing shorts, to visit his brother at the barracks, and Alexei's winks and talk of boys and of the pleasure in life that had no equal. Najeeb finished his cigarette and I finished my ogling of his thighs, but he kept on standing there.

I decided to leave. I looked at my watch and shook my head. He asked me if I was waiting for someone and I answered that I had to go, so he threw himself at me to kiss me. I felt insanely angry. I could have choked him instead of kissing him, and my head started ringing, but I kissed him anyway, my lips quivering with anger, and set off at a run. I went into the café near the Ampère Cinema, where I calmed my nerves with a glass of cold beer. Then I went back outside and waited, but she didn't come out, and that meant that she'd gone while I'd been sitting in the café.

That is the true story, sir. No, I didn't do anything with the young Mansurati at the barracks, for I know that that is not only a sin but a crime too. Even with *Malfono* Haleem I didn't. Others maybe; I don't know, and I wouldn't presume to say. But me, no.

That is why I suggest that the explosives file be closed at the point when Yalo met Heikal close to the Araysi Building in Ashrafiyeh, Tabarees Square. I also believe that this confession is good enough to hold up in court. The judge can use it against me or he can cite mitigating circumstances, such as that it is to be supposed that Yalo fell victim to his former comrades' blackmail and he was afraid for his relationship with Shireen so he got mixed up in their business, but he didn't have any direct connection to either the planning or the execution. Similarly, his relationship and that of *Khawaja* Michel with the person named Ata Ata didn't go beyond the miracle. It's a terrible shame to pick on *Khawaja* Michel. Anyone but the *khawaja*, that noble human being who rescued me and made me a man again after fate, in Paris, had brought me to a state lower than an animal's! It's enough that he's become a laughing stock and that his visits to Lebanon have tailed off following the Ata scandal at the villa. I believe that the Ata incident destroyed his influence in his own home. Just imagine, sir: his daughter, Ghada, who used to regard him as a god, now makes fun of him. If that's how it is with his daughter, what must it be like with his wife, Mme Randa, who had always mocked his obsession with Byzantine icons and the little spray bottle he used to spray the icons to keep them clean and fresh? I'm sure the lady must have come to despise him, and that she chose me as a way of expressing her contempt. I was a just a tool, sir, and realizing that has helped to cure me of love. I was a tool for Randa and she was a tool for her husband and he was a tool for Ata and Ata was a tool for I have no idea who. Or, I was a tool for my grandfather and he was a tool for my mother and she was a tool for Elias El Shami and he was a tool for his wife and she was a tool for her illness and I don't know what.

All of us are tools, sir. No-one exists in and of himself. So why did God create us? Could it be so that we might be tortured, and torture?

Yalo does not agree with me that life has no meaning. It's as though he's discovered another meaning for life that he doesn't want to tell anyone about, not even me. I move close to him and read to him and he turns towards me for a moment, then averts his face and returns to his private world that transports him I know not where.

Yalo, sir, has discovered that a man exists only when he becomes the lowest of the low. There, at the bottom, no-one is anyone else's tool any more. There, he becomes a sheep sacrificed for all, and his soul flies above the world because it is free.

I fear for him, though. I write because I fear for him. I feel a great pain mounting from my backside to my neck and throttling me. I sit on the site of pain and I write of him and for him, and I hope that he will descend and come back to me. There he stays, though, up above, neither hearing nor seeing. Or rather, he hears voices that come from inside him, and sees when he closes his eyes. I envy him and I fear for him and I am afraid of him and I don't know. Is it my right to call on him to descend, so that he may return to me and we may leave the prison together and begin our life anew? I want to start my life. I have come to understand the meaning of life. When I leave here, I shall open a small joinery workshop, look after my poor mother and make up to her for her life, and I shall forget Shireen, and the story of Shireen and my love for Shireen.

The story's clear now, to you, to me and to him. Poor Yalo! Did you know, sir, that all the rapes attributed to me during a period of a year and a half amount to no more than ten? Of course, to those we have to add some twenty cases of theft, intentional or unintentional.

The charges are without foundation, sir.

I am aware that one case is enough for you to throw me in prison and give me hell, but things have to be taken in context and mitigating circumstances considered. I personally believe that the sole charge on which Yalo should be tried is that of being a peeping tom.

Here, I'd like to go into the charge of rape in a little detail. Who is the true accused, sir? Yalo, or the men and women who used their cars for indecent behaviour in the Ballona forest? Lebanese law is explicit on this point. Indecent behaviour in public places is forbidden. It may be argued that the law is unjust because it infringes on individual freedoms, and that is true but has no meaning in law. The law states that a woman who is arrested in suspicious circumstances inside a vehicle in a public place is to be treated as a prostitute until proven otherwise.

Why, then, are you only applying the law to Yalo?

I know you don't want me to be a smartass. The officer told me when I was on the throne that he wanted a story "without any smartass stuff or other crap". And I've told you the facts as I lived and witnessed them. But wouldn't you agree that the case treats me unfairly?

I don't want it to be understood from what I've just said that I'm trying to deflect the accusation onto Shireen. Shireen is innocent and pure, and she only came to the forest with that spineless cuckold Dr Saeed El Halabi because she had despaired of life and of her fiancé's fatuousness. All of you saw him, sir – how he sat at the interrogation with his fat thighs pressed together saying he was an engineer and a graduate of the American University. What is a donkey like that who falls over his fat thighs going to engineer? How could she choose him and leave me? Can't she see what's right in front of her eyes? How could anyone leave a tall, slim young man who walks on tiptoe so as not to disturb the dead who cover the surface of the earth for that mule who's afraid of his own shadow? And how can he pretend that he was with her at Ballona? Damn it, what a miserable liar! He was happy to show off his horns just to get me thrown in prison. I swear to God, sir, if I see that fatuous little bastard with her, I'll shoot him and scatter his body round the forest and leave his soul to moan among the pine trees for all eternity. But I've never killed anyone. If Yalo was a criminal, he would have killed them all and made a forest for the dead like the woods of Ein Ward.

I'm not going to stray from the topic now, even though the shade of my grandfather fills my head and his voice, which he swallowed during his final days, rings in my ears. I will not stray and tell you about the sobbing willows of the dead. In fact, I'm going to tell you the truth about Yalo's loves and his thefts, and about how he would go down to the blind, unlit cars in the middle of the night of pines and make off with the plunder that God saw fit to grant him, in money, watches and rings. I agree, the ring he gave Shireen was one of the spoils of Ballona, and when he saw it inside the handkerchief opened by the interrogator the tears sprang from his eyes, not because he felt guilty or because he wanted to appear pitiable, as you supposed, but because he was upset at Shireen's betrayal of their pact. That wide silver band with ancient Egyptian symbols engraved on it was the symbol of love that he gave to Shireen. They were sitting in the Rawda Café and there was the sea. That day she took the ring and her heart opened up to him and he felt that the girl loved him. She took the ring and said thank you and spoke as though she were an open book. She talked about her family and about how her two brothers had emigrated to Canada. She said she was sick of life with people like them, who didn't know how to enjoy it. She said she envied Yalo. Yes, she told Yalo that she envied him because he lived life and enjoyed it. She thanked him for having taught her how to eat and have fun. She talked about her mother, who cared about nothing except cosmetic surgery and facelifts, and about her father the contractor, who went every night to the Casino du Liban and gambled. She said she'd decided to go back to university to study French Literature and told Yalo about the poetry of Jacques Prévert, which she loved. Yalo saw himself climbing up her words and swinging on them and embracing them. Then she put out her hand and he did the same, and the two hands embraced. She said she thanked him for everything before looking at her watch and saying she was going to go home now.

The ring of love had become the ring of accusation. Shireen didn't want the ring any more and preferred to wear her fiancé's gold band in its place. She's free to do as she likes, I don't dispute her freedom, but why did she give the ring to the interrogator?

The interrogator knows the ring is worthless. If it had been valuable, she wouldn't have accepted it. Why did the honourable interrogator not ask her why she had accepted a ring from a man who stalked her and whom she hated and wanted to be free of? The interrogator considered the ring material evidence and he was right, but did he ask Shireen when she had taken the ring from Yalo? Of course not. Even if he had asked her, she would have lied and never acknowledged that she'd taken it six months before bringing the case against me. I will not request that you ask her what happened during those six months and how many times we ate fish and *kibbeh nayyeh* and drank arak.

Let's slow down a little, though.

I confess I stole, and the penalty for stealing is prison, and I confess that I fornicated with women at Ballona, and my punishment for that will come from Almighty God. I will write how these things happened and try to remember, and I beseech you to forgive me for the gaps in my memory, for a person's memory is full of gaps which none but God can fill. God alone possesses perfect memory. Human beings, on the other hand, remember only to forget.

You want the beginning of the story, and the beginning of the story was Ballona.

The story began when I saw a car stop in the forest at night and turn off its engine and lights for about half an hour. Then it left. I, in my capacity as guard, was concerned. The darkness was intense, but in my head I drew up a plan for the defence of the villa in case of armed attack. I knew, from things I'd overheard *Khawaja* Michel say, that the villa might be under threat. The *khawaja*, as you know, is an arms dealer, owns a hotel in Ras Al Khaima, has dealings with the big clothing designers in Lebanon, organizes visits by Lebanese fashion models to the Gulf and things like that. I squatted in the darkness, ready to face the worst, but nothing happened, thank God.

The second night I heard a similar sound and saw the same scene more or less, though things took a more complicated turn. While the first car was there with its lights turned off, a second car came and stopped not far away. It too turned off its engine and its lights. After a while, the first car left, but the second car waited for about half an hour more before departing. This excited my fear and my misgivings. I thought to myself that they were reconnaissance vehicles, and that the presence of two cars together meant that the operation was organized and coordinated.

It occurred to me to go down to the second car, but I was afraid of falling into an ambush. I decided instead to bide my time and watch with my weapon at the ready. Suddenly, however, the second car turned on its lights and left. I decided to tell Madame about what I'd seen, but then I dropped the idea; the man had put me in charge of the security of his house and his family and told me to make my own decisions, so I decided not to frighten Madame and to act as events dictated.

I went on like that for about a fortnight. Each night I'd announce the call to arms and build in my head imaginary fortifications among the pine and willow trees. Then one day I realized the truth.

The moon was full. A car stopped beneath a willow tree, as though deliberately seeking cover under its weeping branches. As usual, the engine was turned off and the lights extinguished. I couldn't see what was going on from my hiding place behind the wall of the villa, so I didn't know what to do. Should I go over to the car and leave my rifle behind the wall, walking like I was just passing by so as not to get caught up before I was ready in a battle with this gang that was plotting to assassinate *Khawaja*

Michel or kidnap his wife or daughter for ransom? Or should I take my rifle and move stealthily towards them, so that they couldn't see me, even though this was risky? Then I thought of the words of our trainer Qusta, about the relationship of the fighter to his rifle, namely that there were three things a man should never abandon or lend even to his closest friend: his wife, his rifle and his horse.

I picked up the rifle and moved slowly and carefully. I left the wall of the villa behind me and advanced in the waddling position they'd taught us during military training. I advanced like a duck and hid myself under a pine tree so I could see the car and those inside it clearly.

This was when the surprise occurred.

I had expected to see armed men, but I couldn't see any obvious weapons. I saw a man and a woman. I thought, That's it. They're using love as a cover. They're pretending to be lovers so they can watch and plan. But they can't put anything over on Yalo. I thought, I'll watch until I see where this all leads. Damn! It's like watching a film in the cinema.

Little by little, however, I started to forget about the gang because I felt that the man and the woman weren't acting; they were practising a sort of sex, meaning the sort of thing teenagers do. And I started to get into it. No, I didn't get aroused at first because I was afraid, and if you're afraid you don't. But gradually my fear left me, my breathing became regular, and I started enjoying myself. It was the first time in my life that I'd witnessed a real-life sex scene. I got very aroused and was afraid I'd fall over because I was squatting and my knees were hurting me, but I decided I wouldn't move. That day I came before the man in the car did, because when I rested my rifle butt in my lap it knocked against my penis and I ejaculated. I'd never seen anything like that before. A man playing with a woman all over her body, the breasts exposed over her dress and so forth. My comrades had told me how they'd catch their parents at night and how they'd have orgasms amid the whisperings of their fathers on top of their mothers. I, on the other hand, was a pathetic case. My father had gone away ages ago, Elias El Shami didn't sleep with my mother in the house, and my grandfather was a desiccated tree trunk.

There, beneath the pine tree, lust consumed me. I saw the man, whose features I couldn't make out, sucking her big breasts and then fondling them. Then . . . I don't know how to put it, but it was an amazing scene. When I heard the sound of the engine, I ran back to my hut to wash, and something strange happened. I got aroused again and came in my hand under the shower, and from then on I'd get aroused every time I went into the bathroom.

After that moonlit night, and by virtue of continued observation, I understood the whole business. It had nothing to do with gangs and attempts to assassinate or kidnap, as I'd thought at the beginning. What was taking place in the cars was just indecent behaviour. I decided to go on watching. Of course, I didn't abandon my rifle, but I made use of the torch that Mme Randa had given me and I put on a white balaklava.

I found the balaklava in the hut. The torch, though, was to do with the power cuts. After I'd been in my job two months, there was a power cut and I heard Mme Randa screaming. The electricity at the villa doesn't usually fail because when it's cut off in the area, a huge generator takes over that distributes electricity to the houses of the village. It seems that this time the generator wasn't working. The darkness was total, and Yalo heard Mme Randa asking him to come up. She was carrying a lighted candle and a slender black torch. She gave him the torch and asked him to turn on the villa's private generator, which was in the garden.

Yalo went down to the garden, primed the generator and got it running, and kept the torch for himself. Or at least, Madame asked him to keep the torch for emergencies, so he put it in his coat pocket and it became his permanent companion, his life soon becoming filled with emergencies.

Yalo didn't initiate the adventure. The adventure came to him in his hut, so what was he supposed to do? His adventure was watching the blind cars that stopped among the trees, the steam of desire rising off them and spreading above the green branches of the pines.

A man meets his fate halfway, they say. Yalo's was the forest. Yalo started waiting for night and living night and breathing night. In his eyes the cars came to resemble tame animals having sex in the dark. The idea pleased him and he decided he wouldn't tell anyone about it. When he told Shireen for the first time, he omitted the scene where he rested the rifle on his thighs. And Shireen believed him. Yalo was convinced that Shireen believed every word he said to her, which is why he was so surprised when he saw her in the interrogation room, which in turn led to his rapid breakdown and confession to everything. Yalo wasn't a coward that he'd confess so easily; he confessed because the presence of Shireen made him lose his balance, and despite the fact that he'd already confessed he found himself in a vortex from which he couldn't escape. Later he realized that what was wanted was a confession about the explosives, so he confessed to that. You, however, found that his confessions were missing certain details, and you were right. The reason was not Yalo's attempts to obstruct the interrogation, as you claimed, but because he didn't know, and that is a story I have explained to you, sir, in detail, and I hope that no more will be asked of me, for I have resigned myself to God's will and to yours.

The first time was by accident.

Yalo was squatting in his usual place, behind the wall of the villa, under the pine tree, when a car stopped in the forest. The car turned off its lights so he couldn't see anything. Most of his nights were like that. He would sit in the dark, count his breaths and imagine. He could only really see when the moon came up, and this made him love Fairuz's song "We and the Moon Are Neighbours", and he'd sing along with her: "Behind our hills his house is. In front of us he rises." However, the moon was not at Mistress Fairuz's command. The moon only gave light when it was full, and because the breasts of his beloved Shireen (so he imagined on that night of wonder when the smell of incense arose) grew larger and smaller, he called them "the moon" and started addressing them as *sahro*, and had to explain to Shireen every time he used it what that Syriac word meant.

That night, with the colour black covering the two heroes of the scene, Yalo heard a scream and saw what seemed to be the shadows of struggling hands. Then weeping could be heard, mixed with a woman's moans. That was when Yalo gave birth to the eagle. He found himself flying, pulled his torch from his coat pocket, released its beam of light and hit the man between the eyes.

Yalo moved as though he were flying and swooped down on the car carried by the air that filled his open coat and made him look like a bird with its wings spread. In a few seconds, which were insufficient for the driver to regain his balance and flee, Yalo reached them and saw how the man's jaw fell open from fright, and saw two arms. True, the man thrust his head and shoulders through the car window and put his hands in the air in surrender; nevertheless, Yalo kept on coming, the light shining on the point between the man's eyes. He reached the car and gestured with his rifle. The man, who was sitting in the car, pulled his head back in and doubled over. Then he opened the door and got out with his hands up, saying, "Whatever you want. You can have whatever you like. You want her? Take her. She's a prostitute. Take her, but please, I beg you . . . "

It hadn't occurred to Yalo to take her. He'd swooped down because he'd heard quarrelling and weeping. The man cringing in front of him never stopped talking: "Please. Whatever you want. Take her if you want, but let me go." Yalo shoved the man aside, went over to the window and shone the light on the woman. It was a young girl, or so she appeared to the hawk's eyes that had opened in the darkness. She became aware of the light and moaned louder. Yalo decided that she wasn't what her friend, who was in his early forties, had said she was. He drew back, kneed the man between the thighs and spat on him. The man, doubled up with pain, started emptying the money from his pockets and holding it out to Yalo. Yalo saw the money, but instead of snatching it and putting it in his pocket, he kneed the man again, spat on him and motioned with the torch, ordering him to go. The man got into the car, turned on the engine and left, the girl still bent over at his side.

Yalo was surprised that the girl consented to remain with the man who had called her a prostitute. He also felt guilty. He ought to have released the girl from that pathetic man, but what would he have done with her?

He returned to his hut. Then he decided to bathe, and under the shower he pictured the girl with him and it was the way it ought to be.

That's how things started, sir.

The first time, Yalo didn't steal or rape. On the first occasion, he discovered – when he came out of the bathroom, drank a glass of arak and ate some tomato salad with onions – that he was a fool. He ought to have taken the woman and the money and perhaps the car too. He got drunk and talked to himself and laughed at his naiveté.

After the first time, things took shape. Yalo didn't plan his operations, because his main activities continued to be watching and peeping. However, from time to time he would swoop down on the lovers and take whatever God granted him by way of spoils. Yalo wasn't greedy since if he'd wanted to he could have stolen what he wished and had sex with whomever he wished. He was economical in his operations because he liked to take a nibble here and a nibble there, to do things in a leisurely fashion, and this had nothing to do with his fear of the police. He was certain that none of the men would file complaints against him. What, after all, could they say? Would they say they'd been fooling around in the cars? And what would happen to them and to their girlfriends if the law of Lebanon were applied to them?

These were the men whose statements the interrogator had

read out to him. They weren't telling the truth. I don't say that their statements were completely false, but I do say that they were missing some details. The police, sir, did not interrogate them seriously. What nonsense! They all came with girls they didn't know? That's a lie. I swear that in all my long experience I only came across one prostitute, and I split with her the money she'd taken from the man. The rest of the women were not "of unknown identity". They were ordinary women, but the interrogation wasn't serious. One taste of the bastinado, just one I swear, and they would have shat the truth and confessed the women's names. I'm not saying they should have been given the water torture or the sack or the chair or the bottle. That wouldn't be right. If you'd just interrogated them, sir, you would have found out the truth about the lovers' forest, but you weren't interested in the truth. You were only interested in condemning me and pinning the explosions and the rapes on me. That's why you let everyone go, and the only one to be caught was this poor slave, who is ascending to his heavenly throne.

My stories in the forest aren't all like one another, but I won't tell them all because I don't know how to describe the difference between one taste and another and one smell and another, which is why I shall content myself with setting out for you the main headings, which are enough, because what I am writing here are my confessions. I am not writing a novel.

1. I don't know the names of the women because I didn't ask their names. I didn't ask so I wouldn't be asked – that's the rules of the game. That is why when you tortured me to force me to mention names, it did you no good, because it would have made me make things up, which is what I promised you, myself and God I would not do.

2. I only stole what was offered. I contented myself with whispering, "Hand over everything," and took what they produced from their pockets. I didn't demand watches or jewellery, but I didn't refuse them. Once I threw a watch away because it looked like a worthless child's watch, and I saw the man bend over and pick it up so I ordered him to give it to me. Then I discovered that my instinct had been correct and it was worthless.

3. I didn't speak much, and then only in a whisper, because I was careful to make sure that no-one would remember my voice or my features. I used to cover my head and face with the white balaklava and speak in a low voice because I believe that a low voice strikes terror into the hearts of those who hear it.

4. I only committed rape in the true sense of the word once. The man threatened me and gave me shit, and that made me force him to get into the boot of the car, which I closed. Then I pulled the girl over to the pine tree and tried to do it with her, but she refused vehemently and tore my shirt, so I threatened her with my gun. It was not an enjoyable experience because the woman was barely open. I felt my member bleeding so I decided to stop having sex with women but was unable to implement my decision.

5. Once it was especially enjoyable, with a woman in her forties who was in the company of a young man of not more than twenty-five years of age, or so I supposed.

6. There were more incidents of theft than of sex.

7. I didn't keep any of the stolen goods because I decided from the beginning that it would be a mistake to do so. I therefore sold everything for very little money, taking

whatever I was offered. I sold them in the gold market in the Aisha Bakkar quarter near the T.V. building motorway, but I made a point of dealing with more than one jeweller so I wouldn't be found out. I squandered the money I made.

This, in brief, is the story of what happened to me with the women of the forest, and as you can see, sir, what I did isn't even one per cent of what anyone else would have done in my place. The take was ample, and the cars poured into the forest in droves.

On the other hand, the tale related by the engineer, when he claimed he was with Shireen in the forest, has no basis in truth. He was not her fiancé and he didn't go with her. If he had been with her, everything would have been different. I'm sure, sir, that you must have noticed, when he was sitting in the inter-rogation room "like a deaf man at a wedding", what a miser he was, and how unkempt. He'd take a cigarette out of his jacket pocket as though he was stealing it instead of putting the pack on the table like everyone else. You, sir, put your pack on the table, and you offered cigarettes to your assistants and your visi-tors. You even offered me a cigarette, though I didn't notice because I'd closed my eyes, which is a habit of mine that is connected to my childhood. He, sir, on the other hand, would put his hand into the inside pocket of his jacket and extract a cigarette, because he's despicable. I swear, if I'd seen that idiot in the forest everything would have been different, because I would have killed him. But God took His precautions, because if I'd killed one person and buried him in the forest under the willow tree, the killing would never have stopped, and the forest would have been turned into a graveyard like the wood at Ein Ward where the children were forbidden to play because of the moaning that came from the branches.

My grandfather told me that what made him go with his uncle Abdel Maseeh when his uncle came back to the village to purchase his sister's son was the sobbing of the willows and poplars that sprang up on the banks of a little river whose name I don't know. That's where the whole story started and where I, God's humble servant Daniel Habeel Abyad, known as Yalo, was tied to the thread of blood that stretches from Tur Abdin to the end of the world.

My grandfather said that I was born under the sign of death because the cord was wrapped round my neck. The midwife, Linda Saleeba, saved me from death by a miracle. She left my mother screaming in pain, forgot about the afterbirth and set about untying the cord from round my neck. It had strangled my cries so everyone thought I'd been born dead.

I was born in a hangman's noose, and a rope of blood is my only inheritance, which is why I will not be surprised if the rope wraps itself round my neck at the end. That way, my end will be my beginning and my life will have been nothing but a dream.

The story was only born in my memory here in the prison, when it came about that I had to sit on the bottle. This made me taste what it's like for a person to live outside of time. True, the pain was great, but living outside of time is a pleasure without equal. This, in my opinion, explains Yalo's insistence on staying there, among the memories of the dead.

I don't know, sir, why I'm writing this story now, when I know that it doesn't interest you and will add nothing to the interrogation. I have confessed to all the crimes, and all you have to do is issue the sentence. All the same, I'm writing for the sake of poor Yalo, for this will be the first time he hears the full story of his grandfather.

The beginning of the story is a child called Habeel Jibra'eel

Abyad, who was born in the village of Ein Ward in the neighbourhood of Tur Abdin in a land that has no name because it is the land of a people who no longer exist. There, at the beginning of the twentieth century, the Turks carried out a terrible massacre that harvested some 1.5 million Armenians. It is the massacre that our brothers the Armenians commemorate each year. My grandfather's massacre, however, is remembered by no-one because it was a little massacre attached to a larger massacre. Woe to a people slaughtered in a secondary massacre, for the butcher will see no need to wipe the blood from his knives! This is what happened at the beginning of the century, when the small Assyrian people was slaughtered.

The armed hosts entered a little village, called Ein Ward, "Spring of Roses", because the red damask rose grew at the edges of its spring, which bubbled over with water coloured gold by the sun. (This is how my grandfather used to describe his village, after which he'd tell his daughter that he was speaking like a poet and that he'd wasted his life because he'd never given his talent for poetry the attention it deserved.) There the massacre to which all the inhabitants of the village fell victim was committed. When the inhabitants of the village sensed danger, they took refuge in the monastery of Mar Yuhanna three kilometres from their village, but the attackers, who had surrounded the monastery, would accept nothing but total surrender. Following negotiations led by *Kohno* Danho, the inhabitants were given safe passage. They emerged with their hands up, having thrown their rifles on the ground, and the massacre began. The attackers put all to the sword, women and men, and only a tiny number of the inhabitants survived. These made their way to the valleys and fled in the direction of the city of Qamishli.

My grandfather doesn't remember the massacre because he

was less than three years old. He tells it as though it were his uncle, whom he hated, recounting it, which is why I'm not obliged to believe the story – not the story of the people of the village taking refuge in the monastery, and not the story of their slaughter and burial in a mass grave dug among the willow trees. What can be believed is that the children under three were not harmed and that the attackers plundered the houses in the village before deciding to settle there. This is why the image of the blood that became my grandfather's mother's *kokina* may be no more than a literary conceit with which my grandfather hoped to establish his credentials as a poet.

The children wandered the streets of their village begging, fear and hunger leaving them no space to weep over their murdered parents.

Then Mullah Mustafa's decision was announced.

All I know is his first name because my grandfather refused to speak about him. The mullah decided that the children must not be left wandering the streets and ordered that they be distributed among the Kurdish families that had taken possession of the houses in the village. My grandfather's luck was great, because he was taken to the house of Mullah Mustafa himself. The child's name was changed from Habeel to Ahmad, and he became a Kurdish boy who spoke Kurdish, Arabic and Turkish and lived in the bosom of the mullah's family as though nothing had happened. The wood of willows alone bore witness, and the children were forbidden to play there because of the moans that seeped from among the branches of the trees that grew there with strange vigour after the massacre.

The story might have ended there, and Habeel Abyad forgotten his origins. He might even have become an officer in the Turkish army, like many who were snatched as small children from their mothers' arms and brought up in the Ottoman army to become pillars of the Janissaries, whose very name inspired terror.

Fate, however, had other plans.

Ten years after the massacre, and following the Ottoman defeat in the First World War and the collapse of their state, some Assyrians from the Tur Abdin district who had sought refuge in Qamishli in northern Syria began searching for their children. It is here that my grandfather's maternal uncle, called Abdel Maseeh Abyad, comes in.

Abdel Maseeh arrived in Ein Ward, went to the house of Mullah Mustafa and said he'd buy the boy for whatever amount was asked, and he asked Mullah Mustafa to swear that he would return the boy to his family, his religion and his kinsfolk. The mullah said he was ready to give the boy Ahmad to his uncle free and without recompense, on condition that the boy demonstrate that this was his own wish.

The mullah called for Ahmad, who came and stood between his Kurdish father and his Assyrian uncle. He heard his story from the mouth of his father and understood that the mullah was giving him a choice between going with Abdel Maseeh and staying where he was.

When my grandfather reached this point in his story, his tears would fall and he would choke up and start stammering. He would say nothing for a long while and ask for a cup of tea before telling how he left with his uncle without looking back.

Instead of the story ending there, in Qamishli it took a new turn because in his uncle's house the boy felt doubly a stranger. He didn't know Syriac, he hated the job his uncle found for him in a bakery, and he felt people treated him as though he was a Kurd.

In Qamishli, my grandfather recovered his original name but lost his identity, because people thought he was a Kurd and he felt he was a stranger. The world closed up in his face, and he missed the smell of the trees that had filled his life in Ein Ward. He was also persecuted at home and exposed to his uncle's fits of insanity when he drank arak and beat his wife and three daughters, after which he would turn on his nephew, whom he wanted for a son because God hadn't granted him a boy, and beat him savagely.

Habeel didn't know what to do. He couldn't go back to Ein Ward any more than he could go on living in that small, dark house, and he couldn't give up the exhausting work at the bakery because to do so would mean he'd die of hunger. The only refuge he could think of was the church of Mar Afram. He took to attending mass there regularly and helping to tidy up after mass, which attracted the attention of Deacon Sham'oun, who entered him in his Sunday school in the church basement.

At this point, my grandfather says, God rescued him. He fell in love with studying, and the boy excelled among his peers and memorized all the Syriac prayers without understanding their meaning.

Once again fate intervened, in the form of Deacon Sham'oun who advised Habeel to go to Beirut, where the world would be his oyster. The boy made his decision, collected his week's wages from the bakery and, instead of going home, got on the bus that went from Qamishli to Aleppo and thence to Tripoli and finally Beirut. Habeel arrived in Beirut carrying only the address of the church of St Sawirus in Museitbeh. He searched long and hard for the church before finding himself at its locked door, where he spent the night.

In the morning, a new chapter of the story began. *Kohno*

Hanna El Dinuhi arrived at the church and saw the boy sleeping on the pavement. He woke him gently and asked what he was doing there, and Habeel gave him Deacon Sham'oun's letter. The *kohno* read the letter carefully, took the boy into the church and led him to a side room to use as a refuge while he sorted himself out. On the second day, the *kohno* gave him a letter of recommendation to *Khawaja* Mitri, owner of the Yazbak tile factory, and told him not to talk too much as his accent sounded strange to the Lebanese ear.

This is where, sir, my grandfather as I knew him began, which is to say, where he became Habeel Abyad. He worked at the tile factory and helped in the church. He studied Syriac and religion and pleased the *malfono* with the record speed with which he memorized the lessons. My grandfather was the best student in *Kohno* Hanna's night school, where a number of Assyrian tile workers from Syria studied. Then the *kohno* married my grandfather to his niece, or so goes the official family account. The truth is that the *kohno*'s niece fell madly in love with my grandfather and went on a hunger strike, thus forcing her family to agree to her marriage to the Kurdish boy who became thereby a legitimate son of the community in Beirut. There was a further development when the *kohno* asked my father to leave the tile factory and help him run the congregation's affairs because he was getting old. My grandfather grew in status and knowledge and devoted himself to the glorification of the Creator, which qualified him, in the opinion of Thrice-blessed Metropolitan Daoud Karjo, to become assistant priest at the church of St Sawirus and then, on *Kohno* Hanna's death, to inherit the latter's position.

My grandfather studied much and toiled much. My mother said that my grandfather studied Syriac when he was fifteen, became obsessed with the debate over the one, or two, natures of God, went to Damascus and returned with the highest theological degrees. At this point, his ambition became apparent, inspired as he was by the fact that God had chosen him from the depths of the earth. Just as Christ had chosen his disciples from among the fishermen, so the Lord had chosen his disciple Afram from among the children of the massacres.

Here the story should end, for my grandfather's story ends, like all stories, with the death of its hero, and my grandfather died, and sated himself on death. Indeed, the story did end there, for all the events that were to happen after his wife's death could have been predicted. The man became old all at once and discovered that his life had had no purpose, and he started inventing books he hadn't written and imposing strange rituals on his daughter and grandson.

Gaby, however, didn't believe that the story should end with the death of his wife. The man had begun to change before his wife's death, and that death was merely an additional factor in a process that began with a strange visit paid by Mullah Mustafa to the *kohno*'s house in Museitbeh. The story seems odd. Why would the Kurdish mullah go to the Assyrian priest's house? Is it true that he asked him to return to Ein Ward, promised him his inheritance and proposed that he marry his cousin once he had repented and returned to his true religion?

My mother said that if she had heard the story from someone else, she wouldn't have believed it, but that she'd seen it with her own eyes and heard it with her own ears. She heard a knock on the door and saw the old man with his white beard and black mantle speaking with her mother in a strange form of Arabic and asking for Habeel. The woman asked him politely to sit down and went to call her husband, who was in his room putting on his priest's robes in preparation for leaving the house. My mother and her sister Sarah went into the reception room to look at the strange man, and he embraced them and kissed them.

My grandfather entered the room and saw the old man fidgeting in his chair, about to stand up. The *kohno* rushed to him like a small child, took his hand, kissed it, placed it on his head, and then kissed it, back and palm. The old man kissed the *kohno*'s shoulder and then sat down again. The *kohno* remained standing, his head bent, before the old man. The mullah told him to sit, so Habeel sat on the edge of the sofa as though ready to stand up again at any moment. Then a strange conversation took place between the two men, in a strange language. They drank tea and smoked hand-rolled cigarettes that the mullah carried in the pocket of his mantle. The *kohno*, whose lips no cigarette had touched since he'd entered the priesthood, smoked like any smoker. The *kohno* wept and the mullah wept. Then when the mullah stood up to leave, the *kohno* bent over his hand again and kissed it.

My mother said that the mullah proposed to his son that he return to Ein Ward because he wanted him to inherit his land there, and that he also proposed that he marry his cousin. My grandfather, however, said he couldn't.

They didn't speak much, for a man like the mullah, whose authority extended over all the villages of Tur Abdin, didn't have to say anything. It was enough that he had made the effort. The mere fact that he had honoured the house was something that could never be repaid, said my grandfather; but despite that he replied that he couldn't.

The *kohno* wept bitterly, said my mother, and the mullah wept quietly. The men's tears ran down their beards, and then the mullah departed, leaving the *kohno* stunned, as though he could neither see nor hear.

My mother said her father had been as if deaf for seven days, that on the Sunday after the visit he hadn't gone to church on the pretext that he was ill and had refused to receive a member of the congregation, and that he had spent an entire week in bed taking only bread and water.

My mother said she discovered that day that her father was a Kurd and that when she saw him speaking Kurdish with the mullah, she saw his true face, which only returned to him once thereafter, at the moment of his death.

The *kohno* changed greatly after the visit, as though a strange spirit had entered his body. The Syriac language took possession of him and he became obsessed with collecting the names of Lebanese, Palestinian and Syrian villages that began with the word *kafr* and interrupting people to whom he was speaking endless numbers of times to explain the Syriac origins of Arabic words, and saying that the air spoke Syriac and standing in front of the icon of Christ and addressing it in the language that no-one but the two of them understood.

My grandfather talked to his wife of his conversation with his Kurdish father only once, when he said that it had been his temptation. Just as Christ had been tempted by Satan, the mullah had been sent to the *kohno* to test his faith. He said he'd been afraid for himself, especially when his Kurdish father had spoken to him of the agonies the Kurds were suffering in Turkey and how persecuted they felt and how their villages were violated every day. The mullah, at whose footfall all trembled, seemed hesitant and sad, as though he had come to seek his son's help. The two men wept a lot and only laughed once, when the mullah reminded his son how he had memorized the Noble Koran at the age of seven, which had been considered a miracle around Ein Ward.

The greater miracle, though, the *kohno* told his wife, was that he had been able to forget, and then the mullah had come and awakened in his heart all the things that he'd forgotten.

Yalo, there, refuses to descend from his throne and come to me. I tell him not to be afraid because he is in the right. Yalo committed only one sin, which he greatly regretted but could not put right, and which he did not realize would lead to his downfall.

The sin wasn't Shireen but Shireen's voice.

The girl whom he loved to the point of death could not forget. She went on numerous dates with him. She laughed, wept, ate and drank. She held his hand, kissed him, slept with him in the small hotel in the city of Jounieh. She loved him and didn't love him, but she couldn't forget that he had broken her voice.

She said, "My voice broke, there at Ballona, so I can't love you properly," and he couldn't understand what she meant. He pictured an earthenware vessel falling to the ground and breaking, but he didn't understand that when a women's voice breaks, it means her heart has been afflicted by a deep hoarseness that has no cure, and that such a heart cannot love.

She said that there, when . . . when Dr Saeed had fled with the car and she'd been left alone in the forest with the tall man, she had tried to scream and shout, but the shock had paralyzed her, so her voice hadn't left her throat. The voice had broken in her throat, and that had broken her.

She said she'd do anything for him, but that she was incapable of recovering her broken voice and therefore wouldn't be able to keep on seeing him and had decided to go back to her fiancé, and she asked Yalo to understand.

Yalo didn't understand, and that was his great sin. He clung to the cords of a broken voice and kept up his game with a broken woman.

That was what brought him to prison and elevated him to his agonies and lost him his soul.

I went over to him. I tried to read to him, but I stopped reading because I saw his tears. I read to him about his grandfather and the Kurdish mullah and the broken voice, and the tears ran down his cheeks and wet his neck.

How can I bring him down from his throne and hug him to my chest?

Yalo is swooping down now, sir. I see him swooping down from the throne and walking towards me. I see him near to the window. I see him approaching. I rise. I open my arms and take him into my eyes.

Yalo looked at the pages. He read for a bit and asked me to stop writing because the story was over.

The clock said 12.00 noon.

The officer entered the isolation cell and ordered Yalo to follow him. The young man picked up his papers and walked down the middle of the darkened corridor. He descended a long stairway and found himself in a large underground hall. The young man with the continuous eyebrows, brown oval face and tall, thin body stood in the half-darkened hall holding his papers and waiting to offer his story to the interrogator and by so doing to pass beyond the long journey of agony and arrive at the end.

I stood and did not see.

The darkness was intense. Or no, not the darkness: the lights you shone in my eyes veiled what was to be seen and created spots of darkness and light everywhere. I closed my eyes so that I could see, which is what I always did. I closed my eyes to allow the darkness to withdraw from them, and then I opened them and saw.

I stood in a heavy silence like darkness. I stood and I waited, holding my papers. I was certain that everything I'd written was correct and that I'd written the story of my life from beginning to end and would never again be sent to be tortured.

And I heard his voice saying, "Open your eyes, man."

I opened them and waited for him to ask me for the papers, but the white man sitting behind the metal desk didn't ask me for anything. I saw the puddles of water scattered over the floor, I smelled the foul smell that filled the place, and I knew that I must go back up. I should not have believed them and descended from my throne.

I felt that I was on the verge of falling and heard his voice saying things I couldn't understand. His words were superimposed on one another and I couldn't decipher the letters. I heard questions about a man called Richard Sawan and a woman called Mary, and all I could answer was that I had not heard those names before. I understood that I was going to be transferred to Roumieh Prison and that I was presently on the bottom floor of the interrogation facility run by Intelligence at Sin El Feel.

The interrogator said my story was a joke, and his laughter rang in my ears. I went over to him and held out the papers.

My hands are suspended in the air. The story of my life from beginning to end is in my hands, my hands are in the air, and the interrogator is laughing.

"Come here so I can see," said the interrogator. "What's that in your hands?"

Why does he ask me when he knows the answer? thought Yalo. Then he answered himself: That's what interrogation is. They ask you things that you've already confessed, and when you repeat your confession you make mistakes. It's inevitable, because you can't tell the same story twice. But not this time. This time I'm not going to answer a single question. All my answers are written in these papers. I'm not going to tell the story again. I wrote it all, from beginning to end, and there's no room left for error. Black on white, and everything is here. I will not rewrite and I will not tell. It's my story, so let them take it and do with it, and with me, whatever they please, I will never . . .

Before Yalo could finish his sentence in his head, he felt a pain in his tongue and felt the answer repeating itself in his throat and the words turning to stones on his lips, and he wanted to answer, but he could not. He held out the papers and went over.

"I'm asking you what those are," screamed the interrogator.

"These . . . these . . . " said Yalo.

"What?"

"These are the story."

"The story!"

"Yes, yes, the story."

"The story of what?"

"The story. It's my story. This is the story of my life."

He waved the papers, gripping them firmly, but the interrogator didn't try to take them from him.

"The story of your life?" said the interrogator in amazement, and he came out from behind the table.

"Yes, sir. You asked me to write it, and I wrote it from beginning to end."

The interrogator burst out laughing and asked Yalo to come over to him.

Yalo approached across the holes full of water and smells, saw the interrogator's hand reaching out to snatch his papers and recoiled instinctively, tightening his grip on them.

"Those are the papers?" asked the interrogator.

"Yes, yes. These are everything."

"Why did you go to such trouble?"

"You gentlemen, sir. You asked me for everything, and I wrote everything. At the beginning, the officer sent me to be tortured because they were missing things. These aren't missing things."

"Great. Great. Dear God, you really are incredible," said the interrogator. "What an idiot! You are an idiot."

"I'm an idiot," said Yalo.

"Are you trying to take the piss?"

. . .

"Who do you think you are?"

. . .

"Do you really think we're waiting for the story of your life to find out the truth? We know everything. Who do you think you are anyway, clinging to those papers? Listen, boy. You're nothing. You know you're nothing. Give me the papers and let's have a look."

Yalo held out the papers and heard a ringing laugh.

"You're an idiot and a bloody fool. Do you know what you are?"

. . .

"Answer when I ask you a question."

"Yes, I know."

And I saw. I closed my eyes so that I could see and I saw. The papers flew in all directions before falling into the holes full of stagnant water and I heard the interrogator's voice saying, "We do apologize, M. Yalo. We do apologize. We've given you a terrible time. Your story's stupid and not worth the bother. We've unmasked the explosives gang and they've confessed to everything and you're in the clear. You're just an arsehole. Why did you try to pull the wool over our eyes with your endless stories? That's what made us suspicious of you, when in fact you're just dumb. You're simply an insignificant little arsehole, and the charge you're going to be tried on is theft and doing dirty stuff with every woman you could get your hands on in the Ballona forest. So there's no need for all these confessions."

Yalo saw the papers falling to the ground and heard the interrogator saying, "Get him out of here."

The papers were on the floor. The story of my life from beginning to end was on the floor. The water and the ink and the story that flows. His voice was saying, "Get him out of here," and on hearing that I wanted to ask him not to step on them, but he stepped on my voice. The words were stuck in my throat and the interrogator was saying, "Get him out of my sight."

"Look at the shit. He thinks he's a big turd, the shit. Go on, get him out of my sight."

I saw myself falling. I saw myself on my hands and knees trying to gather the papers. I saw his feet. They were stepping on my hands and fingers and he was grinding the papers under his heel while I tried to gather them up and drowned in the water and the smell and felt kicks up my backside and heard roars of laughter. I saw my forehead hit the floor and the smell of my tears was like the foul smell coming from the holes full of water.

. . .

And I saw him.

He had left his clothes behind, climbed onto the metal desk and jumped up to the window. I saw him there, up above, and he had regained his throne.

They dragged me along the ground.

Two men with bulging muscles appeared and they dragged me. I dug my nails into the floor because I couldn't leave Yalo there. I couldn't leave the story of my life to be ground to pieces beneath their shoes.

I saw myself being carried, and I saw me in an army jeep that was taking me to prison, and my tears were coming out of my eyes and my hands and my ears and my nose and my face and my chest.

I entered the common cell and they put a blanket on the ground for me near the door. I looked at the small, high window with its iron grill, and when I saw him my tears ceased.

Yalo was there, waiting for me.

SENTENCE

IN THE NAME OF THE LEBANESE PEOPLE

The Criminal Court of Mount Lebanon, composed of assigned judge Ghassan Diyab and advisors Nadim Jha and Niqula Abd El Nur

after perusal of indictment bill no. 223 dated 18/3/94, the declaration of Mount Lebanon's advisory prosecution no. 9355 dated 2/8/93 and of the entire lawsuit bill

finds that the following accused was arraigned before this court:

Daniel Habeel Abyad, also known as Yalo, mother's name Mary, born 1961, Beirut, Lebanese, who was arrested following oral proceedings on 8/6/1992 and who has remained in detention since that date

to be tried under the provisions of article 640/693 (Penal Code) and 739 (Penal Code) for committing, in the region of Ballona, at a recent date, a number of crimes of robbery and rape, at night and under threat of the use of arms.

Further to the public trial in the presence of the parties, it appeared that:

1. THE FACTS:

It appeared that the accused, Daniel Habeel Abyad, was employed during the years 1991 and 1992 as a watchman at a villa located in the region of Ballona, property of M. Michel Salloum, lawyer, and situated on a hill providing a view of the surrounding minor roads which in turn were a favoured haunt of lovers where a young man and a young woman might frequently be found in a car with lights extinguished exchanging embraces and kisses, and by virtue of the location of the villa providing an overview of the minor roads, witnessed on a continuous basis what took place inside any car that might stop on one of these roads.

It appeared that the accused, Daniel Habeel Abyad, repeated the process of theft after the manner described approximately thirty times and likewise of rape approximately thirteen times, the following being among his victims: N. S., A.F. and M.D.

It appeared that the accused, Daniel Habeel Abyad, had been given by his employer, Michel Salloum, an automatic rifle, make Kalashnikov and licensed to the latter, for use in guarding the precincts of the villa, and that he had access to the military revolver belonging to his employer, which the latter placed on a permanent basis in the glove compartment of his car, whose keys he had entrusted to the accused Daniel for purposes of the care and cleaning of his car, the said revolver being licensed in his name. The automatic rifle and revolver have been seized by members of the Jounieh Judicial Department and restored to their owner.

It is apparent that the accused, Daniel Habeel Abyad, has confessed to the events outlined above before the Jounieh Judicial Department and the investigating magistrate and has written out the text of his confessions in his own hand. He has, however, retracted his confessions before this court, claiming that they were made under torture. The report of the forensic examiner has not, however, confirmed that the accused has been subjected to torture, either physical or mental. Daniel has also stated that named witness Richard Sawan was attempting to rape the girl who was in his company and that he prevented him from so doing and did not subject him to theft.

Richard Sawan has been interrogated in his capacity of plaintiff and has affirmed that the accused Daniel was the person who robbed him and raped Mary, full name unknown, the young woman who was with him in his car.

Daniel also declared that he did not rape named witness Shireen Raad, but that she on the contrary requested that she spend the night with him of her own free will following the flight of her fiancé Emile Shaheen. It appeared that named witnesses Shireen Raad and Emile Shaheen, having dropped their charges against the accused, Daniel Habeel, and responding in their capacity as witnesses, have both affirmed that the accused threatened Emile Shaheen with murder before ordering him to leave the forest and then raped Shireen Raad three times in his hut situated below the Salloum villa.

It also appeared that the representative of the Public Prosecution presented his case and requested the inculpation of the accused. The attorney of the accused designated by the court also presented his case pleading the innocence of the accused for lack of evidence. The final statement was given to the accused, Daniel Habeel Abyad, who threw himself on the mercy of the court.

These findings are supported by the following:

1. The institution and dropping of legal proceedings

2. The minutes of the preliminary interrogation and the seizure of the coat and torch from Daniel's residence
3. The minutes of the interrogation
4. The confession of the accused during the preliminary interrogation and before the investigating magistrate, as well as the confessions written in his own hand
5. The purport of his declarations before the court
6. The declarations of the witnesses
7. The seizure of the automatic rifle and revolver, which were returned to their owner in view of their being licensed
8. The minutes of the trial and the entire lawsuit bill

2. THE LAW:

Whereas it became established before this court, on the basis of the confession of the accused, Daniel Habeel Abyad, before the Jounieh Judicial Department and before the investigating magistrate, on the basis of his written confessions, on the basis of the seizure of the automatic rifle and the revolver and their return to their owner, and on the basis of the seizure of the coat, balaklava and torch, that the accused, Daniel Habeel Abyad, undertook, unaided, a number of acts of robbery, by night and by force of arms, and a number of acts of rapine, by night and by force of arms

and whereas this court has been convinced by the purport of the declarations made before it of the accused, the witnesses Michel Salloum, Randa Salloum, Shireen Raad and Emile Shaheen, and the plaintiff Richard Sawan

and whereas it follows that the commission by the accused, Daniel Habeel Abyad, of a number of acts of robbery and rapine, by night and by force of arms, constitutes a felony as set out in article

639 (Penal Code) and article 640 (Penal Code)

and whereas the court, acting on the powers vested in it, thinks it proper to recognize with regard to the accused mitigating circumstances as per article 253 (Penal Code)

consequently,

the court, following hearing of the statements of the Public Prosecution, the Defence, and the Accused

1. Finds the accused, Daniel Habeel Abyad, guilty of a felony as per article 639 (Penal Code) and article 640 (Penal Code), sentences him to the penalty of temporary hard labour for twenty years, as per the first text, intensifies the penalty and increases it to hard labour for life as per the second text, and reduces it as per article 253 (Penal Code) to ten years hard labour, to be calculated from the time of his detention

2. Holds the convict responsible for legal costs and expenses.

This sentence was pronounced publicly and in the presence of the parties and the representative of the Public Prosecution on 6/6/1994.

MARCH 1995 – ROUMIEH PRISON – CELL 12

I share this cell with a large number of other prisoners. I am, however, on my own and have nothing to do with anyone else. I asked the guards for paper and pens, but they refused. One of the guards, Nabeel Zeitoun, took pity on me. All the other prisoners ask for food and tobacco but not me. I've gone off food and I crave tobacco, but I haven't asked for it. I asked for blank paper. I want sheets that look like those ones of mine that were wiped clean in the basement of the interrogation facility, because when I look at my life, I feel it's a story. I want to read that story so that I can bear the pain that wracks me. I can't tell my story to anyone because they'd think I was insane, not to mention that no-one would understand. I wrote my story by myself and for myself.

The other prisoners here look at me strangely. They think I'm the "Sex King". That's what the cell boss, a professional hashish smuggler who lives here like he was in a palace, named me. The prisoners wait on him as though he wasn't a prisoner like them. When I entered Cell 12,

M. Abu Tariq El Arnaout – that's his name – gave me a place to sleep at the edge, by the door, and told the prisoners to watch out for me because I was a sex monster who was never satisfied.

I don't want any of them. I look at the window with its iron grill and I see him, and feel a need to weep.

After I was sentenced to ten years in prison, I was moved to this oblong cell from which rises the smell of men's sweat. Sweat, not fear. I no longer fear anything. My innocence of the explosives crimes was announced for all to hear, while the incidents in the forest of lovers and the activities associated with them made the judge laugh several times, especially when he asked me to describe the details. That made me feel certain that the sentence would be light. When they told me that my sentence was ten years, I was overcome by a sadness that has never left me. My only request to the court was for my papers that the interrogator had crushed underfoot, and that made them laugh too.

I couldn't explain that it was for him that I needed my papers. How could I tell them about Yalo, who has returned to his heavenly throne and is sitting near the window and doesn't answer me?

The prisoners look at me strangely because they are longing to hear my story, after all that's been said about my sexual exploits, and that I didn't only rape women but men too! How disgusting! I see the prisoners' eyes open wide with lust for the stories, but none of them dares approach me lest they be accused of wanting me.

I don't want them, and I have no desire to speak to any of them. I want to speak with my soul, to cure it of its pains. I look towards the window, I address a person that no-one but me can see, and I try to remember the stories I wrote, but my memory does not come to my aid.

No-one has the right to say I owe him anything. I have paid the price for everything. Life and I are on the same plane now. If we were put in the two pans of a scale, they would balance, which is why I feel no pangs of conscience or regret for all the things I did – not because I'm happy about what I did, but because I've paid the price in torment and blood.

I long for the scent of pine resin and the smell of incense that surrounds the Villa Gardenia. I long for those two smells, that's all. As for the people whose lives crossed mine and whose lives mine crossed, I feel nothing whatsoever. I don't even long for my mother, in the real meaning of that word. I knew longing when I was in love and foolish. Longing bites and hurts. Now I long for my mother without pain. I long for her because I pity her. The poor woman visited me once in prison. Visits here are strange. The prisoners stand behind iron bars and their relatives stand opposite them and the yelling starts. My mother came once and didn't bring me anything like the rest of the families, who bring food and tobacco to their sons the prisoners. She came and stood with the rest of them and didn't see me. How weird! I'm the tallest prisoner here, and I feel as though I'm getting taller even though that's impossible scientifically speaking because people stop growing when they're adolescents, but I've got taller and thinner – I know it and I know it's strange. Even so, my mother didn't see me. She stood there with her untidy *kokina* looking right and left while I was standing right in front of her. I yelled at her, so then she saw me and wept. She put her hands over her ears and bowed her head. She covered her ears because the noise was hurting them, like my grandfather, whose ears grew larger in his last days, so he took to opening his hands and then closing them so the sounds wouldn't enter his brain and pulverize it.

I yelled at her so she covered her ears and asked me to speak softly. I asked her how she was and she answered in a low voice, but I could hear her. I heard her voice in spite of all the other voices and I gathered that they had thrown her out of the house in the Mreiyeh quarter in Ein El Roummaneh, and when she went back to her house in Museitbeh she found it occupied by a family she didn't know. She said it was her house and they threw her out and threatened to call the police. She said she was now living in Wata El Museitbeh. She'd rented a small room in one of the shacks where the women who work as domestic servants and the Syrian and Kurdish cement workers live. She said she paid a hundred thousand lira a month for the room, that she would end up begging so that she could eat and that she didn't have a penny.

Nabeel Zeitoun, a guard at the prison, took pity on me. He saw that no-one came to visit me and that I didn't put anything in the storage lockers, and he noticed how insistent I was in my request. Nabeel Zeitoun gave me twenty blank sheets of paper and a biro and said he couldn't get me more than that. I decided to write the story of my life over again in small handwriting, so that the words would be like ants and no-one could read them. I don't want anyone but me to read this story. I saw with my own two eyes how the interrogator ground my papers under his feet. He read with his shoes and soaked the papers in common, foul-smelling water. The smell is still in my nostrils and it mixes with that of the men's sweat and urine, and that prevents me from remembering. I try to see everything in black on white, but I can't read. It's as though I were reading in a dream. I see letters whose meaning I cannot decode.

I will write very small words on these papers so that I can get a whole page into a line. My pains never leave me. The prison doctor diagnosed a hernia in my large intestine from the bottle and said it needed an operation. However, he advised me to be patient and not have the operation done in the prison hospital as the result couldn't be guaranteed.

I'm not writing for my own sake but for him and his mother. I want him to come back to me for the sake of his poor mother, and we have to find a solution for her because she is going to be the hero of the story. I don't like stories whose heroes are men. The hero of my story will be Gaby, with her *kokina*, her long hair that turned to gold by the sea, her lover the tailor, her father the *kohno* and her son, who lost his life.

My mother only visited me once. I worry about her a lot. I haven't heard from her for a year, and I don't know how to get in touch with her, which is why I have only written one page. A whole year in which I've written only a page, which is nothing to do with my being lazy but is because I don't know what to do. I want a happy ending. I don't want my story to end with its hero, Gaby Habeel Abyad, my mother and my sister, walking alone through the streets of the city, stumbling over her shadow.

I want another ending.

I try to imagine a different ending, but my imagination refuses to help me. I don't have enough imagination to find an ending for Gaby equal to the story of her love, and if I can't find the ending, how can I write the story?

FINIS